# THE
# BATTLE

BOOK THREE – THE STORY

# EC LARTIGUE

*The Battle*
*Copyright © 2017 EC Lartigue*
*All rights reserved.*

*Printed by CreateSpace, An Amazon.com Company*

*Books may be ordered from Amazon.com and at www.eclwriter.com.*

Book Cover Design: Buffy Cooper

ISBN: 13: 978-0692984239
ISBN- 10: 0692984232

# DEDICATION

To my biggest fan and best friend, Carol, my love.

# ACKNOWLEDGMENTS

Special thanks to those who assisted me in the process. Thanks to Sherry Bass for her clear insight and keen eyes. Thanks to Linda for her love of the story and assistance. Thank you Buffy for your gifted design and talents. And always thanks to my partner and biggest fan, Carol.

Thanks to the many readers who have pressed me to complete the work and for their excitement and encouragement.

Most of all, I give thanks to the heart and inspiration given me by the greatest writer of all, the Lord Himself. No one writes a better story than the Creator and Savior of my soul. *Et gloria Dei est.*

The present danger was that the Story was moving to its conclusion and too few recognized the peril. But even this was foreseen in the Story. And so, once again, the memory of many would be stirred. The deep truth of the Story that lay buried, twisted, or ignored in the souls of many would soon be re-ignited.

The darkness was growing. But light, though dim at the start, would come. It was time for the Story to be told once again in unmistakable fashion. There would be no excuse. The lie and the scheme would be exposed for what they were. In the end, the Story would remain as it was from before the beginning.

But first, comes the Battle.

Before the beginning was the Story,
But then a Lie was declared and believed.
But in the end,
Everyone will know and understand
The Story.


"And the LORD will be king over all the earth;
in that day the LORD will be *the only* one,
and His name *the only* one."
Zechariah 14:9

# Chapter 1

*The Chronicle of Eli*

The first indication of trouble was the dogs. A single dog barking broke the deadly stillness of the late night. It wasn't long before several more joined in. But then it all changed. One dog after another went from a deep bark to a high pitched painful yelping. One by one they each went silent. In the distance a long lone howl echoed down the alleys.

Then came the shots. It sounded like fireworks but different. The howling of the dogs had stirred Armand Cohen. But when he heard the shots he sensed approaching danger.

He immediately woke his wife, Emily. They both listened. They heard more shots and then the screaming began. He went to the window and heard it coming from down the street. Lights in some houses were coming on only to be followed by more shots and screams. Houses were on fire.

Emily's voice was trembling. "I thought we were safe here?"

They had lived in the diplomatic compound for over a year. The Lebanese government constantly assured them that they were safe. But in a world going mad, such assurances resembled wishful thinking more than guarantees.

Personal weapons were strictly forbidden. The State Department provided protection, but at night it reduced it to a minimum. Depending on the strength of the attackers, the two men downstairs might only delay disaster.

Armand's mind raced for a plan. With each minute his options dwindled. The security men downstairs yelled out to them.

"Ambassador Cohen, remain upstairs! The perimeter has been compromised. Try to stay calm. We have called for help. It should be here soon. Lock yourselves in your room."

Emily screamed frantic. "Armand, Eli!"

Armand raced down the hall and went to Eli's bedroom. He decided not to turn on any lights. He saw his young son soundly sleeping. His nightlight dimly lit the floor. Even at eight years old, the boy loved his baseball nightlight.

Armand softly shook his son's shoulder. Eli barely stirred. Armand didn't want to make any needless noise so he gently picked him up wrapped in a light blanket. He quickly made his way to their bedroom.

When he reached his room he placed Eli on their bed.

More shots and screams. They were getting closer.

The noises woke Eli. He rubbed his eyes trying to see his surroundings. The only light in the room came from the half-open closet.

"Mom, Dad, what am I doing in your room? How did I get here?"

His dad placed his finger over his lips to silence him. Eli saw the distress in his Mom's eyes. The sound of a nearby explosion shook the windows. His mom bolted to sit on the bed next to him. She wrapped her arms around him. He felt her trembling. The fear immediately transferred to him. He began to softly cry.

Armand tried to remain calm but feared he might buckle. He remembered his training. Panic is the enemy of survival. He looked at his wife and son and sensed a coming inevitability.

The shots were now very close. He went over to the window and dared a peak. In the distance he could spot emergency lights. Help was on its way. He also saw the house next door on fire. He realized that help would not arrive in time. He had decisions to make.

"I want you both to go into the closet and close the door."

"Darling, no."

Armand swallowed hard and nodded yes. From the look in his eyes she almost fainted. The touch of Eli's hands on her arm shocked her back. She sobbed as she took him by the hand. They walked to the closet.

"Get into the deepest corner. And no matter what, don't come out."

"Daddy!" Eli struggled to get free from his mom's grip.

"Son, go with Mommy. Please. And pray."

Eli lowered his head and yielded.

They went into the closet. When they closed the door the darkness engulfed them.

The downstairs rocked from an explosion that blew the front door directly into the body of one of the guards. He died before he hit the ground. The other guard fired his weapon but quickly dispatched by the charging figure in black.

Six hooded men blasted through the entrance with weapons sweeping the room for any other resistance. The presence of guards told them they had found the right house. After they cleared all of the downstairs, the leader pointed up the stairs.

He directed three of the men. "No prisoners."

They grinned and nodded.

Weapons ready, they slowly walked up the stairs.

Armand had heard it all. He knew they were coming. He had always wondered what he would feel like if and when such a time came. The training had said one thing. Now he realized something more. He slowly moved to his knees.

"Lord, I have always put my trust in You. Now comes my last test. I am in Your hands. Keep me safe in You."

Emily held Eli tight. "Pray darling, pray."

"I am mommy. I am."

Shots sprayed the door and easily tore through it. Among the many shots, several found their mark on Armand's kneeling body. He softly fell to the ground. He never felt a thing.

Emily heard the shots. She trembled so intensely she imagined that the ground moved. She heard Eli's soft prayer. Calmness suddenly poured over her. She began to faintly hum a tune her sister-in-law had taught her. Tears gently rolled down her cheeks.

The closet door flew open and the light came on. A dark hooded figure stepped in. It didn't take him long to find them. He grabbed Emily and yanked her to her feet.

Eli screamed. 'Mommy."

"Stay in there, boy, don't move," the man yelled.

As they dragged into the bedroom she called out to Eli. "Keep praying, honey."

"Yes, Mommy."

The man threw her to the ground. She lightly screamed, more out of the pain than of fear. The man looked down at her.

"Well infidel, do have anything to say before you die?"

Emily's gentle eyes looked at her captor and softly spoke.

"The Lord is my shepherd."

"He cannot protect you, so die infidel."

One quick shot dispatched her. Her serene smile disturbed and then angered the man.

One of the others interrupted his thoughts.

"What about the boy?"

"Yes. We will make him see his worthless parents before he meets his fate." They both laughed.

Eli silently prayed and then began to hum the little tune his mother had sung moments before.

All three of the men grinned as they took a step toward the closet.

Suddenly a bright light threw them back and they tripped over the bodies on the ground. In the fall, they dropped their weapons. When they looked up, they had to shield their eyes from the intense brilliance emanating from the closet.

It took them a moment to adjust to the light. When they did they saw a man standing at the closet door. But what sort of man?

He stood at least seven feet tall. Dressed like some peasant shepherd, he stood looking at them with his arms crossed. His eyes were strong and fearless but he carried no weapon.

When they realized that he was weaponless, they looked at each other and grinned. They each reached for the weapons and rose to their feet.

The tall figure extended his right arm and opened his hand toward them. Fire shot out. The flames divided and flew toward each of the men. The fire struck and ignited their weapons. The flames quickly traveled down the rifles and flowed like a fiery river across their arms. The blaze then grew and engulfed their entire bodies. The men screamed as they ran in various directions. Running into furniture, soon the fire engulfed the whole room.

The tall figure turned and entered the closet. He extended his hand toward Eli.

"Come on, my son. We must leave this place. Cover your eyes."

The deep calmness in his voice chased away any fear from the young lad.

The tall man wrapped Eli in his cloak. He lifted him up and carried him out of the burning room.

Downstairs the leader had heard the shots. He and the others were pillaging the house assuming that his men had done their work.

He heard footsteps coming down the stairs. It shocked him to see the tall figure coming down carrying the boy. He screamed out to his men to come as he raised his weapon toward the man.

Like before, the tall figure only needed to raise his hand. The same fate overcame all of the murderers downstairs. Their flaming bodies caught the remainder of the house on fire.

With the fading sounds of their screams Eli fainted in the arms of his rescuer.

The next thing he remembers is the sound of sheep and the smell of a stable. He looked up and saw the man sitting by a fire. He softly hummed a tune. It was the same tune he had heard his mother sing.

✡   ✡   ✡

Brandon Rivers closed Eli's chronicle. He laid it on his lap. He sat on a porch outside a small but comfortable home of his Bedouin host Ibrahim. A warm midday breeze ruffled the top pages of the story. He put down the narrative as he looked across a field pondering what he had just read. There in the field walked the two enigmatic figures that had turned his world upside down.

A few weeks before, with his own eyes, he had witnessed the unexplainable. He and his small band of friends had crossed the Dead Sea on dry ground. Pursued by a madman named Osgood, set on killing them, they had driven across on the dried up seabed. No, that's not exactly right. The sea had not dried up. It had been split open. When they were crossing, the waters stood towering on either side of them, held by a power he could not explain.

That same power closed the sea after they reached the western shore. The crashing waters swallowed up all of their pursers. The whole event arose to the level of . . . biblical proportions. He whispered those two words over and over again in his mind.

Could it actually be true? Were those two men walking in the field, in fact, biblical characters? Had the Bible accurately predicted the arrival of two prophetic witnesses before the coming of the end?

The whole idea stretched beyond his present ability to accept. And yet, he could not deny all he had seen. Perhaps that's why he had remained.

George and Emma Franklin had returned to the United States. At first they didn't want to leave their friend, Oliver, aka Moshe. Moshe had practically ordered them to leave and to do so quickly. And so they did.

Freddy Collins, Brandon's former cameraman had left as well. With funds for Brandon's earlier project dried up, curiosity couldn't hold him. In fact, the earlier events had frightened Freddy. He had attempted to persuade Brandon to join him. Freddy had said that he had bad feelings about the direction of it all; "Bad ju-ju," or some mumbo-jumbo like that. He almost convinced Brandon. But in the end, the sheer inexplicability of everything forced him to stay behind. With everything else happening in the world, he would not walk away from what could very well be the biggest story of his life. It could very well be the biggest story in everyone's life.

So with all of the "what ifs" rumbling around in his mind, he watched the two men in the field walking toward him. They obviously enjoyed each other's company.

Brandon knew who they claimed to be. He had read the Biblical account that spoke of them. If their claims proved true . . . the time for laughter would soon be over. The possibility of such things and every ramification coming out of it slammed his mind like a boulder.

Brandon rubbed his forehead in mental exhaustion. He whispered to himself, "Brandon, you better get this one right."

The two men noticed Brandon's troubled look. Eli spotted the chronicle sitting on Brandon's lap.

Eli sat down beside Brandon. "I see you've been reading my story."

"Yeah, thanks for letting me. You told us the whole story earlier. This gives me a chance to go through it slowly. There's a lot here."

"Yes, there is."

"Who wrote it?" Brandon felt nervous. He didn't understand why, but he did.

"A friend."

"You mean the big guy who rescued you?"

Eli nodded.

"I don't suppose I could . . . talk to him right now, could I?"

Eli answered slowly. "No, . . . he's not around at the moment."

"When was the last time you saw him?"

"The night we arrived."

"That's when you and others went out with the ferret."

"Snoop."

"Yeah, Snoop. The night he . . ."

"He went away."

"Yeah." The word slowly floated off his lips. Brandon remembered Moshe's story about how he had met Snoop and about the Island.

Eli placed his arm around Brandon's shoulder.

"Brandon, why do you think you stayed? You could have left with the others. Do you have a reason for not leaving?"

Brandon thought for a moment. "I guess I have too many unanswered questions."

"About what?"

Brandon chuckled. "About what? Are you kidding me? You guys . . . the power of God thing . . . the Dead Sea. I mean seriously, I started this whole thing looking for a story. Instead, I end up supposedly in the middle of some battle and the end of the world!"

As he finished, Brandon seemed emotionally exhausted. He lowered his head.

Eli could empathize with Brandon. He patted him on the back and rose to get up.

"For you to want your questions answered so badly, you must have a strong desire for certainty."

Brandon looked up at Eli. He knew that he looked as puzzled as he felt.

Eli smiled. "Keep reading. You might find some of your questions answered. Don't get in a hurry. There's still some time before . . ." His voice trailed off.

"Before what?"

Eli didn't answer right away. "We're leaving tomorrow."

"Leaving? Leaving for where?"

"We'll talk about it tonight." Eli took a few steps before turning to look back.

"Keep reading."

# Chapter 2

**B**randon waited about an hour before continuing to read. He wanted to clear his mind. He spent the time watching his host lead his small herd out to pasture. It provided him with some amusement as he studied how the shepherd guided the smallest in the herd. He listened to the sounds of sheep as they scurried along. The clanging bell acted as a guide for the other sheep. He watched how they all followed. He remembered someone saying how sheep always needed a shepherd. As he watched, he better understood why.

He quietly asked himself. "Who am I following?"

After the herd crested the hill and the quiet returned, Brandon picked up the chronicle to continue reading.

✡   ✡   ✡

### *The Chronicle of Eli*

Shock!

Like being shot with a nail gun, the horror of his parent's murder lodged deep in Eli's soul. Though leaving no outward scar, the wound remained like a deep splinter. A gnawing reminder lingered deep within. The sum total of the shock had literally stolen his voice.

Eli had become a mute. He would not; no, could not utter a word.

For months Shamer and the young shepherd Ibrahim made no demands on the boy. They provided for his needs but asked no questions. At times the boy would break down and silently weep. Ibrahim's mother, Layan, would go to the boy and wrap her arms around him. Eli would receive the momentary comfort and continue a soundless cry.

As the months passed, the crying episodes decreased. From time to time they came unexpectedly like a wave seeking to knock him down. Eli had learned to brace himself and weather the pain by burying it deeper. But hiding it never took it away. It would remain like a dormant seed waiting its season.

Shamer knew the time would come when Eli's past would explode from within. His duty to the boy remained the same, guard and protect. The rest remained in someone else's hand.

As the years passed, Ibrahim, in his late teens, became like an older brother. Eli shadowed him daily into the fields with the sheep. Even though he never spoke a word, he and Ibrahim found a way to communicate. Eli learned and lived the life of a shepherd. Most days Eli found ways to have fun in the work. It amused Ibrahim to watch Eli silently laughing at the antics of the sheep. Sometimes the sheep frustrated Eli. At times his aggravation bordered on the edge of a brewing rage.

It always surprised Ibrahim that at just such times, Shamer would quickly appear. Shamer would take the boy aside with a gentle firmness. Eli would give only momentary opposition before finding comfort in the strong hands of his protector.

In one such incident Eli's anger reached the point of tears. He resisted anyone's attempt to comfort him. He fell to his knees, and with his face in the dirt, pounded the ground in silent anguish. Shamer waited until Eli had collapsed in exhaustion before he walked up to him.

Shamer stood looking down at Eli. "Young one."

Eli looked up wiping away the dirt caked tears.

"What angers you lad?"

Eli raised his fist and pointed at the sheep.

Shamer gently smiled. "The sheep?"

Eli affirmed with pouting lips.

"Young one, they are sheep and nothing more. They cannot be anything but sheep. They have their purpose and their limits. That is why they need a shepherd."

Eli looked down.

"But you already know this. Ibrahim has explained this to you before. The source of your anger is not the sheep. It comes from your hidden pain. It is so deep that I cannot reach it. And it seems neither can you."

Shamer cast his gaze across the valley and beyond. Eli followed Shamer's stare trying to see what had his friend's attention.

After a moment, Shamer looked back down at the boy.

"At the right time, your healer will come. Until then, know that you are never alone."

Shamer turned and signaled to Ibrahim. The shepherd immediately ran over to them. Shamer stepped aside as Ibrahim helped Eli get up and dust off.

Afterwards, they both turned around. Shamer was gone.

Ibrahim chuckled as he placed his arm around Eli's shoulder.

"Your friend is a strange one. He comes and goes like the wind. Let's go and make us some tea."

✡   ✡   ✡

Brandon stopped at the sound overhead. Three military jets screamed across the sky. Such sights were never uncommon in the region. Yet he had noticed an increase in frequency. He wondered if this area would ever settle down. With so much talk of war, it was no wonder that people greeted one another with words of peace.

He looked back down and read.

✡ ✡ ✡

Eli's thirteenth birthday arrived with much less fanfare than normal. There were no party decorations or a table full of gifts from family and guests. Ibrahim came from a poor and simple family, yet they provided the very best for Eli. That night, away from the house, they erected a special tent reserved for such occasions. Beautiful rugs were laid down around a center area readied for the coming meal. Handmade cushions lined the edges of the rugs. In the corner of the tent, mint tea brewed on a small stove. Special lanterns hung from the tent poles and filled the tent with a soft amber light.

Ibrahim's father, Ahmad led them into the tent. Ibrahim and Eli followed. Removing his shoes, Ahmad found his place on the right side. After Ibrahim and Eli removed their shoes, they found their place. Ahmad nodded his head as a signal. Ibrahim's mother, Layan came in carrying a large tray with several teacups. Behind her was her niece, Sasha with her friend Minera. They were each carrying a tray with assorted baked treats. They served the men before the ladies took their place opposite them with their tea and treats. They all shared conversations about the day, men with men and women with women.

The women gathered the teacups and exited. They soon returned and filled the center area with large trays of food. Eli's eyes went wide as he scanned the feast before them. It included Bedouin pita bread, salads, rice, and vegetables. In the center of these sat a Matfuna dish. This was a whole stuffed chicken along with delicious homemade kebabs and assorted side dishes.

But before they began, Ahmad rose to his feet. Though Bedouin in tradition, Ahmad and his family were followers of Yeshua. All bowed as he opened his palms and spoke a prayer and asked a blessing. Eli kept his eyes open. He remembered the times of prayer with his mother. Since that terrible night, Eli had not lifted his heart in prayer. He felt unable to direct his affections toward heaven, as if a vault had shut over his soul. He missed the serenity that prayers had once provided, but he didn't know how to recover it. So once again, he buried it and turned to the moment for relief.

Everyone enjoyed the meal. Though Eli remained silent, he seemed to enjoy the festivities. This carried great value for the hosts.

Eli noticed that Ibrahim would often look over to his cousin's friend. Minera, in turn, would shyly acknowledge his attention with a slight smile. It made Eli happy for his friend. He wondered if anyone would ever be attracted to an orphaned mute like himself.

✡   ✡   ✡

Brandon looked up from the chronicle. The Chronicle provided fill-in information on Eli's life. It also created as many questions as anything else. He wondered how the shy mute boy had become a vociferous yet gentle man. He knew his answers were found in Eli's story. He also realized that he needed to get up and walk around. He put down the narrative and decided to go look for the shepherd.

The early autumn afternoon sun on his back invigorated Brandon. He walked up a rise and spotted the flock. They looked to be about a mile away so he decided to walk to them. The distance turned out a little greater than it first appeared. The ups and downs of the terrain made the trek a bit more challenging and not as direct as he had assumed. Hearing the clanging bell of one of the sheep, he knew he was almost there. He stopped when he crested the hill just to take in the scenery.

The scattered flock grazed on the hill, into a small valley and onto an adjoining hillside. The surrounding hills seemed to quiet the air. It amazed Brandon how this place could exist so close to areas full of struggles and dangers.

Not far below him sat Ibrahim. His dog sat to his left, constantly scanning the flock. Moshe sat to the right of the shepherd, his Rod lying across his lap. Funny how he had taken to using the man's new name rather than the one he knew when they first met. Another reminder of how things had all changed so quickly.

The dog acknowledged his coming. His ears and head perked up. He turned and watched him as he walked toward them.

14

Brandon admired how the dog didn't bark so not to startle the flock. Instead, the dog remained alert until he recognized him as no danger to the flock. Brandon wished he possessed the same ability.

The dog prompted Ibrahim to turn. He waved Brandon over and returned to a conversation with Moshe.

Not far from the shepherd, Brandon almost slipped to fall. The dog softly growled. Ibrahim patted the dog's head to calm him. He called out Brandon.

"Are you okay sir? Excuse the dog. His main concern is for the flock. They startle very easily. He is ever vigilant. Come, have a seat."

Brandon parked himself on the hard ground next to Moshe. For a moment, no one said a word. Moshe finally broke the silence.

"The desert has a splendor all its own. It isn't colorful or fragrant, but it has a rugged tranquility to it, don't you think?"

"Yes, I suppose it does. It's certainly quiet, especially when you think how close we are to the activity nearby."

Brandon thought a second and asked. "Was it like this on that island of yours?"

"I don't think of it as my island. But I certainly would describe it as peaceful. But unlike this desert, the Island teemed with life. It filled in the air, the water, and in the light itself."

Brandon snickered. "You make it sound almost magical."

Moshe had a distant look. "Magical? No, wondrous is a better word. Magic involves tricks and illusion. But I learned that wonder is real and true. More real and true than anything else."

"You're talking about the God-thing again aren't you?"

Moshe chuckled. "You see, you talk about God like He's an idea or a thing. What I'm talking about is that He's more real than anything else. I know that because you can't see Him, you doubt His existence or relevancy. But trust me, He's real."

Moshe wrapped his fingers firmly around the Rod.

Brandon saw Moshe grip the Rod and the look on his face.

"I'm having trouble wrapping my mind around all you've said and all I've seen. I just . . ."

Moshe turned and looked directly at him. He brought the Rod up against his chest.

"Trust me, I know exactly what you mean. You can't imagine how hard I fought it. It practically killed me."

Moshe's eyes widened. "But when I met reality, when I met Him, it laid me low. He lifted me up and rescued me from myself."

His voice now trembled. "And then I saw. I best describe it as a blind man seeing color for the first time. I saw how utterly foolish I had been. I . . ."

Moshe looked firmly at Brandon. "When you first came to us, I wondered what it was you were up to. Now I realize that your motives are irrelevant."

He paused a moment to catch his breath. "Brandon, God has something very singular in mind for you. Don't stop with the questions. The answer is coming to you. It will both surprise and amaze you."

Without another word, Moshe turned and looked off into the distance. A few moments later he took a deep breath and used the Rod to help him stand.

Not speaking to anyone in particular Moshe declared, "It's time to go back."

Ibrahim immediately clapped his hands and his dog went into action. He scurried around moving the flock barking at the scattered sheep and moving them in the direction of the shepherd.

Moshe had already made his way halfway up the hill. Rather than pursuing Moshe, Brandon stayed with the shepherd and watched the process of gathering and then moving the flock home.

The slower pace suited him better. All of his adult life had been one hurried task after another. He enjoyed this pace that allowed him time to think.

Brandon watched Ibrahim's care and concern for the sheep.

Witless as sheep were, he took the time to guide them safely along. He even whistled and sang to them, calling them by name.

Brandon whispered to himself, "Who am I following and where is it taking me?"

The question bounced around in his mind as the shepherd whistled a soft tune to his flock.

# Chapter 3

Eli and Moshe sat on the porch waiting for Ibrahim and Brandon to return. They had declined an offer from Minera for some late afternoon tea. They heard a distant sheep bell and knew the flock wasn't far away.

As they both looked in the direction of sheep's the bell, Eli spoke. "So you're sure about Brandon?"

"If you mean, if I am certain how he will do, who can truly say? But I know that the Lord has chosen him for this task. And I trust that He knows what He's doing."

Eli chuckled, "That's the one certainty in this whole thing."

"Is it just me, or is all of this a bit surreal? I know what's about to take place. Yet the fact that we are somehow a part of it all stretches my mind."

"Yes. I never imagined such a thing. I mean, look at us. Everyone thought we were dead. I suppose, in a way we both had to die in order to live."

"Seems to be that way, doesn't it? It just helps me to realize that He always knows what He's doing. He's definitely proven that with both of us."

"He certainly has." Moshe gripped the Rod in his right hand.

The flock crested the last hill.

Eli let out a long sigh and looked at Moshe. "Minera told me that all of the families have arrived."

"Good. It's nice to know that they will all be safe in Him."

"As we all are."

"Truly."

The festive mood filled the room that night. All of Ibrahim and Minera's children and grandchildren were present. Son, Yousef, his wife Miriam and their children had come. Their daughter, Anya and her husband Anis, and their children were there as well. Their daughter Sasha and her husband Marwan, had just arrived.

The women were busy with all the preparations as the men sat and enjoyed their tea. Brandon still felt odd being served and watching both men and women seemingly living out roles he didn't understand.

He leaned over to Eli and asked, "I almost feel lazy just sitting here and being waited on like this."

Eli chuckled. "First of all, you are a guest. Hospitality is very important in this home. These are century old customs. You'll be back in the modern world soon enough. Enjoy the evening."

After the teacups were gathered up, the food arrived. A lavish spread filled the center floor. With it all laid out, the ladies sat together opposite the men.

Ibrahim rose. He looked across the room and smiled. "My heart is full to have you all here tonight. I am honored to ask my friend Eli to proclaim a blessing on our time tonight."

Eli stood as Ibrahim sat back down.

Eli opened his palms upward and began. "Lord God, maker of the universe, protector of our souls, we give thanks to You this night. You alone are our provider. Grant us the joy of Your presence in our every step. Bless this meal and the delight of its fellowship. To Your glory and kingdom forever, Amen."

Whispered amen's echoed quietly across the room.

Moshe placed his hand to his heart and whispered, "Truly."

Brandon listened as he ate. Laughter and stories filled the evening as everyone enjoyed the food and family affections. Brandon had to smile as he watched the grandchildren climb on Ibrahim's lap and ask their questions.

As Brandon took it all in, he realized a certain isolation. He alone had no family present. In fact, like Eli and Moshe, he had no spouse. He had never taken the time. But Moshe and Eli had each other. He had no one. Even in the middle of all the festivities, he felt alone.

With the meal completed, Eli looked over to Ibrahim who knew what to do. Ibrahim called for everyone's attention. He then turned to Eli.

"It is so wonderful to see everyone enjoying themselves. It saddens me to have to say what I must now say. Tomorrow morning, my friends and I must leave. Unless the Lord provides otherwise, this will likely be the last time we shall see you as we see you now. I have spoken to Ibrahim and I now tell you all. You must leave very soon as well. Things are happening and soon the government will be closing all unregistered cities in Israel. Provision has been made for you in Galilee and you must all go there."

The families looked at each other and at Ibrahim, who nodded in agreement.

Eli continued. "As I said, do not worry. Complete provision has been made for you all. You are safe in the Lord."

Eli paused, allowing the words to sink in. "We . . .," he looked at Brandon and Moshe, "our path takes us in a different direction. Our trust is in the Lord's provision as well. If nothing else, we know that we shall see each other in the Kingdom."

All of them slowly nodded.

Eli saw a certain sadness overtaking the room.

"Brothers and sisters be of good cheer. He is with us."

At this Moshe stood up. He took the Rod and raised it slightly in his right hand. Suddenly drops of light began to float up and out from the Rod. Minera walked over and turned out the room lights. The tiny droplets filled the room like a canopy of stars in the night. Some of the children reached out to touch them. When they did, they giggled as the droplets tickled their fingers.

Ever so gently some of the tiny pearls of light floated down and into those reaching for it. When they did, it was like a waterfall of light filled their being. Some would cry and some would laugh. All of them, even the children, fell with their face to the ground.

Among those gathered, only Eli and Moshe stood. Tears ran down their faces, as light radiated from their clothing, and as the light drops engulfed them.

Brandon sat alone among all the others with their faces down. He had reached over to touch the tiny lights. It amazed him that when he did, he could actually feel the light. It had substance and it did tickle his fingers. But unlike the others, it remained only on the surface of his body.

He looked over to Eli and Moshe. They had sadness in their eyes and yet they smiled. They had an expectation of Brandon, a hope beyond the moment. He looked again at the floating lights and sighed. Even though alone, he didn't feel abandoned.

One by one, the tiny lights began to fade. And one by one, the people got up to leave without saying a word. The last ones to leave were Eli and Moshe.

Brandon walked into the living area the next morning and immediately sensed it. Ibrahim and Minera stood in a corner talking quietly with Eli. Moshe, who sat in a chair near the door, looked over at Brandon. His expression spoke volumes. Everyone's eyes were sad and moist.

The host couple embraced and whispered a few more words to Eli. When the quiet and intimate scene finished, Eli picked up a small knapsack off the floor and walked past them and out the door.

Moshe looked over to Brandon, "Do you have all of your things ready like we told you?"

Brandon nodded.

"Good. Get them and meet us outside. We're leaving right away."

Brandon looked over to the weeping couple in the corner and then to Moshe. He turned and followed Moshe out the door.

Brandon placed his bags in the back of the vehicle that they had arrived in two weeks before. Eli sat in the driver's seat with Moshe sitting next to him. As soon as Brandon got in and closed his door they left.

No one said a word for the first fifteen minutes. Finally Brandon broke the silence.

"Just out of curiosity, . . . where are we going? And will we be coming back here later?"

Eli remained stoically silent.

Moshe turned to answer. "We are presently heading for Arad. As to your second question, it is not likely. As you could tell they were saying goodbye."

Brandon didn't know what to think about the answer. He also knew not to ask more questions. The look on Moshe's face only confirmed his thoughts. They rode in silence the rest of the way.

✿  ✿  ✿

Arriving in Arad, Eli pulled into the circular drive of the Inbar Hotel. Eli led them into the lobby where he checked Brandon in. After he had finished, he looked over to Moshe who was sitting with Brandon on a couch in the lobby.

Moshe turned to Brandon. "Alright Brandon, I need you to listen carefully. We are leaving you here. We'll be back, but not for at least a month, maybe more."

"What?"

"Listen." Moshe's spoke firmly. "Your hotel room is covered for at least two months. This includes breakfast and evening meals here.

You can have lunch here as well or choose somewhere else."

He handed Brandon an envelope.

"There is more than enough in this envelope to cover any expenses you may have while we're gone. If for some reason you need more, talk to the front desk clerk, he'll know what to do."

"But what am I suppose to do?"

Moshe grinned. "Brandon, you're a grown man. That's for you to decide. It's the end of summer and almost fall. You can do the tourist thing in Israel. The money I've left won't cover that, but I think you can figure it out. If you want our story, you're going to have to wait until we return. And we *will* return."

Brandon looked around the small lobby trying to get his thoughts together. He suddenly felt Moshe's hand on his shoulder.

"I know this is a bit much. If you continue hanging out with us, it won't be the last time you'll feel this way. Try to use the time to relax and think about all you've seen and heard. You can also finish reading Eli's story."

With that said, Moshe turned and walked out of the hotel.

Brandon noticed the front desk clerk holding up a key and waving at him.

Moshe got into the vehicle.

Eli looked at him. "How did your friend take the news?"

"He'll be fine. He's got some things to figure out, as will a lot of people in the days to come."

"Very true. Well, I know a place we can pick up a few supplies before we leave."

They actually stopped at a couple of places. Considering how long they might be gone, it wasn't much. Eli then took Highway 31 toward Neve Zohar in the direction of the Dead Sea. About five kilometers out, he pulled off to the left on an unmarked road. It actually looked more like a goat path than a road. He drove for approximately another kilometer and then stopped.

"This is about as far as this vehicle can take us. I left word with a friend back in Tel Sheva on where he would find the vehicle. He'll come retrieve it in a few days."

Moshe took a deep breath as he looked out at the barren terrain stretched out all around them.

Eli grinned. "You ready?"

Moshe's eyes looked down before turning to Eli. "I hope so. I truly hope so."

Eli nodded. "Truly."

✡   ✡   ✡

Brandon sat in his room and considered his options. The front desk had given him maps of both Arad and of Israel. He decided against an exploration adventure just yet. Looking over at his bed he spotted Eli's chronicle. When he picked it up he had to smile. He thought it humorous that the cover had a title on it, "The Chronicle of Eli."

"Who names their own story a chronicle?" He chuckled.

"Well let's see what you're made of Mr. Eli." He found the little piece of paper he used as a bookmark.

✡   ✡   ✡

### *The Chronicle of Eli*

Almost four years to the date had passed since his thirteenth birthday. Ibrahim had left early to Be'er Sheva for supplies and left Eli to graze the flock. In truth, Eli enjoyed the solitude. He enjoyed the quiet sounds of the morning along with the serenity of the sheep innocently foraging the hillside. His major duty involved insuring their safety and protecting the serenity of the flock.

At first glance all of the sheep looked alike, yet Eli knew each one by name. And though they were simple and ignorant creatures, he knew that they depended on him. It made him feel needed and necessary.

Something suddenly caught his eye. On an adjacent hill a lone figure approached some of the scattered flock. The angle of the morning light prevented Eli from immediately identifying the person. But when he heard the whistle and the sheep's response, he had no doubt.

"Shamer!" the words shouted in his mind as he rose and began to run toward him. Although he only saw him on occasion, the bond between him and Shamer grew ever stronger. From the very beginning, Eli viewed Shamer as a protector. For years he had wanted to find a way to tell Shamer how he felt, yet he remained powerless to utter a single word. It left him frustrated even to the point of anger. He also carried a deep sadness that taunted him.

Shamer saw young Eli running toward him waving. He smiled as he watched the young lad express such eager excitement. He had watched over him these many years from childhood to now young manhood. He knew that the boy had experienced enough trauma as to make grown men scream. And yet this young life had a profound strength granted to only the noblest heroes. He understood that Eli's life would never be one of ease and comfort. His destiny would take him down the path of pain known by the great.

Shamer gave thanks in his heart that he had been chosen to share in this portion of the Story. He knew that one day Eli would look back and remember the importance of this day.

# Chapter 4

Brandon put the chronicle down on his lap, feeling tired. The emotion and events of the past few weeks had drained him on several levels. He wanted to get back to reading but he didn't want to fall asleep doing it. He looked over at the bed. Suddenly a nap seemed like a good idea. With no pressing schedule the idea seemed more appealing. He made his way to the bed and in no time he was asleep.

It surprised many how quickly the video went viral on the Net. Someone on the western bank had recorded it on their phone camera. The video had captured the waters of the Dead Sea parting. The waters stood like giant churning towers of frothing turquoise. It seemed as if some invisible hand held them back. And then the waters came crashing down. The images left no doubt that some vehicles and people were on the seabed when the waters came crashing down. Screams from some on the shore were clearly audible on the video

Initially, people reacted in amazement to the clip. But it didn't take long before skepticism about the footage's authenticity arose.

What happened next, changed everything. Freddy Collins could have never predicted the reaction. If he had, he would have done things differently. Freddy felt he had to warn Brandon.

Brandon's mobile phone sat on the hotel dresser. The vibrating phone and the loud ring tone woke Brandon in a start. He strained to focus. He wondered how long he had slept.

As the phone continued a buzzing ring, he stumbled to finally get it. He saw the time. He had slept for almost five hours.

He didn't recognize the number, but knew it came from the U.S. He decided to answer it.

"Hello."

"Brandon!" The intensity made it easy to identify the voice.

"Freddy, this isn't your number. Where are you calling from?"

"An undisclosed location."

Brandon chuckled. "What's up?"

"Are you kidding me?" He muffled his excited voice. "Have you been online at all lately?"

"No, not really."

"Well, maybe you should have."

"Why? What's going on?"

"I'm sure you remember that little incident we had on the Dead Sea not long ago?"

"Yeah…"

"Well, you'll also remember that there were people on the western shore when we got there."

"OK."

"Someone on the shore captured it on video and published it. It's gone viral."

Brandon sighed. He remembered discussing with Freddy the importance of keeping it quiet. He'd forgotten about witnesses.

"So what's been the reaction?"

"Crazy! At first people were gaga over it. Then, as expected, the weirdo's chimed in. What I didn't expect was the vile skepticism. The comments were brutal."

Brandon shook his head. "Well, just leave it alone. It'll die out on its own. It's only one video."

Freddy hummed. He had more to say.

"What is it Freddy? What else is there?"

"Well . . . when some people started trashing the whole thing, it kinda' ticked me off. I mean I was there. I saw it. They were turning it into some sort of alien UFO nut job thing."

"Freddy, you didn't? Tell me you didn't download your footage?"

"I'm sorry man, really I am, more than you know. But I just couldn't sit back and say nothing. My footage was not amateur. It was professional and clear. The waters parted, stood up and then came crashing down on those low life's who tried to kill us. I can't explain how all of that happened, but I know it happened."

Freddy could hear the frustration in Brandon's breathing over the phone.

"Freddy, I thought we agreed . . ."

"I know. Believe me I know. I've kicked myself a hundred times."

"So are you getting some push back on it."

"Push back. Ha! I could have predicted the skepticism. What I didn't expect was the threats."

"Threats? What do you mean?"

"What I mean is that I get a call at home at three in the morning. A voice tells me to pull the video and declare it a hoax or else."

"Or else what?"

"That's when a rock came through my bedroom window. I ran out and saw a black SUV driving off with my mailbox on fire."

"Did you call the cops?"

"Oh yeah. They wrote it off as teenage vandalism. The next day I went into my office and it had been broken into. My computers and hard drives were all gone. I rushed home only to find my place on fire. This was a professional job."

"How do you know?"

"Back at my office I had two micro-cameras that captured the whole thing. I saw three guys all in black. They wore masks and moved around in skilled precision. They were armed and knew what they wanted. They were in and out in two minutes."

"So what are you going to do?"

"What I'm doing is disappearing. Luckily, I always have a stash of mad money. I'm off the grid and in a remote location. I'm gonna' lay low and occasionally peak back in."

"Seems a little radical Freddy."

"Look Brandon, I don't know who those two guys are you're hanging with, but after Jordan and now this, they've got some powerful enemies. I prefer to steer clear. I just wanted to call and warn you. Watch your back and stay low. I gotta' go. Take care."

"You too, Freddy."

The line went dead.

✡   ✡   ✡

Eli and Moshe trekked into the Judean Desert with only a general sense of where they were going. They each carried a small pack of supplies and dressed as any Bedouin would. The rugged terrain ran mostly uphill. Eli led the way, following no path or trail. By the end of the day they had traveled about fourteen kilometers northeast. Their conversation remained minimal, processing the nature of the trek individually. This would soon change.

By evening they reached a plateau and decided to camp for the night. Eli built and ignited a small campfire. The chill of the desert night would soon fall on them. They had a small meal of smoked meat, dried dates, and water. After the meal, they both laid back staring out into the night at the vast star field above them. Moshe softly hummed a tune and Eli joined him after learning it.

After about an hour, they heard footsteps approaching on the rocky ground nearby. They looked at each other and wondered who or what could be coming. Eli heard a whistled song he knew well.

He whispered, "Shamer."

He soon came into sight.

Eli ran and wrapped his arms around Shamer's waist. Moshe watched and smiled, knowing the special bond that existed between them.

Eli released his grip and stepped back. "Greeting to you my friend. It's good to see you."

"And greetings to you both, servants of the Most High. I come bringing a message."

"We're all ears." Moshe had many questions running through his mind since Eli had told him about their journey into the wilderness.

"Our Lord has sent me to tell you the path you are to take once you begin."

Eli and Moshe traded glances and nodded.

Shamer reached into a pouch hanging from his side. He looked at Moshe and held out his hand.

"Moshe, I have some mint leaves collected from a special garden and sent to you from my brother and your friend. You need use only one every time you brew some tea. Save the rest for later. The tea will strengthen you both. After tea I will share the instructions I bring."

Moshe recognized the leaves and remembered sharing such tea on the Island. He grinned as he took the leaves and turned to prepare the tea.

✡   ✡   ✡

### Osgood Castle, St. Gallen, Switzerland

Hermann Lanzig knew all of the secrets of his former boss. With the horrific death of Malcolm Osgood at the Dead Sea under yet unexplainable circumstances, Lanzig took practical possession and ownership of the Osgood Corporation and the Swiss estate. Lanzig used the fact that Osgood's body was never found to his advantage. He held power of attorney over all of Osgood's holdings. He had taken steps earlier to protect himself from the treachery of his former master.

Even with its namesake dead, the corporate machine continued undisturbed. Lanzig had thoroughly secured his position. He now sat as master enjoying unimagined wealth and power.

The meeting taking place that night had been planned for some time. Lanzig now played host for the elite. He would sit among the powerful in place of Osgood.

All furniture from the Great Hall had been removed and replaced with a massive thirty-six foot long table brought in and positioned in the center of the hall. Thirty-six large ornate chairs lined the table. Two chairs were placed at the southern end of the table. One of them sat singularly and noticeably larger.

The long draperies were pulled and the lights were darkened. Six large lamps occupied spots along the center of the table in the otherwise dark room. An amber light from the lamps spilled down on the table and onto the faces of those around it. The two ends of the table remained dark.

All of the guests had arrived and were seated in their assigned places. At the southern end two chairs sat vacant. All of the soft mumbling ceased when the final two guests entered the room and found their place. One of the two pounded the table with his fist to get everyone's attention.

"Gentlemen, welcome. For those of you who do not know me, I am Yacov Besnik. This evening it is my honor and pleasure to introduce you to the director of this evening's events, Anton Cheva D'bar."

Everyone stood and applauded. Yacov directed his arm toward Anton. This continued until he directed everyone to sit.

Anton remained seated as Yacov continued.

"Thank you all for coming. Like me, you have longed for this time and this meeting. Before we begin, let me first thank our host, Herr Lanzig. We are sorry that Herr Osgood is unable to be here. But in essence, Lanzig sits in the place of Herr Osgood. So, thank you for your care and attention for this evening."

Lanzig bowed his head in recognition. No one else at the table looked toward Lanzig. All attention focused on the man seated in the large chair.

"Very well. Without further delay." Yacov bowed his head to the man next to him and immediately sat down.

Anton waited a few seconds before rising from his seat. Even in the darkened shadow of his end of the table, he obviously stood tall and lean. He surveyed his audience.

Then he spoke. "Welcome." His voice resonated with a deep, rich and instantaneously alluring tone.

"We all know why we are here. For years the plan has been in motion. We have worked, positioned, and waited. It is almost time to begin. Each of you are here because of your positions, power, or influence. All of you know what is at stake. All of you will share in what awaits us."

He began to slowly walk around the table beyond the light. Only his voice and footsteps revealed his position. His words came out slow and deliberate. With each word a sense of something growing and building filed the air.

"We all know that in order to build something new, old things must be replaced and sometimes destroyed. As we move forward, do not allow the smoke and ashes of the dying order trouble you. None of you have achieved your present place by attending to weaker instincts. You must not allow sentimentalities or emotion to lessen your resolve. You have seized your place by strength of will. That will is about to be tested. Harden your resolve for the purpose we are sworn to."

Everyone's hearts raced. His words electrified the air. He now stood against the wall, a tall silhouette of shadow. He swept his arm across those at the table.

"We are no strangers to power. We have all obtained it in various ways. We each hold it jealously. But we each know that this power is nothing compared to the real power that binds us together tonight."

Suddenly an unseen energy began coursing through everyone at the table. They wrapped their arms around themselves as if to keep it from escaping. Even Lanzig felt a hot shiver bolting through his body. The sensation both frightened and excited him.

D'bar raised both his arms into the air. He had complete command of the moment.

"All of us are partners and servants to this power. Some of you are chosen for positions but all will share in the prize. Yield and obey it and your reward is immeasurable. Resist or betray it and your punishment is unspeakable."

The speaker spread his arms as if reaching out across the whole room.

"Are you with me?"

Everyone at the table rose to their feet and screamed in reply. "Yes!"

"Will you swear your devotion to me and to the power!"

"Yes!"

"Then repeat it to me. Swear your oath."

As if in some mesmerized stupor they all raised their right arms into the air with their palms open toward the man. The words entered their minds and came out of their mouths.

"By the power that binds us and fills the air, we declare our unfailing allegiance. We have no god but the power and the one who holds it. We swear ourselves to you our Master. You will bring us through collapse, destruction, and chaos into a new world. To you and to this we swear ourselves. Peace, Prosperity and Order. Peace, Prosperity and Order. Peace, Prosperity and Order."

They repeated it with increasing volume.

Anton whispered it to himself in unison with their shouts. He then raised his arms and pressed them forward toward them and shouted, "Receive the power."

As if struck by an invisible hand, they were all thrown back onto the ground. They remained there for several minutes. As they each regained consciousness, they looked over to Anton seated in the large chair. One by one they got up and went over to the man. He extended his hand. Each in turn kneeled before him and kissed his hand. The man would then bend over and whisper into their ear. They would then rise, nod their head and leave the room.

Lanzig didn't understand all that occurred but he in turn followed the others. He listened to hear what the man would say to him.

As he bowed, the man whispered to him, "Although you are new among us, you will share in all I have to offer. Serve me well and power is yours."

Lanzig, never an emotional man, kneeled almost helpless to stand as the words shook him to the core. The man reached down and helped him up. D'bar leaned over and whispered into his ear. "I will be here until tomorrow afternoon. We will talk before I leave."

Though electrified, Lanzig felt a slight uneasiness. Something in the man's smile seemed familiar. As he left the room, he racked his mind to recall it. Like a forgotten name at the tip of the tongue, it finally hit him. He had seen the same smile on Osgood. He mulled over the apprehension. Time would answer his questions.

# Chapter 5

Each of them felt a light chill in the breeze as they sat around a fire drinking their tea. It didn't take long for the Judean desert to cool down.

Eli closed his eyes as he slowly sipped his cup. "I've never tasted anything like this tea before."

"And most likely, you never will," Shamer responded with a smile.

Moshe chuckled. "I remember this taste. I used different water, but the taste is the same. Thank you Shamer. And thank our friend for sending it."

They each enjoyed the isolated quiet as the last traces of the day faded away. Finishing their tea and a small meal, Shamer rose.

He turned to Moshe. "Allow me to borrow your Rod."

Moshe handed it to him. Shamer stepped away a short distance and traced something a long and somewhat narrow image on the ground. He then handed the Rod back to Moshe.

He stepped into the image at one end and motioned for them to come see. As they looked down, they recognized the image. Shamer had drawn a perfect outline of the nation of Israel.

"Observe and learn, for this will be your path. As decreed, for three years and a half you will deliver the Story in word and deed."

Shamer stepped to a place in the Negev. He reached into a pouch and placed a stone on the ground. "Tel Sheva."

Almost next to it he placed another. "Be'er Sheva."

He took one step to the west and one step north and placed another. "Sderot."

Shamer looked at them. "This is your first year."

They both nodded.

Shamer walked along the coast. Midway he stopped and placed a stone down. "Tel Aviv-Jaffa."

Moving further up the coast he again placed another stone down. "Haifa."

Stepping slightly down and eastward he placed another. "Nazareth."

He looked at them. "This is your second year."

They nodded again.

He then stepped to a place near the northern end of the Dead Sea and placed down a stone. "Jericho."

He took a step and a half southwest. He looked at them and then placed two stones down. "Jerusalem."

Shamer sighed deeply. "This is the last year and a half."

They looked at each other and then back at Shamer. They again nodded.

"Nine stones I have placed down but one remains." He reached into the pouch and looked at the remaining stone. "This is the tenth."

He slowly bent down and gently placed the last stone in Jerusalem.

"These ten stones represent ten messages. As you journey to these cities, you will declare and demonstrate the message you are given. To some it brings salvation and a miracle, to others, judgment.

Healing or a curse, such is the fate of men before their Maker."

Shamer detached the pouch and handed it to Moshe. "Gather up the stones. Use them as a reminder and a sign."

Shamer looked up into the night sky. "The autumn feasts will begin soon and so will your work. The blessing of the LORD is upon you both."

He vanished.

✡ ✡ ✡

To divert himself, Brandon spent the next three weeks taking a few day trips. The hotel arranged for him to join tour groups going to the Dead Sea and to Masada. He also traveled to Be'er Sheva to attend an orchestral event. He had considered traveling further north but decided against it. He couldn't explain it but he detected a strong nervousness all around him. The Fall Jewish holidays were approaching. Increased military alerts added to the discordant feelings of the populace. So Brandon returned to Arad. He settled into a daily schedule, which provided him a sense of stability.

Each day he set out on a two-mile walk after breakfast. He began to meet and develop surface relationships with merchants he met as he browsed their shops. He began to pick up and learn some Hebrew and Arabic. Most of the people he met helped him and seemed to appreciate his attempt.

As per Freddy's advice, he kept a low profile on the Net, answering mail from only a select few individuals. He also decided to finally finish Eli's story.

✡ ✡ ✡

### The Chronicle of Eli

Shamer waited for Eli on the hill. When Eli reached Shamer, his instructor wrapped his strong arms around him. Shamer could see in the young man's eyes a measured eagerness mixed with the frustration of silenced lips.

Rarely did others see or know of Shamer's visits with Eli. Yet, a week hardly passed that Shamer would not meet with Eli. Shamer would use the visits to teach Eli on a variety of subjects. While Eli's tongue remained silent, his ability to hear and comprehend allowed him to learn unhindered. Shamer taught Eli sign language. This skill gave Eli an avenue of expression that would have otherwise taken years and a special school.

Being raised in a Bedouin home, Eli attended school just as any other Bedouin boy. The teacher's at Eli's schools were constantly amazed at his proficiency and breadth of knowledge. Whenever they congratulated him, Eli only smiled. He knew that Shamer's tutelage gave him an advantage. No one knew about Eli's secret world and he let no one else know.

Eli also secreted away other parts of his life. He feared what would happen if he ever let it out. He kept it buried but not forgotten. This day would change all of that.

Shamer pointed to a small grassy area. "Let us sit down. The sheep are in no danger."

Eli smiled as he looked into Shamer's ever-watchful eyes. The confident tone of Shamer's voice reassured Eli. He trusted Shamer completely. Eli sat down next to him.

Shamer looked out across the terrain. He closed his eyes and listened. He slowly opened his eyes and turned to Eli.

"I am glad that the silence of your world is limited to your lips. The songs and sounds of the world are not silent to you."

Eli looked down. He slowly nodded.

Shamer took a deep breath. "I am here today to tell you of the Story and your part in it. I know your heart suffers with pains hidden deep in shadowy memories. I also know that it is those memories that silenced you. But in these years, your silence has also protected you in ways you will someday understand. But the days of silence will one day come to an end."

Eli wrinkled his brow trying to understand.

"I hear a voice crying out from the wilderness. It is a voice strong and mighty with God. All of the world will one day hear this voice and tremble. The words from this voice will cause the great and small to take heed. This voice will deliver the words of God's judgment and of His mercy."

Eli's heart raced at hearing Shamer's words.

Shamer looked directly into Eli's eyes. "Yours is the voice I hear! And God will empower your words so that all the world will hear the Story proclaimed once again in power."

Eli touched his throat. He used signs to ask, "How can this be?"

Shamer chuckled, "Nothing is impossible with God."

Again Eli signed, "Will He do this now?"

"As always, He will do it when the time is right."

Eli's signs animated his frustration. "What's wrong with now? He is able and I am ready."

"Yes, He is very able, my young friend. But perhaps you are not as ready as you think. The task He has for you far exceeds the ordinary. There are matters in your heart that remain unsettled."

The words stung quick and deep. He wondered how Shamer knew. He had never shared them. He assumed that he had thoroughly masked them. With Shamer's words, a floodgate tore open and torrents poured out uncontrollably.

His hands exploded with words. "You have no idea what it is like! Evil invaded my home and stole my parents away from me. Why did God allow this? He could have saved my parents! He could have stopped it. Tell me! Tell me why!"

Eli collapsed face down pounding the ground. Shamer knelt down and placed his hand on Eli's trembling shoulder.

Shamer waited a few moments before speaking. "I am not the one to answer such questions. The answer will come one day. And on that day, your voice will sing and you will know more than you imagined."

Eli heard but his will refused to listen. He could only convey his anger by pounding his fists into the ground. He continued until his hands ached and the tears ran dry.

Shamer placed both his hands on Eli and looked up. "Into this restless soul, sing Your song of peace."

He then vanished.

In subsequent visits, neither of them ever brought up that day. Eli preferred that the matter be forgotten. He imagined that if left alone, it would fade away. The opposite was true.

Shamer continued to visit and teach him. Eli politely listened. He learned many facts and truths, but the wall remained. Outwardly, Eli lived an exemplary life. No one around him could guess the gnawing turmoil. No one knew his struggle to hide from Shamer's words. With every passing year the wall grew taller and thicker. Eli prided himself in his ability to outwardly hide it. Occasionally doubt crept in and shook him. He avoided hard eye contact with Shamer. He overcompensated with brash attempts at humor. And so it continued. Year to year, he assumed that the hidden anger had gone away. Then came the wedding.

Eli and Ibrahim lived in every way as brothers. From the day he came to stay in their home, everyone in the community assumed Eli belonged to Ibrahim's family. Few secrets existed among the Bedouins in their small village. Their mutual hardships as Bedouins bound them in history and life. Although Ibrahim's family was not Muslim, everyone highly respected them. People never questioned Eli's relationship to the family or within the community.

As Eli and Ibrahim grew into manhood, they shared family responsibilities and privileges. They each owned a portion of the flock and a share of the small family enterprise. Eli admired Ibrahim's unconditional acceptance of his silence and peculiarities. He never doubted Ibrahim's loyalty or love. He knew he could ask anything of Ibrahim. He also knew that he would do the same for his friend and brother Ibrahim.

Yet it caught Eli by surprise the day Ibrahim and Minera stood before him and announced their intention to marry. Outwardly he embraced them both and clapped his congratulations. But inwardly he felt a wall cracking. He excused himself, signing that his tears embarrassed him. He saw the joy in Ibrahim's eyes. He knew that the couple did not suspect the truth.

Later, Eli joined the celebration of the whole village. Even Shamer made a rare public appearance at the party. For the most part Shamer stood back and watched. Every time Eli glanced over to him, Shamer nodded. Eli wondered if Shamer even suspected the earthquake rumbling through his heart at that moment. Eli walked around and faked joyous greetings in order to avoid looking at Shamer. Weary of fighting the obvious, he decided to confront Shamer. But when he looked up, Shamer had left. Eli maintained the charade of enjoying the festivities for the rest of the evening.

Sleep eluded Eli that night. The next morning he felt as if he were suffocating. He knew he had to get away. Sensing a loss of control, he concocted a lie. They all noticed his haggard state that morning. He signed to the family that he needed to go into the wilderness to fast and pray. He told them that God had commanded it. With the mention of God, the rest of the family rejoiced and prepared provisions for his time away. The lie stung deepest when Ibrahim patted him on the back and wished him God's presence and mercy.

Some distance from the house, he turned and saw Ibrahim waving. The lie burned his soul. He hated the feeling but couldn't find a way to turn back and face it. So into the wilderness he went. He had no idea what awaited him.

# Chapter 6

## *Osgood Castle, St. Gallen, Switzerland*

**M**any of the dignitaries had departed in the night. Those who remained had scheduled meetings with D'bar including Lanzig.

Lanzig waited patiently for his appointed time. He pondered how to decipher all of the angles of his new arrangements. He tried to never proceed without a plan and concurrent contingencies. He had learned that such endeavors often ended tragically.

All of the morning meetings were taking place in the main office and adjoining library. There were other places and computer stations throughout the castle but no other computer had the security available in his office. He knew that to do the kind of research he wanted to do on D'bar required proceeding with supreme caution. He received a text message. D'bar would meet with him in five minutes in Osgood's old office.

Lanzig had left Osgood's office unchanged when he moved into the castle. The design of the office and library communicated power and intimidation. Yet today he entered it, not as master but as servant.

D'bar stood by the large window facing out.

Without turning, he spoke. "Come to me."

Lanzig walked over and stood next to him. He remained silent, waiting for Anton to begin.

"This office is magnificent. Osgood knew how to project power in architecture. I have learned much about him simply by walking around in here. But enough about the past, it is the future that now concerns us, wouldn't you say Herr Lanzig?"

"Yes, indeed sir. You said you had something to tell me?"

"Very direct and to the point. I like that."

He turned to face Lanzig. "You have become a part of our special group almost by default. You took over Osgood's enterprise with surprising speed. For that, I commend you. But I'm sure you have many questions."

Lanzig's silence said much.

D'bar nodded. "I know that you are man of action like myself. But action without direction is foolishness. I wish I could take the time to fill you in completely, but my schedule is tight. I have much to tend to and little time to make things ready. Even though you come into this late, I have a place for you. If you serve well, there is no end for a man of your particular talents."

Lanzig half smiled as he nodded. He wanted to portray complete willingness.

"Very good, Lanzig. I am sending you to Israel. There you will assist Yacov Besnik. He is the Regional Transition Czar for the Middle East. He will instruct you on your assignment. As you know, that region is most troublesome to world stability. We have plans in place to solve the turmoil plaguing the region. It is vital that these plans are carried out."

Anton saw the look on Lanzig's face.

"As I shared last night, there is much in store. Acquiring Osgood's fortune is only the beginning. You must prepare yourself for possibilities surpassing anything you have ever done before. Do well in Israel and you will be among my great ones. The conquerors of old only dreamed of what we will accomplish."

D'bar's fists tightened as he fixed his gaze on the mountains surrounding the castle.

"If it were possible, even these mountains would bow down when we are finished with our plan. We will become gods among men."

He slapped Lanzig on the back as he turned to leave. Lanzig stared out the window. He heard the man's laughter behind him but fixed his gaze outward.

Just before leaving the room, the man repeated the phrase, "Gods among men." He laughed even louder as he left the room.

✡   ✡   ✡

### *The Chronicle of Eli*

Eli walked into the wilderness without a true sense of direction. Although he was no stranger to being out alone in the desert, he struggled that first evening. He despised the false pretense that had brought him there, but decided that returning and admitting it wasn't an option.

The past serenity of time alone eluded him. Night sounds that usually calmed him, now stirred an almost predatory fear. The small campfire did little to dispel his nervousness. It frustrated and angered him to experience such feelings. He scolded himself for acting like a frightened child. But he couldn't shake it away.

His aggravation finally gave way to the need to sleep. Sitting against a boulder, he drifted off. He slept so hard that he didn't even notice the soft footsteps. He never realized the presence of his visitor.

The sound of a piece of wood falling into the heart of his campfire stirred Eli. It startled him to see someone standing next to the fire. Unable to say anything, he simply stared, waiting to see what his unknown guest would do next.

Having finished his work on the fire, the visitor sat down facing

Eli. He noticed the strained look in Eli's eyes. He was a young man close to Eli's age. His clothing betrayed a higher income but not westernized. It calmed him that his features were in every way similar to the Bedouin's he knew.

"Sorry if I startled you. You were asleep when I arrived and I noticed your fire dying down. What I've added should do for the night. My name is Hassam."

Hassam waited for Eli to respond. Finally Eli used signs to let him know that he couldn't speak. To Eli's surprise, Hassam answered in sign language.

"I have a family member who has no voice. Are your ears silent as well, or is it only your tongue?"

Eli replied, "It is only my tongue. I can hear you clearly."

"Ah, excellent. From your small provisions, you're not on a long journey. My guess is that you are on the run."

Eli looked down without answering.

"Don't worry friend. I've run away from home myself. I've had enough of rules and boundaries. How about you?"

Eli slightly nodded. Then he noticed something that made him ask.

"Where are your provisions? You don't seem to have anything for someone out on your own."

"Oh that. My provisions and transportation are not far from here. I came over when I noticed the light of your fire. Since you're running like me, if you want you can join me. I'm leaving north in the morning."

Hassam saw that the idea interested Eli. Hassam looked out toward some distant lights.

"I don't know about you but I'm tired of others telling me what I should do with my life. I think I should decide that on my own. I need to be true to myself. That's what I say. What about you?"

Eli considered Hassam's words. For the first time in his life, he considered the idea of being on his own. He looked at his meager provisions and realized the futility of such a plan. Hassam watched Eli and jumped right in.

"Look, I can see you don't have much. Don't worry. I have more than enough for the both of us. Don't worry about what your parents may say, decide for yourself."

The mention of parents caught Eli off guard. He quickly responded.

"I have no parents. They were killed when I was a boy."

"I'm so sorry friend. You truly are on your own. Well look, I won't abandon you. Stick with me and we'll go places. You don't need to live like this anymore. I can help you make a new life for yourself. I have money and connections."

As Eli listened to Hassam, questions swirled in his mind. Then a thought came to him. "Hassam, if you are so connected, why are you out here?"

"Yeah, it looks strange I know. I just needed to get away from the grind of . . ."

"Liar!" A voice boomed from behind them. The intensity immediately shut Hassam up.

Eli turned toward the voice. He instantly recognized it. The next moment Shamer stood in the light of the fire.

He pointed directly at Hassam and once again shouted. "Liar from the pit, return to your master and declare these words to him. This one belongs to the Most High."

Suddenly Hassam's countenance devolved into something akin to an angered lizard. His eyes blazed fiery red even as he cowered under Shamer's words. In place of words came hissing sounds and a foul odious smell.

Shamer took another step toward Hassam. The creature hissed louder as he scurried out into the darkness.

Eli sat trembling, uncertain of what he had witnessed. Shamer stood looking out into the darkness for several minutes. When he finally turned, Eli saw sternness in his eyes like never before. Shamer calmed himself before looking directly at Eli.

"Pray, for your visitations are not completed for this evening."
He vanished.

Eli fell face down. He wept as he recounted his lie and the subtle
dark pull he had experienced. He lay face down for quite some time
pleading for forgiveness. His cries of remorse turned into pleas of
loneliness. Eventually his heart hit a wall. It was the wall he had
avoided and even run from. He had bargained with himself that it did
not exist. Now its reality stood undeniably right in front of him. The
wall could be described in one word, surrender.

Eli pounded the ground. The word rang over and over in his
mind. Each time it repeated, other words would follow. "Surrender
your pain. Surrender your will. Surrender your desires. Surrender your
past. Surrender your present. Surrender your future. Surrender . . .
surrender."

With each phrase his heart yielded. And with each yielding came a
lifting. In the end, though lying flat on the ground, his heart felt
weightless.

He soon became aware of a hand softly patting his head. With
each touch his body quivered.

Then he heard a voice. "Speak my son, tell me what your heart
longs to say."

Eli rolled over and looked up into the face of someone he had
never seen before and yet . . .

Again the man spoke. "Speak to me."

At first it was like a fire in his heart fighting to move up into his
mouth. His cheeks and lips trembled. He finally opened his mouth
and spoke. "Lord."

Eli quickly turned face down. He reached out and touched the
scarred feet of his Lord.

Eli whispered the one word over and over again. Each time he
said it, the strength of his voice increased.

After a time, the Lord reached down and helped him to sit up. Eli gleamed as he gazed into the eyes of his master. The Lord sat down next to him.

Eli took a deep breath. "I can speak."

"Yes you can. And you will be My voice to the world. But for now, I need you to listen to My instructions concerning the mission for which you are chosen."

Through the rest of the night Eli listened as the Lord revealed to him the portion of the Story he would play. As the first rays of the morning crested the horizon, the Lord completed His instructions.

Eli had listened intently. It amused him to hear his voice as he asked questions. When the Lord had finished, they both sat and watched the sun rise.

In a voice as calm as the gentle breeze moving across their faces, the Lord spoke. "I always love to watch it come up. It's like a fresh reminder of a promise I will keep. It brings Me delight. What about you Eli?"

Eli felt embarrassed discussing the subject with its creator. And yet, . . . his heart danced with the opportunity. He felt like a little boy.

"Whenever I take the time to stop, watch, and ponder it, I think of . . . I think of better. That today might be better than yesterday. A part of me hopes for better days, to be a better friend, a better son, . . . just better."

The Lord smiled and whispered, "Hope."

Eli heard Him. "Yes Sir. Hope."

"Good. Very good."

They both sat silent for several more minutes until they heard the sound of footsteps. Shamer stopped when he saw that they had noticed him.

The Lord invited him over. "Come sit with us Shamer. I have some final instructions for both of you."

Shamer moved quickly and sat next to Eli, each facing the Lord.

"Eli, as I have said, in time you will be My witness. There is another who will join you. Until then, you are to return home.

Confess to your family your deception and My restoration, but say nothing of the mission I have for you. Shamer will continue to guide and guard you."

The Lord looked at Shamer, "This is and has been My mission for you. The enemy now knows that Eli is My chosen servant. Teach him to recognize the enemy and the battle he will face."

The Lord turned and looked into the distant horizon. "The days for My return are approaching. But before then, My witnesses will declare My Story with boldness and clarity."

He turned to look directly at Eli. "This work I have for you will be a source of great joy and sorrow. For the great and terrible day of the Lord comes. Many will hear and believe. But evil is multiplied in the hearts of men and judgment is also coming. Be strong and courageous. I will come again to you once more before you come to Me."

He was gone.

Shamer placed his arm around Eli's shoulder. "My heart never ceases to tremble at the sound of His voice. The Lord has honored His call on you. The heavens rejoice at the coming of this day. Now return home."

Shamer got up and helped Eli to his feet. Walking back, Eli poured out his heart in words. He now gave voice to all of the years of teaching. Eli's mind ignited with clarity of thought that exploded from his lips. As they walked along, Eli would often stop and laugh out loud. It delighted him to hear the sound of his own voice.

Shamer listened and smiled. He reveled in the joy of his ward. Yet his eyes never ceased in their vigilance. Such is the diligence of a guardian.

In the years to follow, the faith and boldness of Eli increased. All were amazed with his transformation. The miracle of having regained his speech was impressive enough. Added to that, his words contained power and wisdom. When asked for an explanation, he would merely smile and point heavenward.

✡ ✡ ✡

As Brandon finished the last page, he wrestled with the credulity in his own mind. Could he believe what he had read? He recalled Moshe's story and the events at the Dead Sea, . . . was it possible?

The roar of air raid sirens interrupted his thoughts. A voice in the hallway yelled out in multiple languages instructing everyone to go the hotel air raid shelter. Brandon grabbed his phone and the chronicle. He joined the people in the queue. Looking around, Brandon saw fear and panic on people's faces. When he arrived at the shelter, a lady asked the hotel worker if he knew what was going on. The worker merely shrugged his shoulders and waved her on.

They spent twelve hours in the shelter. Food and water were brought in, but they permitted no one to leave. A military official came on one occasion and whispered something to the hotel manager.

When they were finally allowed to leave no explanation was ever given. Very quickly one thing became obvious. The world had changed.

# Chapter 7

Brandon returned to his room. He immediately sat on his bed and turned on the television. Everything about the news broadcast was chaotic and frightening. He surfed the channels looking for any definitive explanations. The talking heads seemed unanimously uncertain about what to say next.

As he sat looking and listening, a numbing apprehension welled up inside. Suddenly a banging on the door startled him. He almost fell off the bed. He looked to the door and felt petrified. Three more loud raps and he heard his name shouted from the outside. He recognized the voice.

He ran and looked through the peephole. It was Moshe. Brandon immediately opened the door.

Moshe wasted no time. "Brandon, do you have a canteen and some water?"

Brandon gave an affirmative nod.

"Get them and whatever you can put in your backpack. Be downstairs and outside in five minutes. Don't delay. We don't have much time."

Before he could say anything Moshe cut him off with an intense stare while pointing to his watch. Moshe turned and took a step before turning back. Brandon stood there stunned.

Moshe practically shouted. "Brandon! Move! I mean it! And don't forget the canteen and some water . . . NOW!"

Moshe exited in the hallway and forced his way through several people who were running in the hallway. Moshe's last word shook Brandon out of his temporary paralysis.

Brandon raced through his room and gathered what few items he could stuff in his small backpack. He almost picked up his backpack to leave when he remembered the canteen and some water. He gathered them and left the room. He could see a crowd waiting at the elevator so he decided to take the stairs. He raced downstairs and outside.

Brandon spotted Moshe standing beside a vehicle. Moshe signaled him to hurry. When Brandon made it to the vehicle he stopped to look around. Up and down the street people were racing around in various states of mounting confusion and unrest. In some places crowds or makeshift gangs were congregating as if they were plotting their next move.

Moshe shocked him back with a shout. "Get in, now!"

Brandon hopped in the back seat and they sped off.

Eli weaved his way through the crowds walking aimlessly in the streets. Neither he nor Moshe said a word as they headed west out of Arad. Brandon waited until they were well out of the city before saying anything.

"Guys, you've been gone for over a month, where have you been? What's going on?"

Moshe and Eli didn't answer. They merely looked at each other.

Brandon waited until he could hold it no longer. "Come on guys. I need something. What in the world is happening?"

Eli looked at Moshe and nodded. Moshe turned to Brandon.

"Did you read Eli's Chronicle?"

Brandon nodded.

"You also remember when I told you my story?" Moshe paused. Brandon simply nodded.

"Our mission has begun. The days of distress and trouble have commenced. You must decide if you wish to continue to travel with us. You will be safe with us but I cannot guarantee as much if you leave us. You don't have long to decide."

Moshe turned and looked forward. Eli gave Brandon a short glance through the rearview mirror. They continued down the desert highway with no one saying a word.

Twenty minutes out of Arad, Eli looked at his watch. Scattered abandoned cars and trucks lined portions of the highway. Eli found a place to pull off.

He again looked at his watch. "This should do."

Both Eli and Moshe got out of the vehicle. Eli began to walk up a small rise. Moshe stood beside the door of the back seat. Brandon rolled down his window.

Moshe leaned in and spoke. "Brandon, now is the time to choose. You are free to take this vehicle and go wherever you want or you can stay with us."

Brandon sat confused. "Moshe, what's going on?"

Moshe looked at his watch. "There's no time to explain. You have to decide. Choose wisely my friend."

Moshe smiled and turned to follow Eli. Brandon pressed his temples. His mind battled with thoughts practically shouting at him. His hands trembled as he looked toward Moshe. He had reached Eli who sat on a rise about two hundred yards off the highway.

Raw fear finally shook him out his paralysis. He grabbed his backpack and exited the vehicle. He ran up the rise. As he looked toward Moshe and read his lips, "Hurry."

Like a baseball runner sliding into a base, Brandon landed to the left of Moshe totally winded. He sat up. He started to ask a question when he felt it.

Like a wave on the sea, the ground in the distance slowly rose and dropped. Then came the sound. Like the roar of an approaching herd of trucks, a growing rumbling moved towards them.

Eli turned to the other two. "Hold on."

The shaking lasted around twenty seconds. They each steadied themselves as best as they could. Brandon fell over and almost started to roll down the rise when Moshe grabbed him. When the shaking and rumbling ceased and moved away, they each got up. As the dust around them cleared, Brandon could see the dust rising in the east.

Brandon then looked back toward the road. The ground had completely swallowed their vehicle. Brandon took a deep breath as he turned to look at Eli and Moshe.

Moshe smiled and slowly nodded. "You chose wisely."

Eli shook the dust off of his clothing and picked up his small bag. Moshe picked up his bag and the Rod. He looked at Brandon, "Let's go."

Brandon picked up his bag and followed right behind them. As he watched Moshe place his arm around Eli's shoulder he wondered to himself. "Could all of this be true? Were these two men really who they claimed to be? And if they were, what did that mean for him and the rest of the world?"

Even as they walked, they enjoyed each other's company while passing the destroyed landscape. They stood tall like mighty mountains in a barren landscape. From this point on, Brandon and soon the rest of the world would refer to them simply as *"the Two."*

✡   ✡   ✡

The world seemed almost paralyzed in a chaotic panic. Air travel worldwide had been temporarily grounded, yet Lanzig's plane landed in Brussels with little problem. Prior to the panic he had received orders to come to Brussels for a meeting.

# Chapter 8

### The Chronicle of the Witnesses – Year One

The recording of all the works and words of the Two Witnesses would require more than time allows. Only eternity's record will fully document the complete testimony of the works and words of Eli and Moshe. This brief record is left as a continued testimony for those who remain. Take heed. Time is short.

The first four months followed a regular routine. It seems a stretch to call the events of those days either regular or routine. Perhaps a better description is to use the word pattern. And so began the work of the *Two Witnesses*.

Both the world and Israel focused their attention on events other than the happenings in the Negev. Stories did eventually begin to trickle out. Initially, they seemed like exaggerated hysteria in keeping with the confusion of the times. But enough reports surfaced that in due course they caught the attention of certain officials. One could call it the beginning of conflicts.

After leaving Arad, *the Two* and Brandon traversed the area of the Negev. They traveled mostly by foot but occasionally caught random transportation. They spent those early months among the unregistered Bedouins villages.

Like most who wandered the countryside in those days, the three of them seemed to end the day in a village. Eli had lived among the Bedouins. He understood their customs of hospitality, which helped them gain acceptance into the life of the villages they visited. Within a day it would become obvious that Eli and Moshe constituted more than regular or average wanderers.

Brandon understood his situation as an outsider. Yet Eli and Moshe extended never-ending love and friendship to him. He realized that they truly cared for him and didn't merely want him as a prize or convert to their cause. Yet it didn't escape his attention that there existed a unique bond between *the Two*. They drew upon each other in a symbiosis of purpose. This both attracted and frightened people they came in contact with.

Every village had a person from a leading family who was seen as the village leader. *The Two* would always begin their testimony with that leader. Their response to *the Two* would either be acceptance, ambivalence or outright rejection.

One day they came to an unnamed village. It sat off a main highway but near enough to spot because of the scattered houses on the hillside. The three of them walked the short distance from the highway to the village. They arrived around twilight. They met a shepherd along a path. He invited them to spend the night in a small shelter on the edge of the village. It humored Brandon that he had begun to acclimate to the Bedouin life.

In the morning the shepherd greeted them with the offer of hot tea at a nearby house. After tea they inquired about the village leader. The leader's name was Sheik Basher Srihan.

The house was not elaborate by western standards but clean and ornately furnished. The floor coverings were elegantly designed and colorful. A simple stove sat in a corner with a steaming teakettle sitting atop it. Along the floor of three walls soft floor seating was arranged for the backs of guests. On the main wall, several very large pillows supported a prominent figure. Servants scurried about to hastily clear away food and drink.

The moment *the Two* walked into the room everyone felt the tension. Bashir had just completed his breakfast. All but one of the servants quickly left the room. It didn't take long to see why Bashir held the position of leader in his village. At six foot five inches tall and an imposing three hundred pounds, everyone else easily submitted to his mere presence. Bashir had intimidated others his whole life. At present, people in the village lived under his domination.

Eli calmed the air with a friendly Bedouin greeting honoring the home and its leader. Bashir smiled at the acknowledgment.

Bashir looked directly at Eli. "I have heard of the two of you. I wondered if we would see you come to our small village. The things I have heard are both strange and intriguing. Tell me, why have you come?"

Eli stepped forward. "We come in peace and in the name of the True and Living God. Our message is simple. The time is come to believe in His name and His Savior before it is too late."

Bashir responded loudly, "Too late for what?"

"The days are approaching when in His coming He will judge this world. From this there is no escape."

Bashir pondered a few seconds before asking his next question. "And which God is this that has sent you? My people worship one God and his name is Allah and he speaks of judgment day. Is this who you speak of?"

"There is but one God. All others are false. His name is not a mystery. He came first to the people of Israel."

At the mention of Israel, Bashir rose to his feet in anger.

Moshe, who stood beside Eli, slightly raised the Rod and softly tapped it to the ground. Bashir flew back as if slammed by a large fist of air. The large man struggled for a moment to catch his breath. Leaning on one elbow, he looked at *the Two* puzzled and frightened for reasons he didn't understand.

Still feeling a pain in his chest, Bashir spoke. "What sort of sorcery is this?"

"This is not sorcery. This occurred so that you may know that we are His witnesses and what we proclaim is true. Most here are your family. As leader, you are responsible for their lives. We call upon you to turn from your ways and believe what we say so that you and your people may be saved."

The mention of family subdued Bashir. Though the claim of Islam was upon him, he had never been a religious man. His faith and its traditions were merely vehicles for his authority and position. Never before had it been called into question to such a degree.

"And what is it that we are being saved from?"

"From yourself and the judgment to come."

"We believe in the judgment. But how are we saved from ourselves?"

"All men have fallen short. You fail, even with your faith in a false god. How much greater is your failure in not believing in the True and Living God. What we could not do for ourselves, God has done in His Son Jesus. He came to rescue all who will trust in what He has provided."

Bashir couldn't explain it, but the words bore deep into his heart. Still on the ground, he recognized that his great stature, the source of his authority, had been vanquished. For the first time in his life he had doubts. How could he continue if his people knew?

As if reading his thoughts, Eli spoke, "Admission of our failure is the only road leading to the Savior's rescue. The Lord does not shame us in our failure but delivers us in His victory. Do not fear."

Bashir stared in astonishment. How could this man possibly know? No one knew of his fear of failure. All of his bravado and harshness were bulwarks against any possibility of discovery. Yet here he was knocked down in body and heart, fearful.

Eli looked down at Bashir. Yet rather than looking down on him in triumph, his eyes were full of care and compassion. Bashir wondered why his conqueror showed grace and not triumphing over him. Could it actually be true? Was it possible?

"Bashir, humble yourself before the truth of God and He will raise you a mighty man."

Bashir slowly sat up. He noticed his hands shaking and his heart racing. He wanted to draw up the strength to express his old self but it had left him. Bashir saw something in these men's eyes that was dismantling his being. Though he fought it, he was drawn to it. Suddenly he knew.

He remembered a time as a little boy and the look in his mother's eyes. The gentle gaze in her eyes shouted unconditional love. He had used the word love when speaking of his family but didn't really understand it. He certainly had never attained what he had received from his mother.

Yet here were these men, firm and resolute while displaying that same look. How could they possibly to be strong and loving at the same time?

Finally he whispered, "What must I do?"

Eli walked over to him. As Eli approached, Bashir lowered his head.

Eli's words were soft yet resolute. "Look up, Bashir." And he did.

"Believe in your heart and confess with your mouth that Jesus is Lord and that God has raised Him from the dead."

His thoughts collided in conflict. How could he betray his heritage? Yet, besides his position of power, what had it provided? He thought of his family and in particular his youngest son. He wondered if his son knew that he loved him.

As his lips trembled a well of strength began to flow upward. He looked directly at Eli. With two words a light seemed to explode within him, "I believe."

Eli reached down and put his hand on Bashir's shoulder. "Yes, so you do."

A man his size rarely felt light, yet nothing else could describe the load that seemed to float away. He had never expressed tender emotions, yet suddenly his cheeks were damp with tears.

He slowly wiped them away, "What has happened to me? What have you done to me?"

"I have done nothing. You have simply walked into a new life, a life given to you by the True and Living God."

Just then Bashir's wife walked in. She stared in stunned silence at seeing her husband kneeling before the visitor. "What is happening? What have you done to my husband?" Fear filled in her voice.

Bashir stretched out his hand. "Misha, come. Come to me."

She cautiously walked past Moshe and Eli and stood before her husband who remained on his knees.

Bashir took her by the hand. "Misha, I am so sorry."

Her eyes widen in shock. She looked at the visitors and then to her husband.

She saw something in Bashir's eyes she had never seen before, tenderness. When the look remained, her disbelief began to yield to what seemed impossible. Trying to make sense of it she could only manage one word, "How?"

Bashir turned toward Eli.

Eli took in a deep breath. "Let us all sit."

For the next two hours Eli and Moshe taught Bashir while Misha listened. Within the first hour Misha had heard enough. She understood what had happened to her husband. She confessed a new faith.

The three visitors spent the next five days in the village. Bashir invited in the heads of the other families of the village. They listened to words of *the Two*. One of the family heads, Foad El Bedoun refused to accept the message. His intense rejection forced him to move his family to a nearby village. As Foad left the village, he screamed a vengeful curse and vow of reprisal.

As for the rest of the village, the transformation and celebrations that had come to the homes of the village were undeniable. Healings of hearts and bodies took place. They even spoke of renaming the village to express its new life.

On the last evening before *the Two* left, the whole village gathered outdoors in the village common area.

Eli rose and addressed Bashir and those gathered.

"What all of you have witnessed in your hearts and the change in the people around you provides testimony to the truth we share. Continue to grow in the grace and knowledge of the One you now follow. For now, what has happened here remains unnoticed. The world and those around you have many troubles to occupy their attention for the time being. This will not continue for long. Great days of trouble are coming. Know that the LORD is with you."

Eli turned to Moshe. "Trust in the name and Savior which you have confessed. He will provide for you. So that you may know that the LORD, He is God."

Moshe stretched out the Rod and tapped a nearby large rock. The ground beneath it began to softly rumble. Suddenly the rock rolled aside and water began to flow.

There were audible gasps. Children began to cheer. Bashir's eyes widened as he placed his hands on his head.

Eli then commanded, "Dig and create several cisterns. Make them large. Channel and collect the water into the cisterns. Work in haste. The water will flow for seven weeks. After that time it will dry up as will the sky. This is a gift and provision from your Lord."

Several looked at each other until Bashir shouted out, "You heard what he said. We must begin immediately. Two families will work together. Each team of families will work for one day and then the next group will continue the work. Begin the first cistern just off from where the water now flows. Place the remaining cisterns downhill nearest the homes."

Bashir pointed to two of the families to begin. They immediately shouted orders to the members of their households. The other families ran off to gather tools and machinery. Simultaneously songs broke out among the people in the joy of the gift and work.

Eli nodded at Bashir to come over to where he and Moshe stood.

Moshe placed his right hand on Bashir's shoulder.

He looked directly into Bashir's eyes and spoke. "Brother, God has blessed you this day. In earlier days you led your people with your own strength. Days of trouble are coming and you must continue to lead them, but not as before. You must lead them in the strength God gives you. Do not fear for He is with you."

Eli then spoke. "Brother Bashir, we must leave tonight."

"Why so soon?"

"It is for your own safety. Be strong in the Lord for your family and for your people."

As *the Two* and Bashir huddled together in prayer, Brandon stood to the side scratching his chin. He looked at the water flowing and the people scurrying about. He silently kept asking himself, "*How much will it take to convince you?*"

He had no answer.

# Chapter 9

The first months the three of them traveled from village to village. They usually only stayed a day or two in a village. Word spread ahead of their visits and nearby villages sent representatives to hear what the messengers had to say.

Some went ahead of them to oppose them. Foad and his family, who had left Bashir's village, led the opposition. They took it upon themselves to obstruct the work and message of *the Two*.

Each of the unregistered villages had distinct names and identities. Every village had their own story when encountering *the Two*. They were stories of fear and rejection along with faith and freedom.

The journey through the Negev took them to places with names like A Zaura, El Chumera, Baat El Saraya, Al A'ra, Bir El Mashash, Sawawin, Wadi El Mashash, A-Ser.

True to his word, Foad gathered to himself groups of like-minded opponents to the message of *the Two*. They took care to avoid direct confrontation. Most often entered a village after the *Two* had left. Where they found believers, they harassed and intimidated. They also recruited among those who had rejected the message. An altercation seemed inevitable.

The five-month journey of *the Two* within the Negev took them in a circuit of villages that moved towards Be'er Sheva. When traveling from the El Mashash toward the township of Segev Shalom a confrontation finally occurred.

Several from El Mashash were traveling with *the Two* and Brandon in a bus on their way to Be'er Shiva. They sang and celebrated the day and the works they witnessed with the visit of *the Two*.

As the bus approached Segev Shalom from the north a long column of perhaps fifty men lined each side of the highway. A barricade of cars and men blocked their approach ahead of a roundabout intersection. Brandon sat near the front of the bus. He spotted the trouble and alerted Moshe.

Silence and fear quickly spread across the passengers, many of them women and children. The bus eased to a stop some distance from the barricade. Eli and Moshe both rose from their seats.

Moshe turned to Brandon, "Stay here. Keep everyone calm."

Eli then turned to the passengers. "Do not be afraid. You are safe. Pray for those who oppose us that they will turn away before it is too late."

Brandon watched as the passengers bowed and did as Eli had commanded. He then turned to watch as Eli and Moshe walked out onto the street.

Foad stood front and center of the group directly ahead at the barricade. Many of those who had lined the street had joined his mob. Together they began walking towards the bus. Foad carried a large scimitar while others displayed either bats or carried large stones.

Eli and Moshe positioned themselves directly in front of the bus. Eli watched the mob approaching. Then both bowed in prayer.

Foad moved forward ahead of the angry parade. Shouts of vitriol and hateful chants intensified until they were within twenty feet of the front of the bus. They stopped and began to chant as one, "Depart in death or in pain!"

The chant increased in volume with each repetition.

Eli and Moshe remained with heads bowed as the furor grew.

Finally *the Two* looked up. Both of their faces were damp from tears shed in prayer.

Eli took a deep breath and spoke. "Foad, why are you doing this? It does not have to be this way. We have come among the Bedouin with a message of peace and hope. This is something your people have longed for and needed. Why do you place yourself and others in danger?"

Foad looked puzzled at the words. Then he shouted back. "Us in danger?"

He raised the sword into the air and then pointed it directly toward Eli. "It is you who are in danger. You two come spreading lies and deception. You corrupt my people to abandon themselves to a false god. This will stop."

He turned to the mob and shouted, "This will stop!"

The mob repeated it in antiphonal shouts, "This will stop!"

The angry chants continued until Moshe lifted the Rod only slightly and brought it down with a thud. The air shook with the clash of thunder.

Silence.

Eli looked around and spoke out loudly, "All of you, we come proclaiming the message of rescue. The Lord, He is God. I plead with you. Listen and believe while you can."

Foad's eyes filled with rage. "NO!" he shouted.

He raised the sword and began to charge toward Eli.

Eli sadly lowered his head.

Moshe quickly lifted the Rod high into the air. "So that you may know that the LORD, He is God..."

Immediately, what could only be described as blue fire shot out from the Rod and spread out towards the advancing mob. The fire consumed them where they stood. In mere seconds all that remained were the ashes of men and weapons.

Those in the bus trembled, as they looked at one another in amazed fear. Soft weeping mothers whispered prayers for themselves and their little ones.

✡   ✡   ✡

Yacov had arrived in his office in Amman, Jordan the night before. His position as Regional Transition Czar (RTC) required him to travel to his offices in the capitals of all of the countries in his region. His task as RTC involved transitioning all of his countries into the new economic, military and governmental reality.

He left Lanzig in Beirut that day with the task of solving a particularly sticky situation.

Yacov's secretary Mina, knocked on the door before entering. Yacov looked up. It always pleased him to see Mina. He had hired her for her skills but most certainly for attractiveness.

He loved his new position and all of its perks. He had worked and schemed hard to gain his place in the new world reality. He also knew that in order to maintain his position, results were expected.

Prime Minister D'bar had made it clear that he did not tolerate failure. If Yacov did not deliver, someone else would. The Middle East region continued as the most volatile area in the world. It also carried immense wealth. The reward for success in his assignment promised untold riches and power.

When Mina reached his desk, she greeted him with the smile reserved for him alone.

Yacov spotted the file in her hand.

Mina giggled and handed over the file. "There's some trouble in the Negev of Israel."

He didn't like the sound of that. "Trouble, what kind of trouble? The whole region thrives on trouble."

He could have read it but asked Mina deliver the message.

"An unknown number of people were killed in some sort of mob protest not far from Be'er Sheva."

Yacov shook his head. The constant frustration of this region exasperated him. Why were these people always either fighting or preparing to fight? He sighed.

"How long did you say Lanzig is stuck in Beirut?"

"Possibly a day or two, Sir."

He tapped the file. If he opened it he would have direct responsibility. He had learned that such risks were better passed on to others.

"Has there been any violent reaction from the incident?"

"No sir. It remains an isolated event."

"Very good. Pass this on to Lanzig and have him look at it and report back to me."

Mina smiled. "Very wise decision, sir. Is there anything else you might need before you leave?"

He grinned. "Yes. Alert security and find us a nice place in this wretched city for our dinner tonight."

"I shall make the arrangements, sir."

"Yes Mina, I know you will."

✡   ✡   ✡

Lanzig occupied a suite extremely beneath his usual accommodations. His security detail had assured him that nothing better could be found which could guarantee his safety. Beirut had suffered multiple tragedies in its history but nothing compared to the recent earthquake and subsequent riots. Although frustrated, he knew he would leave by the end of the day or morning at the latest. Even though he resented his position as a subordinate to Yacov, he continually worked on plans to change the current arrangement. He knew that such plans required time and careful maneuvering.

In the meantime his position afforded him the free use of power he had never had before. The absence of the usual governmental oversight made his work go more smoothly. He had the authority of the government at his disposal. Getting results remained the only criterion. That reality consistently dogged him.

Lanzig recruited only the best operatives for his assignments. The local trouble in Beirut was close to resolution. The three leading figures behind the current local trouble needed some convincing, but their public profile complicated the situation.

Lanzig had spoken to each of them individually. Now he only needed to decide which of the three to eliminate as a means of bringing the other two in line. He waited for a report from a senior operative to help him finalize his decision.

Even though he had an assistant traveling with him, he intentionally limited how much he allowed her access to either his time or his plans. He had little doubt that Besnik had placed the assistant as an informant. He knew the game.

Lanzig didn't remember whether her name was Charlotte or Charlene. Her beauty seemed an obvious part of Besnik's plan.

She knocked on the door before entering. Lanzig stood by a window overlooking the interior of the hotel grounds. She carried a file. He knew it had nothing to do with his work in Beirut.

"What is it?" His voice conveyed both irritation and dull interest.

"Heir Lanzig, you have a dispatch from RTC Besnik."

Lanzig hated titles, especially presumptive ones bestowed yet unearned.

"Leave it on my desk." He pointed with his head to a desk in a sitting area.

She placed the file on the desk before walking over next to Lanzig. He kept looking out the window but saw her peripherally. Her posture made it evident that she wanted his attention.

Without turning, "Is there something else?"

"No sir, unless you need something." She said the words slowly.

He turned and looked at her for a second. She had been well

coached. In other situations he'd taken and discarded such a woman at his leisure. But he recognized a spider's trap.

"No, you may leave." Abrupt and to the point, he would not give Besnik an inch. He knew what he wanted and no pretty face would stop him.

He waited a few minutes after she left before picking up the file. He broke the seal and carefully read the overview.

As many as a hundred men were missing and assumed dead. Details remained sketchy. Few individuals were willing to provide information. Only one full account existed. The witness asked to remain anonymous.

Lanzig read the action report. From the details in the report he recognized the pattern. The sudden death of as many as one hundred men by an unexplainable cause said all he needed. He turned to the end of the report and read the addendum.

> Addendum: *All attempts to locate the two survivors have been unsuccessful. It is believed that the two survivors are possibly in the Tel Shiva area or possibly any number of the surrounding unregistered villages.*

Lanzig dropped the report. A sudden chill ran up his arms. Was it possible? He had never put much stock in PTSD. But he also knew what he had experienced and what he felt at the moment.

He slowly scratched his forehead. Only once in all of his life had he failed to understand his opponent. That one time had almost cost him his life. He had no satisfactory explanation for what he had witnessed.

The thought of another such encounter unnerved him. This mission requires a cautious approach and careful attention. Were these the same two? How does he prepare to defeat what he could not explain.

# Chapter 10

As his jet taxied, Lanzig's phone rang. Very few people had his phone number. He could have guessed the caller. He looked at the screen, Besnik.

"Yes."

Although Besnik held a position superior to Lanzig, he rarely acknowledged the fact. Besnik knew it and resented it.

"Did you receive the file I sent you?"

"Yes I did." A long silence followed.

Besnik hated the power maneuvers Lanzig played. He would have eliminated him had D'bar not personally positioned him. He wondered if the placement might be a test. He thought it better not to seek to outguess the Chancellor. Others had tried before. Their disappearance testified to the foolishness of such endeavors.

The silence continued. "And what did you discover?" Lanzig gave no more than demanded specifically.

Lanzig smiled. He loved the game and played it well.

"We have no more details than those spelled out in the report. No one else is willing to provide further information about the incident or the whereabouts of the two men. We believe they are somewhere in the Tel-Sheva area."

"Has there been any reaction or blame attached to the incident which would hamper our transition plans?"

"No. The incident involved Bedouins. They are a closed group. They are accustomed to tragedy. The reason for the mob is unknown. I will continue looking for the two men. They seem to be at the center of the incident."

"Very well, keep me informed. The Chancellor has made it clear that nothing should impede the success of his seven-year transition plan for the region. Is that clear?"

"I'm quite aware of the Chancellor's plan and intentions. I believe this incident will have no bearing on his plans. Is there anything else?"

"Something may be coming up in the next few days in Egypt which may need your attention. I will contact with the details."

"Very well." Lanzig ended the conversation. He did not trust Besnik.

Besnik decided to do some checking of his own. He would make a trip to Tel-Sheva to see for himself.

✡   ✡   ✡

Brandon walked to a small market in the early morning to purchase some food for the group. It puzzled him how they always had funds. It seemed that Moshe had some arrangement with a jeweler in Jerusalem who provided money on a regular basis. They maintained a low profile for several weeks after the incident. He wondered how long this could continue. They had discovered that government officials were making inquiries concerning their whereabouts. The *Two* had already decided on an appearance in the next few days at the center of Tel Sheva or Tel as-Sabi as it is also known. Beyond that they had shared nothing else with Brandon. The *Two* had spent the previous day isolated in prayer.

Brandon returned to the small Bedouin house where they were staying. Many had accepted the message of the *Two*. Brandon called them the followers. They had found refuge among the followers. Through unknown sources, much needed supplies arrived into the village for distribution. The general distrust of the authorities worked in their favor in keeping them hidden from those looking for them.

When Brandon entered the house he saw Eli teaching a group out on the patio. Moshe sat in the middle of several children and their mothers. The enigma of his two companions continued to puzzle him. One minute they were firm and frightening and another moment gentle and loving.

Moshe spotted Brandon and called him over.

"Did you have any trouble?"

"No, not at all. I went where you told me. The man there said everything will be delivered as you requested."

"Good." Moshe smiled as a toddler crept onto his lap.

Brandon took in the scene. "Can I ask you something that's been bugging me the last few days?"

"Sure."

"Where's the money coming from to buy all of the things I bought today and the supplies we've been handing out?"

Moshe chuckled. "I'm surprised you waited so long before asking. Do you remember me sharing of my time on the Island?"

Brandon nodded.

"When I left the Island I was given some stones. They were not relics or mementos. They were in fact priceless gems. With the help of a jeweler in the U.S. and in Israel, the proceeds from their sale have funded our work. They will continue to do so long after we are gone."

The mention of their death troubled Brandon.

"Brandon, do not trouble yourself with our demise. Such things were decided long ago. Your main concern should be your own destiny."

Brandon turned inward. Moshe's words were firm yet his eyes communicated calm warmth. Brandon knew the inevitability of a decision on his part. He feared and strangely amazed himself to be entertaining such a decision. He watched Moshe play with the children. A part of him wished he could accept life with the simplicity of a child.

Moshe saw Brandon struggling.

"You want to talk about it?"

"You guys confuse me."

"What do you mean?"

"Where do I start? Look, I get your message of love and redemption. I'm not saying I accept it yet, but I get it." Brandon paused.

"The other day with the mob, was their destruction necessary? Couldn't there have been another way?"

Moshe sighed. "I hear your question. No, ... I feel your question. Watching us I can see how you might think that we use this power at our discretion. You must understand something. This power that you have witnessed is not at our disposal to exercise as we wish. His power is never at our disposal. We are at the disposal of His power. The battle against Him and His message is just beginning for us."

Moshe paused as tears trickled down his cheek. "I started this journey as a doctor. As a doctor I helped heal and save lives not destroy them. I feel . . . it pains me deeply . . . to be . . . to do this. But I have also seen the darkness of evil. It is coming upon this world in unimaginable ways. We are here to shine the light and rescue all who will receive it. The time is short. The King is returning to judge the world. People must be warned."

Moshe rubbed his forehead. Brandon could tell that Moshe battled the question in his own mind. He excused himself and left.

RTC Besnik arrived unannounced in Tel-Sheva. Government officials practically fell over themselves to accommodate him. They quickly set up an office next to the chief city official. He smiled as he watched them scurry about getting things in place for him. He enjoyed instilling personal fear into subordinates. He made it clear that he wanted any and all information concerning the incident, and especially regarding the two unknown participants. He would get to the bottom of it.

Eli stood at the door looking up into the sky. The morning started with a light cold February rain with darkening clouds promising heavier showers approaching. He bowed his head and whispered a short prayer. When he had finished he turned to Moshe and Brandon.

"It's been six months since we started. Today is the day. We should go now."

Moshe nodded and picked up the Rod ready to leave. Brandon recognized the look in their eyes. It meant they would soon have another confrontation. This excited and frightened him. He swiftly followed Moshe out the door.

Word spread quickly that the *Two* were making their way to the Municipal Weekly Market area. Crowds gathered and were growing. Something akin to a parade accompanied them as they walked toward the market. With the local government offices nearby, government informants picked up the news and immediately passed it on to Besnik.

Besnik sat at a desk, planning how to handle the situation. He wanted to use this to his benefit. He called out to his assigned government liaison.

"Assemble a security detail to assist my team. I want the government to have a ready response for anything that may occur. Also alert the local news organization."

Besnik turned to Mina who never strayed far from him when he traveled. "Where is Lanzig at the moment?"

Mina looked on her phone. Using a monitoring application, she located him. "Sir, he is still in Beirut. Seems his plane has some maintenance issues they are seeking to resolve."

A sly smile emerged on Besnik. Mina saw it.

"And sir, he also received word about the developing rally. He had planned to land at the air base west of Arad. He will not be here in time."

"Excellent Mina. It seems I will have to take the lead on this."

He turned to his security chief. "Let's go."

It surprised Brandon how quickly the crowds developed. They made their way to a large open area south of the market. Along the way Bedouin women and children cheered. Some cried and hailed them as prophets.

Other faces expressed looks of outrage and contempt. Word had spread concerning the incident in Segev Shalom. Fear tempered their anger into silence.

Brandon saw the determination on the faces of the *Two*. No doubt, a confrontation would occur. He only wondered what shape it would take. The sky darkened by the minute. Light showers misted the air and a cold breeze sent shivers down his arm. Finally a crack of lightning immediately followed by exploding thunder had everyone jumping.

Eli and Moshe traded glances and a mutual nod. The ground began to get muddied by the foot traffic. They pressed forward quickly as the market came into sight. Even traffic halted, allowing them to cross the highway leading to the market.

Many of the parade accompanying them began to run beyond the market seeking to find a place among an already large crowd. Brandon and the *Two* now approached those gathered.

Someone had set up a makeshift platform on the north side of the area. The crowd parted like the proverbial Red Sea. Several reached out to touch the *Two* as they passed. The crowd closed in behind them.

The *Two* had never seen such a large audience. Easily five thousand had gathered. Brandon's nerves stood on edge while the

*Two* seemed unfazed.

As they reached the platform, Brandon noticed the presence of police and security forces surrounding a small group of government officials. The media had their cameras partially covered from a steady light rain.

Moshe turned to Brandon and smiled. "Relax and enjoy the moment. This is only the beginning." Eli and Moshe then stepped up unto the platform.

Moshe stood to Eli's right side. They both smiled as they surveyed the crowd. Cheers arose from segments of the crowd. Others hissed them to be silent.

Eli raised his right hand calm to quiet them. He wiped some raindrops from his face and began. "Ladies and gentlemen, we greet you in the Name of the True and Living God and His Son Jesus."

Murmurs rippled through the audience. Whispered questions arose among separate groups. "Why is he speaking in Hebrew?"

"No," said another. "He's speaking in Arabic."

"No, it's English," said another.

With a booming voice Eli brought everyone's attention back to center stage. "Hear the words of the LORD, the days of His patience are coming to an end. You must repent, turn and accept His mercy while there is time. These last six months we have been among the Bedouin proclaiming liberty from the darkness which has held you captive for too long. But the days are running short. A great and growing wickedness is coming upon the earth."

Besnik's anger grew as he listened to him speak. He had positioned himself near the platform for just such an incident. He had come prepared.

Besnik wasted no time. He grabbed a wireless microphone.

"I am Yacov Besnik, Regional Transitional Czar for this area. You speak of liberty. It is the Chancellor who has brought stability to this region. How dare you speak of such nonsense to us. I speak on the authority of the Chancellor and the government. By what authority do you come speaking before us here today?"

"We come by the authority of the True and Living God."

"Which God? There are many gods among men and many who claim allegiance to no god."

The rain began to come down more steadily.

Ignoring the comments from Besnik, he turned to the audience. "The Maker of heaven and earth implores you. Turn to Him and His Savior."

Eli's comments further angered Besnik. He shouted out louder as the rain intensified. "There is no maker of the universe. The cosmos made itself and we make our own destiny. We have no need of a god from heaven. If your God is the maker, then let him stop the rain."

A silence hung over the crowd in the face of the challenge, as the rain beat against umbrellas.

Eli looked over to Moshe and nodded. They bowed for a second. The crowd watched spellbound, waiting to see what would happen next.

Besnik displayed a wicked grin. He shouted out once more. "You see, reality silences dreamers and false prophets."

Eli Lifted up his eyes in the pouring rain. He then turned to the audience. "So that you may know that the LORD, He is God, except by my word it shall not rain upon the earth."

At that moment Moshe lifted up the Rod. A bright light flashed from it into the sky. Instantly the rain stopped and the clouds vanished. The bright sun lit up a blue cloudless sky.

People looked at each other in astonishment. Their clothing was no longer wet. It was as if the sun had licked the air dry. No trace of wetness remained anywhere including the ground. Fear began spreading among the crowd. Some ran away, while others fell to their knees and wept.

Besnik looked around. He had no words only an unexplained feeling of helplessness. He looked up at the platform as Eli stared directly at him.

Eli leaned down towards Besnik. He whispered, "This is only the beginning."

With that, the *Two* stepped off of the platform. They walked towards those kneeling and began to pray for them.

Besnik clenched his fist and commanded his team to leave immediately.

# Chapter 11

Besnik ordered all media present at the square to surrender any and all recordings. He did it under the auspices of an investigation. In truth, he knew he wanted to minimize his exposure. Unfortunately for him, the media were not the only ones recording the event. Several civilian videos were captured through phone cameras. It didn't take long before they were quickly traveling the worldwide airwaves. The entire world had witnessed the event.

Lanzig arrived at Besnik's hotel. He paced the floor as he waited for Besnik to enter the living area of his suite. In typical fashion, he intentionally delayed coming out. Lanzig knew the game and it angered him.

Besnik finally nonchalantly walked out, casually chewing on a pear. "Ah Lanzig, how are you today?"

Lanzig's responded immediately. "You fool! What were you thinking directly confronting the two men? You don't understand what you're dealing with."

"Oh, and I suppose you do?" He maintained his coolness.

The question momentarily caught him off guard. He pierced Besnik with his eyes. "You're right, I don't. And that's a problem. You should never deal with an opponent from a position of ignorance."

Besnik whipped back in angered retort. "How dare you call me ignorant. You…"

Lanzig's cold stare stopped Besnik before he could say anymore.

"You expose your naïveté. I'm not talking about intelligence as against ignorance. I'm referring to actionable intelligence. Adequate intelligence on an adversary is the guarantor of success. If you walk into a situation without fully understanding your opponent you will lose."

Besnik realized the truth of Lanzig's words. He had been outmaneuvered and he knew it. His silence invited Lanzig to continue.

"This is why you have me. You went into it with power but did not understand just *who* you were up against. Osgood made the same mistake and it cost him his life."

Lanzig paused, remembering the incident at the Dead Sea.

"So you've encountered these two before?"

"Yes. I also came very close to sharing Osgood's fate. But I recognized it in time."

"Recognized what?"

"I don't know how they do what they do."

"What do you mean? Listen, they are hucksters. Yesterday they boasted and timed it with a break in the weather. When it rains again, they'll say that they made it rain. We control the media. We'll expose these two for what they are."

"Timed it? Really? I read the witnessed accounts. Where did all the water go?"

Besnik twitched, unable to answer.

"You see what I mean? People told me that the Dead Sea event was a freak storm as well. They weren't there. I saw it with my own

80

eyes. It was freakish. No storm does what I saw."

The heaviness in his eyes unnerved Besnik. "What are you saying?"

"I don't know. That's what I'm saying. And it's the not knowing that troubles me."

"It's a trick. What else could it be?"

Lanzig scratched his chin. "I don't know. They could be aliens for all we know."

Besnik's face squinted in incredulity. "You're not serious are you?"

Lanzig shouted. "Of course not. I'm simply saying that we don't know. And until we do know we need to avoid further direct confrontations."

"Then what sort of strategy are you suggesting?"

Lanzig thought for a moment. "Use the media to shape public perception all we can. This will buy us time to get to the bottom of what's behind this. We need to understand how they are doing what they are doing. There is a source and that should be our target."

"They say it is God."

Now Lanzig had the look. "Don't even go there. That's no better explanation than the alien angle. No, there's a source and I *will* find it. You do what you do and allow me to do my job. Unless this is solved, all the plans for the region are in danger of collapse."

The words cut Besnik to the quick. He thought of D'Bar's orders and the unacceptability of failure.

They both nodded to each other. Despite their differences, they had common cause in survival and they knew it.

✡   ✡   ✡

Brandon and the *Two* moved around fairly unnoticed for several more weeks moving from house to house in the Tel Sheva area. They spent the time instructing and teaching among the Bedouin followers. After a week they sent out word for a meeting of the family leaders among the followers.

Brandon looked around the patio and recognized many of the persons in attendance. He remembered encounters where each of those present had become followers. The unmistakable transformation amazed him. Their somber and angered countenances were replaced with a winsome delight of being in each other's company. Once hardened men now acted like someone newly in love. If he hadn't witnessed it himself, he wouldn't have believed it. The evidence of the message of the *Two* continued to mount.

Eli and Moshe walked into the patio area. All attention turned toward them.

"Greetings and the peace of the Lord Jesus be upon you all." The words rolled over everyone like a cool breeze. Eyes were either turned upward or heads bowed in reverence.

Eli waited for a few moments before continuing.

"The hand of God has visited the Bedouin. You were once a forgotten people, but no longer. The True and Living God is now among you. But our time among you has come to a close."

A soft sigh floated across the group.

"You now have a foundation. Build on it through the Word of God. Difficult days are coming and you must strengthen your people. Do not fear. The Lord is with you. Trust in Him and know that He will not desert you. The Bedouin gave me a home in my time of distress and the Lord will protect you as well. Now our faces are turned to the Jews in order to complete our mission."

"How will we know what to do?" asked one of the men.

"Ask the Lord for wisdom and He will provide it to you. You are His children, trust Him in simple faith and He will manifest Himself to you in ways you've never imagined. You are all people of the land. Where you lack wisdom He will supply."

Moshe saw the fear on their faces. "Gather around. We shall pray for you and the Lord will answer us."

They looked at each other and moved quickly into a tight group.

Eli looked at Moshe and nodded.

Moshe raised the Rod over them all and prayed. "Lord of heaven and earth, grant to these wisdom and the ability to lead Your people. Declare Your fame and message through them. Let Your love and mercy become a beacon shining through them in the darkness of these days. We pray this in the name of Your Son, Jesus. Amen."

Like a breeze coming down from above they were all forced down to their knees as the Holy Spirit filled them.

Moshe began to sing.

> *Servants of the Living God*
> *Filled with life and courage.*
> *Rescued from the darkness*
> *And sent to shine His light.*
> *So all who hear and all who see*
> *Are left without excuse.*
> *A message simple, a Story true,*
> *The Lord He is, He truly is,*
> *The Lord is very near.*

Those gathered began to softly pray aloud. As they each took their turns, Eli, Moshe, and Brandon slipped away and left.

✡  ✡  ✡

Curiosity more than anything else brought people out in the beginning. The ever-spreading videos and rumors on the web created an interest of the inquisitive. The *Two* began making frequent appearances throughout Be'er Sheva. Followers made it a practice to post messages at synagogues announcing places where the *Two* would be speaking. And then it would happen.

Eli and Moshe would go to a location, usually a park or public garden and begin to pray. Brandon sat nearby and watched. Within an hour of the *Two* commencing to pray, people would arrive. They seemed to trickle in as small groups or individuals. Before long a crowd formed and waited. Initially the groups numbered only between twenty and fifty.

At some point the *Two* would cease praying, turn to the group and begin.

Eli spoke. "Children of Abraham and others, greetings in the name of the Lord and His Messiah Yeshua. We have come to bear witness and deliver His message to you. The time has come to turn again to the God of your Fathers. The times of difficulties have begun. The days of judgments are upon you. Turn and believe in the Messiah sent to rescue you from your sins while there is still time."

Every one of his messages followed this form of introduction. Eli went on to explain how Yeshua had come to provide the only way to God.

People responded in a variety of ways. Some shook their heads and walked away. Others openly laughed or mocked before they turned away to leave. But some remained and asked questions. When only the questioners remained, both Eli and Moshe engaged individuals in private conversations.

Brandon moved in close to listen in on the dialogues.

One such incident involved a middle-aged woman. With fiery eyes she asked, "I don't understand how Yeshua dying on a cross makes me right with God. Can you explain this to me?"

Eli deferred to Moshe, "That is a good and honest question. It does seem strange that someone dying over twenty centuries ago has any meaning to us today."

"I will answer you in this way. Let me begin with what I will call four realities. These are four things that we all recognize in life. In fact, these realities are even used by some to argue against God's existence. You will see what I mean."

"The first of these is Justice." Moshe took the Rod and used it to write the word *Justice* in the dirt.

"Everyone knows and understands this reality. From our earliest days we recognize and demand fairness. There are many forms of Justice: Legal, Social, and even Personal Justice. When something is wrong, *Justice* requires that it be made right. In light of so many things that are wrong in life, people often cry out and demand that God make things right. Do you understand?"

The woman nodded in agreement.

"The only problem with this reality is that *Justice* brings out the reality of personal guilt. We are all guilty. There is not an innocent person here. I don't know what you are guilty of, but I know you are guilty. While you may decry the evil in the world, you have no answer for the evil within your own life."

Moshe took the Rod and three feet below the word Justice he wrote the word *Guilt*.

The woman looked at the word and lowered her head, feeling the weight of the word in her heart.

Moshe continued. "The next reality is *Love*. There is a universal desire and need to love and be loved. Songs and stories are written about love. Love is seen as the highest of all virtues. And God is Love."

A foot below and to the left of the word Justice he wrote the word Love. "Now some acknowledge this when they accuse God saying, If God is love why is there so much evil in the world?"

Moshe allowed this to sink in. "Just as *Justice* demands punishment for *Guilt*, *Love* cries out for *Mercy* and forgiveness."

Moshe wrote the word *Mercy* two feet directly across from the word *Love*.

"Herein resides the dilemma and the answer to your question. Our guilt demands justice, yet love cries out for mercy. These all stand juxtaposed from each other. So how can these realities be reconciled?"

The woman remained silent. Moshe took the Rod and drew a line down from Justice to Guilt. He then drew another line from Love to Mercy. The lines formed a cross.

Moshe pointed the Rod directly to the center of the cross. "It is here and only here where these realities come together. There is no other philosophy or religious ideology where these realities are reconciled. It was on the *Cross,* through Christ where God reconciled all things unto Himself so that we might be made right."

Tears began to flow as she fell to her knees. She looked up at Moshe, "How can I be reconciled to God?"

"Confess your sin. Believe in your heart that Christ has died for your sins and has risen from the dead. Proclaim Him as your Savior and Lord. Ask and you will receive this gift from God. Do you believe this?"

She raised her eyes upward and confessed. "I do." She placed her face to the ground and began to pray and make her confession to God.

Brandon watched and listened. She finished her prayer and raised her head up. He couldn't explain it. Her appearance had radically changed. She seemed younger with almost a childlike glow to her countenance.

He looked down and realized that he had been clenching his hands tightly. They were blanched by the intensity. When he opened them up he saw that his fingernails had even scratched his palms. As he looked at them, they were shaking.

He looked down at the Cross drawn in the dirt and trembled. He recalled how he had wanted to pray along with the woman but didn't. His bloodied hands reminded him of his battle. He didn't understand his resistance but recognized its reality. He knew sooner or later he would have to decide.

# Chapter 12

Lanzig sat in his hotel room completing his study of the latest intelligence report. He had operatives assigned to attend all of the open rallies of the so-called prophets. He learned that people referred to them as "*the Two.*" Individually, they went by the names Eli and Moshe. Brandon Rivers always accompanied them.

Lanzig considered using someone to infiltrate the band of followers but decided against it. He recalled the failure of that strategy with Osgood. Their spy ended up a follower. D'bar would not accept that type of failure.

The location of the *Two* changed constantly. They had no permanent residence or headquarters. They continually moved around and rarely stayed two nights in the same place. The *Two* had no electronic footprint. Perhaps they suspected surveillance or it was simply the nature of their vagabond life. These factors complicated surveillance. It required intense manpower with constant monitoring. Having more people involved increased the chances of detection.

All of his combined resources brought him no closer to

comprehending the *Two*. Without that understanding, he lacked a viable strategy in dealing with them. He hated not having a plan. It left him responding rather than manipulating events to his purpose.

He received a message on his phone. *"Besnik and several of his staff members are on their way to assess regional transitional progress and plans."*

Lanzig cursed under his breath. Not only did Besnik like exercising his oversight authority, he enjoyed displaying it in front of others. The loathing rage he felt for Besnik simmered. The problem with the *Two* had distracted him from his plans to undermine Besnik and forward his own position. Some things would have to wait until he had those two under control.

Lanzig reviewed the reports he knew Besnik would want to discuss. Perhaps the situation with the *Two* wouldn't come up.

✡   ✡   ✡

Brandon sat outside on a patio looking over some notes and letters sent to Moshe and Eli. It had become his job to sort through the correspondences reaching them. They contained requests for prayer, invitations to speak, or countless questions about life. He wondered how any of these people expected the *Two* to respond to all of their wishes.

Brandon organized the correspondences into categories so that Eli and Moshe could make some sense of it all. To do that, he had to partially read them. Some of them made him smile or laugh, while others stopped him cold. They included the exact questions that he had. He made sure those questions reached the top of the pile. Eli and Moshe would take the letters, sit them down and to pray over them. After their prayer time they would blindly pick a few of the letters out and respond to that particular one.  He sat and watched them, thinking of his own situation.

After the Two finished, Moshe came and sat next to him. "What has you so troubled, my friend?"

Brandon looked at him. "It's all of these letters and requests. I don't know how you and Eli know which ones to respond to."

Moshe smiled. "I can see how that might puzzle you. Actually it's the same way we know where to stay every night."

"What? I mean, what do you mean? I assumed you worked that out in advance."

Moshe laughed out loud. "Brandon, every day we move forward trusting the Lord to show us what comes next. Even the general plan about what cities to visit is something the Lord gave us. And the every day things, we trust Him to show us."

"And how does He do that exactly?"

Moshe thought before answering. "For one thing, we pray a lot. He reveals it to us in our minds and hearts and then confirms it as we go forward."

Brandon wasn't getting it.

"Look, we have a meeting, rally or whatever you want to call it. Every time, either during or after the meeting, someone asks us to stay with them. If we have more than one invitation, God makes it clear which invitation to take."

Bandon's expressed his frustration. "But how exactly does He do that. I don't understand."

Moshe looked directly into Brandon's eyes. "I know you don't. And a person in your position never will. God's Spirit lives in us. He is real and we know it. You on the other hand … you don't. To you God is a speculative possibility. To us, He is a reality. I have no better way to explain it than that."

Brandon chewed on the words. "You're right. I'm still debating if the whole God thing is real or not. I can see that if He is truly real something as simple as what I'm asking is no big deal. The real clincher is whether or not He's real. Everything else flows out of that, I guess."

Moshe grabbed Brandon's arm. "I'm praying for you my friend."

Brandon looked down at the ground and quietly responded. "I know. Believe me, I know."

They both remained silent for a moment. Finally Moshe got up.

He gathered up all of the letters in a single swoop.

"Brandon, you know … you really don't need to separate them like this. After what we talked about you should see why it isn't necessary."

Brandon half chuckled and nodded.

Moshe bunched all of the papers in one hand. "Well, let's see what the Lord has in mind for today."

Moshe walked off whistling some tune Brandon had heard him sing before. With everything else going on in the world, he wondered how anyone could be happy enough to have a song. These two men possessed nothing and what little they did have they gave away. And yet, he found himself envying them in a peculiar way. Maybe that's what kept him hanging around.

✡ ✡ ✡

At the same moment that he heard a knock on the door, Lanzig received a message from one of his operatives: *Ben Gurion University of the Negev, 3:00 pm.*

Two knocks and the door opened. Besnik and his entourage pranced in with every intention of impressing. Lanzig feigned mild interest and looked back down to reread the message.

When Lanzig finally looked back up, he calmly asked, "What's with the parade. Yacov?"

Lanzig knew how it irritated Besnik for anyone to address him by his first name and not by his title. He especially loved doing it with straight face. It added to the sting.

Besnik waited to calm himself before responding to Lanzig.

"The office of the RTC requires a large staff. These are the essential personnel needed when I'm traveling. A great task requires sizeable resources."

Lanzig had a great many irritating retorts but chose against it for the time being. He had more important matters to deal with at the moment.

Besnik took his silence as a small victory and proceeded.

"So Lanzig, I saw the progress report you sent me. What is your assessment?"

Besnik took a seat opposite Lanzig. His minions found chairs and positioned themselves behind their master like so many sycophants.

He picked up his copy of the report.

"All of the transitional issues are under control. All political resistance is eliminated. We should be able to move forward as scheduled. Ample enticements and warnings are in place. If any snags arise we can respond with adequate speed to neutralize them."

Lanzig dropped the report on the coffee table between them. He anticipated the next question.

With a raw smugness, "What about the religious problem in Israel?"

"No problem. The Jewish leaders are very enthused about the progress on the Temple and the requisite security measures. They are completely in tune with all transitional plans. I have assured them that D'bar's agreement addresses all of their previous concerns."

Lanzig answered Yacov's question, yet not really. They both knew the game.

With a sly smirk Besnik responded, "Hermann, you know that's not what I'm asking about. I want to know about the two religious pretenders wandering about in Israel. What about them?"

Lanzig rechecked his phone. More information had come in.

"I don't regard them as religious leaders. As to their status... it seems they are having a rally this afternoon. My sources reveal that it will occur on the campus of the Ben Gurion University of the Negev."

"And what are you doing about it?"

"Doing about it? I already have operatives on campus. The location for the rally is in a common area called the Kreitman Plaza. We have cameras set up on top of the Kreitman building that overlooks the plaza. It gives us complete view of the entire area."

"Cameras, operatives, that's it?" Besnik raised his voice.

Lanzig remained calm. "What else would you have me do, Herr Besnik?"

Yacov's grew increasingly irritated. "Have them arrested, kidnapped, or whatever, just get them out of the way. Eliminate them if you have to. You are capable of accomplishing that aren't you?"

Lanzig waited, scanning those listening. "Ordinarily I would agree with you and take such actions. But these two are anything but ordinary. I don't think we need another public failure on our part, do you?"

Besnik seethed. He recalled the incident in Tel Sheva and the consequent publicity.

He leaned over toward Lanzig. "Then what exactly *is* your plan?"

Lanzig held his response. He looked over Besnik's shoulders to the others in the room. "Perhaps the answer to that question is better held in a more secure smaller circle."

Besnik caught the meaning. His team were all looking at him.

"Perhaps you're right."

He turned to his lackeys. "Leave us."

One of them commented, "But sir."

Besnik shouted, "I said leave us! Now!"

They moved out quickly. When they were gone the two of them continued.

"So, what is this strategy?"

"I still haven't reached a conclusion as to the source of their abilities. Their persuasive or oratory abilities I can understand. But they continue to demonstrate yet unexplainable capabilities. There is an explanation for how they do what they do, I just don't know what it is. And I promise you, I *will* get to the bottom of this."

"And then what?"

"Then we expose them publically. We completely discredit them. Once that's done, we eliminate them. The sooner the better."

Besnik nodded. "So we agree. What's your plan for today?"

"As I said, we have set up an operational center in the Kreitman Building. You are welcome to join me there. Only you must remember, it's my operation. You're there to observe not to control."

That comment chafed him, but Besnik agreed. He realized that if things went wrong, Lanzig carried the blame. The thought of failure angered him, while the idea of attaching responsibility to Lanzig pleased him.

He grinned. "Of course Hermann. Of course."

Lanzig wanted so much to strike out at the snake standing opposite him. Instead he clenched his fists behind his back. He would find a way to destroy this weasel.

✡  ✡  ✡

Brandon gathered together some incidentals for the afternoon. Moshe told him they were going to a university campus. He wanted to make sure he had plenty of water. The last few weeks they had held meetings in parks in different sections of Be'er Sheva. The meetings were getting progressively larger. The one at the university today could have well over a thousand present.

Brandon looked at his watch. Their ride would arrive within the hour. As with earlier times, Moshe and Eli were in their time of prayer. When they were finished, they would leave.

✡  ✡  ✡

Naomi Goldman and her ten-year old son Jesse walked out of the Children's Hospital. She and Jesse had completed his bi-monthly evaluation visit. Naomi's husband had been killed in a car bomb attack a year earlier near the Gaza border. She had never imaged herself as a single mother raising their severely autistic son.

Often after their appointments they would visit Naomi's sister Yudi. She worked as a Neurosurgeon at the Soroka Hospital, which was a part of the large medical center where Jesse came for his evaluations. Today, Naomi had plans to visit the university library.

The Ben Gurion University sat on the north side of Ben Gurion Boulevard across the street from the hospital. The library had special books that Jesse loved for his mother to read to him. Yudi taught an occasional class at the university and that allowed Naomi access to the library. All together it made for a convenient way to spend a nice a portion of the morning with Jesse.

When they crossed the street heading to the library, Naomi noticed a large crowd gathered in the plaza adjacent the library. Unlike most autistic children, crowds did not upset Jesse. In fact it calmed him. Jesse seemed particularly attracted to them. It was being alone that frightened Jesse.

Naomi always kept a close eye on Jesse. He easily wandered off into a crowd. Whenever he did, he would stand and watch people. Jesse could not speak. He would simply stare and smile at people with a large innocent grin. This unnerved some people until they realized Jesse's condition.

When Jessie saw the crowd, he immediately picked up his pace and headed for the throng. It was obvious that their visit to the library would be delayed.

# Chapter 13

They arrived via taxi. Brandon chuckled. Here he was crowded into a cab with two supposed prophets, one of them carrying a long wooden rod.

The humor of it all wasn't lost on Asher Peretz, their cab driver. At five foot five, one word described Asher, winsome. Meeting this thin jovial man, one could never guess his troubled past. He had once struggled with anger after the loss of his family from a rocket attack in Ashqelon. The tragedy had driven him to the edge of suicide. He went to hear the *Two* speak several days earlier and had become a follower. He practically pleaded for the honor of transporting these special passengers within Be'er Sheva.

Moshe noticed the two of them grinning. "We are a sight, aren't we?"

With that said, they all laughed. Moshe started a song. Eli happily joined in. They worked to teach it to Brandon and Asher. It made the trip enjoyable.

Asher slowed his approach when he noticed flashing lights. The mood quickly changed. Eli and Moshe looked at each other. They knew something.

Brandon looked at the traffic ahead. "Asher, what do you think?"

"I don't think I will be able to turn onto Ben Gurion Boulevard and get to the south entrance of the campus. They have the street blocked off. I think it's best if I turn around and take you to the northwest entrance. There's a large parking lot there not far from the plaza. I can show you how to get there."

Eli nodded. "That sounds like a good idea Asher. Thank you."

"No problem sir. I will stay around and take you wherever you want to go afterwards."

Asher made it to the parking lot entrance. A campus security officer stood there blocking entry. He waved for Asher to stop.

Asher pulled up to the officer. He rolled down his window.

"I'm afraid you will not be allowed to enter here. There is a large event here in the plaza and vehicle access is restricted."

Asher smiled and pointed to his passengers. "I have the speakers for the event in my cab."

The puzzled officer looked in the back seat. He saw two men who resembled throwbacks to ancient times. They both wore long woolen pullover cloaks. They each sported full beards and their skin had obviously seen many hours of sun. One of the men gently smiled while holding a long wooden staff in his right hand.

"Pull to the side and wait while I get verification." The officer began talking to someone on his communication device.

Asher pulled off to a side space. He turned to Brandon. "Sorry for the delay. Hopefully this will not take too long."

Moshe answered from the back seat. "Do not worry yourself Asher. The gentleman is merely doing his job."

As the officer carried on an animated conversation, Brandon asked the *Two*. "What sort of event do you foresee today?"

Moshe shrugged his shoulders.

"But I thought you two had inside information on such things.

Isn't that the prophet sort of thing you guys do?"

Eli chuckled and Moshe answered. "Brandon, we are not clairvoyant. If we ever have inside information, as you call it, it's only as God reveals it. We approach today as we do any day, in faith. We believe Him and trust He will show what is necessary for the day."

Eli added, "Sometimes we get impressions." Moshe nodded.

"But as Moshe said, we simply trust the Lord to lead us and speak to us."

Brandon thought for a second. "By impressions, do you mean hunches? Or is it a reasoned deduction? And what do you mean, speak to you? Do you hear a voice?"

Eli answered. "It's a bit hard to explain, especially to a skeptic. The Lord said that His sheep hear His voice and follow Him. I know His voice when I hear it. It's very different from mine."

Moshe nodded "He's right, Brandon. When it's my voice speaking, it's often frightened, confused, and uncertain. His voice is always calm, resolute and ... winsome."

Moshe looked at Eli. They both smiled and nodded.

Asher's eyes filled with tears as he listened. He felt excluded from the fraternity of experience the others were sharing. Silence continued as they each reflected on the conversation.

This all ceased when the officer tapped on the window. "I ask that you gentlemen wait here. Security is sending over someone to verify your claims and then perhaps escort you where you need to go."

Asher nodded. "Thank you, officer."

The officer took one more look inside the cab. He walked away scratching his chin.

Within a few minutes, three Israeli soldiers arrived and walked over to the cab.

A young woman tapped on the window. "Can I have you all step out of the cab please?"

They were directed to stand against the cab. Two of the soldiers scanned the surrounding area as if looking for something. The young woman concentrated on the group, holding a sheet of paper in her hand. She repeatedly looked at the paper and then at the group.

She folded up the paper and put it in her pocket. "Very well. My name is Mya. Welcome to the university. I am responsible for your safety while you are here today."

Brandon interrupted. "Excuse me Mya, but what were you looking at on that paper you had? Was that a picture of us? And how did you get it?"

Mya simply smiled and went on. "As I said, I am responsible for your safety today. There is a very large group of people here. We don't expect any problems and hopefully our presence will facilitate that."

Brandon almost said something. Eli put his hand on his shoulder and spoke. "Thank you Mya. I appreciate your concern. I don't think we are in danger, but I am glad you and your fellow soldiers are here. Perhaps the Lord has something for you as well today."

Mya looked at her fellow soldiers and shrugged. "Yes, well be that as it may, we are here so let us proceed to the plaza."

She looked at Asher. "You must remain here with your vehicle or you may leave."

Asher looked at Eli, "I will be here when you need me."

"Let's go." Mya took the lead and the other two soldiers followed at the rear of the group.

They crossed the parking lot and weaved in between a few buildings. They approached the plaza from the north. Just before entering the opening Mya stopped them and turned.

"Gentlemen, as you can already see, the plaza is very crowded. I am informed that the faculty has set up a small speaking platform up against the Kreitman building." She pointed to a large building stretching across more than half of the plaza on the east.

Several more soldiers joined their group before they continued on. As they traversed the northern edge of the plaza they heard shouts from groups or individuals in the crowd.

"Speak to us prophets of God," yelled one young man.

"We don't need more religious division among us. Leave us alone," shouted another.

Individuals waved signs with a variety of slogans: We Don't Need God; Repent; NO MORE RELIGION; Reason Not Religion; Love, Not Faith;

When they almost reached the platform, a young boy came running up to the *Two*. He grabbed the robes of both Eli and Moshe. When they stopped to look down at the lad he simply smiled and looked at each of them with strained intensity.

Immediately a woman came running behind the boy. "Sirs, I am so sorry for my son's intrusion. His name is Jesse. He is a special young boy. He cannot speak but is immensely curious. He is … autistic."

Eli waved off any concern as he got down on his knees. He looked directly into Jesse eyes. Time seemed to stop as the two stared at each other. Eli placed his hand on the side of Jesse's face. He remembered his own life trapped behind the silence.

Eli looked at the mother as he rose to his feet. "Do not be afraid. Jesse is here for a reason. Trust in God and you will see and understand."

Brandon looked over to Moshe who intently watched the interaction. Eli and Moshe shared something with their eyes. The little boy took Eli's hand and they continued to the platform. Naomi suddenly became part of the group.

✡ ✡ ✡

Lanzig and Besnik arrived at the operation center in the Kreitman Building. Multiple viewing monitors lined an entire wall.

Lanzig turned to his operations leader Marcus Neumann. "Is everything in place?"

Lanzig had selected Marcus for his size and prowess. At six foot four he modeled the ideal Aryan warrior. His cold steel blue eyes betrayed nothing but hard efficiency. Even his voice communicated his trained competence.

"Yes sir. As you can see, we can view the entire plaza and all adjoining area along this building and the area surrounding the library. We have operatives and snipers atop this building and the student center on the north side. We have scattered operatives within the crowd as well. Members of campus security and IDL soldiers are handling the platform area."

"Well done. And what about sound?"

"The platform sound will come right into us. We have selected monitoring devices with our operatives within the crowd. This should give us all we need to know in this situation."

Lanzig smiled and looked over to Besnik. Turning back to his man, "Very thorough. We should find out what we need."

"Yes sir."

Besnik stepped up close to Lanzig and whispered. "Snipers?"

"It's not what you think. It's only a precaution. We don't need martyrs at this point."

"Marcus!" Lanzig remembered something. "Do you have emergency personnel nearby?"

"Yes sir, just as you requested. A unit is stationed in the parking lot behind the student center."

"Excellent." He looked at Besnik. "Well, now there's nothing left to do but wait and watch the show. Everything is recording."

✡ ✡ ✡

Reaching the platform, Moshe turned to Brandon. "The three of you stay here."

Naomi took hold of Jesse's hand, preventing him from following Eli onto the platform.

Two microphones were on the stage several feet away from each other. A university professor stood in front of one of them.

Eli and Moshe walked up onto the stage. They quickly assessed the day's format. It seemed the faculty desired a debate. Eli took his place in front of the other microphone. Moshe stood to his right. They waited for the professor to begin.

"Good afternoon everyone. May I have your attention? Thank you all for attending this afternoon's event. Many of you know me, but let me introduce myself nonetheless. I am Dr. Alon Goldman, Professor of Science and Dean of the Sociology Department."

Weak and scattered applause accompanied some chuckles.

Goldman cleared his throat. "I will ask the other gentlemen to introduce themselves."

Eli waited for a long minute and a half. He looked over the crowd and an obvious section of faculty. They were strategically positioned in front of some microphones provided for questions from the audience. As the silence continued, Alon grew nervous.

Eli finally addressed the crowd. "We come to you in the name of the True and Living God. The days are short. You must repent from your prideful ways and humble yourselves before the Lord."

Suddenly a faculty member jumped in front of a microphone and shouted. "Who are you and what gives you the right to speak to us like this?"

"I am a voice sent from God to bear witness to you of His intentions."

Alon sensed his control slipping away. "Please, there's no need for shouting. Let's remain orderly."

Another faculty member shouted into a microphone. "We are men and women of reason. We have no need for any god or his prophets."

Eli looked at him. "Your reason has left you blind and senseless. You neither see nor understand the danger you are propagating."

"How dare you speak to me in that manner!" he yelled out.

Eli ignored the man and turned toward the crowd. "People of Israel, awaken yourselves while you can. Remember the Lord who has returned you to this land in these last days."

An obvious orthodox student ran up to a microphone. "How can you say you speak for God? I have studied the words of God and I have no need to hear from you."

Eli looked directly at the young man. "You display your righteousness outwardly but it is not so in your heart."

Eli pointed directly at the young man. "Woe to those who deeply hide their plans from the LORD, And whose deeds are *done* in a dark place, And they say, "Who sees us?" or "Who knows us?" [1]

The young man looked all around. He sensed a multitude of eyes bearing down on him. His shoulders drooped as he quickly slinked away.

Alon jumped in. "Listen here sir. It is completely improper to address our students in such an accusatory manner. The young man seems sincerely religious so you shouldn't speak such condemnations."

Eli did not respond. His silence increased Alon's boldness. "And anyway, why should we receive anything you say. Many here prefer not to accept the reality of God."

Most in the crowd shouted their agreement. When Eli did not respond they shouted their accusations louder against the *Two*.

Finally Eli's booming voice silenced the crowd. "Do you not remember the words of the Lord?"

Silence carpeted the air.

Eli looked to the crowd. "Hear the words of the Lord." He stretched out his hands. "You are My witnesses, declares the LORD, And My servant whom I have chosen, So that you may know and believe Me and understand that I am He. Before Me there was no God formed, And there will be none after Me. I, even I, am the LORD, And there is no savior besides Me. It is I who have declared and saved and proclaimed, And there was no strange *god* among you; So you are My witnesses, declares the LORD, And I am God. Even from eternity I am He, And there is none who can deliver out of My hand; I act and who can reverse it?"[2]

The faculty and many in the crowd grew increasingly angry at every word Eli spoke. Hearing the words of the scriptures seemed to ignite a furnace of rage. The soldiers detected the reactions intensifying. Suddenly a spark was lit.

Shouts and screams exploded everywhere. Faculty members and students began throwing their books toward the stage. The soldiers tightened their formation and more assets were quickly coming into position.

The whole scene frightened young Jesse. He held on tight to his mother. Brandon nervously tried to calm his mother. He wondered what would happen.

Eli looked across to Alon who had begun hurling vile curses toward him. He scanned the audience and saw a boiling caldron of vindictiveness. He sighed and looked over to Moshe and nodded.

Eli's voice rang out like a roar over the shouts and screams, "So that you may know that the LORD, He is God, noise and silence shall exchange places."

Moshe raised the Rod high and brought it down with a thud. It sounded like thunder.

All across the plaza the shouts and screams ceased. Men and women grabbed their throats. They tried to speak, but could not. The harder they tried, the more a pain attacked their throats. Alon grabbed his throat knocking over his microphone.

Those who had not participated in the angry shouts looked around in shock. They whispered questions to one another, unable to explain what they saw.

Now muted, the anger that once spilled from their mouths now filled their eyes. The anger turned into a raw hatred.

Little Jesse saw it on the faces. It frightened him.

He shook himself loose from his mother's grip and ran up onto the stage. His mother tripped on the steps as she ran after him. She quickly got up but was unable to catch him.

Jesse ran past Eli and picked up the fallen microphone. In a voice deeper than his size he shouted out, "Do not be fools, hear the words of the prophets."

Naomi fell to her knees as she heard him speak the words.

# Chapter 14

Besnik shouted at the monitors, "What is happening?"

Lanzig had the same question but his concentration focused on the how and why of the question. He knew if he could answer those two questions he could undermine and extinguish the *Two*.

He turned to Marcus. "Move your men in. Quietly isolate all of those affected. I'm talking about the people who have become mute. I want them examined. I want to know what has happened to them."

Besnik reacted differently. Incredulous, he shouted, "What about arresting the two who caused it to happen? They're the ones behind this whole thing. Apprehend them!"

Lanzig took his arm and pulled him aside. "I don't think that's a wise move. If you didn't notice, we weren't the only one's recording what happened. There were dozens, maybe hundreds of cameras in the crowd. We can't change the reality of what happened. But we can come up with an alternate explanation."

Besnik didn't seem convinced.

Lanzig whispered, "Listen, I don't know how they are doing

these things. But I don't want to be outsmarted in front of a camera. Instead I want to expose them. For that, I need to know how they're doing it."

Besnik quieted a bit. "I'd prefer a more direct approach but I'll defer to you for the time being. But you better get this right. Both of our heads are on the line in this."

"I know." Lanzig's mind raced through strategies and angles. He always measured the stakes.

✡ ✡ ✡

When Naomi finally reached Jesse she found him standing next to Eli, holding his hand. She knelt down and hugged him tightly.

"Jesse, you can speak. How is this possible?"

"Yes Mommy, isn't it wonderful?"

Naomi trembled as she looked up at Eli. She slowly rose to her feet and took his other hand and kissed it.

Meanwhile, down in the plaza, chaos rolled across the crowd. The people who had previously screamed at the *Two* were now writhing in pain. The more they attempted to talk, the greater the pain gripped them. It frightened people around them to watch the writhing faces.

Suddenly, men within the crowd began grabbing the silenced ones and carrying them off. Pushing and shoving ensued. Some students protested as they watched some of their professors subdued and hauled away.

One student fought angrily against the fierce pain attacking him. He had been among the most vitriolic skeptics. He watched the *Two* on the stage and his rage only intensified. He had watched others taken away and knew they would seize him as well. In the midst of the pain, his rage against the *Two* exploded. He wanted to attack them, but the pain worsened with one step toward the stage.

He looked around for anything he could use. He finally spotted a rock the size of his fist. He pushed through the pain to grab the rock.

The torment felt as if a collar of spikes were tightening around his throat.

As he lifted the stone to throw it, the agony tightened even more. By force of sheer will he reached back to hurl the projectile at the stage. His brain practically exploded as the pain attacked him with a vengeance. He completed the throw but the stabbing pain altered the trajectory.

As if in slow motion, Naomi watched the projectile coming toward them. She saw it but couldn't stop it. The stone struck Jesse squarely on his temple. The little boy collapsed.

In an instant, Naomi's earlier joy came crashing down in horror. Jesse lay on the stage bleeding and unconscious. She screamed in horror as she fell beside her little boy.

Down on the plaza the assailant rolled on the ground gripping his throat. Blood poured from his ears as his eyes rolled back into his head. The payment for the crime of his willfulness had only begun.

On the stage Moshe stepped quickly toward the boy only to be stopped by Eli's hand. Eli slowly shook his head to say, No.

At first Moshe didn't understand. He was a doctor. He held the Rod of God in his hand. Why prevent him from helping? Eli placed his hand over his face and Moshe understood.

Naomi screamed out, "Someone help me. Someone get a doctor!"

Security had already dispatched the nearby medical team. They arrived very quickly and assessed the situation.

"The boy's pulse is rapid. We need to transport him right away. Alert the hospital."

Naomi frantically cried out, "Will he be ok? Please tell me."

The medical personnel had only one response. They pointed her to the ambulance.

Fortunately, the Soroka Hospital sat immediately across the street from the university. The crowd parted for the transporting ambulance. They arrived at the emergency room within two minutes.

Eli and Moshe watched the ambulance ride off.

Eli looked at Moshe, "Now, let us go."

Several people desiring prayer delayed them. They finally arrived at the trauma center forty minutes later. When they walked in the attending doctors had just left. Naomi and her sister stood embracing each other beside the gurney bearing the lifeless body of Jesse.

A hospital security officer moved to stop the *Two*. One look from Eli changed his mind. Several hospital personnel gathered around, curious about the unfolding situation.

Naomi heard their footsteps and looked up. Despair shrouded over her.

Through her tears she managed only one word. "Why?"

Her sister Yudi demanded, "What are you doing here? Who are you?"

Naomi struggled to answer. "These are … ah … these are the men I told you about."

Yudi's eyes hardened as she leered at them. She turned to her sister. "Nimi, you need to stop…"

"Do not despair." Eli's words halted Yudi from completing her sentence.

He walked over to the body of Jesse. He gently stroked his hand. Tears began rolling down his face.

He turned to the sisters. "So that you may know that the LORD, He is."

Moshe walked around Eli and stood beside the gurney. He stood over the body of the boy and began to silently pray.

Yudi tried to force her way to stop Moshe, but Eli held out his arm and restrained her.

After a moment, Moshe took the Rod and placed it on the body. He then put his face directly over Jesse's face. He closed his eyes and gently exhaled onto the face of the lifeless boy.

One long second hung frozen when suddenly Jesse coughed.

Moshe placed his hand under the boy's head and lifted it up. Jesse opened his eyes and smiled.

Jesse looked at Moshe and tipped his head to one side. "Hello, what's your name?"

Moshe smiled and answered. "My name is Moshe. What's yours?"

"I'm Jesse. Do you know where my Mommy is?"

Moshe stepped aside and pointed to Naomi. Both she and Yudi stood together in shock.

"Mommy!"

Naomi ran to him. She wrapped her arms around him and continuously kissed him all over his head and face.

Yudi stood frozen in place. Her face said it all. Her mind raced trying to come up with an explanation. She looked around the room and saw reactions ranging from joy to shocked disbelief.

Yudi's stunned state broke with Eli's voice.

She turned to him. "Madam, we should like to dine with your family tonight."

"What?" She struggled to register his words.

"I said, we would both like to dine with your family tonight."

Naomi heard the request and answered for her sister. "Yes, certainly yes!"

A nurse's aide had caught the whole event on her phone camera. She wasted no time to upload the video. Within moments its journey across the globe would take less time than anyone imagined.

✡ ✡ ✡

Yudi sat in her living room as her sister served their guests. Her mind raced as she continued to contrive an explanation for her nephew's present condition. Before leaving the hospital she had obtained copies of all of Jesse's emergency room records. The medical record provided a clear and concise timeline of the event. The staff had furiously worked on Jesse for over fifteen minutes attempting to revive his dead body. After all attempts failed the attending physician declared him dead.

No doubt existed as to the reality of his death. Another twenty minutes had passed before the two men sitting in her house had walked in and did what they did.

Eli sat on the floor and listened to Jesse as he read a book to him. Naomi peeked out from the kitchen. Hearing his voice, she wanted to jump up and down like a schoolgirl.

A thought occurred to Naomi. "Where is the other man who accompanied you?"

Eli answered. "You mean Brandon? I sent him out to make arrangements for our transportation. We must leave after dinner tonight."

"So soon?"

Eli looked over to Moshe before answering. "Staying any longer would put you all in unnecessary danger."

Yudi voiced her question. "I don't understand. What sort of danger are you talking about?"

"It's best we leave it at that."

She pressed the matter. "Where are you going?"

Eli smiled but gave no answer.

Moshe had noticed Yudi wrestling with Eli's comment as well as the events of the day. She didn't even notice him walk over and sit next to her on the couch.

"You know I was once a doctor."

"What?" Her voice carried a hard edge. She then noticed Moshe. "I'm sorry, what did you say?"

"I once practiced medicine."

She squinted. "Really? What kind of medicine?" Her voice communicated her skepticism.

Moshe smiled. "I was an orthopedic surgeon in San Diego."

Yudi knew that such credentials were no small matter. She understood the requirements of a specialty surgeon.

She decided on a strategy. "Well then, medically speaking, how do you explain Jesse?"

Moshe chuckled. "As a doctor I could never explain it. He was autistic, correct?"

"Severely so."

"And he couldn't speak?"

"Not at all."

"And he was declared dead and left unattended in that condition?"

"For almost twenty minutes." Her voice cracked.

"So there's no reason or natural explanation as to why he should be alive, much less speaking?"

She simply nodded.

"I could tell you my whole story, but I won't. I'll simply say that I've seen things, many amazing things that have no natural explanation. And although I can't provide a scientific explanation, I do have an answer." He paused. "There is a God and He is real."

"How can you be so certain?"

"Because He rescued me."

For the first time Yudi scrutinized him. "Wait a minute. You're that guy they found out on the ocean. You had been missing for all those years?"

"Yeah that's me."

"You say God is real? How do you know?"

"Because He spoke to me. He still speaks to me."

"How do you know that it's not anything more than your own mind speaking?" She had used the same argument with her sister and it had always silenced her.

Moshe smiled at Yudi. He held the Rod and he rolled it in his fingers. He turned to Jesse.

"Jesse, would you please come here for a moment?"

Jesse happily bounced up and ran over to them.

"Jesse, have you and I talked about what happened to you today?"

"No sir."

Yudi squinted. She wondered about what Moshe had in mind.

"Jesse, do you remember when you were asleep at the hospital?"

"Uh huh."

"What was happening?"

Jesse thought for a mere second and then began to recall in detail the whole scene in the emergency room as the doctors tried to revive him.

Moshe and Yudi listened intently. The conversation also had everyone else's attention.

"And Jesse, what were you doing?"

"Standing with the man."

"What man?"

"The big man." Jesse stretched up his hands above his head.

"And what happened then?"

By this time Naomi's stood with eyes and mouth open wide.

"He told me not to be afraid, 'cause everyone else looked afraid."

"Did he say anything else?"

"Yeah, he told me that Aunt Yudi was afraid."

"Afraid of what?"

Yudi could feel her heart pounding.

"He said that she was afraid of dying."

Yudi began to tremble. She had never told anyone. She had battled that ever-growing fear from the time she witnessed death first hand. No one knew.

Jesse looked directly at Yudi. "Aunt Yudi, you don't have to be afraid if you know."

Yudi swallowed hard before asking. "Know what, honey?"

"That God is real." He smiled and turned to his mother.

"Mommy, I'm hungry."

He turned to Moshe. "Can I go now?"

"Yes Jesse, thank you."

He bashfully lifted his shoulders, "You're welcome." He ran to his mom.

Yudi felt a wall inside of her collapsing. She looked down at her shaking hands as tears began falling on them. She slowly looked up at Moshe.

"How did you know?"

Moshe sighed and looked down a moment. Looking back at her, "Like I said, He's real."

He paused a moment. "And He told me."

Yudi could barely see through the tears but didn't even try to wipe them away.

"I am afraid. I … I want Him to be real. I just don't know how I can know."

Moshe took her hand. "Why don't you simply talk to Him?"

"Can it be that easy?"

Moshe nodded. "He's as close as the mention of His name. Talk to Him, right now."

"Really?"

Moshe slowly nodded.

Yudi wiped her face once and closed her eyes. "God … Lord Jesus, I ah … I want to know You're real. I want to believe You are. I just don't know how. Help me. Forgive me. Speak to me."

Without another word, Yudi dropped to her knees. In inaudible whispers she began to confess unspoken things from her heart. The room remained silent as they whispered prayers of their own.

After several minutes Yudi's prayers ceased. She remained on her knees for a moment as if catching her breath. She finally opened her eyes and looked around to a room full of smiling faces.

Yudi's eyes glistened. Her face seemed to glow. Her whole

countenance communicated the essence of a smile.

Moshe helped her to feet and asked. "Well?"

"Light." The word jumped off her lips like a song. She looked at everyone and repeated it. "Light!"

# Chapter 15

Besnik knew right away once the phone rang. He knew the incident had not escaped someone's attention. After two rings he picked it up.

"Good morning, Master." His sheepish voice betrayed him.

"I don't believe it is a good morning, Yacov." The cold steel in the voice said it all.

"No sir, I suppose it isn't. Please let me explain."

"Yes, enlighten me."

"Well sir, Herr Lanzig…"

D'bar's shouting stopped him. "Besnik, I do not place people in positions of power to blame others! I put them there to accomplish what I command. Your job is to eliminate ALL obstacles to transitioning your region under my control."

"But sir."

"Do not interrupt me. I expect results! I expect silence and submission from your region, not religious renewal. Your region above all regions cannot afford any reignited fervor for any mythological deities."

"But sir, we are placating both Islam and Judaism in the treaty structure? The Jews have agreed to build their Temple on a site other than the Muslim area. That will encourage religious excitement from both sides."

"Please, their leaders are more interested in power than faith. They think they are gaining something in all of this. Their hunger for power has blinded them to my true intentions. Time will betray them both."

Besnik chose silence rather than response.

"Unlike the leaders I spoke of, these two independents and others like them cannot be allowed to exert influence. We must command the stage of ideas. People are like sheep and we must be their shepherds. Old ideas have to die if we are to command the world into the new order."

"But what of Lanzig?"

"Who is in command there? He is an excellent tool but a tool nonetheless. Either take control of the situation or I will find someone who can. I shall speak to Lanzig. From you, I expect results."

"Yes Master."

"Peace, Prosperity and Order." He hung up.

"Peace, Prosperity and Order." Besnik whispered the words to an empty line.

✡   ✡   ✡

"Marcus do you have that report?" He sat at his desk rubbing his chin. He expected to hear from Besnik soon and wanted a complete grasp of the situation beforehand.

"Yes, Herr Lanzig."

"Good, I'll read the whole thing but give me an overview."

"I personally interviewed, as best we could, the individuals we took into custody on campus."

"Explain."

"Well sir, they were all unable to speak. Any attempt to do so caused them intense pain. Even writing these facts down for us initiated pain. We had them checked by physicians and they could find no physical reason for their conditions."

"What of the student who died, the one who threw the rock at the child?"

Marcus found the student's medical report. "As you said, he is dead. An autopsy says I quote, *He died from massive cerebral hemorrhage seemingly precipitated by the crushing of his brain.*"

"What?"

"Yes sir, it says that the brain appeared crushed by an unknown immense multi-directional pressure or blunt force. At the same time no injury or damage occurred to the skull."

"How do they explain that?"

"The medical examiner can offer no medical explanation nor provide an explanation for the fatal anomaly."

Lanzig sat tapping his fingers on the desk. "Well, that's great. No one's to blame but something terrible and unexplainable occurred."

"What about the little boy?"

"You have copies of all of his medical records. It seems the boy suffered from severe autism. He could not speak and communicated only through grunts and pointing."

"And yet he spoke at the rally?"

"Yes sir."

"Go on."

"When brought to the trauma center he was non-responsive, dead. Physicians worked on him for about fifteen minutes before declaring him dead. The boy's body remained unattended another twenty minutes before the arrival of the two ... whoever they are." Marcus stopped.

"Why stop? Go on."

"Well sir, this is where the video records the events. One of the men leaned over the boy, prayed and then breathed on him. The boy then revived."

"I'm guessing the doctors didn't have an explanation for this either?"

"No sir. In fact, after examining the boy, even the wound of the rock appeared as a mild abrasion. No indication of any blunt force trauma remained."

Lanzig sighed in anger. "So let me get this straight. We have faculty members who are painfully silent? We have the assaulting student dead with a crushed brain without injury to his skull? We have a mute boy who suddenly speaks? This same boy is struck and pronounced dead? And then after as much as thirty-five minutes he is alive for no explainable reason?"

"Yes sir. That's a fair assessment."

Lanzig looked down.

Without looking up, "Have we spoken to the little boy and his mother?"

"Yes sir. I did so myself this morning."

"And what did they have to say?"

"They claim it as a miracle from God. They said that the men are prophets."

He looked up. "Of course. Why not? It's understandable in their situation. Do they know where they are?"

"The mother told me that they were together last night. She also said they left after dinner."

"Does she know where they were staying or going?"

"She asked the same question of them but they did not tell her."

Just then the phone ran. Lanzig looked at the number. "D'bar."

He looked at Marcus, "Leave."

✡  ✡  ✡

Brandon sat in the front seat with Asher their driver. They had all spent the night at Asher's home but left before dawn. They had stopped for breakfast in the small city of Netivot. The *Two* didn't seem in any hurry so they spent the morning walking about. It didn't take long before some people recognized the *Two*.

Both of them engaged in several conversations and prayed for those who requested it.

By noontime Eli decided it was time to leave. He looked to Asher, "We need to make our way to Sderot. Do you know it?"

"Yes sir."

"Then let us go."

✡ ✡ ✡

D'bar let the silence on the line create the needed effect.

"Herr Lanzig?"

"Yes Chancellor."

"I assume you have expected my call?"

"Yes."

"Then let us not waste my time. Tell me your plan of action."

"My plan is two-fold. First, we will undertake a thorough discrediting of these two in every area of the media and society. I am beginning this program within Israel and will move it internationally. Secondly, as soon as they are located they are to be apprehended. I plan to use the cover of Israeli proselytizing laws. This will give the whole matter legitimacy."

"Very good. I received a report on the two incidents in Be'er Sheva from Besnik. The report contains merely the facts, which are indeed puzzling. Have you reached any conclusions?"

"All of the evidence so far does not yet yield anything conclusive. We have verified the medical results of all of those involved. We just don't know how they were accomplished."

"You do know the conclusions being promoted?"

"Yes, but those are ridiculous. Part of our media campaign will attack those ideas and those who promote them. We have many weapons in our arsenal to intimidate people into submission."

"Very well Lanzig. I am going to trust that you have this matter under control. I don't wish to be troubled with this again. Take whatever steps necessary to stabilize your region. Understand?"

He hung up not waiting for an answer. Lanzig understood clearly.

✡  ✡  ✡

Brandon walked in and saw Moshe sitting looking out the back window. Moshe smiled as he watched Eli and their host talking about some domestic issue.

Though they had remained in the area of Sderot, every few days they would relocate to a different home. For almost three months they had avoided any public appearances. They had restricted themselves to small venues in homes where mostly families would come and visit them. After a few days a visitor would extend an invitation to come to their home.

Brandon stood beside Moshe and looked out to see what had Moshe's attention.

"Everything's seems to fit very easily for Eli in this setting doesn't it?"

"This is home for him. It's where he grew up."

Moshe turned to Brandon.

"How are you today?"

"I woke up this morning and it hit me. I can't believe it's been almost a year since we started on this little adventure."

Moshe chuckled. "Yes, time passes when you're having fun. So, what are you up to today? I haven't seen you all morning."

"I caught a ride up to the college. I wanted to get an idea about what's going on."

Moshe turned back to look out the window. "So, what's going on?"

"I think it's a good thing we've been laying low these past months. They are ravaging you guys in the media. Everywhere I looked there were stories and articles slamming you as kooks, troublemakers, or enemies of society. All of the videos showing the things you've done are either gone or relegated to bizarre sites."

Moshe smiled and turned to Brandon. "Is that what you think, that we are laying low?"

"Well, aren't you?"

Moshe chuckled. "As a media expert, you should know that contrast is the best form of clarity. We are, quote, "laying low" because that is what we've been led to do. In the meantime, the enemy has done what they do best. They have spread their lies. But those lies will stand in contrast to the truth as it's revealed."

"I don't understand."

"Look Brandon, this is not about us. This is about God. We have spent almost a year proclaiming the message concerning the reality of God. All of the propaganda of the Lie has one goal, that He is not real. As His messengers we are targets of the Lie as well."

Moshe could see the look in Brandon's eyes.

"Did you suppose that we reduced our public profile out of fear?"

"Maybe."

Now Moshe's eyes became fixed and determined. "Brandon, our mission is set by God Himself. We will accomplish that mission in His way and according to His timing. But one thing is certain. The enemy can do us no harm until our mission is completed."

Moshe turned to look back out at Eli. "No, if anyone should be fearful it should be those who oppose the Living God. He, and He alone is to be feared."

Brandon knew the conversation had concluded. He looked out the window and then at Moshe. He sensed that the tranquility of the past months coming to an end.

✡ ✡ ✡

Lanzig sat in his Jerusalem office looking over reports when he received a text from Marcus.

"We've located them. Be there in two minutes."

"Yes! Finally some progress." Lanzig clinched his fists.

Over the office intercom, "Charlotte, when Mr. Neumann arrives, send him right in."

She replied, "Yes sir. Is there anything else you need?" Her voice always carried a seductive lilt.

Lanzig gave her credit for her persistence. "No, that will be all."

Marcus arrived on schedule. Lanzig greeted him with palms open. "Well?"

"They're in the area of Sderot. They keep a low profile, move around a lot, and don't stay in one location more than two days. But my sources definitely have them there. I have resources and inquiries spread out across the area."

"Excellent. The media campaign has obviously quieted them publically. There are no more large rallies or gatherings. Now we simply have to grab them without too much of a show."

"I suggest a small squad of five." Marcus suggested.

"Make it ten."

"Yes sir. I'll have them dressed as Israeli Police. We can arrest them and bring them here to Jerusalem."

"Very good, Marcus. I want you on this mission supervising it. I want video feed of the arrest. I'll link Besnik and the Chancellor so they can see it."

Lanzig walked up to Marcus and put his arm around his shoulder. "I want this done swiftly and thoroughly. But take care."

Marcus looked puzzled.

"Do not underestimate these two."

"What do you mean sir?"

Lanzig exhaled a tense breath. "I'm not exactly sure. I simply know that they can be dangerous. So once you find them don't give them a chance to plot a response."

He paused for a second. "If necessary the use of deadly force is authorized. Do you understand?"

"Yes sir. Don't worry. We'll get these guys. I'll find them and put an end to all of this."

Lanzig half smiled and he patted him on the shoulder. "Very well Marcus. Day or night let me know when you locate them and begin your move."

Marcus nodded and briskly made for the door.

Lanzig whispered, "Take care."

✡   ✡   ✡

Brandon walked out onto the back porch. They had spent the night as guests in the kibbutz of Gevim, south-southeast of Sderot.

The early morning sun remained somewhat hidden behind some low clouds. The air felt cool for an August morning. Moshe and Eli sat facing the south. They both held warm cups of tea.

"Beautiful morning," Brandon had a cup of the same mint tea.

The *Two* looked up at Brandon and nodded.

Moshe spoke. "Brandon, come sit."

After he did, Moshe continued. "Brandon, you've been over to the Sapir College campus haven't you? What's the activity like at this time?"

"Well normally this is the summer and there are no classes. But due to some attacks from Gaza in June, they were unable to have classes. It took a couple of months to make repairs so they are making up for the lost time before scheduled classes begin in September."

"Good. We're going there today. You know the campus. Spread the word. Choose a spot for all of us to meet. Make it for around noon."

"Really? Is a public gathering wise?"

Eli looked at Moshe and then at Brandon. He chuckled.

"Yeah, OK." He looked at the heavy cloud cover coming in from the east. "Normally clouds like that would indicate a chance for rain.

But since it hasn't rained in almost nine months ..."

Moshe spoke. "It's not going to rain today."

Brandon nodded. "Well, you would know."

Brandon took a deep drink of his tea. "Noon, today?"

Moshe nodded.

"OK, I'll get on it." He finished his tea with a gulp.

"Here we go!" Brandon turned back toward the house.

Eli and Moshe both whispered, "Here we go."

# Chapter 16

Marcus received a text. "Sapir College, noon today."

He looked at his watch, 11:30. It left him no time to waste.

He screamed at the squad leader. "Let's go! We leave in five!"

It took every bit of the five minutes to assemble and pull out. The team required two police jeeps and a van. They contacted Lanzig and completed all the communications link ups.

Marcus and the squad leader looked over a campus map in the back of the van.

Marcus took control, "Let's assume they'll choose some place central. Here."

He pointed to an open area between the student housing and the Administration Office. "This would be my guess. It's open and it's central. We'll approach from the west."

The squad leader nodded. "I'll break the group into three teams. One will come in from around the admin building. I'll send another around the housing and come in by the library. The main group will approach from the west."

A squad leader injected. "Sir, normally the campus is empty at this time. But because of certain circumstances, students are on campus for exams."

Marcus puffed his frustration. "We definitely don't have a controlled environment."

He tapped his communicator in his ear. "Sir, should we proceed?"

Before Lanzig could answer, Besnik gave the order. "Proceed."

Marcus passed on the order. "Everyone listen up. We have a go. You all know the suspects. Isolate and arrest them. If they resist, lethal force is approved."

Lanzig watched and listened. He felt the tension and adrenaline of a mission.

Besnik sat watching in his office feeling proud to be the one who gave the go ahead.

The Chancellor sat alone in a dark room with a clinched face as he watched and waited.

✡ ✡ ✡

The campus sat due west from Gevim within short walking distance. They left the house around 11:20.

Accompanied by Brandon and their hosts they walked and talked as if they were out for a midday stroll. Brandon watched the *Two*. They didn't seem at all nervous or fretful. Their winsome mood put everyone at ease. Brandon kept looking around wondering.

When they crossed the street to enter the campus, groups of people were waiting. Word had spread quickly. By the time they passed the School of Art and neared the Library, nearly one hundred people had joined them. When they entered the meeting place, another one hundred waited for them. The growing crowd did not go unnoticed. Curious students began to join the gathering.

The *Two* situated themselves on the eastern edge of the open space and waited.

Brandon stood next to them. He nervously looked at his watch. 11:50. "What are we waiting for?"

Eli looked west toward the opening and a parking lot where three vehicles had pulled up.

He looked at Moshe. "We can begin now."

A college administrator quickly walked over to the policemen emptying from their vehicles. "I'm so glad you came right away. We have a large crowd gathering not far from here and I'm not sure what is happening."

Without looking at him Marcus answered while checking his equipment. "Don't worry about anything. We've got this under control."

"Under control?" He didn't understand.

Marcus turned to him with a cold stare. "Return to your office immediately."

The man meekly nodded and hurried away.

Even from two hundred yards away, Marcus saw the size of the crowd.

"Sir, are you seeing this?"

Lanzig responded. "Yes. Not what we expected."

Before Lanzig could continue, D'bar's cold calm voice interrupted. "I don't want these men getting away. Do whatever is necessary."

"Yes sir."

Marcus turned to the men. "Alright, we follow the plan. I'll be with the main group coming in from the west. Everyone clear?"

Weapons ready, they all shook their heads.

"Let's go."

Eli raised his hands to quiet the crowd. His voice boomed across the open space, "Welcome. For many days now you have heard the lies. Voices and images have been raised to distort and dispel the truth of the Living God."

A student shouted, "Aren't you seeking to trick and lie to us yourself?"

Eli roared. "Do you not remember the words from the prophet?"

"I am the LORD, and there is no other; besides Me there is no God. I will gird you, though you have not known Me; that men may know from the rising to the setting of the sun that there is no one besides Me. I am the LORD, and there is no other," [3]

"Do you proclaim yourselves as prophets from God?" someone yelled.

Eli quickly responded, "What we have declared is true. We have provided signs from God so that you may know that what we say is from Him and that our words are true."

Another shouted, "How do we know?"

Eli answered. "Has it rained upon the earth since I spoke?"

Murmurs spread across the crowd. Another shouted, "That's simply climate change!"

"I speak to you in the Name of the One who made the heavens and the earth. The day of signs is here for you today. But even these are not enough for some. It is also a day to believe. You must all choose before it is too late."

"To late for what?" shouted someone.

"Before the great and terrible day of the Lord. In His love I plead with you. For even today you shall see the salvation and judgment of God."

A handheld loudspeaker broke in. "Attention! Attention! In the name of the government we are here to arrest these two. They are under arrest for the breaking several offenses. We ask that they give themselves up peacefully. We also ask that everyone else step away from them so that we..."

Marcus's voice dropped out. Moshe stood tightening his grip on the Rod.

Lanzig asked, "Marcus, what's wrong?"

"I don't know sir. The loudspeaker has stopped working."

Eli continued. "For all who can hear me, the time has come to decide. Come in faith and draw close. Know that He Is and that there is safety here. Otherwise stand your distance less you be harmed. Hear the word of the Lord and decide."

Moshe lifted the Rod. The top of it began to glow bright like the sun. At the same time a glowing fog began to form below his feet and spread.

People began moving. Some stepped back in fear while others ran away.

The two squads started their approach from either side but were hampered by the panicking crowd moving in multiple directions. The main squad halted their approach for the same reason.

The bright cloud continued to expand and then float upward. Eli invited the people to come and to do so quickly.

Marcus and his men were pushing through the panicking students. Lanzig watched with mouth open wide. An odd feeling churned in his gut.

The fog now formed into a large glowing cloud.

Eli's voice screamed out, "Believe. Come quickly while you can."

While many had already chosen, a few more heard his voice and ran swiftly toward him.

Within the cloud almost two hundred gathered close around Eli. "Because you have chosen to come, you shall see the salvation of His hand. This is so that you may know that He is and that He saves. Be still and see."

Moshe lowered the Rod and pounded it to the ground. The cloud intensified in brightness.

Marcus and his men stood around the cloud looking and wondering how to proceed. The brightness intensified to the point the squad employed their desert sunglasses. The large number who had run away stood at a distance and watched.

Marcus looked at his men. "Sir, are you seeing this?"

"Yes."

"Instructions sir."

Besnik yelled out. "What are you waiting for? Get in there and get them."

Marcus pointed to the four men to his right and waved them in.

With weapons employed they cautiously moved forward. The cloud churned like bright white liquid smoke. They stood two feet from it and looked at each other.

Besnik screamed. "Get in there!"

They all took a deep breath and ran forward.

Everyone stood stunned and they watched. The second they contacted the cloud their bodies ignited into flames. Those that fell forward were completely consumed. For the one who fell backward, only half his body remained. It quickly vanished in flames.

Lanzig held his face in his sweaty hands and as he watched.

Besnik's open mouth remained silent.

"Sir." Marcus's voice quivered ever so slightly. "Instructions?"

Again D'bar responded. "Surround the thing and fire at will. They must not escape."

"But sir, there are women and children in there. Innocent civilians."

"There is no one innocent in there. Now do as you're told."

"Yes Sir, Mr. Chancellor, sir."

Marcus positioned his men encircling the cloud. He discovered that his loudspeaker now worked.

"People inside listen to me, this is the police. Come out now! If you do not, you will be fired upon. You are all now accomplices to the deaths of government officials. This is your last warning."

Marcus waited one minute. He looked at his men and shouted, "Fire."

At the sound of the weapons many inside the cloud began to

scream and cover the smaller ones around them.

Eli's calm voice called out, "Do not fear. You shall see the salvation of the Lord."

The bullets pierced the cloud. Instantly, bullets of fire returned back to their point of origin. Marcus and all of his men fell and their bodies ignited from within. Their screams sent many in the crowd falling in fear and tears. They could not believe what they were seeing.

Marcus' body camera captured footage of the flaming projectiles before he fell. It continued to transmit from his fallen position. It captured the remaining events.

Inside the cloud Eli raised his hands to silence the ones with him. "Do not fear. Remember the words of the Lord."

> "I, even I, am He who comforts you. Who are you that you are afraid of man who dies and of the son of man who is made like grass." [4]

Eli raised his voice even louder, "So that you may know that the Lord, He is…"

Moshe raised the Rod again and struck it to the ground.

Suddenly the cloud vanished as well as everyone inside of it.

✡  ✡  ✡

Lanzig fell back in his chair. His hands trembled as he remembered the Dead Sea and looked at the empty place where the cloud had just been.

Bensik looked like a trapped mouse in a room full of cats. His mind raced as he tried to make sense of what he had witnessed.

D'bar screamed as he stomped over to the screen and smashed it with his foot.

✡  ✡  ✡

Their memories were varied and fragmented. One thing remained constant. One moment they were at the college in the cloud. The next instant each person found themselves at their homes. Stunned in shock, they all fell to their knees and voiced prayers of thanksgiving.

Eli, Moshe, and Brandon sat on the beach in Ashdod watching the waves.

Moshe looked over to Brandon. "Well, what are you thinking?"

"I'm afraid and confused. I don't know what's wrong with me. I've seen enough, that's for sure. But I'm still afraid. I know that doesn't make sense."

Moshe nodded. "Actually it does. You just have to come to a point of deciding."

Brandon's moist eyes looked over to Moshe. "Deciding what?"

Moshe picked a small pebble and tossed it toward the water. "Who and what to fear."

# Chapter 17

**The Chronicle of the Witnesses – Year Two**

Besnik and Lanzig sat alone in their respective offices. They both waited for the Chancellor to come online for their meeting. Two weeks had passed since the incident in Sderot. With after-action reports and an investigation completed, the Chancellor wanted a meeting between the three of them. A large 52-inch screen sat immediately in front of each man's desk.

Lanzig sat fingering through some reports. One of them contained personnel files on a new security team. The losses in Sderot had seriously damaged his network in Israel. Regardless of attempts to control information on the Sderot event, leaks had occurred. Lower level informants had broken off or scurried into hiding. Rumors were becoming harder to manage.

Besnik, for his part, sat fairly motionless. He had many of the same reports as Lanzig but his mind worked differently. He rehearsed various angles of approach for his position going forward. His plans always included steps to maximize power and minimize damage.

The computer screen alerted them of the Chancellor's online

status. They both saw him sitting down and placing the files on his own desk. The clarity of the image made it seem as if the Chancellor sat immediately in front of them. Besnik and Lanzig's had considerably larger screens in front of them, making the point all too clear.

D'bar cleared his throat. "Gentlemen, I'm sorry for my tardiness."

Besnik spoke, "Sir, you..."

"Silence." D'bar's firm voice said it all. "You will speak when I have a question for you."

He nodded.

"As I said, my apologies for holding up this meeting. I have a world to manage and it does have its demands. Now to your region."

He cleared his throat as he opened a particular file. "Let me say Herr Lanzig, your after-action report is extremely thorough. Let me begin by commenting that although you were in charge of this attempted arrest, I acknowledge that both the RTC and I did issue the commands. We both in turn carry partial responsibility for the results."

Besnik tried to interject. "In my defense sir."

"I said silence, Yacov." Hearing his first name made the point. He folded his hands and lowered his gaze.

"Lanzig, let me also say that I am sorry for the loss of your men. I realize the value of those assets and hope you can quickly rebuild your operation. How long do you estimate before you will be back at full strength?"

"I have already begun recruitment and my plan is to have personnel in place and ready within a month."

"That long?"

"Well sir, it is not merely personnel but also the network they had established. Each team member had regional responsibilities connected to their contact networks. I have detailed intel on all of the networks but the incident has affected morale within the network."

"Explain."

"Rumors and leaked information concerning the incident has created a level of fear with several informants. Some have gone off the grid, while others have become reluctant to continue. Once my team is complete, my plan is to encourage their continued work with us. My team will know what to do to achieve those results."

"Very well. Let me ask. Do either of you have some plausible explanation for what occurred?"

Lanzig waited to see if Besnik had something to offer. Yacov's eyes moved back and forth. He had nothing.

"Sir, as I stated in my report, the material facts have not yielded anything actionable. I have shared all forensic data with trusted experts and they are equally at a loss. As you know, I have a history with these individuals. Both their tactics and methods are a mystery to me. Since I do not accept their stated source behind their actions, I am left trying to find another explanation. I have yet to do that. Quite honestly, it has me baffled. Without knowing how they are accomplishing their ... what they do ... it is very difficult to plan a winning strategy."

Besnik now spoke up. "If I may, sir? I join you in saying that you and I and not Herr Lanzig did in fact give the orders. So he does not bear that responsibility. But may I also add that perhaps the size of the force and timing of the arrest fell short for successful results."

Lanzig smirked. He recognized Besnik's tactic and decided not to defend himself. He assumed D'bar would recognize the obvious.

"Thank you Yacov for that observation. Yet you haven't provided an answer to the puzzle Lanzig brought up. Do have an explanation for how they were able to defeat our attempt to arrest them?"

His silence provided the answer. Lanzig didn't provide further comment either.

D'bar had another question. "Do we have any idea as to their whereabouts?"

"No sir." Lanzig responded. "Their exit from the scene provided no traceable means of tracking them. Since video feed coming from Marcus's camera provided a limited view. We were unable to capture any usable footage for facial recognition of any of the other individuals involved. This has left us with no other persons of interest to question."

"Do you think they still are in the Negev area?"

"There's no way of knowing sir. We will have to wait until they choose to show up or we receive further intel."

"So you are looking?"

"Absolutely."

"So what are your plans?"

"Well sir." Besnik tried to pipe in.

"Yacov, I was speaking to Lanzig"

Lanzig smiled. "We are continuing our media campaign, pressing a conspiratorial angle. While they remain low profile, we will pursue promoting an image of a more clandestine nature. When we do locate them I would like to move with an assassination from a safer distance. I am acquiring assets with exactly those skill sets."

D'bar laughed. "Lanzig, I like the way you think. And Besnik, I want you to provide him with whatever resources he requires. Is that clear?"

"Yes sir. But what did you have for me to do?"

"I want you to concentrate on the Jewish matter. I want the conditions of the treaty initiated and moving toward completion. I want the Jewish religious leaders on our side in this whole matter. I DO NOT want any so called prophets stirring up any religious fervor that we are not in control of."

"Yes sir."

"Speaking of religious fervor, Lanzig, I have received reports of some incidents in different parts of the world. They're scattered. I want to know if they are related. See what you can find out about that."

"Certainly Herr Chancellor."

"Well, I have to get back to other issues. Let's see if we can learn from all of this. Our goal has not changed and neither has our schedule. Peace, Prosperity and Order."

His image feed went dead. Both Lanzig and Besnik repeated the words in whispered voices. "Peace, Prosperity and Order."

Lanzig spoke up. "I'll get back to you in a week." He closed his feed.

Besnik steamed as he looked at the blank screen. "Don't think you're getting the better of me Hermann. Don't think that for a moment."

✡  ✡  ✡

The three of them had spent several days in Bat Yam, a coastal town not far out of Tel Aviv. Through the invitation of a fellow believer, the last few days were ones of quiet and regrouping. The *Two* spent their usual hours in prayer. Brandon, for his part, enjoyed the break from their usual pace. He hated to admit it, but days on the beach let him feel the old normal. It provided a small respite in a world increasingly out of control.

Late afternoon and walking back to the house from the beach, Brandon spotted the *Two* sitting on the patio overlooking the shore. Looking at them Brandon chuckled.

When he reached the house he had to comment. "You should see you two. This is the beach, guys. Can't you two lighten up a little? Most people here are dressed in shorts and swim wear. But you two still look like you just came out of the desert."

Moshe smiled. "Well Brandon, believe it not I've had more days than you can imagine on the beach. As for Eli, he's lived with Bedouins all his life. This is his normal. Anyway, we're leaving in the morning."

Brandon stepped up and sat next to them. "Wow, so soon? Don't you want to lay low a little longer? I mean, after the last thing the media attack has only increased. They are accusing you of killing

137

police officers. The public is sympathetic with the police, most of the time."

Eli seemed less patient with their companion. "Brandon, why exactly are you still with us?"

Moshe grinned. "Patience my brother. The Lord knows the true answer to that question. But it is a good question nonetheless."

Looking directly at Brandon. "Back when Freddy and the others left, why didn't you? And then after we picked you up in Arad, what made you choose to come with us?"

The questions pulled him back into a different setting. He recalled all of the events that led to his decisions. Moshe had hit it squarely.

He thought about how to say it. "It's a fair question and one you both deserve to have answered. First, let me thank you for the privilege and also for saving my skin more than once."

Eli responded before Moshe could. "Actually it was the Lord who did the saving."

"Yeah, you see that's all part of my answer. You say it's God and I'm not sure about that whole thing. What got me to stay and then join in, involved getting an answer to my question. I couldn't … no, I can't explain you guys."

He cleared his throat. "When I first started this whole thing it concerned getting a story and making a movie. Well, that's all gone now. Now, it's about finding out. It's about … I need to know. For myself, I need to know. That's the best I can do in explaining why I'm here."

Moshe patted him on the shoulder. "I understand. I think we both understand that kind of question."

Eli played back his own memories and sighed. "Yeah, questions like that do drive you to distraction, don't they?"

Brandon waited several minutes. "Speaking of questions, I've got one. What's the plan now?"

Moshe nodded to Eli. "We've completed our first year. We

focused on a single message: He Is. The Lord now commands us to build on that message."

"Ok, I get that. You're talking about the existence of God? I think the things you've done have definitely got people thinking about it. But what's next?"

Moshe answered. "Brandon, it's not enough to simply concede to His existence. It also includes the reality of that existence and its significance."

Eli joined in. "Exactly. His reality has implications to all of life. No part of life is exempt from the applications of that reality. If He Is, if He is God, then He is Lord. He holds sovereignty over all of life. He is to have no competition to His position over all of life."

Moshe added. "Many people agree to the idea of God. I know that before I believed, I would give assent to the idea of God. For instance, for me, my mother's faith in God existed like some preference, like a choice in music style."

Eli jumped in. "Precisely, in this world people treat all ideas about God as equal, as merely a matter of taste or preference. It's as if we can create God to suit our tastes. But there is, in reality, a True and Living God. He is not subject to modifications or alterations to our dispositional fancy. He Is who He is."

Moshe continued. "And that reality has implications. The True and Living God is sovereign over all of life, over all institutions and over all other pretenders to the divine."

Brandon sat stunned under the barrage of what he heard. "Wow, I never thought of it like that."

Moshe nodded. "Most people don't. I know I didn't until I met Him."

Eli's voice quieted. "And that's why He has sent us to proclaim the message that He is and that He is Lord. It is important for people to understand it before it's too late."

That last line sent a chill down Brandon's arm. "Too late?"

Moshe answered. "Brandon, you used to make movies. They

were in essence, stories."

Brandon nodded.

"Imagine if the characters didn't know that they were actually in a story. They believed that they were creating all of the reality around their lives. But in actuality, there was a larger story they were participating in and they didn't even know it. They didn't know the real plot. And worst of all, they didn't know the main character of the story. They lived their whole lives and never knew the story or the hero of that story. How sad would that be?"

Eli lowered his head. "God wants people to know that the story is coming to a close. It's important for them to know Him. Time is running out."

Brandon tried to absorb it in while not letting the implications get too close to his own life. He remembered. "In a movie or story there is a principle that all story writers understand."

"What is that?" Moshe asked.

Brandon looked out toward the sea. "It is a fatal error to be on the wrong side of the hero at the end of a story."

Eli nodded. "Yes, yes it is."

Moshe whispered, "Truly."

# Chapter 18

Asher got a call and responded in swift fashion. He had become their unofficial official driver. At least that's how he referred to himself.

"Where to sirs?" His voice rang with delight.

"You're in a fine mood today, Asher." Moshe commented as they loaded his cab.

"It is always a fine day when I am allowed to transport you sirs."

Brandon asked. "Asher what does your boss think of you taking off to move us around?"

"Oh sir, I am my own boss. This is my cab. I often transport local families and even tourists. I am a certified tour guide here in Israel."

"Excellent." Eli added. "It seems God has brought us all together for His purpose. You will be most helpful."

"We will make sure you are amply rewarded for your service." Moshe said as he reached into his bag.

"Oh no, sirs. The Lord has blessed me greatly in my years and even more so now that I recognize the source of my blessing. It is I who should be paying you. I feel this is my contribution to the great work God is doing through you."

Eli placed his hand on Asher's shoulder. "God's blessings will be upon you my brother. And you shall see the return of our Savior and He brings His reward for you."

The words of blessing gripped Asher as he sensed the presence of the Lord fall upon him. In his heart he knew the assurance of the promise he had just received.

He whispered a prayer. "Blessed be our Lord and Savior Yeshua."

Moshe finished, "Truly."

Brandon, sensed the presence of beauty while equally knowing his exclusion.

Eli took a deep breath. "Asher, take us to Tel Aviv. Actually we go to Holon."

"Yes, I know the place."

As Eli sat back, Brandon asked. "What's in Holon?"

"I'm glad you asked because it involves you."

"Me?

"Yes. We will visit a friend there but you and Asher have a task to fulfill."

"What?"

Moshe reached into his bag and pulled out some money. "This should be enough."

"Enough for what?"

Eli grinned. "We're about to put your movie making talents to work."

"What do you mean?"

"I mean, we want you to make a video for us. We want to announce our next event and we need you to produce it and send it out, email it, or whatever you need to do. We need people to know about it."

Brandon nodded. "So we're losing the low profile approach and going all in with this next thing?"

"You might say that." Moshe added.

Brandon looked at the money in his hand. "Yeah, I can do it and this is more than enough money. Asher, looks like we have our orders."

"Yes sir, Mr. Brandon, we will get it done. You tell me what we need and I will find the places."

Brandon began making a list.

They reached Holon and dropped off the *Two*. It took most of the afternoon to track down the items on his list. They made it back to Holon by late afternoon.

Brandon readied a place in the living room to tape the message. By early evening he had everything set in place to shoot the message.

"Alright gentlemen, who's going to speak?"

Moshe grinned and nodded toward Eli.

Brandon sheepishly smiled. "Oh yeah, I forgot. Will both of you be in the picture though?"

They looked at each other and nodded.

"Ok then." Brandon put them both in place. He gave Eli the signal to begin.

"Greetings in the Name of the True and Living God and His Savior Yeshua."

Moshe stood silent on Eli's right side.

Eli continued. "Know that the Lord has commanded us to declare His message to Israel and to the whole world. One week from today we invite you to join us in Tel Aviv and hear the word of the Lord. He has a particular message on that day. Specifically the message is for the nations of the world. We invite, no, we admonish representatives of the embassies and consulates located in Tel Aviv to come."

Eli took a breath before continuing. "We will gather at mid-day at

Ganei Yehoshua Park HaYarkon. We invite all who wish, to come. But we strongly encourage the ones mentioned to attend. It is to your benefit that you attend."

Eli finished and lowered his head.

"Ok, if that's it, we'll end it there."

Brandon reviewed the video on the computer and readied it for editing.

Moshe walked up. "Brandon, we want it to go out tomorrow morning. Is that possible?"

"Oh yeah."

"Also," Moshe continued. "Our host has the means to distribute the message in such a way that it is untraceable. I trust you to get with him and make it so."

Brandon nodded. "You got it. It'll happen just like you want. Any other instructions you want going out with the video?"

"No, that should do it. Thank you."

"My pleasure. I'm glad to help out."

Moshe patted him on the shoulder and turned to walk away.

✡ ✡ ✡

Lanzig got word within an hour of the video's release. He called together his special team for a morning meeting.

Lanzig had spared no expense in assembling a deadly and talented team. They came from all around the world but shared one thing in common; their lethal skills knew no equal. The team consisted of eighteen men and two women. Each of them had specialties yet all of them spelled danger for any opponent.

"Alright, each of you have reviewed the video and read over the dossier on the two subjects. In most cases our approach would be intense and direct. That is not our strategy. Our subjects have proven to have resources, which we have yet to explain and quantify. Therefore we will use stealth and distance. Our goal is their elimination."

Looking around at his fellow team members, one of them asked. "Isn't this a bit of overkill for these two? They don't appear to carry any weapons."

"Let me begin by saying that no one in this room should underestimate them. My previous team of ten did that and they are all dead. They were good men. They were very good men."

"Let me get this straight," another asked. "I read the report. You still don't have an explanation on how they accomplished what they did?"

"That's correct."

"So what are we dealing with here?"

It frustrated Lanzig to not have an answer. He cleared his throat. "I have been dealing with these subjects for over a year. They have displayed and utilized abilities and resources, which I cannot yet explain. It is all in the dossier. We are tasked with eliminating them. They are a clear and present danger to the world order."

One of the team looked up from the reports on his lap. "They claim their power comes from God."

"We don't go there." The question angered Lanzig. "Complete this mission and all of you will be rewarded handsomely beyond our current arrangement. The highest authority is behind this action."

They all looked at each other and nodded with big smiles.

"Ok, let's look at the current situation. We have location and time. The larger team is tasked with securing the perimeter. Two of you have the job of taking the shot. Let me introduce you all to Eduardo Santos and Alexandre Ferraz. They've made a study of the layout. I'll ask them to summarize their plan."

The two walked to the front and Eduardo spoke. "The park is very large and does not provide an adequate setting for us to station ourselves within the park. The Ramat Gan Stadium is located just across the Yarkon River directly east of the park. The rest of the team will act as local security and move the event to the far northeastern section of the park. This will provide us with a clear line of sight from the stadium."

One of the female team members spoke up. "Which of you two will take the shots?"

They looked at each other and Alexandre answered. "We'll probably flip for it."

Everyone in the room laughed except Lanzig. He did not doubt the plan's soundness or the team's skill. His worry lay in what he couldn't pin down.

Lanzig walked back to the front. "Alright, everyone. Get busy. We have seven days to prepare. That's more than enough time to make sure this goes smoothly. Let me stress, we want No, I repeat, No collateral damage. The two subjects are the only targets."

He waited a second to let it sink in. "You're all dismissed."

✡ ✡ ✡

Brandon reviewed a second video set to release at noon three days in advance of the rally. It went live right on time.

Eli spoke with Moshe standing next to him. "I again invite as many as can to come at noon, to Ganei Yehoshua Park HaYarkon. I plead with the dignitaries from the countries represented in Tel Aviv, come. And so that you may know that He Is and that He is Lord..."

Moshe stretched out the Rod only slightly. He then tapped the ground. The screen went dark.

In that very instant at the eighty-seven embassies across Tel Aviv chaos broke out. Every one of them experienced an immediate outbreak of massive infestations. For some, rats came streaming out of vents and sewers. For others it took the form of snakes or frogs. Others experienced unending swarms of flies and crawling insects. Whatever form it took, personnel in all of the buildings began evacuating. Screaming and cursing employees stormed out of their buildings and refused to reenter.

City services couldn't cope with the scale of the infestations. They all closed until the situation could be brought under control.

Lanzig watched the news coverage with clinched fists. The connection between the video and these seemed unmistakable. The coordination necessary to carry out this incident strained credulity. He slammed his fists onto his desk. Only three days and he wondered what else these two had up their sleeves.

✡ ✡ ✡

Asher arrived on time. Brandon walked outside the house where they were staying. Brandon tapped on Asher's car window.

"Nice ride."

Asher looked confused by the comment.

"I'm just kiddin'. So you did as Eli requested. This vehicle is a one-trip car? It isn't a stolen car?"

"Oh no sir. It is an old disposable car, which has no owner. After today I will dump it. I'm not sure why I can't used my regular car."

"Eli said he didn't want it traced back to you."

"They are so kind to think of me."

Eli and Moshe walked out. "Are we ready?"

Brandon gave a thumbs-up.

"Then let's roll."

✡ ✡ ✡

Eduardo and Alexandre were in position well in advance. They measured a slight breeze of 2 mph coming from the west. The conditions were optimal. An hour remained before the scheduled event. The team had moved the growing crowd to the northeastern corner of the park. Lanzig had arranged for a small raised podium and sound system. Everything moved according to plan.

Lanzig sat in the back of the operations van stationed in a parking lot at the northwest end of the park. He watched the various video feeds provided by the other team members.

The communications specialist reported. "With less than thirty minutes all assets are in place and all communications are clear."

Lanzig rubbed his chin. "Now we wait."

Very close to noon the radio came alive. "Sir, we have a car pulling in through the north rim of the park. Orders sir."

Lanzig responded. "That's them, let them continue. Santos, have you spotted them?"

"Affirmative. Just let me know when."

"Let them get in position. I'll give the order."

"Si Senor." Santos grinned. He turned to Ferraz, "This will be an easy one." They fist bumped each other.

Brandon sat in his usual place in the front seat. Security personnel directed Asher to drive toward the northeastern end of the park. Eli could see Brandon's nervousness.

"Calm yourself Brandon. Everything's fine."

Brandon looked over the large crowd as they passed them. More security directed their car toward what looked like a small stage. Brandon turned toward the back seat.

"I didn't arrange this. I don't like the looks of all of this. Someone else is directing all of this."

"So they think." Moshe fingered the Rod as he looked down at it.

The car stopped by the podium. Eli spoke. "Asher, I want you to stay in the car. Turn it around and have it ready to exit. We may be pulling out quickly."

He looked at Brandon. "You can get out, but stay next to the car. Ok?"

He nodded.

Before exiting the car the *Two* whispered a short prayer.

Eli stepped out first and walked to the podium. Moshe stepped immediately behind him.

Scattered applause broke out. Eli raised his hands to silence them.

Eduardo looked through his scope and spoke up. "I have a shot. Awaiting your orders."

Lanzig looked at the screen ready to give it.

Moshe squeezed the Rod in his hand. The top of the Rod instantly ignited a controlled but intense white.

Eduardo grimaced and almost screamed in pain.

Lanzig said it loudly. "Take the shot."

Eduardo held his right hand over his eyes. "Something blinded me. My eyes. All I can see are spots. What is that bright light?"

Lanzig looked at the screen and cursed. "How about Alexandre, can he take the shot?"

"He's gone down to the van. We have a scope filter to neutralize the light. With this happening at noon, the sun is directly above us. We had no reason to expect this."

Lanzig slammed his fist against the van wall.

Eli did not even stopped to acknowledge the glowing Rod. "For over a year we have declared words of witness for our God. I can see and give thanks that some of you have come as representatives of the nations. The word of the Lord speaks concerning you:"

> "For I know their works and their thoughts; the time is coming to gather all nations and tongues. And they shall come and see My glory. I will set a sign among them and will send survivors from them to the nations: Tarshish, Put, Lud, Meshech, Tubal and Javan, to the distant coastlands that have neither heard My fame nor seen My glory. And they will declare My glory among the nations." [5]

Lanzig screamed even louder. "What's taking so long? We need to take the shot."

"He's just arrived. He is prepping the scope. It should only be a minute or two."

"Hurry!"

"We have come to bear witness that the nations may hear and understand."

"Oh, that You would rend the heavens *and* come down, That

the mountains might quake at Your presence - As fire kindles the brushwood, *as* fire causes water to boil—To make Your name known to Your adversaries, *That* the nations may tremble at Your presence!"[6]

Eli looked across the audience. "He and He alone is sovereign. No king or ruler is above Him. All the nations and their rulers will answer to Him. These words are true and sure. And so that you may all know that He Is and that He is Lord."

Moshe took the Rod by one end and raised it high. He then slammed the glowing end into the ground. An explosion of light flashed out in every direction. All those in the audience shielded their eyes from the glow.

Alexandre raised his weapon and began to take aim. The filter had reduced almost all of the light. He took a deep breath and began to squeeze the trigger.

Across the park, moving toward the river, the ground began to shake. Both Alexandre and Eduardo grabbed the stadium edge to steady themselves. The shaking increased and they heard the cracking. The shaking became violent and then it happened. The entire western half of the stadium collapsed. Both of the men screamed as they plunged and were buried under tons of concrete.

The quake moved across the city. People heard it, but only a few felt it. Without exception, every embassy in the city collapsed. Buildings immediately next to them remained undamaged. As if an unseen hand grabbed each building and shook it until it fell, while buildings adjacent to them remained unaffected.

In the park, everyone present rubbed their eyes to clear up the spots floating in their field of vision.

The quake had knocked the operations van on its side. Several in the van were unconscious. Lanzig shook his head trying to get his bearings.

In all of the chaos a single car drove out of the park and away from the scene.

# Chapter 19

One story filled the news across the world. Countries were
scrambling to handle the destruction of their embassies in Tel Aviv.
Governments were demanding that their embassy be secured. Police
and military worked tirelessly to assure that the no one entered the
rubble until national representatives arrived to supervise any action at
their embassy. Each nation had national secrets to protect. All of this
hampered any investigation as to what had occurred. No one even
knew if there were bodies under the debris.

Lanzig sent both Besnik and the Chancellor an after action
report. They all had viewed the footage and audio record of the
event. Besnik and Lanzig waited in their offices for D'bar to begin
the meeting.

Besnik felt at ease. It pleased him to know where the
responsibility would fall.

The screen came to life as D'bar dropped a file on his desk.

"Well, that didn't go as planned, did it?"

"No it did not." Lanzig sported a bandage on his right temple.

"Any theories, Hermann?"

"Nothing that explains what occurred."

"And what of this stick, or rod, or whatever it is? I remember Osgood believed it was key. Is that your opinion?"

"It does play some part. Every time we have one of these events, the rod is utilized."

"In the video it seems to glow. What exactly is happening there?"

"Spectrum analysis indicates that the light is possibly some kind of energy resulting from hydrogen fusion."

"How is that possible?"

"Well, what we saw wasn't thermonuclear fusion. What occurred more resembled cold fusion. But cold fusion is more hypothesis than something someone has actually accomplished. And yet, ... it happened. It appeared and manifested itself from an otherwise ordinary wooden stick."

"What are you suggesting?"

"I'm not suggesting anything. What I am saying is that there's no way it should happen."

"And yet it did?"

"Yes it did." His frustration outweighed any fear of reprisal from D'bar.

"What is your plan now?" Besnik chimed in.

Lanzig answered without reacting to Besnik's intent.

"Some team members have suggested drones or even a smart bomb."

"Well, it might come to that. Do you know where they are?" D'bar added.

"No. The vehicle they arrived in had no plates. We found it abandoned in the Negev east of Tifrah, basically in the middle of nowhere. We can assume they know we are trying to locate them. They are not sophisticated, but they are not dumb."

"Wasn't one of them a former doctor?"

"Yes, the one now known as Moshe previously went by the name Oliver Cohen. He was an accomplished orthopedic surgeon."

"What about all of the embassies?" Besnik again inserted himself.

D'bar grunted. "We'll let the Israeli's worry about that. They are responsible for the safety of sovereign embassies on their land. Actually we could work this to our advantage. The confusion provides good cover for our transition agenda."

He paused to think. "Besnik how is the religious portion of the transition going?"

With excitement in his voice, Besnik answered. "Excellent sir. All plans are approved and construction for their religious shrine has begun. Completion is scheduled within a year's time."

"Very good, Besnik. We must placate these religionists. Sometimes they're worse than politicians."

"Speaking of religionists, I didn't see anything in the report on the scattered accounts of zealots."

Lanzig's frustration increased even more. He picked up a new report he had received.

"Yes sir, just this morning I received communiqué from all my foreign sources. As of yesterday, we have counted over one hundred and thirty thousand proclaimers, preachers, or whatever they are. They seemed to be mimicking the two here in Israel. Although they do not have the same kind of unexplained events accompanying their preaching, their message is very much like our subjects."

"So the cat is out of the bag, so to speak, Herr Lanzig."

Lanzig did not answer.

"All the more reason to cut this off at the root." D'bar paused for affect. "You are running out of time Hermann. Our schedule is moving on and delays are not an option. Am I clear?"

"Very clear, sir."

"Excellent. Peace, Prosperity and Order." The screen went dead.

Besnik happily repeated the phrase. "Peace, Prosperity and Order."

Lanzig sensed the dark weight hanging over him and for the first time felt fear.

✡  ✡  ✡

Asher returned late in the day. His winsomeness always encouraged Brandon.

"So Asher, where did you dump the old car?"

"Ah yes sir, it sits in the desert. I removed all numbers from it and set it on fire. No way to trace us. All very good, sir."

Brandon laughed at Asher's mannerisms and attitude. "That's great. There's food in the kitchen, help yourself."

"Thank you sir, so kind of you."

As Asher bounced off, Brandon whispered to himself. "Don't thank me. Thank the people here."

For the last few days they had lived in Petah Tikva east of Tel Aviv. A newly gathered congregation of Messianic Jews had taken them in. The warmth and love of the group greatly resembled what he had experienced with the Bedouin believers. They all knew of his unbelief yet received him as family. The whole atmosphere disarmed him completely.

As on other evenings, they gathered in a large room and the singing began. Brandon didn't know the words but enjoyed the shared joy filling the room.

After the singing, either Eli or Moshe would speak and teach. Just as Eli walked forward to begin, they all heard the loud knock on the door.

Almost everyone tensed up. Thoughts of danger raced through many of them. They knew that taking in the *Two* had its risks.

Moshe calmed everyone with his relaxed tone. "Do not fear. There is no danger. We have a visitor."

He walked to the door and opened it. "Hello Charles, come in."

Everyone watched a bit stunned. Not everyone recalled his name but they recognized his face. The news had covered his coming to

Israel. The sheepish smile of Australia's Prime Minister seemed totally out of place among the small gathering.

"I'm so sorry to interrupt your meeting."

Moshe put his arm over his shoulder. "Think nothing of it Charles."

Turning to those gathered. "Please continue. My friend and I will visit together elsewhere."

They walked back out onto the rear patio. "Have a seat Charles."

"Thank you."

"So Charles how did you find us?"

"I have friends. I made inquiries. Don't worry. You're safe. I came by myself. I knew what sort of people to ask. I told them my story and they trusted me. So here I am."

"Yes, here you are, again."

Charles seemed nervous. He didn't know where to begin. "Where's your little animal friend?"

"You mean Snoop? He's with friends. I'll see him soon. But that's not why you're here is it?"

Charles gripped his trembling hands. Lowering his head, "Oliver, or Moshe, do you remember the last time we spoke?"

Moshe nodded.

"Things were bad then and worse now. I remember the things you told me. You said that the time would come when great numbers would see. News of your work has spread across the globe. And as you said, it has frightened many people. You also said it would bring hope."

Moshe added, "... to those who believe."

"Yes ... yes that's right. You also said that God had chosen me." Charles stopped to catch himself. His voice quivered.

"You ... you also said that when I reached a point when I ran out of answers to look for you."

He looked up at Moshe. His eyes were filling with tears. "I'm here. I'm here because … because I'm out of answers." He pressed his hand over his mouth as if trying to hold control of his failing emotions.

"Then you've come to the right place." Moshe's kind eyes and warm smile provided instant relief.

"The help and answers you need are right here. The Lord has journeyed with you. You need to call upon Him. You need to trust in the Savior, in what He has done and will do."

"How do I do that?"

"He's as close as the mention of His name."

"Really?" The words came out like that of a little boy.

Moshe nodded.

Charles gulped, took a breath and whispered the name. "Jesus."

Only those who know can describe in clear fashion the wondrous encounter of His coming. The flood of love and cleansing and the reality of His being are beyond simple descriptions.

Charles fell to his knees at the encounter. In whispers meant only for the Forgiver, the heart of Charles Owens was emptied and remade. The wonder of redemption and new life became a reality once again in the trusting heart of a man before the Living God.

If one could perceive it, celestial songs rang out as another soul found rescue.

Long moments passed before Charles looked up. A different man came up than the one who had gone down. Born again.

Moshe spent another hour teaching Charles Owens of the new life. With every passing moment new truth began taking hold of a redeemed soul. The old fear melted away replaced with a fresh strength. They spoke, they laughed and they embraced as if age long friends.

After a time they walked back to those gathered. Many clapped as they instantly recognized the change. The beaming smile ignited fresh tears of joy. New songs were sung and stories shared. This continued late into the night.

Brandon watched feeling increasingly alone in the party of joy. He wondered if such a thing were possible for someone like himself. Doubts and fears badgered him into a hardened silence. He finally stepped out of the house alone.

Charles prepared to leave early the next morning. Many in the congregation trading contact information with him and promised to keep in touch.

It surprised Charles how quickly he had bonded with people he barely knew. He began to realize a life link that would always secure a connection of common faith worldwide.

Standing at his car door, he looked at Moshe. "It's like coming home to a large family?"

"Yes it is."

He put his hand on Charles' shoulder. "Grow in the faith. Discover the family. Fulfill your part in the Story. Until we meet again."

"Yeah, until we meet again." He got in his car and drove off. On his way back to Tel Aviv he laughed in joy. He could hardly believe the difference from just yesterday. "Amazing! Simply amazing."

Eli walked up next to Moshe putting his arm over Moshe's shoulder. "It never gets old does it?"

"No ... no it doesn't."

Brandon walked out. "So is the Prime Minister gone?"

Moshe simply nodded.

Eli turned to Brandon. "Tell Asher to make sure his car has plenty of fuel. We leave early afternoon."

Brandon nodded. "Where are we going now?"

"Haifa."

"Haifa? What's going on in Haifa?"

Eli answered, "War of the gods, Brandon. War of the gods."

# Chapter 20

Asher had traveled to Haifa before. The journey from Tel Aviv would normally require slightly more than an hour. Yet it actually took more than three weeks. After about the third stop he understood. People were more important than the destination.

Whenever they would leave one place, the *Two* would have a time of prayer alone. They would then tell Asher the name of their next stop. Even with Asher's extensive knowledge of the land, some villages were so small he had to resort to a map.

The stops varied from small kibbutzim of only a few hundred to larger beachside tourist cities. Both Brandon and Asher turned it into a kind of game trying to locate their next stop. Some of their names were Ga'ash, Udim, Kafar Vitkin, Sdot Yam, Or Akiva, Jisr az-zarqa, Ma'gan Michael, and HaBonin.

Brandon once asked how they knew of these places and the people in them. Moshe answered with only a shy grin. Brandon didn't press it. He knew that the answer involved God and at present he didn't want to go there.

Sometimes the stops would only be for a day. Eli would direct Asher to the house of what he called, "the person of peace" in the town. Once they arrived, the circumstances determined the length of the visit. But long or short, one thing became obvious; each visit provided an occasion for the interaction of human need and divine provision.

One such visit occurred in the town of Caesarea. When they pulled into the driveway of Ben and Emily Shapiro, she ran out and immediately fell to her knees.

As Eli stepped out of the car Emily cried out, "Praise to the Living God." Her husband stood on the porch holding his hand over his mouth in astonishment.

After tea they revealed their story. It seemed that the Shapiro's had moved here from Miami. They had come on a visit as part of the sister city partnership with the neighboring Or Akiva. They fell in love with the area and made the move. In the chaos of the past year, Emily came to faith in Messiah Yeshua. Her husband strongly resisted her new faith. Yet nine months ago she began praying that God would direct her. Her husband laughed at her when she told him that God would reveal Himself by sending a messenger to their home. When he saw the news of the *Two,* he challenged her and her God to send them. She then prayed fervently to that end. God had answered her prayer.

That evening new life entered that home and into the lives of specially invited guests. In the same way the *Two* had continuing life-changing encounters with people in every stop they made.

Yet with every life celebration, Brandon seemed to harden his resolve. He relegated these events to mere religious proselytizing.

They finally made their last stop before reaching Haifa. Tirat Karmel lay at the southern base of Mount Carmel. They were guests in a home as at other times. But unlike before, no visitors arrived. The *Two* slipped out late in the afternoon and hiked north into some sloped area at the base of the mount.

They made it clear that they would be back in three days. Eli had given Asher very specific instructions where he wanted to go when they returned. He and Brandon worked on the best route to the destination, even doing a practice run. The winding roads up the mountain proved to be tricky. Their instructions also included planning a strategic egress toward Nazareth.

Both Eli and Moshe were nearing exhaustion. The last few weeks had been non-stop day and night ministry. They both sensed the necessity for this time alone. They also both knew the approaching event demanded time of prayer and fasting.

When the sun went down, a chilly March breeze had them bundled under heavy wool blankets given to them by Bedouin friends. They had each spent several hours in separate prayer times before drifting off to sleep. The next day they trekked farther into some isolated hillside terrain. By midday they decided to stop and remain there for the night.

On the third morning, they prepared to begin to make their way back. By afternoon, they decided to camp on a hilltop that overlooked Tirat Karmel. Not having had any food and little water for three days, they were physically weak but spiritually focused. When evening came, they wrapped themselves in the wool blankets. They both looked forward to return in the morning.

Late into the night they both lay shivering under their blankets. Very slowly and almost unnoticed their bodies ceased shaking. Simultaneously they both looked up. Two men sat admiring a low burning fire. Its warmth exceeded the fire's size. It came as no surprise when they realized the identity of the two.

They each whispered the names. "Shamer." "Keeper."

They jumped up and ran to embrace their friends. After exchanged greetings, they all gathered around the fire. The fire burned steadily but interestingly no wood burned.

Moshe chuckled as he admired the phenomenon. A tea-kettle and pot of something delicious sat cooking on the fire.

Shamer nodded toward the food. "It is here for you. Careful not to burn yourself."

The Keeper provided them with plates and utensils and they dug in. They weren't sure what they were eating. They only knew that it satisfied them completely.

Moshe considered introducing him to Shamer.

When the Keeper detected it, he smiled. "We've know each other long before ... for a long time."

They all laughed. They shared a few minutes of short reminiscence before Shamer cleared his throat.

"It is good that you both are preparing yourselves for the coming event. Your human adversaries are struggling in their denials. But know that your real enemies are very aware of your work. They know that you are near. They are preparing. On the other side of the mountain is a shrine where they are gathering their human confederates. It is there where you will confront them."

The Keeper spoke next. "Before, your adversaries came armed with guns. Their destruction came in response to their plans against you. Tomorrow's enemies have no guns but they are no less dangerous. Our Lord sees them as a plague upon this land."

Shamer picked up the comments. "You must not hesitate to execute God's judgment in keeping with the message He has given you. Many will die. They have willingly chosen death by the master they serve. This is the will of God. Accusations will be made against you because of this. Do not fear. Days of healing are coming."

The Keeper continued. "Be strong in the Lord and in the power of His might."

The two visitors vanished.

Eli and Moshe fell to their knees and prayed for several hours as the fire slowly faded out.

Two hours after dawn the *Two* approached the house where

Brandon and Asher had stayed.

After a quiet breakfast Eli spoke. "I take it we are ready and you have a route?"

"Oh yes sir. For two days we have prepared."

Eli looked over to Moshe. "Very well. We need to arrive at our destination before midday, so I will trust you to let us know when we should leave."

"Yes sir, that would be 10:30 I believe, sir."

Moshe so enjoyed Asher's joyful attitude of service. "Thank you so much Asher."

"My great pleasure, sirs. All is ready."

Eli sighed, "All is ready indeed."

✡ ✡ ✡

The Universal House of Justice had planned the event for over a year. With all of the worldwide disorder, they felt compelled to act. As the Supreme Governing Institution of the Bah'ai faith, they saw the event as a way to unite all the world's faiths together under the goal of solidarity. The past few days they had sponsored a series of conclaves and seminars in keeping with their stated core principles of unity: Unity of God, Unity of Religion, and Unity of Humanity. The Chancellor had assisted and provided guidance under his motto of Peace, Prosperity, and Order.

They had spared no expense to assure the success of the events and worldwide media attention. Representatives of every major religion attended and lead in the festivities. This day's events included spiritual dances, group chanting, multi-faith prayers and spells for peace. No expression of human spirituality was excluded. A full array of events ran down all nineteen terraces and across the forty-nine acres of the Bah'ai Gardens. Worldwide media provided lengthy coverage and commentary on the events. They had one instructed goal. Mankind could unite around the varied ideas of God that existed within.

Asher and Brandon dropped off Eli and Moshe. The *Two* immediately walked out and onto the upper grounds of the Bah'ai Gardens. Right away they encountered several leaders coming from the Universal House of Justice. Its white facade almost glowed in the sunlight against the manicured green lawns. One of those gathered instantly recognized the *Two*. He whispered to someone next to him and walked straight up to Eli.

"I'm sorry sirs but you are not invited participants to our festivities."

Eli looked past him toward the other leaders. "Is this not a gathering of the gods?"

"I'm not sure what you are implying by that remark, sir." His voice smacked of condescension.

Eli now looked directly at the man. "Is this not a conclave of voices on behalf of the deities of man?"

"Well, in a manner of speaking, I suppose so, but..."

Eli's voiced his interruption loudly. "Then we come as a voice of the True and Living God."

With that, both he and Moshe walked down into the terraced garden. Along the center of the garden and down through the terraces ran a long stepped walkway. On both sides of the walkway were pavilions and celebrations. The walkway ran through the garden and down each of the nineteen terraces. On each level the *Two* would stop and Eli would make his proclamation.

Eli began his message with the same words. "We come in the name of the True and Living God. Turn from your ways and to the Lord while there is time. The days of your ignorance and His tolerance have come to an end. I implore you. Leave this place while you can. Your gods cannot save you from the wrath of the Lord. Turn to Him that you might find rescue and forgiveness."

At first people ignored or curiously smirked. Before long some began jeering or shouting derogatory remarks at them.

Eli would respond.

"I am the LORD, that is My name; I will not give My glory to another, Nor My praise to graven images. Behold, the former things have come to pass, Now I declare new things; Before they spring forth I proclaim *them* to you." [7]

Before they descended to the next level down, Eli would make one more appeal. "How long will you chase after those who are not gods? Turn to Him while you can. If you do not turn now, there will be no escape. Hear and know that the Lord Himself calls out to you. Hear and understand that we are His witnesses."

At those words Moshe would lightly tap the Rod on the ground and all across that particular level the ground would shake. The *Two* would then move down one level and repeat their message.

As they descended down the levels, they captured the attention of the media as well. Within minutes people around the world were hearing and seeing it all. Networks broadcasted portions of their message along with lengthy commentary and criticism of what they labeled as intolerant intrusion. Any attempt to stop them proved unsuccessful. Security personnel tried to move upon them and Moshe would simply squeeze the Rod in his hand. The person's moving toward them suddenly stopped as if paralyzed. They would remain in this state until the *Two* left the area.

When they had descended to the level containing the Shrine of Abdu'l Baha, Eli added to the repeated message.

"Turn to Me and be saved, all the ends of the earth; For I am God, and there is no other. I have sworn by Myself, The word has gone forth from My mouth in righteousness and will not turn back, that to Me every knee will bow, every tongue will swear *allegiance.*" [8]

✡   ✡   ✡

The door burst open. Shannon Fegan stormed through. Lanzig had given Shannon one assignment, locate the *Two*. She held a crumpled paper in her hand.

"They're in Haifa!" She practically screamed it.

Lanzig clenched his fists. "Load up the team."

Shannon hesitated only a second before Lanzig shouted. "What are you waiting for? Now! We leave in five minutes."

On the way, Shannon briefed Lanzig and the team on the events taking place in Haifa.

Lanzig asked the operations pilot. "What is our ETA?"

"Thirty minutes sir. We've cleared all air traffic between here and there. We should land on the top of area where they were spotted. We'll have the high ground."

"Excellent." Lanzig tried to hide his nervousness. "I want everyone sharp. We need the element of surprise on this one."

He wondered what sort of surprise the *Two* might have. He trusted the violent skills of his team. His only doubt lay in not fully comprehending his opponent.

✡ ✡ ✡

With every descending level, the crowd of hecklers increased. The media highlighted the open hostility displayed against the *Two* and ran continuous negative commentary. And yet it puzzled the reporters that all protest remained at a distance. What they didn't see or recognize were the repeated failed attempts to physically approach the *Two*.

As Eli would begin to preach, the anger against them ignited some to action. Yet whenever anyone would begin to run toward the *Two*, they would immediately fall to the ground. The legs of the perpetrators would seize in uncontrollable cramps. The sight halted others attempting to follow suit. This pattern occurred enough that further incursions toward the *Two* ceased. Attempts to throw anything toward the *Two* met with similar results.

The protestors and agitators followed the *Two* on their journey down the terraces but from a distance. The media commentators interpreted the crowd's action as a way of forcing the *Two* off the mountain.

When the *Two* reached the bottom terrace of the garden, the sky darkened to a peculiar greenish tint. The clouds were also unusual in that it had not rained in over a year.

The large crowd of hecklers stepped back even more as Eli turned to face them. The size had grown to the point that they stretched up two whole terraces. Eli slowly scanned across a sea of hate-filled faces. He softly sighed and turned to Moshe.

Moshe nodded to Eli as if to signal for him to begin again.

In a thunderous voice, Eli projected his message. "How long? How long will you hear and not believe. Hear then now the word of the Lord."

> "You felt secure in your wickedness and said, 'No one sees me,' Your wisdom and your knowledge, they have deluded you; For you have said in your heart, 'I am, and there is no one besides me.' But evil will come on you which you will not know how to charm away; and disaster will fall on you for which you cannot atone; and destruction about which you do not know will come on you suddenly. Stand *fast* now in your spells, and in your many sorceries, with which you have labored from your youth; Perhaps you will be able to profit, perhaps you may cause trembling. You are wearied with your many counsels; let now the astrologers, those who prophesy by the stars, those who predict by the new moons, stand up and save you from what will come upon you. Behold, they have become like stubble, fire burns them; they cannot deliver themselves from the power of the flame; there will be no coal to warm by, *nor* a fire to sit before! So have those become to you with whom you have labored, who have trafficked with you from your youth; each has wandered in his own way; there is none to save you." [9]

Eli caught his breath and turned to Moshe. Moshe felt the Rod in his hand and trembled.

Eli looked up to the sky before turning back to the crowd. "So that you may know that the Lord, He alone is God."

Moshe raised the Rod. The crowd stepped back farther. Moshe kept the Rod held high. When he did nothing else immediately, some in the crowd began laughing and launching curses at the *Two*.

Suddenly Moshe slammed the point of the Rod to the ground in front of him.

Fire ignited the green grass.

## Chapter 21

The second the Rod struck the ground, the green grass ignited. Fire spread out and up the hill. The speed and intensity at which it widened out and up shocked everyone. Panic broke out immediately. People ran pushing and screaming. Within seconds the fire reached the first and second terrace. Those among the terrified crowd who tripped were trampled over. Bodies piled up in its wake.

Media personnel on the ground became part of the flood of the panicking. All camera coverage on the ground ceased. The news headquarters dispatched a nearby helicopter to get a sense of the situation.

Most fires dissipate and weaken as they move past an area and consume ground fuel. Not so with this fire. It continued burning in place even as it spread. Chaos spread as quickly as the flames. Within two minutes the fire had traveled halfway up the terraced garden.

Eli and Moshe remained where they were with their heads hung low. Eli turned and noticed that Asher and Brandon had parked on the street behind them waiting.

Eli looked at Moshe. "It's time to leave. It will finish on its own."

Moshe looked at the horrific scene unfolding on the mountain garden. His hand trembled and as tears ran down his cheek.

He raised the Rod as well as his eyes. "Oh Lord, that the world may see and know that You are Lord."

Moshe pointed the Rod directly at the greenish cloud above them. The cloud began to glow as if some mighty light stood behind it. Suddenly bursting through the clouds fell a huge ball of bluish flame. The size of the fiery ball had people across the entire city and out in the bay screaming in terror.

The fireball struck directly upon the Universal House of Justice on the top of the mountain. The impact exploded in a flowering expanse of fire. Once the flames struck the ground it flowed like a huge river of burning wax. Those remaining on the mountain found themselves trapped between two vicious walls of fire. There would be no survivors.

✡  ✡  ✡

Lanzig and his team were eight miles out when they felt the helicopter halt its forward motion. The question on everyone's mind received a quick answer. The pilot pointed to the sky.

They all stared with open mouths as they watched the immense fireball falling from the sky. When it impacted the top of Mt. Carmel, they looked at each other in shock. Within seconds the shock wave of the impact reached them and the helicopter began shaking violently. The pilot worked hard as alarms rang out.

After he gained control, the pilot spoke to Lanzig. "Sir, as you can see our landing zone is destroyed. What are your orders?"

"Get as close as you dare and let's assess the situation."

As a precaution the pilot increased altitude before moving in closer. They began to hover a quarter mile away and around the area. Even for battle-hardened soldiers, the scene unnerved them.

The ground fire had begun to dissipate. Yet the fire from the fireball continued its flow downward. It's bluish flames made it easily identifiable.

As they circled, one of the operatives tapped Lanzig's shoulder and pointed to the ground. "Sir, isn't that strange?"

Lanzig squinted and shook his head. He didn't understand.

"The fire is still burning but it hasn't moved beyond the garden area on the mountain. How is that possible?"

Lanzig grabbed his chin and squeezed it. He had no explanation, at least not one he would accept.

As they circled again Lanzig called to the pilot. "Contact the authorities. Tell them we will have representatives in on the investigation of this incident. I want to know what happened and if they know how the *Two* were involved in all of this. Is that clear?"

"Yes sir."

"Alright, find us a place nearby where we can land. I want to see this at ground level."

When they finally reached the area, the whole team had to put on gas masks. The smell of burnt flesh and rotten eggs permeated everything. Fire and HAZMAT teams worked across the huge scene gathering corpses and taking ground samples. Just as they had seen from the air, the fire had somehow stopped at the edge of the garden boundary.

Those working in the area continued to shake their heads in disbelief at what they were finding. All of the world networks devoted continuous coverage to what the called the "Mt. Carmel Tragedy." Endless theories were proposed as to the cause including alien invasions.

After an hour, Lanzig had seen enough. He ordered the evacuation of his team. A few remained to gather intelligence on the investigation. Lanzig and the rest returned to Jerusalem.

On the trip to Jerusalem Lanzig ignored several calls on his phone. He had little doubt what awaited him. He would wait to confirm his suspicions.

✡ ✡ ✡

As per instructions, Asher drove them north along the coast and then southeast toward their destination. The route didn't take the most direct path, but it did provide a long quiet time for everyone. Moshe told Asher of a family in Bethlehem of Galilee, a small rural community where they would stay the night. The *Two* sat in the back sleeping in exhaustion. Neither Brandon nor Asher had either the will or ability to speak. They traveled lost in their own thoughts over what they had witnessed.

When they reached their destination, the *Two* woke up. The host family stood at the front door as if they knew the time of their arrival. Few words were exchanged at the meal table. Everyone felt the weight of the day, yet no one knew how to break the silence.

Finally Moshe's quivering voice broke the barrier. "Everyone is probably…trying to find a way to process what happened today. I know I am. Whether in person or watching from a distance, death on the scale and manner seen today is tremendously difficult." He stopped to catch his breath.

Eli didn't look up. He kept his gaze on the plate in front of him.

Moshe continued. "I hope you know that both Eli and I are deeply troubled. We are simply men, who by the providence of God find ourselves … we find ourselves…" He could not finish. He placed his right hand over his face and left the table weeping. The Rod remained next to where he had sat.

Without saying a word, with trembling hands Eli pushed himself away from the table. He left in silence.

The rest silently finishing their meals.

✡ ✡ ✡

That evening Lanzig sat alone eating his meal. His laptop sat open on the coffee table. It didn't surprise him that he didn't receive any phone calls as before. He knew the reason.

Lanzig had always prided himself in his meticulous approach to his life and work. His motto, "Good decisions are made with good information."

When it came to adversaries, this played out in knowing and understanding everything you could about them. It kept surprises to an absolute minimum. It also provided the groundwork for plans and counteraction.

Just as with Osgood, he planned for every contingency. At the beginning of taking his position he had put in place ways to monitor all of Besnik's communications. He did not risk doing the same with the Chancellor. Covering Besnik would be enough. It had proven the correct move. The Chancellor viewed the Haifa event as Lanzig's failure. He had communicated to Besnik that such failures were no longer permitted. His services were coming to an end.

Though he hated the idea of it, Lanzig had foreseen this possibility. He understood Besnik's incompetence in such matters and planned appropriately. From his information, he knew that Besnik had no exact plans on how to eliminate him. Lanzig would not wait around to allow him the opportunity. He would vanish for the time being in order to plan further.

A previously hired confederate would arrive for him within the hour. His go bag sat at the door. He took his time and enjoyed his last meal for the time being as Hermann Lanzig.

✡   ✡   ✡

Moshe sat enjoying the coolness of a June morning. Eli had greeted him earlier as he left for a morning walk. Their hosts were busy inside the house preparing a breakfast and a packed lunch. They would leave around mid-day.

Moshe had almost finished his tea when Brandon walked out and joined him on the porch.

"Do you mind if I join you?"

"Not at all. Please do." Moshe's heaviness seemed to have passed.

As Brandon sat down he wasted no time in getting to the

question he had struggled with all night. "You seem better this morning?"

Moshe smiled. "Well, you have to admit, it's a lot to process. But, I can tell something's on your mind."

Brandon sighed. "Yeah, you might say that. We've been together for a while now. You know my ... doubts?

Moshe nodded but didn't say anything.

"A lot of people died yesterday. Now you've told me all about your mission and all. But I'm having trouble reconciling everything. You say you serve a loving God and yet, all that death?"

Moshe waited a moment. "I can understand your question, trust me. You know that as a doctor I swore to do no harm. I became a doctor because I wanted to help people. So from the very beginning, I have wrestled with this issue."

Brandon inadvertently spoke. "What about the innocent?"

"Brandon, no innocent person died yesterday."

Brandon looked stunned by the words. "What do you mean? How can you know that?"

"Because no one's innocent, not you, not I. We're all guilty."

"I understand what you're saying and you're right I'm guilty. But death?"

"What do think is at stake here Brandon? Do you suppose it's some kind of battle for dominance? There is no battle. God is who He is; He has no competitor in that. Every other pretender is a liar. And that lie keeps men and women from rescue."

Brandon sat there. He had never thought of it in those terms before.

With Moshe's passion ignited he continued. "Brandon, what if as a doctor I had the cure to a fatal disease. And what if every time I tried to share that cure, someone came out and blocked me. They told lies about the cure and me. Who's the villain then?"

Moshe paused briefly, remembering. "The scriptures tell us that the enemy has come to blind the minds and hearts of men. I was once an enemy of God. I slandered His name, I laughed at the cure, I … I even mocked Him."

Now Moshe's eyes were moist. "The Lord tried to reach me through my wife. I would not listen. My stubbornness cost me the most precious person in my life, my…my wife. Even then I wouldn't listen. He had to take radical steps to rescue me from myself."

Brandon remained silent as he listened.

Moshe caught his breath and composure. He looked at Brandon directly. "I understand how reconciling death and His love bothers you. Truly I do. If love and death raises deep questions for you, perhaps life from death will provide you with the answer."

Moshe got up and took hold of the rod. Without another word he walked back into the house.

# Chapter 22

Aaron Spealman existed as a constructed identity carefully crafted by Hermann Lanzig. Among the many false identities Lanzig created, Spealman had all the traceable aspects of a real person. Aaron possessed citizenship and residency. During his time under Osgood, Lanzig invented and filled out the person of Aaron Spealman.

Lanzig had hired a person matching his general physique and having all the characteristics of the fictional Spealman. Through secret funds, Lanzig paid and arranged this person to make weekly visits to homes in Cyprus and Jerusalem. His movement kept him from forming any attachments yet allowed confirmation to his reality.

Lanzig assured his substitute could not know his identity and promised reciprocal anonymity. Lanzig arranged lucrative compensation for his surrogate. For several years this person lived high and well under this situation. The substitute also knew that if he revealed the arrangement or failed in his obligation, the funds and his life would end.

Lanzig viewed this as an avenue of last resort. He used other identities for mere secretive travel. The present situation made activating his use of Aaron Spealman a necessity. He informed his surrogate. As per their arrangement, he received a sizable and final compensation. Lanzig had also arranged for his termination. He hated loose ends.

Taking on the Spealman identity would keep Lanzig safe while allowing him time to resolve his current dilemma. He didn't fear Besnik or his ability to find him. He could not say the same for the Chancellor. He knew that only way to regain favor with D'bar meant getting behind the secret of the *Two*. This became his present mission. The new identity provided him the time and opportunity. He would carry this mission to the end.

✿  ✿  ✿

Yacov Besnik could hardly contain his excitement. The Chancellor had basically given him the green light to eliminate Lanzig and take complete control of his operation. Lanzig's earlier connection to the Chancellor had kept his distain in check. Now he could act and savor the destruction of his insolent subordinate.

He knew not to underestimate Lanzig or his shrewdness. He decided to take his time and surprise him. Hermann had not returned his calls. This troubled him at first. He'd let Lanzig feel safe and then pounce.

As Besnik sat finishing a meal, he whispered to himself. "You think you're so smart. You won't see this coming."

He took another bite then laughed out loud.

✿  ✿  ✿

Asher considered it a great privilege to be the driver of the *Two*. He constantly prepared himself for whatever assignment they gave him. He kept a vehicle ready for whenever they wanted to leave.

Eli walked out of the house and found Asher standing beside his vehicle reviewing a map. He whispered a short prayer of thanksgiving for the gift of their driver.

"Asher?"

"Yes sir?"

"We will be leaving in the hour."

"All is ready sir. Where are we going today?"

"Nazareth."

"Nazareth?" Asher's looked surprised. "Sir, you do know that the city of Nazareth is almost completely Arab. People refer to it as the Arab capital of Israel. You are sure of this?"

Eli saw the man's concern and smiled. "Yes, I am sure. Nazareth is the one-time home of our Lord. For too long hurt and hatred have reigned in men's hearts. We will go and once again reveal the healing love of our Savior."

Asher didn't understand the nature of Eli's words but he nodded in acceptance. "I am ready when you are sir."

"Thank you, I know you are. One other thing. When do schools let out for the year?"

Asher thought for a second. "June 30th sir, why?"

"Excellent, which gives us most of the month. Find us an elementary school. It will be our first stop."

Asher squinted. "Ah ... very well sir.

"Don't worry yourself Asher, God has a plan." Eli turned back toward the house.

Asher shrugged his shoulders. He then set out to find what Eli had requested.

Brandon assisted Asher with directions. They made their way to a school just as Eli had requested. Neither Eli nor Moshe revealed what they had in mind requesting a school.

When they pulled up to the school, a small bus had just begun unloading its passengers.

Asher turned toward the back, "This may be a while sir. This bus carries handicapped children."

Eli smiled broadly. "Don't worry Asher, we will get out here. The

Lord knows exactly what He's doing."

Eli and Moshe existed the vehicle and walked toward the bus. When they arrived, a young girl's wheelchair was being lowered onto the sidewalk.

A female teacher turned and noticed the two men smiling. They looked familiar to her.

Eli saw her questioning look and spoke. "Do not fear. The Lord has come to help."

Moshe looked down at the little girl of eleven, returned his warm smile. "*Alwuquf fatat saghira*, stand up, little girl."

Moshe extended the Rod to her. She looked at it and then at Moshe. Something in his face communicated trust.

She grabbed the Rod and suddenly felt it. She had never before had any feelings in her legs. But now a glowing warmth filled them. She giggled as the sensation ran up her legs.

Moshe nodded. The little girl took a deep breath and used the Rod to pull herself up.

When she stood straight up, strength entered her legs. She released the Rod and took a step. Tears filled her eyes as she looked at teacher. "*Astatie almashi almaelam*, I can walk teacher!"

The teacher fell to her knees, holding her hands over her mouth. The little girl ran and wrapped her arms around her teacher.

Eli walked to the door of the driver. "Let us unload the rest of the children. Today, all of them will be made whole."

Within twenty minutes all seven of the handicapped children were dancing in a circle. News spread quickly throughout the school. A great celebration replaced the day's classes.

Before noon that day, they visited six other schools resulting in similar healings. In the afternoon the *Two* visited a hospital. Within three hours every bed in the children's unit became vacated. From the crippled to the once terminal, all were healed. Reactions varied from astonishment to celebrative weeping. Physicians and medical personnel could not explain it but the reality left them speechless.

In the remaining days of June, the *Two* moved across the city and surrounding towns visiting all of the schools. Anywhere they found youth or children they ministered healing and delivered the message of redemption in Jesus. In earlier times such a message would face immediate rejection. Now all resistance fell away in light of the demonstration of power behind the message. The work and message of the *Two* spread quickly across Nazareth and the surrounding towns. Their presence and work became common knowledge among the Arab community. They knew they wanted status of the *Two*. Therefore, they kept news from getting beyond their people.

One thing could not be hidden; the changed lives within the Arab community. Israeli authorities took notice in the obvious drop in crime and misconduct among the populace. With troubles all around them, they welcomed the new development. Only one group expressed curiosity behind the change, the local Jewish religious leaders. On an evening in July, three such leaders tracked down the *Two* in the town of Reineh northeast of Nazareth at a large family celebration. Many changes would occur that evening.

Earlier in the day, the mother of the family encountered the *Two*.

Having heard of their work she made her way through a crowd to get to them. Several years earlier, an automobile accident had left her paralyzed in one leg. She forced her walker through the crowd.

"Holy men," she shouted, "Hear my cry. Show mercy."

Eli immediately heard her. "Woman, what do you desire of us?"

"Can you not see? I am broken of body."

"That we can see. But can you see your greater brokenness?"

The words silenced her. Many in the crowd saw her reaction.

Her eyes darted around nervously. *How did they know?* She wondered. Finally she lowered her head under the weight of Eli's gaze.

"Fear not woman. We come in the name of the Lord who heals the brokenness no one sees."

"What must I do?"

"You must turn away from your gods, confess your sins and believe in the name of Yeshua. He alone can rescue you."

She pondered for a second, looking around. She half expected ridicule from those around her. It surprised her to see people smiling and affirming her to decide.

The weight of the moment pulled her down to her knees. She covered her tear filled face with her hands. The struggle, the guilt, the pain all came together crushing her and yet she knew. Somehow she knew.

"I ... I believe. I turn to Yeshua. He is my Lord."

With those words she collapsed face down on the ground. A few moments passed and she felt a hand on her shoulder and looked up.

Moshe stood in front of her. Her quivering lips smiled in response to his warm smile.

"Woman, the Lord who saves you now heals you."

He took a step back and held out the Rod. She reached out a tentative hand and took hold of it. Warmth coursed through her arm and down into both legs. She trembled as she wondered. *Could it be true?*

She looked at the waiting crowd. Several nodded. She took a deep breath and attempted to stand. But more than an attempt, she stood straight up. As if hearing music in her head, she stepped out a little dance. Several people clapped. She spun around and danced some more. The clapping took on rhythm and others joined in her dance. A song of praise caught the beat of the dance and soon many were singing.

Above all the music the woman shouted, "Praise to the Lord who gave me a new heart and new legs."

After a few more moments she stopped her dance and looked at all around. "I must go tell my family. I must show them what God has done today."

She took a step to leave but then stopped. She looked at the *Two*. "Please come to my home tonight. Teach us the ways of God."

Then she turned to the crowd. "Come all of you and invite friends. Tonight we celebrate and honor God and His prophets."

Eli nodded. She clapped her hands and swiftly ran toward her home. Someone mentioned how she had left the walker. Everyone laughed.

The once lame woman could not stop welcoming people into her home. With each new guest, she gave testimony of her new faith and miraculous healing. She and her family spared no expense in the celebration.

Brandon sat next to Eli at a center patio table. Asher stood outside the circle of guests as Moshe taught and told stories. Everywhere in the house, and spilling into the streets, the celebration continued.

Asher happened a glance toward Brandon and noticed something. His countenance contrasted to everyone around him. He couldn't miss his friend's struggle. He walked up behind Brandon and put his hands on his shoulders.

Asher leaned over and whispered. "With all of this celebration, how is it you are so troubled my friend?"

Brandon felt exposed. He thought he had hidden it. He wondered if anyone else saw it. Conversations around him continued unaffected. He half-smiled and excused himself. He got up and walked to a small garden area. Asher followed him.

Brandon's hands shook as he turned to face Asher.

"What is it my friend."

His words came out shaky. "I ... I'm not sure. Look around. Everyone has a reason to celebrate. I should be ... at ... at least happy with them. Instead, I'm ..." He couldn't finish.

"Take your time my friend. I remember the feelings." Asher paused. "It is like you are outside and you don't know how to come in. It even frightens you that you want inside."

Brandon breathed hard as he nodded. He gathered his thoughts.

"Asher, for months now I have watched. I thought I could simply do so and remain outside of it all. But something began to happen. What I saw and heard exposed the cheapness of the mortar holding me together. It was crumbling and I couldn't stop it. I feel like even a small wind could blow me away. I'm afraid."

Asher felt at a loss on how to respond. Before he could attempt a word they both heard the commotion.

Three men stood at the gate of the house. Their clothing immediately gave them away. They were decked in full orthodox Jewish attire. Their demeanor made it clear that they were not in the least intimidated by those around them. Shouts broke out at their obvious intrusion to the evening's celebration. The woman hosting the event pleaded with others to show hospitality.

Then one of the three shouted. "We have come to speak to the ones called the *Two*. Is it not allowed?"

Tensions were rising. Eli and Moshe approached. Eli spoke to their host. "Sister, what is your desire concerning these men?"

She meekly bowed her head thinking of the question. "My desire? My desire is to follow the will of my new Lord."

Her words immediately calmed everyone.

Moshe smiled as he placed his hand on her shoulder. "Then we shall invite them in, sister. Perhaps their eyes can be opened to what you now see."

He looked at the three. "Come. Sit with us."

The crowd parted for them. They followed Moshe and Eli into the garden area close to where Asher and Brandon stood. The rest of the crowd went back to celebrating while keeping their distance from the new visitors.

Eli spoke. "So, why have you come?"

The obvious spokesman began.

"I am Aaron and we have questions."

Eli nodded and waited.

"Yes well, we are leaders in our community. We, like many others of our people, have followed your work with great interest. We know that you are both Jews like us, but not like us."

Eli said nothing.

"Let me begin by commending your work here in Nazareth. Everyone has noticed that tensions and crime have decreased here and anywhere you have been. It is good for people to live together in peace. And we have heard the stories of miraculous healings."

Eli nodded but said nothing.

"But as Jews, why are you working here among these people? In these terrible times, is there not enough work among the people of Israel?"

Finally Eli responded. "The message we have is for the people of Israel and for the gentiles. Our Lord has spread His messengers all around the world. Even now they are proclaiming His testimony across the globe."

"Yes, yes we know these things. And like here, the conduct of men is changing but what of the Law?"

"Do you think this is simply about the conduct of men and the making of a better world? The kingdom of God is more, so much more than that." Eli's eyes displayed his passion.

He would have continued except again commotion at the gate caught everyone's attention. A man stood talking desperately with the host. He had in his hands a large bundle wrapped in heavy cloths. The host looked over to the *Two* before signaling for the man to wait.

She quickly ran over to the garden. "I beg your pardon at the interruption sirs. The man at the gate, he pleads that you come. He has … he … please sirs come."

Eli looked at Moshe. They both knew. Eli looked at the three visitors. "Follow us. The hand of God is at work."

They all walked over to where the man stood. Many gathered around.

When they arrived, the man gently lowered the bundle to the ground. Tenderly he unwrapped his package. Many gasped. Lying in the midst of the cloth lay an obviously dead young girl.

The father, on his knees, looked up. "This is my daughter Eva. She has been ill for a long time. She could not attend school and we had brought her home from the hospital. We attempted but failed to get to you. Now she is dead." He broke down in tears.

Eli asked, "When did she die?"

The father gently touched the child. "Yesterday."

People shook their heads in sadness. Many of them knew the pain of loss. Even Brandon pitied both the man and the *Two* in this situation beyond anyone's ability to resolve.

Eli and Moshe looked down at the weeping father and his dead child. They both understood the pain of death's loss. Warm tears ran down their faces.

Eli took a deep breath. "Brothers and sisters, cease your weeping." He looked directly at the three visitors.

"The Lord did not come and die so that evil could be replaced. There is a word for evil. That word is Sin! The end result of sin is death." He pointed to the dead body.

"It cannot be eradicated by the changing of the conduct of men or the keeping of the Law. The Lord came not to replace evil with good. He came to destroy death with life. So that you may see and know that He is the Lord of life and the destroyer of death!"

Moshe quickly knelt before the body of the young girl. He placed the Rod on top of the girl and his hands on her cold face. He lifted his eyes to heaven and prayed aloud.

"Lord of Life, come upon this little one for Your glory."

He closed his eyes as she opened hers. She breathed.

All around the garden people fell to ground or onto their knees. Even the three visitors lost their footing and fell back.

The little girl rose to her feet and she alone stood beside Eli.

She looked down at her father. "Papa, where are we? Where is mama?"

It took several minutes for any form of normalcy to return to the celebration. Once it did, the celebration returned with greater joy. The three visitors remained by themselves. They could be seen arguing with each other. After a time, one of them came to Eli. He tore away his outer garments and knelt before the *Two*. After a prayer, he too joined the celebration.

For his part, Brandon sat silent beside Moshe. He smiled courteously on the outside but continued to crumble within.

At one point, the young girl sat talking to Eli when she noticed Brandon. Her curiosity got the best of her. She got up and stood in front of Brandon. Then without a word sat on his lap. She looked directly into his eyes.

"I was dead." She smiled and said it again. "I was dead, but now ... now I'm alive."

Was it her smile? Was it the way she said it? Like the blush of a cool breeze, a gentle wind pierced Brandon to his core. What remained of his wall crumbled like dead leaves.

As he sat there his body began to tremble all over. The girl got up not certain what to do. And then it happened.

Brandon began to weep uncontrollably. The tears poured from his eyes. He fought to catch his breath. He didn't understand it but as his inner wall collapsed a new strength immerged. Instead of a sense of falling, he felt a great weight lifted from within.

He looked at Moshe and Eli. In quivering and broken words, "I... I can see. I... I believe."

He looked up. "Lord."

In all of the events that evening no one took notice of the stranger who had slipped in earlier and witnessed all that occurred. They certainly didn't detect the confusion rifling through the mind of Aaron Spealman as he pondered his next move.

# Chapter 23

*The Chronicle of the Witnesses – Year Three*

Desperation, a word often used recently in the media and in day-to-day conversations. The worldwide drought had continued for eighteen months. The suggested explanations pressed against all credulity. Some proposed man-made climate change as the cause. Others declared the result of Mother earth or Gaia reacting to man's acts against her. Along with these, and others, the video of the *Two* making their declaration kept reappearing. Every attempt to eliminate those videos met with failure. The sustained mission of the *Two* only added credence and annoyance to their message.

The cumulative misery and confusion of the days left many in despondency. Only time and opportunity remained before these same feelings turned to anger if properly directed.

**Rome**

The Transition Leadership Council came together by order of the Chancellor. D'bar waited to enter the room. The ten members engaged in a passionate debate over the many issues facing the world and their individual regions. They had no consensus as what to make of the multitude of crisis arising since they had launched the world transition initiative. D'bar watched the entire discussion. He would make his entrance at the appropriate moment.

After thirty minutes of heated debate, D'bar knew the time had arrived. D'bar walked in without a word. His silent appearance quieted everyone. Besnik made his way to his seat along with all the others. No one said a word. They waited for D'bar.

D'bar waited. He straightened up papers on the table before him. His delay had its desired effect. The anticipation and tension intensified.

He finally looked up speaking to no one in particular. "So gentlemen how are things?"

The table instantly broke out in unrestrained voices. They practically shouted over each other. D'bar allowed this for only about thirty seconds.

He rose up and slammed his palm down on the table. "Silence!"

His fiery eyes scanned the faces and powered them down. They all yielded.

"I have chosen you as leaders. You are acting like schoolchildren. I have heard your words. The world can panic and we desire a bit of that. Such fear works to our advantage. But we must not, we cannot, allow it among ourselves."

One of the members ventured a word. "But your Honor, the problems are real."

"Of course they're real. We live in a real world not some make believe fantasy."

"But the people?"

"What about the people?"

"How can we help them?"

"Help them?" His face curled at the question. "Perhaps you have misunderstood. We are not here to help them. They are here to help us. Our only concern is that the people comply with the new order. We direct their desire in ways that forward our plans. We teach them what to think and feel. And we do so in such a way that they believe that we serve them. But in truth, they serve us."

Some of them struggled to process D'bar's words. A few exchanged glanced questions. D'bar saw it.

"Do my words frighten you? Perhaps they should. Power is frightening to the weak. But to those who wield it, it is exhilarating. Have you all forgotten the display of my power?"

D'bar began to walk around the table behind the members. "Already we have had defectors from our original group. These ten seats are the culled remains. Some have failed in their duties. Others have sought to walk away in fear."

As he paced around, the members shivered from the crushing fear invading the room. One by one they succumbed to its grip and surrendered themselves.

One within the group fought it and gave voice to his resistance. "This is wrong!" He shouted.

D'bar grinned as he slowly made his way to the lone resistant.

"I'm so glad you have spoken up. You have provided a great example to the others."

The loner and the others seemed confused at the words. D'bar put his hands on the loner's shoulder while looking at the others.

"As I said, this brave soul has done us all a great service in expressing his doubts about our plan. From this point forward I want you all to know the nature of our endeavor, the resolve of my will and the reality of my power. Never doubt my will or my power."

With that said D'bar closed his eyes and looked to the ceiling and whispered indistinct sounds. He slightly squeezed the loner's shoulders. Suddenly the man shook and screamed horrid sounds of agony. Within a few seconds he collapsed head down onto the table. D'bar lifted his hands away from the man. Everyone noticed a foul odor in the room. Some gagged at the stench. No one complained.

D'bar called as he walked back to his seat. "Instead of arguing with each other prior to my arrival, you should have read the folder in front of you. The details for this year's plan is in there. Your job is to focus on the plan. Let nothing divert you from it. Eliminate all obstacles to the plan. Every crisis is merely an opportunity to forward the plan."

They each looked at the folder in front of them. Some stole a glance at the corpse at the table.

"Don't concern yourselves about our fallen comrade. His replacement is already selected and will be properly instructed."

D'bar walked toward the door. Before leaving the room he lifted his right arm and shouted the words, "Peace, Prosperity and Order."

The door closed behind him. The council members sheepishly looked at one another and picked up their folders. One by one they exited the room without saying a word.

✡ ✡ ✡

Asher expressed his concerns to the *Two* as they drove toward their destination. Everyone sat in their usual places.

"Sirs, I know what you instructed. But I feel that as your driver and someone knowledgeable of the area, Jericho is a hotbed. Entering the West Bank area by itself is dangerous. But Jericho is, how can I say it, practically suicidal."

Eli smiled. "Dear brother, I am always thankful to God for bringing us together. Your knowledge continues to help us and will be valuable in the future. But you must understand our mission."

Moshe spoke up. "The Lord has commanded us to proclaim His message without restriction. Time is running out and everyone needs to hear."

"But to our enemies?"

Brandon, who had listened, softly answered, "Even enemies."

Eli nodded. He put his hands on both Asher and Brandon. "Truly, we were all once enemies of God at one time or another. But in His providence we yielded to His grace. Whom He rescues says everything about Him. Who and why some willfully reject Him says everything about them."

"I'm new at this." Brandon shyly injected. "But everyday I can see more clearly. You are right Eli, God surprises. I would have been the last one on the list to rescue. He never crossed my mind. I saw no reason to make Him a consideration in any part of my life. And yet, ... He took thought of me. I've never known anyone ... anyone like that before." His voice broke.

"Nor will you ever." Moshe added. "None of us will."

Everyone in the car nodded. They all remained silent for the next thirty minutes.

Fifteen kilometers out from Jericho, Eli prayed in the back seat. As he finished, he raised his head and spoke. "Asher, tonight we will stay in Netiv Hagdud. Do you know of it?"

"Yes sir. It is one of the Jewish settlements northeast of Jericho. It is a good choice."

Eli chuckled. "We are still going to Jericho. It's simply that there is someone there we must see."

Moshe looked at Eli. Eli smiled and shrugged his shoulders, "Such is the mystery of our adventure."

When they arrived Asher looked in the mirror. "As you can see it is very small. Where do we go?"

Eli thought for a second. "Drive around. I think we shall know when we see it."

Brandon tipped his head to one side. Asher got the unspoken message, *Let's see.*

Only one road led into the village. Quickly they came to an intersection. Straight ahead would take them to into a central park of the village. Right or left and the road formed a modified circle with a few roads branching out to the homes of the settlement.

Asher stopped at the intersection. "Which way, sirs?"

Eli thought for a second. "Go right. And drive slowly."

"Very well, sir."

Approaching the first intersection, Asher slowed down, awaiting instructions.

"Keep going."

As they approached the third intersection they spotted a man standing by the road. When the man saw the car he placed his hands over his mouth.

Eli laughed. "There's our appointment."

Asher stopped right beside him. The man then leaned in and looked inside the car. He clapped his hands and fell to his knees.

Looking upward, "Praise to the Living God, for He has revealed Himself in a mighty way."

Eli and Moshe exited the vehicle and helped the man to his feet. The man reached out and touched both of the *Two*.

He clapped his hands again. "Last night in a dream I saw you both. A voice told me to expect you today. The voice said to wait here by the road and you would come. And now, here you are."

"Yes, here we are."

"My name is Aram Levinston. Come, my house is down this street. I told others that I expected visitors from God today. Many of my neighbors laughed at me but I convinced them to come this evening."

And they did come. They shared a meal and Eli shared a message. They listened out of courtesy but some remained leery.

One of them voiced his doubts. "If you are prophets from God as some say, why are we being punished? We are farmers here and the drought has left us desolated. Are not the children of Israel special in the eyes of God?"

Eli responded. "God has a plan for the people of Israel, of this you can be sure. But God has no favorites. But He does have intimates."

"What do you mean?"

"God desires a relationship with men. He is our Creator, the Father of all life. But we have rebelled and isolated ourselves from Him. He came to heal the brokenness and provide a way to be reunited with Him. That way is Jesus, Yeshua, the Messiah."

They remained silent but not yet convinced.

Moshe rose to his feet. "You must each decide for yourselves. God extends His mercy to you this night. And by this you shall know that He is Lord. Go each of you and fill seven buckets with sand. Take them and drop them into your wells."

"Are you mad? This is your answer from God? Our wells are already dry. Putting sand into them does nothing. In fact, it seals their fate."

Aram spoke up. "Brothers, do not respond in this way." He turned to Moshe. "I shall go now and do as you say. I have already witnessed God's hand and desire to see it again." He immediately left out the back door.

The remaining guests looked at each other. One of them spoke up. "I know it sounds crazy but Aram is a good man. I came here tonight because of that. If he does it, then so shall I. My well is dead already so what have I got to lose?"

All but one nodded and left to follow Aram's example. That loner shook His head. "Go and waste your time. See if I care. As for me, I'm petitioning the government for assistance. That's what makes sense to me."

He nodded in courtesy at the *Two* and left for his home.

With everyone gone, Brandon and Asher busied themselves picking up the table. Eli walked up to Moshe and whispered something in his ear. Both of them left out the back door. They had their own appointment for the evening.

Hidden in some bushes twenty yards from the house Lanzig, aka Aaron Spealman, monitored the evening's events. He had placed listening devices on a window. He had heard everything. He also used several well-placed micro cameras on all of the windows to see what he wanted. He watched the *two* slip out the back door with a night vision scope. He remained determined to discover the secret behind these two so-called prophets. He had no idea where that determination would lead.

# Chapter 24

Eli led the way out into the night. He walked out past the freshly plowed field to the outskirts of the town. Aram's farm sat on the southwestern limits of the town of Netiv Hagdud. Just beyond it, the desert controlled the landscape. The two of them soon found themselves walking in a dried ravine that normally carried the areas limited rain down from the surrounding hills.

Another hundred yards and they noticed a campfire burning along the hillside. Eli would have recognized the fragrance of that campfire tea anywhere. As they approached the light of the fire, Eli smiled when he noticed who tended the fire.

Without looking up from pouring some tea, Shamer's warm voice greeted them. "Welcome brothers. Greetings in the name of our Lord."

Eli ran up and hugged his friend. Moshe smiled, remembering the same special relationship he shared with another.

"We will drink tea together and then I have much to share with you."

For Eli, the evening campfire brought back countless memories of similar evenings as a young man.

After finishing their tea, Shamer rose. Before he began, Shamer looked out into the night.

Moshe asked, "Is everything alright?"

Shamer grinned. "We are being watched."

Eli looked out trying to see into the night. But the light of the campfire had stolen his sight in the darkness.

Shamer looked at them both. "Don't worry yourself. The one who watches us can see but not hear us."

Eli looked at his friend. "You know who it is don't you."

Shamer only grinned. "As I said, don't trouble yourselves. As I was saying, I have an important message to deliver to you both."

They now focused on Shamer.

"Up to this point your confrontations have been limited."

Moshe wondered at the statement. He had enjoyed seeing those who had accepted God's grace but it troubled him when people rejected it.

Shamer continued. "You now enter the final stage in your mission. The opposition to your mission and message will intensify greatly. The enemy is fully aware of your identity and mission. He would destroy you if he could, but the hand of God always limits his reach."

Shamer paused briefly before continuing. "The return of our Lord approaches. Man has turned their back on the Lord. They follow after many things as substitute gods. In the days remaining the Lord shall judge their gods. As you proclaim our Lord's return you shall also declare and demonstrate our Lord's judgment."

They both let out a heavy sigh at hearing the word "judgment."

Shamer locked steely eyes on them both. "Seven judgments are determined against the gods of man. They shall begin after you enter Jerusalem. In this manner shall you declare and execute them."

For the next twenty minutes, Shamer shared the message from God concerning the coming judgments. Several times Eli and Moshe's hands trembled as they listened to the troubling words from Shamer. On one occasion tears ran down Moshe's face.

After Shamer finished he sat down.

Moshe responded first. As if speaking to himself, the words escaped his lips. "So many people will be affected. Is there no way to avoid this?"

"The heart of man has turned against his Maker. As you both know, mankind's time is running short. You are His voice to declare His mercy while there is time. For those who reject it, their rebellion will reveal itself in judgment. There are many who will receive the rescue of our Master. But sadly, many more are hardened in their rebellion."

They both understood the truth of what they heard. It saddened them both to contemplate the cost of mankind's war with God.

Shamer looked up at the night sky teaming with stars. He turned towards the *Two*. "Be strong in the Lord. Fear not the enemy. He has no power over you until your mission is completed. Peace to you both."

He vanished.

Lanzig had watched the whole event. The tall figure at one time had looked directly at him. He wondered if he had been spotted. It frustrated him that he could not listen in. He even tried reading lips but gave up after a short time. Instead he concentrated on watching for any other visitors or any suspicious actions.

The whole thing seemed pretty boring until...

He immediately fell backwards when the tall man vanished from sight. He refocused his scope and then scanned the surrounding area with night vision goggles. Nothing. His mind wrestled trying to come up with an explanation. He again carefully scanned the area. The terrain did not provide any hiding places, especially for someone as large as ...

A thought crossed his mind. He fought to avoid panicking. There had to be an explanation. There just had to be.

✡  ✡  ✡

Early morning Aram returned from visiting his well. He burst into the living room where everyone sat.

He shouted, "It's a miracle!" as he fell to his knees at the feet of the *Two.*

Moshe placed his hand on Aram's shoulder. "Arise brother and give praise to God. He alone is due honor."

Brandon and Asher traded grins as they listened to Aram tell how he discovered that his dry well now brimmed with fresh water. Brandon continued to be amazed at all of the new thoughts and feeling that flooded his soul's once dry well. He never would have believed it possible. Yet here he sat astounded and surprised.

Aram rose from his knees and shook Moshe's hand. Instantly a thought struck him. *He had to go tell his friends.*

"Please excuse me brothers. I have to go tell others about what God has done." With that, he scurried out of the house.

An hour or so later Aram returned with many others. They all shared stories similar to Aram's. The wells of every farmer who had followed Moshe's instructions had similar results. Though initially reluctant, they all sat out on the back patio and were eager to hear the message from the *Two.*

Moshe began. "Brothers, your faith, though small, is now rewarded. But you must not misplace your faith in us. Understand the true source of this wondrous provision."

Eli continued. "The days of your ignorance are over. The day of mercy has come. The gift from God is more than water. There is a water come from God which will flow not from the ground but from your hearts."

"What is this water? How can we attain it?"

"The water is Yeshua, your Messiah. He came and gave His life to provide your redemption. Turn from your ways and come to Him. He will rescue you from your sin. Then He will create in you a river flowing with living water. Such water cannot be purchased; it is the gift from God and received in faith."

The words captured Brandon. At that very moment he sensed the living water flowing and filling his heart. He shook his head, struck with wonder at the reality of Eli's words. He whispered to himself, *I never imagined.*

Eli stretched out his arms.

> "Ho! Every one who thirsts, come to the waters; And you who have no money come, buy and eat. Come, buy wine and milk without money and without cost. Why do you spend money for what is not bread, and your wages for what does not satisfy? Listen carefully to Me, and eat what is good, and delight yourself in abundance." [10]

Hearing these words, they all knelt and prayed. Only the sounds of soft weeping and whispered confessions could be heard. After a time Moshe arose and began singing a song.

> *Cleansed by the water*
> *Flowing from His hands,*
> *Freed from the torment*
> *Of life lived in vain.*
> *Filled in the wonder*
> *The new life does bring,*
> *Ever in new song,*
> *My heart free to sing.*

Over the next four weeks this group of men and their families met every evening to receive teaching from the *Two.* Great boldness and love blossomed within the small community. It didn't take long before they carried the message to some of the nearby settlements.

Lanzig/Spealman continued his monitoring. He remained hidden but always listening. He had begun with the idea of obtaining information to help undermine the *Two.* Instead, he caught himself actually listening to what they were saying. It surprised him that neither sedition nor deception lay at the core of their message. Their message and tactics differed from any other adversary he had ever encountered. He refused to accept the reality of their stated motive. He knew if he kept digging he would get to the bottom of it all.

For the first time in his life Brandon felt the pain of leaving. In the short month they had been in Aram's home, deep attachments had formed that he had never experienced. It warmed his heart to ponder how he cared so deeply for people he had only recently met. He now realized what Moshe meant when he spoke of the fellowship.

Moshe and Eli walked out with Aram. Many others from the village and outside the village had come to say goodbye. They all shared the same pain of parting.

When the *Two* reached the car Eli turned. "Brothers and sisters, the Lord has shared His blessings among you all. Freely you have received it, freely share it. Take caution. Troubling times are approaching. The water in your wells shall last for one year. The drought will continue a time beyond that. Plan appropriately. May the Grace of our Savior be among you in peace. Truly."

With that, they entered the car and drove off.

After traveling a short way Brandon spoke. "Is leaving always this hard?"

Both Eli and Moshe answered in softened tones, "Yes."

Moshe elaborated. "The only consolation I have is that we will see each other again. That encourages and comforts me."

Both Eli and Asher nodded.

Lanzig walked among those leaving Aram's house. He blended himself among those from surrounding villages. He approached Aram.

"Did they say where they were going from here?"

"Jericho." Aram answered trying to see the face of the questioner.

But Lanzig took care to keep his face mostly hidden.

"Thank you brother. Peace on your home." He made a quick exit.

The information would assist Lanzig in following them. He had placed a limited range tracker on the vehicle. The information would give opportunity to catch up. He wondered what they had in mind for Jericho.

✡ ✡ ✡

Besnik had sent just enough information in his message to D'bar to stir up his curiosity. It didn't take long to get a response. His private line rang.

"Have you found Lanzig?"

"Well, no sir, not yet. But I have located the whereabouts of the two so-called prophets."

"Then arrest them. Why are you troubling me with this?"

"I thought it would be more strategic if we had someone else do the dirty work."

"Who did you have in mind?"

"I have it on good authority that they are moving toward Jericho. With the troubles they caused in Haifa, the Muslims in Jericho might be good candidates."

"Very clever. Let me know when it's done. And find Lanzig!"

D'bar hung up. Besnik had expected more credit from the Chancellor. He texted his contact in Jericho and then quickly made arrangements for travel. He wanted to be nearby for the takedown. Who knew, maybe Lanzig would be nearby. One could hope so.

✡ ✡ ✡

As per instructions from Eli, Asher pulled off the road just outside of Jericho.

Eli immediately began. "Gentlemen, we are about to begin a new chapter in this journey of ours. From this point on the hostility level is going to increase. It is important that you know this and that you stay close to us. No matter how intense it becomes do not be frightened. As long as you are near, you are safe. We will let you know when it is time for you to leave us."

"Leave you?" Brandon looked surprised.

Moshe touched his shoulder. "Yes Brandon, there will come a time for us to leave you. It's meant to be this way, don't worry. In time you'll understand"

Though it troubled him, he trusted Moshe.

Eli continued. "Let us all pray for one another. The things we will witness will be difficult. We will all see ..." Eli choked up.

Moshe continued. "We will all witness much death and tragedy. The Story is moving to its conclusion. Soon the Lord will return, but not before this world is shaken to its core. The reality of our message is about to collide with this world. Our enemy knows this as well and his resistance is wicked and vile."

Asher finally spoke up. "Sirs, isn't there still some hope?"

Moshe answered. "Yes brother. In the middle of the coming darkness, God's light will shine in many unexpected places and hearts. We are not alone. Let no one forget this."

Brandon shyly raised his hand. Moshe smiled at the changed man in front of him. "Yes?"

"I ah ... I know I'm sort of new at this but ... can I pray for us now?"

Moshe sat back and closed his eyes at his humble and childlike request. "Please do brother. Please do."

They all bowed their heads.

"Lord, You know that this is all new to me. My heart, my heart is full in ways I ah, ... I never imagined. I love my new brothers here. I don't know all they know but I know that danger awaits us. Keep us all safe in You. Teach me and ah ..." A long pause of beautiful silence filled the air. "Teach me so I can help them in some small way. Help me help someone just as blind as I was. I never thought I'd ever say this but ... I love You. Thank You for loving me. Thanks

... I mean, ... Amen."

Each man sensed the calm whispered music stirred in each of their hearts. With their eyes closed, the music ignited in unseen colors of soft joy. They each felt as if they would explode in the presence of the moment. Then they heard it, one voice. A voice familiar, yet...

"I am with you."

# Chapter 25

Asher drove into the city from the northeast. He waited for Eli to give him some instructions but they never came, so he continued driving around the city.

Finally he slowed down and asked, "Sirs, is there somewhere in particular you wanted me to go here in Jericho?"

Eli chuckled, "I'm so sorry, Asher. I was actually enjoying the town and daydreaming a bit."

"I can understand sir. Jericho is an unusual city out here in the dry wilderness. The Arabs call it Ariha, City of Palms."

"I can see why." Moshe said as he turned to Eli. "It seems rather tranquil."

"Oh very much so, sir. It is a city that enjoys more quietness than others in the area. Tourists enjoy coming here."

"And why is that Asher?" Brandon asked.

"The Mountain of Temptation is nearby. It is reported to be where Jesus faced His temptation. Also Qasr al Yahoud on the

Jordan River where it is said John baptized Jesus. Also Maqam an Nabi Musa. Palestinian folklore says it is the resting place of Moses."

Moshe chuckled. "I always thought Moses to be buried near Mt. Nebo?"

Brandon also chuckled, remembering their recent trip to Mt. Nebo.

"But of course. As I said, it is folklore. But it is good for tourism. Anyway, where would you have me go sirs?"

Eli scratched his chin before answering. "I'll tell you what Asher. For our first night in Jericho we will stay in a hotel. You pick it. Make it small and quaint where they don't ask too many questions. Also they must take cash."

Asher thought for a second. "I know just the place. It is a small inn southwest of the center of town. I remember the owners."

Brandon wondered. "Why the change in the routine?"

Moshe answered. "The Lord works in mysterious ways."

Brandon nodded. "I can certainly attest to that."

Asher pulled up to a small white house. "This is the Auberg Inn. I think you will like it."

And they did. The feel of Israeli autumn flowed in the air. Each of them retreated to their rooms hoping for a good nights sleep. None of them noticed another guest checking in that evening. Lanzig/Spealman also wondered at the change in the group's earlier routine. Late in the night he placed a fresh tracking and listening device on their car, undetected.

They checked out in the morning after breakfast. As instructed, Asher drove to the center of the city and parked.

Before they got out Eli instructed the group. "You may not realize it but we are being followed and watched."

Brandon looked surprised. "Who is it?"

Eli continued. "That's not important. The time of hiding is over. We will spend several weeks here in Jericho. The Lord has much to say to this city and the world before we leave. We will walk from one side of this city to the other fulfilling our mission. The Lord will provide and protect. Any questions?"

No one said anything. "Very well, let's go."

And off they went. It didn't take long before someone took notice. At first people would simply stare and point. Soon people followed them and some took pictures. After a while and with sufficient people nearby, Eli stopped. He then began to speak. In the early days he spoke a very simple message.

"To everyone who has ears to hear, we come declaring a word from the True and Living God and His Savior Yeshua. The days of grace are coming to an end. He is Returning to judge the earth. Turn to Him while you can. Days of trouble are approaching. Come and find hope and healing in the Lord. The time is now."

He would then stop and wait. If no one asked a question or stepped forward, he would turn and they would continue on. This occurred several times that first day without any response. Some of the crowd would continue to follow them while others dropped off. At first, the responses came in the form of questions. Moshe would step up and answer. Later in the day someone stepped forward and asked if they would come and stay in their home for the evening.

This became their pattern day-to-day. And day-to-day the crowds grew. Residents and tourists alike came. And as in Nazareth, healings occurred, which in turn caused many to believe their message.

But not all responded positively. The work of the *Two* affected local tourism in ways that did not please many in that trade. People were flocking to hear and see the *Two* rather then the normal sights.

Local Muslim and some Jewish leaders took offense to the constant message and its implications. On several occasions individuals shouted out angry words at the *Two*.

Local police took note of the growing crowds and added their daily presence. Whenever tensions rose they would inject themselves to calm the situation. Soon tensions would rise beyond their control.

Always present and never far away Lanzig watched and listened. He took every precaution to avoid detection. He changed his appearance daily. He employed extensive and elaborate disguises to prevent any discovery of his true identity. He constantly monitored people's use of cameras at the daily events.

The growing crowds made what he did easier, he wondered at what point the tensions would spill over into some action. He had little doubt that Besnik and D'bar were aware of the events taking place in Jericho. He wondered when they would respond against the *Two*. He also knew the price on his head. All of this only heightened his caution.

After about six weeks the growing tensions reached a point of crisis. As the *Two* gathered with a very large crowd in an open field on the southeast part of the city another group plotted and prepared for a confrontation. This group had financing and weapons provided by intermediaries of Besnik. Fed fiery propaganda, the group's anger reached a fever pitch.

Just as Eli prepared to speak, shots rang out in the distance. People turned to see the source of the gunfire. A mob of over one hundred approached with weapons raised. Panic quickly spread as people looked around for a place to run. Their location in an open field left them with no place to hide. Lanzig quickly realized his situation compromised. He couldn't believe he had allowed himself to be caught off guard. *I should have seen this earlier*, he whispered to himself. He knew he had less than five minutes before the mob arrived.

Brandon looked over to Asher. They both turned to Moshe. They could make out his lips saying the words, *"Relax, don't worry."*

Another burst of gunfire and screams broke out from the people. As Eli and Moshe made their way through the crowd, they repeated over and over again, "Please, do not fear. No harm will come to you."

When they reached a position between the crowd and the approaching mob, Eli turned to the crowd, "You may pray, but do not fear. You are all safe in the hands of the Lord."

Another burst of gunfire and the mob began to chant. *Death to the infidels, death to the infidels.*

Eli called out to the mob. "By the mercy of God, turn back while you can."

Simultaneously, Moshe raised the Rod in his right hand. Instantly a cloud of dust formed and stood between the screaming mob and the *Two.*

Again Eli raised his voice.

> "Now what will you do in the day of punishment, And in the devastation which will come from afar? To whom will you flee for help?" [11]

He turned to the crowd behind him. "Do not fear. Put your trust in the True and Living God and His Savior, Yeshua. This day you shall see and know that He saves."

Eli turned once again toward the dust cloud and the mob fighting its way through it. With a shout he called out to them.

"Turn back. This is your final warning. If you do not, your fate is sealed by the folly of your deception."

The first of the mob broke through the dust cloud. They rubbed their eyes and coughed trying to shake off the effects of the dust before pressing forward.

Eli raised his eyes to heaven.

> "Woe to you, O destroyer. As soon as you finish destroying, you will be destroyed; as soon as you cease to deal treacherously, *others* will deal treacherously with you. O LORD, be gracious to us; we have waited for You. Be their strength every morning, our salvation also in the time of distress." [12]

Moshe raised the Rod and pointed it directly toward the mob. Instantly fire shot out from it. Like a burning river the flames, it first encircled the mob. Around them it whirled several times. Then the flames rose like a wall and formed a domed orb over and around them. Moshe then slammed the Rod to the ground. The ball of fire came down like a fist of flames. A cloud of smoke formed like a silent explosion.

The crowd fell to their knees in astonishment. After a moment a soft breeze blew across the field away from them and toward the city. As the cloud thinned a gasp moved through the kneeling.

Nothing remained of the mob. No bones or remnants of the weapons remained anywhere. The smoke lingered for a short time before floating away.

The people began coming up off their knees. Lanzig felt embarrassed and shocked to discover himself on his knees. He looked around wondering if someone would notice him in particular. In truth, everyone focused on the *Two*.

Eli turned to the people. "Remember this day. You are all witnesses to the hand of God. Believe in the God who rescued you today. Proclaim what you have seen to all you know. In three days we shall return to this very place to proclaim to you and to the world the word of the Lord."

With that, the four of them left. Some people mingled in groups. Whispered attempts at an explanation failed to make sense of what they had witnessed.

Lanzig walked over to the scorched area. He bent down to touch the ground. It remained hot to the touch. He finally walked away scratching his head. Someone heard him whisper as he passed by, "There has to be an explanation."

Rumors spread quickly throughout the city. Circulating stories finally reached the media and authorities. The so-called incident led to witnesses being questioned and the area scoured. The investigation confirmed that the ground had truly experienced an intense heat or a fire event. Yet, evidence or traces of anything biological could not be found. Some authorities were willing to allow it to remain an unsolved mystery. Others wanted clarification.

✡ ✡ ✡

Besnik waited for the expected phone call. It finally came.

The voice did not wait for any acknowledgement. "What can you tell me?"

"Excellency, I have people on the ground accessing the event. The rumors floating around are too preposterous to accept. All I know is that I have over one hundred men missing."

"What you mean missing?"

"Well, their families know that they left for the rendezvous point. We have eyewitnesses to them walking as a group toward an open field area fully armed and angry. And that's the last we have. Some witnesses have indentified seeing some of the missing beforehand."

"How were they able to do that. What I read reported panic. How could they identify some of the men?"

"They knew them from the community."

"What did those witnesses say happened?"

"Well…"

"What?" D'bar shouted.

"They said that a ball of fire swallowed them up."

"What? What do you mean a ball of fire? Do they mean an explosion?"

"No one at the scene or in the city reported any explosion or shock wave, which would accompany an explosive event."

"Did this ball of fire come from the sky?"

"No. The witnesses said it formed and then arose from the ground."

"What do you mean it formed?"

"A witness said that the fire seemed to emerge from the stick held by one of the two men whom they were there to kill."

"Ok, you're right. It is too preposterous. What about the two leaders?"

"Our assets on the ground are among of the missing. Witnesses stated that the two suspects left the scene. No one knows where they went. One report mentioned their intention to return to that same place in three days. Beyond that we don't have any idea."

"What are your plans?"

"If they spoke the truth, we have a where and when on their whereabouts in three days. The area is an open field so a sniper is not a possibility. There should be a large gathering. Using a revenge motive for the action, I thought about using a very small team to launch an RPG, (Rocket propelled grenade) at them from within the crowd. Collateral fatalities will likely occur. We can accept that."

D'bar calmed down. "Sounds like a good plan. Make sure it works this time. I have big plans and don't want anything interfering with them. Do you understand?"

"Yes sir."

"Good." He hung up.

Besnik sighed, glad to have concluded that conversation. He had three days to assemble the team and assets. Once he had those two out of the way he could concentrate on locating and eliminating Lanzig. Three days would be enough time.

**Chapter 26**

Early on the third day they traveled to the location. Asher and Brandon recognized the troubled look on Eli and Moshe. Neither of them had spoken, but the feelings were palpable.

Asher parked the car a good distance from the field. Many people were already gathered and walking toward the area. When people spotted them walking, they immediately parted to allow them through. Some reached out seeking to touch the *Two* while others pushed to avoid getting too close.

Stakes and yellow tape marked off the area where the mob had perished. People made sure to walk around it on their way to the gathering. The crowd had reached over two thousand by the time the *Two* arrived.

The event had also drawn local and international media. Asher and Brandon made sure to stay very close to the *Two*.

With all of the media attention, no one took any particular notice of a television van parked parallel to where the *Two* would stand. Within the van two men prepared the weapon for use. The plan involved launching the RPV followed by a quick exit.

In disguise, Lanzig positioned himself on the outer edge near the front. He did not want to find himself blocked in if another incident occurred. He held a bag containing a high quality mini-camera. If something happened, he would have footage to examine. He felt increasingly determined to find the answer behind these so-called holy men.

Eli and Moshe turned to face the crowd. An immediate silence coursed through the crowd. Eli took a deep breath.

"As I declared to you three days ago, the Lord has a message for you today and the entire world. For too long man has chanced his vain desires and fallen prey to the Lie. Many gods have arisen and carried away men's hearts into destruction. We come to bear witness that seven judgments are determined by the Lord. These judgments will come so that you may know that He is the Lord and that we are His witnesses. Hear the Word of the Lord."

> "You are My witnesses," declares the LORD, and My servant whom I have chosen, so that you may know and believe Me and understand that I am He. Before Me there was no God formed, and there will be none after Me. I, even I, am the LORD, and there is no savior besides Me. It is I who have declared and saved and proclaimed, and there was no strange *god* among you; so you are My witnesses," declares the LORD, "And I am God. [13]

Eli paused to take a breath. "And so that you may know that the Lord He is God and that the return of His Messiah approaches, for seven weeks you shall witness His first judgment."

Moshe raised the Rod and stabbed one end into the ground.

Immediately a horde of creeping creatures poured up out of the ground. It consisted of insects, worms, and snakes. Also in the distance and all around, dogs howled and birds filled the air. They all proceeded in mass toward the city. Some screamed as the crowds parted for the virtual river of creatures flowing past them.

After the creatures passed, people quickly followed after them trying to understand the nature of the phenomena. Some even laughed at the determined march of the creatures toward some unknown destination.

In all of the confusion no one noticed a man climbing on top of the nearby television van. He placed the weapon on his shoulder. Lanzig saw it only a second before the explosion. The rocket detonated within its launcher the instant the man pressed the trigger. Instantly the van exploded in an incinerated mixture of fire, metal and flesh. The explosive concussion hurled nearby people to the ground.

Though shocked by the event, Lanzig watched and recorded as Moshe slowly walked over toward a bleeding child. The mother screamed for help as she fell beside her helpless bleeding child.

When he reached the child, Moshe bent down and whispered into the wailing mother's ear. "Do not weep but rejoice. The Lord's mercy is with you."

She looked up through her tear-filled eyes wondering who had spoken to her.

Moshe kneeled down and placed his hand on the large scarlet spot on the boy's chest. He closed his eyes and placed the Rod on the boy's body. Immediately the boy opened his eyes.

"Momma?" he cried out.

"I am here my son."

"What happened? Who is this man?"

Moshe rose to his feet and looked at the mother. "Take him home and clean him up. Teach him of Yeshua who saves and heals."

Though shocked, she quickly nodded. "Yes, blessed sir. I see you are a holy man and I will follow the God who saves."

Moshe smiled and turned to leave. Lanzig lowered his head as Moshe approached where he stood. Just as he passed Lanzig, a portion of Moshe's clothing brushed against Lanzig. Instantly he felt an intense shock. The pain raced across every extremity of his body.

He could not afford any attention, so he struggled to keep to his feet.

Moshe rejoined Eli, Brandon and Asher. They quickly made their exit.

Only after they left did Lanzig allow himself to fall to the ground in agony. He had experienced pain before many times. But the intense nature and cause of this left him completely baffled. He saw no puncture wounds. At one point he couldn't decide what troubled him more, the pain or the mysterious cause. The whole matter had him on the edge of madness.

As to the river of creatures, the nature of the event soon became evident. The initial flow of creatures swarmed a nearby mosque. Birds from the air and creeping creatures of all kinds filled and covered the building. Men came out screaming and covered with all manner of creatures.

All across the city, the event repeated itself. Mosques, churches and any place viewed as religiously revered fell victim to beastly swarms overtaking the premises. The same thing occurred all across the globe. Creatures suddenly poured out of the ground and from around the surrounding areas and overtook any and all holy or revered places. Fire, explosives, or chemicals were eliminated as options for fear of destroying the holy places. Due to the continuing drought, water could not be utilized. Every attempt to evict the creatures failed.

Complaints poured in from religious organizations into government offices demanding some action. Adherents and leaders began to lose interest after weeks of failed attempts to retake their holy sites.

In all of the confusion no one gave thought to the whereabouts of the *Two*.

## Rome

D'bar reassembled the Transition Leadership Council. They waited in the council room for D'bar to enter. They each traded the troubles facing their regions seeking to lessen their responsibility.

214

D'bar watched and listened. It annoyed him to have to deal with such small minds. He sighed at the necessity of working with lesser lights to achieve his goals. He gave them a moment more before entering.

He marched to his seat and dropped a stack of papers in front of his chair. "Take your seats."

They immediately obeyed and turned toward D'bar.

"I have read all of your reports. You are all progressing in good order in your respective regions."

He raised his hand to stop anyone from commenting.

"I am also aware of the recent incident in Jericho and around the world. As I said in earlier meetings, you need to utilize your positions to forward our purposes."

He saw the questions on their faces. He stood up and began walking around the table.

"Take for instance this attack on these so-called holy places. I know about the complaints by the leaders. Forget them. The followers are the ones that interest me."

He laughed out loud. "These two prophets have done us a favor. People are abandoning their former gods. And yet they need something to bring them together, something to believe in. We shall provide it for them. We shall unify them behind our cause."

The council members smiled as they listened.

"It has always been our plan to unify mankind. Religions have always divided them. All their gods have abandoned them so we will unite them in another way. Let me show you."

D'bar snapped his fingers and the room darkened. A large image filled a screen along one wall.

"Behold, my monument of unity."

An image appeared of three large pillars erected on a large stone platform. The three were spaced evenly from each other in a triangle. Each pillar had a word chiseled on its base. Words were also inscribed all along the base of the platform on which the pillars stood. As he magnified the image, names of peoples and nations came into focus.

"All mankind are represented on the monument. No longer are they divided. They are all brought together in unity."

A voice in the darkness asked. "What is it that unites them?"

D'bar chuckled as he answered. "Great question."

An animation of the monument immerged. This time dark maroon banners draped down and waved from atop the pillars. An indistinguishable symbol could be seen on the flags.

"I still don't understand," came another voice.

"Patience, my friends. What is the mantra of our plan that we always repeat and we have promoted wherever we act?"

Besnik answered. "Peace, Prosperity and Order."

"Excellent Yacov Besnik, excellent. That is our goal and that is our plan. Each pillar has a word carved on its base. Those three words are the essence of our plan. Yet, every plan or philosophy needs a symbol, which captures its essence."

D'bar pointed again to the screen. "Behold."

Suddenly a large deep red flag appeared. The center of the flag began to give way to a growing field of black. Within the black area a bold white letter "P" appeared as ominous music accompanied the animation. Beside the letter "P" others letters appeared. The word Peace then formed and then faded leaving only the letter. Again another letter "P" appeared except it turned in an opposing image of the other letter as a backwards "P." Again letters appeared and finished the word "Prosperity." When the accompanying letters faded all that remained were two opposing mirrored letter "P's."

The intensity of the music grew as a large letter "O" appeared surrounding the two other letters. Below it, the word "Order" appeared. Now only black filled the surrounding field. Suddenly a maroon diamond appeared behind the image formed from the three letters. Then an image of simply the symbol appeared on the screen. This is our symbol. Around it we shall unite mankind.

**ORDER**

One in the group spoke up. "It's a bit frightening, don't you think?

D'bar's smile grew even bigger. "Yes I suppose it is. Fear is a great instrument to control men. Those who oppose us should learn to fear us."

Another comment arose. "It almost looks like a skull, like something evil."

This time D'bar clapped his hands in glee. "Excellent observation. Have you never noticed that there is a certain allurement to evil? And anyway, what is evil? Isn't evil simply a construct hoisted upon man by their gods? We are freeing man from evil and guilt."

Many of the men looked confused.

D'bar laughed. "I can see that you don't yet comprehend what I am saying." He rubbed his chin a moment then snapped his fingers.

"In earlier times, the gods held charge over men's will. We have taken that away from their empty deities. Don't you understand? We've just stolen fire from the gods. How can you talk of evil if god is dead? I will tear down the fortresses erected by their gods. Together we shall define our boundaries."

"But men are natural followers," someone said.

D'bar almost jumped as he clapped his hands loudly. "Yes! Thank you. You are absolutely correct. We shall enlighten them to their new freedom. And we shall fulfill the desire for someone to follow. I shall lead mankind's new reign of freedom."

He pointed to the screen once again. An image of the monument appeared and in the animation a statue floated and landed between the three pillars. Three fourths as tall as the pillars stood an image of D'bar in a grand and noble stance with his hands outstretched.

As the council gazed at the completed monument a shiver ran down their backs. A part of them feared but a part of them swelled up in adoration. Though a part of them resisted the idea of a Caesar among them, even they longed for someone to follow.

After a long silence, someone spoke up. "Where will this monument be constructed?"

D'bar smiled. "An excellent question. The monotheists will resist the idea of either the death or replacement of their god. This idea has divided mankind for long enough. I shall construct man's monument of unity in Jerusalem. It shall sit on the southern edge of what is called the Temple mount. It will sit between the great mosque and the newly built Jewish Temple in the old City of David. Our monument will overlook them both and unite us all once and for all."

"There will be violent resistance," Besnik commented.

D'bar turned quickly. Anger and rage filled his eyes. He shouted. "If they dare, I will make an example of them before all mankind. They have destroyed our freedom with their imaginary gods for long enough. If they indeed resist our monument of unity, I will place within their so-called holy places my image as proof of the end of their reign. I will show them that their gods are dead."

Besnik meekly voiced another comment. "But what of these two and the others who claim themselves as voices for their God?"

D'bar regained control of his rage. "Thank you Yacov for reminding us of this lingering reality." He stretched out his arms across the entire council. "I swear to all of you. All mankind shall see it. By my word, in due time, I will destroy those two and the idea of their god. And when this is done, all the others will see. All mankind will know the futility of resisting me."

D'bar marched himself toward the door. Once more before leaving he shouted. "I will tear down all the fortresses holding men captive. I will free them and unite them."

He held up his arm. "Peace, Prosperity, and Order."

He left the room, slamming the door behind him.

The council members each whispered the words with quivering lips. "peace, prosperity, and order."

# Chapter 27

As predicted, for seven weeks the first plague besieged the earth. Any attempts to enter the various religious or holy places failed. The creatures defended and held their conquered territories. There were exceptions. The creatures did not invade or bother the gathering sites of those who followed Yeshua.

The people's attitudes ranged from ambivalence to curiosity. D'bar and his confederates in the media castigated the fallen deities. Those wanting to hold to their old ways didn't know where to turn. Unable to fulfill their religious duties, they began to doubt.

Questions arose as to why the followers of Yeshua seemed unaffected by the plague. The weeks passed and day-to-day life moved to the forefront of people's attention.

On the very day at the end of seven weeks, few even noticed how the animals had vanished overnight. Authorities avoided providing any explanation. If anything, D'bar made sure the media made no mention of it at all.

✡ ✡ ✡

Eli and the others had quietly slipped out of Jericho. They made their way toward Jerusalem. They visited homes in and around Jerusalem. They remained under the radar for the time being.

Ten weeks passed before they appeared anywhere publically. The New Year celebrations had passed. In their absence, Besnik directed his attention to more pressing matters. This would change quickly.

As before, Eli and Moshe took to the streets preaching. They visited the small towns north and west of Jerusalem. The towns were both Palestinian and Hebrew. They included Nabi Samuil, Beit Iksa, and Beit Zayit.

Not many in the communities showed any interest as the *Two* walked and preached in their towns. After a week and a half some events began to spark people's interest. Rumors of some healings reignited attention from the populace and the media.

As they walked, people followed them. Eli would suddenly turn and declare a message. Day-to-day, as the size of the crowds grew, so did the intensity of the message. A nervous dread moved through the crowd at the conclusion of each message.

This did not escape the attention of the reporting media or the authorities. Once again Besnik secured the services of a small squad of assassins to perform a quiet elimination.

Lanzig maintained a disguised presence. He noticed the out of place strangers. He recognized their operational posturing and surveillance. It surprised him that a part of him wanted to warn the *Two*. Prudence convinced him otherwise. He reminded himself of his purpose to observe and collect information. He would watch and listen, nothing more.

Always ready but ever observant, Asher also noticed the out of place strangers at several of the gatherings. At the evening meal, he felt compelled to share it.

After the blessing he spoke up. "Sirs, I've noticed something."

Moshe spoke up. "That we're being watched?"

Asher looked surprised. "So you've noticed. They look... they look like hard men, dangerous men."

Moshe swallowed a bite of bread. "In this world they are dangerous. I suppose they have killed others. But don't concern yourself. We are safe for now."

Brandon had a question. "I suppose, no... I know that the Rod... I mean God has the power to destroy men. But what if you don't see it coming?"

Moshe put his hand on Brandon's shoulder. "Don't worry. We are safe in the Lord."

Brandon sighed and nodded. Moshe's words relaxed and comforted him. Everyone went on with the meal.

Lanzig sat in a room of a nearby house he had rented for the night. With the resources at his disposal, he knew that almost anything could be purchased at a price.

As at other times, he planted night vision cameras and sensitive listening devices to monitor any and all activity. Long after everyone had retired for the night, a motion detector alerted him of movement around the house where the prophets slept.

Lanzig got out of bed and looked at the displays from several of the cameras. Four men dressed in black were circling the house. He recognized the pattern and the weapons. They were setting up thermo explosives on the sides of the house. Instinct wanted to do something. He decided to merely watch and record.

One by one the men attached the explosives and began arming them. Suddenly a large man appeared behind one of the assassins. The large man's hand came down with a single blow and knocked him unconscious. The large man then went to each of the other assassins and did the same thing. He dragged the unconscious men together to one side of the house. The large man then detached the explosives and brought them to the place where the assassins lay.

Lanzig sat glued to the screen. The size and strength of the large man intrigued him. It surprised him that he had missed that the prophets had hired protection.

Lanzig's eyes widened as he watched the large man attach the explosives to the assassin's chests. *What is he planning?*

Then Lanzig almost fell out of his seat as he watched. The man began to grow. He now easily stood at a height of eight to nine feet. The man draped the assassins in a cloak. He then wrapped his arms around the cloaked bundle of men and picked them up.

The large man then looked up toward the sky. Though muffled, the sound of the explosion shook the glass on windows for several blocks. Flames and ignited smoke filled the screen. He ran to the window to see. Neighbors came out to investigate the loud noise.

When the smoke finally cleared only the seared ground remained. Police arrived later. The absence of any evidence left the authorities puzzled.

Lanzig tried to replay it in his mind. Then he remembered that the whole event had been recorded. He sat stunned as he replayed it. The event played back just as he had remembered it with one exception. A chill ran down his arm as he watched. The large man did not appear on the video. He watched the men fall to the ground and be dragged away, but no large man. He watched the cloak appear and drape over the fallen assassins, but no large man.

He played it over and over many times and still, no large man. He paced the floor throughout the night repeating one question, *How is it possible?*

He slammed his fists into the wall. The words screamed in his head, *It's not possible!*

Lanzig fell asleep in sheer exhaustion two hours before dawn.

Had it not been for the motion sensor's alert, Lanzig would have slept through their departure. Though groggy, he managed to watch their driver making preparations.

Asher readied the car for their departure. As per instructions, he loaded the supplies they would need for the day. The chilly morning air helped wake him up. He had slept hard until the late night events ruined any chances of a restful sleep.

Eli walked over to Asher. "Brother Asher, today we go to the place we have been announcing."

"Yes sir. On Mount Scopus by the university there is a place southwest of the university right across from the Hecht Synagogue. It's small but adequate and it overlooks the city as you requested. Our friends have all been informed."

"Very good Asher, thank you."

"My pleasure sir. It will not take us long to get there. I am ready whenever you say."

When they arrived, people from the Hebrew University along with some from the nearby medical center had joined the expectant crowd. News had also reached the media concerning the appearance of the *Two*. A few curious representatives were present. Word had gone out to not make a big deal of any appearances by the *Two*.

Eli and Moshe stood on the top edge of a memorial area. On this clear, crisp January morning they gazed over the city. The gathered crowd waited.

"O Jerusalem," Eli began. "For so long you have witnessed the affairs of God and man. Today is no different."

Eli now turned his attention to those gathered.

"As before we come to declare to you a word from the True and Living God. One has been spoken, now six remain. You shall now see and know that the Lord, He is God and His reward comes with Him. For seven weeks you shall discover who you trust."

Eli took a deep breath.

> "Come now, you rich, weep and howl for your miseries which are coming upon you. Your riches have rotted and your garments have become moth-eaten. Your gold and your silver have rusted; and their rust will be a witness against you and will consume your flesh like fire. It is in the last days that you have stored up your treasure!"[14]

Moshe lifted the Rod slightly and gently bumped the ground. A low rumble ran through the ground and a soft push of pressured air passed by them. Both Moshe and Eli immediately turned, got into their automobile and left. After earlier demonstrations by the *Two*, those gathered stood puzzled. They asked each other questions, "What just happened?"

They left the area wondering. Within the hour their wondering ended. Instantaneously, a worldwide banking collapse had occurred. Though no one understood the cause, the effect was inescapable. The global informational network remained unaffected and carried the economic news everywhere.

Governments issued statements seeking to ease the panic. Banks closed temporarily. Retailers followed suit. Without the banking network they could not continue business. Then the panic came. The need to purchase food and other necessities ignited mobs and riots. A prevailing mood spread quickly that without immediate answers, chaos and collapse would soon follow.

## Rome

The council chamber echoed the panic in the cities. The members argued with each other as they shouted out their opposing solution proposals. D'bar waited in the next room. Once again he watched and let the drama play out. As conditions approached possible physical brawling, D'bar entered. He slammed the door behind him. The noise echoed throughout the room and silenced everyone.

D'bar calmly moved to his chair and sat down. He casually looked over some papers in his hand. He tapped them down on the table to straighten them and attached a paperclip to them. The council members felt the coldness in D'bar's eyes. They all quickly made their way to their seats and waited.

With everyone's undivided attention, D'bar rose.

"Gentlemen, panic is always deadly. Knowing what to do in a crisis is the difference between survival and destruction. As I have stated to you all before, crisis is not necessarily our enemy. I have heard all of your solutions. I am disappointed with all of them. You know our ultimate goal. How is it that none of you have seen it?"

The members looked at each other.

D'bar slammed his hand down on the table. Many of them jumped. D'bar grinned. He loved fear and how men cowered under it.

"I see I will have to instruct you. It has always been our plan to restructure the world's money system. I don't know how they did it, but it seems these so-called prophets have done us a favor. They have given the world a reason to accept our new money system. It has come earlier then we had planned, but don't worry. Tomorrow the banks will issue special credit vouchers to anyone who can prove they have a bank account. Other vouchers will be issued to anyone needing special assistance. We will also announce the new worldwide monetary system and its hardened built-in security structure. We will show the world that their valuable assets are safe and secure in this new system."

One of the council members raised his hands.

"Yes?"

"What if someone attempts to defraud the bank by making a false claim concerning their account?"

D'bar's grinned. "That's a very good question. I'm glad you asked it. We will make an example out of them. This event provides us with an opportunity to demonstrate our resolve for the common good. Beginning tomorrow, we roll out of the new system and launching our campaign of accusation. We will convince the world that this event is a terror attack against humanity. Women and children are starving because of the uncaring violation of our very economic life stream. We will express our shared misery and the culprits who caused it. Anyone who attempts to defraud the common shared value of our livelihoods attacks us all. They are enemies of mankind."

D'bar let out a villainous laugh. "You should see the ads we have created. They would make a grown man cry and then scream out in rage. The emotion and the campaign will continue until we make the necessary repairs and changes to the banking system. When the smoke clears, we will all be heroes."

He slapped the table again. "It's sheer genius I tell you. This is all going better than I imagined. Sheer genius. Oh well, you'll all be given specific instructions and directives for the coming days. Follow them exactly as written. Stay on script. Oh, one other thing, none of you should worry about your personal fortunes. When this phase is completed, each of you will be rich beyond your imagination. We will control the wealth of the world."

D'abar turned to leave. Just before leaving through the exit door, he raised his right hand.

He shouted out. "We will control the world. Peace, Prosperity and Order." Laughing as he left.

The council members looked at each other. Greed filled their smiles as the chanted. "Peace, Prosperity and Order."

# Chapter 28

Lanzig found himself outflanked. Few times in his career had he been out-maneuvered. He had not foreseen the so-called banking crisis. He suddenly found his assets thinned out. He could attempt to reestablish some of his bank holdings, but this could allow possible discovery. He still had considerable resources, but they required tapping into some gold and precious metal reserves. He had viewed these as assets of last resort. Even doing that carried a degree of risk. Reports of firm and drastic punishments for those seeking to profit from the crisis were widely circulated. He had to congratulate the Chancellor. When he had first seen that part of his future plans, he had thought it as something unachievable. But the current situation and public opinion called for it.

He finally decided to utilize some of his reserve and remain hidden. He stayed close to the *Two* who kept themselves out of public view.

Seven weeks passed and the crisis became a memory. Banks reopened for business and D'bar's plan began to implement his process. The new structure would take almost a complete year to extend down to the personal level. The process had already implemented a new international financial infrastructure. The world would have a single digital monetary system and each individual would connect to that system. All commerce would flow from that system. The arrangement promised safety and security. Life went on.

During the seven weeks, no reporting implicated the *Two's* connection to the banking event. All focus concentrated on the depth of the crisis and the brilliance of the Chancellor's solution. D'bar wanted the *Two* to vanish from the public's view. With their absence, he assumed he had succeeded.

Yet, the *Two* did reenter the public arena. As before they began walking the streets proclaiming their message. They concentrated in the area northwest of Jerusalem in Abu Ghosh and Mevaseret Zion. Brandon noted that their message took on a more somber tone. After the previous crisis, people's reception to the message waned. Some listened out of curiosity while most turned away. The general mood of the people and the world found expression in a story headline the second week into their preaching: *"The World Has Had Enough Misery."* The story focused on people's weariness of troubles and crisis. People began repeating the campaign mantra: "Peace, Prosperity, and Order." People wanted to be left alone to enjoy life.

As they entered the third week, Eli's messages seemed increasingly harsh. Besnik utilized media coverage to paint them as divisive and mean-spirited. Protestors began attempting to harass the *Two* and any who came to listen. Mockery replaced civility. Besnik made plans to use the growing mood to once again attempt an assassination.

Brandon recognized the effectiveness of the negative campaign. He worried that it could get out of control but Moshe continued to assure him. Brandon, for his part, spread encouragement across a worldwide network he had created. It greatly helped Brandon to feel useful in his newfound faith. On the night before the last day of the three weeks Moshe pulled Brandon aside.

"Brandon, tomorrow we travel back to Jerusalem. Passover begins at sundown tomorrow and we have made arrangements to celebrate in the home of a brother."

"Wow, I've never celebrated Passover. I was sort of out of the loop."

Moshe chuckled. "Yeah, I guess you were."

Moshe turned serious. "Brandon, this Passover is a very important one for all of us. You will understand it better tomorrow. But for now we have a message we want you to pass on to all fellow believers around the world."

Brandon looked surprised. "Ok, what's the message?"

"To the Jews, Passover commemorates the deliverance from slavery. When Jesus came He marked it as a remembrance of His sacrifice for our sins, which is symbolized in the original celebration. Tomorrow the Lord adds another dimension to the celebration."

"What do you mean?"

"Tomorrow Eli will once again declare a judgment from the Lord. It shall come upon the whole world. But as a sign of the Lord's protection He offers an escape from what is coming. Tell all of our brothers and sisters that before sundown tomorrow they must remain in their homes from sundown to sundown."

"What's happening?" Brandon felt frightened.

"A plague of pestilence is going forth tomorrow. It will spread across the earth in a single day. Yet people in homes that bear the sign of our Savior's sacrifice on their door will be spared. There are no exceptions. We have chosen a large house in Jerusalem where we will celebrate Passover."

"This is kind of like Moses and the ..."

Moshe nodded.

"When did you want me to start getting the word out?"

"Immediately. Tell them to warn others and to spread the word."

"Do you think people will respond to the warning?"

"The faithful will. The Lord will confirm it in their hearts. As to others, most will ignore or scoff at it. But if some at least respond in fear, they will witness a protection and perhaps come to believe. Such things are in the providence of God."

The weight of the message made Brandon sigh. "Wow, I'll … I'll get right on it." He caught himself in a thought. His hands began trembling.

"Ya know, ah … if God hadn't rescued me I would … ah … I'd be out there with the scoffers. I know that now. Thank you for ah … for not giving up on me. Thanks, really."

Moshe put his hands on Brandon's shoulders. "I know what you mean. Not a day goes by but I don't think the same thing. God rescued both of us for a reason, to help rescue others."

Brandon smiled through misted eyes. "Yeah, it's kind of neat."

Moshe got up and left. Brandon paused a moment. He slapped his knees and retreated to a back room. He had a mission for the night and felt excited to do it.

As instructed, the next morning Asher stood ready to transport the team. He stood whistling some tune when Eli walked out.

Eli smiled seeing him. "Brother Asher, I'm so glad the Lord sent you to us. You have already helped lift my heavy heart."

Asher seemed surprised. "It is I who is most happy to be at your service sir. I don't understand all of this but I know God is using you in a mighty way. To be here with you both is enough for me. So, where are we going today?"

"Jerusalem. Do you know where the Knesset is?"

"Oh yes, most certainly sir."

"We will start there. We will walk through the park that sits next to it and on to the Supreme Court building at the other end of the park. Then we will go back into the park."

"Ah yes, the Rose park. Beautiful place. Although with the

drought I think there are no roses. The ground is too dry."

"Yes, yes it is. This too is according to God's plan." Eli drifted in a thought. "But not to worry, that ground will one day bloom in fullness. But for now ..."

Eli turned and walked away. Asher whispered a short prayer for him. He saw the heaviness in Eli. He wondered what the day would bring.

A short distance away Lanzig watched. He didn't know the content of the exchange with the driver, but could see that the man called Eli seemed troubled. He wondered about the day.

Moshe placed his arm around Brandon. "How did it go last night?"

Brandon looked tired. "The word is out. I got a lot of questions but I just let them know what you said. I told them to take it seriously and to spread the word."

"Good job."

Brandon looked at Moshe. "Everybody's wondering. It's kind of ... scary I guess. We know something's coming, we just don't know what."

Moshe nodded. "I know. Don't worry. Soon everyone will know."

The group got to Jerusalem around noon. Word had gotten out among the faithful to meet in the park. They in turn had invited others. Since Passover would begin at sunset, they found the area around the Knesset practically empty. A tour bus had made a stop and a guide had the group walking toward the building when Asher pulled up.

"As I expected sirs, with the coming of Passover few people are out. I'll let everyone out and park nearby."

Moshe spoke. "Excellent Asher. Remember what I mentioned. We are celebrating Passover very near here. The house is large enough for many guests, as well as our group. Our host expects a crowd. He has also provided a bus for all who wish to join us. There will not be much time to get to there when.... when we must leave."

Asher nodded. "Very well, sir. I will park the car."

All but Asher exited the car. They began walking toward the Knesset building. It didn't take long for someone in the tour group to recognize them.

"Look honey," a woman named Margit said. "It's those two men we saw in the news. What are they doing here?"

"I'm sure I don't know. Ignore them." her husband Franz sneered. Margit remained curious.

The tour guide attempted to keep the group's attention, but failed.

Eli stopped and shouted out. "Let everyone who can hear, listen. The god of pleasure, the god that is your flesh and the love of self has come under the judgment of the True and Living God. You will desire pleasure but will not find it. Hear the word of the Lord."

> "Do not love the world nor the things in the world. If anyone loves the world, the love of the Father is not in him. For all that is in the world, the lust of the flesh and the lust of the eyes and the boastful pride of life, is not from the Father, but is from the world. The world is passing away, and *also* its lusts; but the one who does the will of God lives forever." [15]

The tour group seemed puzzled by Eli's words. Out of an impulse Margit shouted, "What should we do?"

Eli looked directly at her. "Return to your place before sunset. Mark your doors with the sign of His salvation."

Moshe raised the Rod. Suddenly a small billowy cloud formed above him and took the shape of a cross. It remained there for a short time before melting in the breeze.

Eli spoke again. "Prepare yourselves. Do not come out until sunset the next day. Take care to heed my words."

With that, Eli and Moshe turned and walked toward the park.

Margit looked at her husband. "Franz, I am frightened. Let's go back to the hotel. Something about what that man said I ... I'm sacred. I mean it. I want to go back, now."

"Margit you're not serious are you? He's a crazy man."

The determined look on her face said it all. Franz talked to the tour guide and arranged a cab for the couple. The rest of the group continued on with the day.

Lanzig had watched from the park. With the help of his listening devices he had heard the whole exchange. He had also seen the cross form and disperse. It troubled him that his arms shivered. He tightened his fists. He had to get a grip.

The police received a call from the tour company alerting them that the *Two* had been spotted. As instructed, the police sent word to Besnik. The police asked if Besnik wanted them to respond. He used the excuse of Passover and told them no. Instead Besnik contacted his latest trio of assassins. They would arrive within minutes.

Asher caught up with Brandon and the *Two* in the park. He walked up to Moshe to give him a report.

"Sir, the bus has arrived. It is parked not far from here. The driver said he will keep the bus running so he can depart right away."

Moshe looked up at the sky. "Good. In fact, you need to ride in the bus with us because we won't have much time."

"But what about my car?"

"You can return for it in a few days. Stay close." Moshe sped up to catch Eli.

Somewhere in the middle of the park a large group of almost two hundred were waiting. Most of them were fellow believers. Also among the crowd were others visiting the park or had come by invitation from friends.

Eli and Moshe smiled and greeted many as they moved north through the park. They continued walking, determined to move on.

At the northern end of the park sat the Israeli Supreme Court Building. When Eli reached the northern edge of the park, he turned to face the trailing crowd. Though still in the park, the beige stone of the court building seemed to almost glow in the late afternoon light.

Eli looked over his shoulder at the building and then turned back to the crowd. As always, Moshe stood beside him.

Eli pointed toward the court building and shouted. "The laws of man are never greater than the laws of God. Men seek to justify themselves by creating laws in order to indulge their own desires, ignoring the Lord God who made them. God is not blind to the affairs of man. The day is coming and is now, when men will once again know the hand of the One who judges all mankind."

Eli took a deep breath. He saw that someone in the crowd had a camera recording his words. "We have come to admonish and to warn you. Time is short. You must hear and believe the word of the Lord."

> "For God ... did not spare the ancient world, but preserved Noah, a preacher of righteousness, with seven others, when He brought a flood upon the world of the ungodly; and *if* He condemned the cities of Sodom and Gomorrah to destruction by reducing *them* to ashes, having made them an example to those who would live ungodly *lives* thereafter; and *if* He rescued righteous Lot, oppressed by the sensual conduct of unprincipled men, *then* the Lord knows how to rescue the godly from temptation, and to keep the unrighteous under punishment for the day of judgment, and especially those who indulge the flesh in *its* corrupt desires and despise authority." [16]

Eli again caught his breath. "Go to your homes and remain there until the sun sets tomorrow. Mark your doors with the sign of our Savior's salvation."

Someone in the crowd shouted back. "Why should we believe you? Why do you create fear and threaten us?"

Eli looked at the man. "We cannot stop the hand of God. We have come to seek your rescue. Do as we say and you will be safe. The devices of man cannot save you. So that you can see and believe in the One who saves."

Moshe raised the Rod and pointed to the court building. Suddenly fire shot out from the Rod and struck the building. A cloud of white dust rose into the air. When the air cleared, the image of the cross was etched into the side of the building.

Eli looked at the crowd who stood staring at the building. He shouted. "Go! Now!"

# Chapter 29

Those who left were believers. Around fifty remained. They could be compared to that type of person who slowdown at accidents out of curiosity. It's like they wanted to see what happens next.

Lanzig hid among the remaining crowd.

Eli looked at Moshe and shrugged his shoulders. He looked over at Brandon and Asher to signal them. He and Moshe began walking back into the park.

They made their way through the onlookers and into the park. Moshe noticed a man in a wheel chair. He felt compelled to stop and talk to him. Eli stopped as well.

Moshe bent down to talk to the man. He noticed that he had tears in his eyes.

"Sir, are you alright? Why are you here?"

"I had planted roses in this garden as a memorial to my family, who were killed in a bombing. Now the roses are all dried up."

Moshe looked around. The once vibrant rose bushes stood dry

and lifeless. He wished he could give him an answer.

Seeing Moshe's face the man spoke. "I don't blame you, just like I don't blame God. I heard what the other man said. I agree. I would flee but I live in Bethlehem and I missed my bus. I can't get home until late tonight. What can I do?"

Moshe saw the longing in the man's eyes. "Do you believe in the Son of Man?"

"Who is he that I may believe in him?"

"His name is Yeshua of Nazareth. He died for the sins of man and rose from the dead as a sign of His victory over sin and the grave. And we are His prophets."

The man looked at the newly etched court building. "The cross? Jesus, Yeshua? The Messiah?"

Moshe nodded.

The man looked down at his dead legs. He looked at the dead roses. He whispered to himself. *"Life from death. A Savior."*

He slowly looked up at Moshe. His lips trembled as he softly uttered, "I believe. Yes, …Yes, I believe."

Moshe's eyes glistened with joy. "Because of your faith, you shall see the goodness of the Lord in the land of the living."

He took the Rod and touched the man's legs. "Rise up and walk."

Suddenly his legs came to life. His whole body quivered. He almost couldn't believe the sensations coursing down his legs to his feet.

Moshe reached out his hand and the man took it. With a strength he had not known for years he rose to his feet. The man shouted and turned in circles, jumping up and down.

Some in the crowd cheered. Others merely stood with their mouths open.

Lanzig, nervously stared while attempting to calm the tightening in his chest. An unexplained fear began rising and he could neither explain nor stop it. He looked around to see if anyone noticed his almost paralyzing unease.

Moshe rejoined Eli and the two of them continued their walk to the center of the park.

A few more people visiting the park joined in the parade following the *Two*.

When they reached the place they wanted, Eli stopped and turned to crowd of about seventy people.

Eli looked up into the sky, then to the horizon. He looked back to the crowd.

"The moment is late. Passover approaches. The time for decision has come. The indulgent pleasures of mankind accept no boundaries. But the Lord declares His judgment."

> "Your dead will live; their corpses will rise. You, who lie in the dust, awake and shout for joy, for your dew *is as* the dew of the dawn, and the earth will give birth to the departed spirits. Come, my people, enter into your rooms and close your doors behind you; Hide for a little while until indignation runs *its* course. For behold, the LORD is about to come out from His place to punish the inhabitants of the earth for their iniquity; And the earth will reveal her bloodshed and will no longer cover her slain."[18]

Eli scanned the crowd and looked at the faces of the people practically one by one.

"You are all in danger. The Lord offers you a chance to escape what comes. But you must not hesitate or delay. To those who do, there will be no place to hide."

People in the crowd looked at each other, seeking to gauge the response of those around them.

Eli took a deep breath. "So that you may know that the Lord He is God and His Word is certain…" Eli looked at Moshe.

Moshe saw that everyone's eyes were fixed on him. He reached down and grabbed a handful of dust in his left hand. In a single movement he tossed the dust high into the air and stretched out the Rod beneath it.

Suddenly the dust exploded into a massive cloud and climbed into the sky. The cloud continued to expand and seemed to swirl as if alive.

Once again Moshe lifted the Rod into the air. Lightening flashed from the Rod and struck the cloud, igniting the swirling mass to expand at a greater rate.

Many in the crowd had fallen down in fear and amazement. They would have continued to gaze upward except for the shout.

Eli's voice startled them back to remembrance. He shouted. "Come with us! Now! RUN!"

Eli, Moshe, Brandon, and Asher broke into a run toward the west end of the park.

The people first looked at each other wondering who would be first. Lanzig surprised himself when he discovered that he was the first one to begin chasing the *Two*. He once ventured a glance up at the churning sky. Raw fear pushed him past caring about the possibility of being discovered. He quickly caught up with Brandon.

When they reached the edge of the park, a large bus waited with its engine running. Eli and Moshe stood at the door and helped people get on board. Moshe smiled as the once lame man walked past him. The man almost giggled as he patted his legs before boarding the bus.

When the last person got aboard, Eli and Moshe entered the bus and the door closed behind them. Immediately they departed.

It only took ten minutes to arrive at the large home of their host.

Before exiting the bus Moshe spoke to the passengers. "Everyone needs to get into the house as quickly as possible. We do not have much time. Once inside we will give you further instructions."

Both he and Eli exited the bus and stood outside admonishing everyone to hurry.

As the passengers exited the bus and walked to the door of the house they couldn't help but look up at the sky. The churning cloud continued to grow. It looked like a brown boiling cauldron of swirling muddy smoke. From the golden underside it became obvious that the cloud had begun to descend as it continued to grow. This realization caused one woman to scream, which in turn ignited a panic for the door.

Eli spoke up. "Don't panic. Get in the house and you will be safe."

As Lanzig approached the door he noticed large red crosses painted on the doorposts. He stole one glance at the sky. An unexplainable fear gripped him. He practically shoved the man in front of him in order to get inside.

When the last passenger and the driver entered the house Eli and Moshe stepped in and shut the door.

The people were directed to a large central patio area of the house. Someone looked up and realized that it had an open roof. The cloud appeared much closer and increasingly sinister. Again a woman screamed and the fear increased exponentially.

Eli stood on a bench and spoke out loudly "You must believe me. We are safe."

"But the cloud. We have no roof. It can get to us."

Moshe now spoke. "It can but it will not. The Maker of this pestilence is the One who protects us this day. As the sun sets across the globe, this judgment will fall upon the whole world. You must each remain in this house until the sun sets tomorrow. If you leave before then, you will fall prey to this plague. You are protected by Yeshua, the Savior."

"But I am not a believer," said one man.

"Yes, I know that many of you are not. But you are spared so that you may witness the deliverance that the Lord provides. You would do well to consider the grace given you this night."

At that moment the woman saw the cloud mere feet above the house. At first it simply hovered. Then it began dispersing away. Soon the clear sky with the last rays of the day's end appeared and people gasped in relief.

The host had meals brought out to the people and they ate on the floor and began sharing their stories.

A large table had been set up in an adjoining room open to the patio. The elegant table arrangement made it obvious to those guests who were Jewish. It was Passover.

The host, his family and a few of his honored guests prepared to take their seats. Eli moved to one end of the table and sat down. At first the wife gasped and almost said something. Her husband took her arm and signaled for her silence.

Many of the bus passengers moved in closer to hear and observe. Lanzig sat at the rear of this group in the shadow of a pillar. He wanted to hear but not be seen.

Moshe sat next to Eli and while the others took their seats.

Before they could begin Eli spoke. "You are surprised that I have taken the seat usually left vacant at this meal. Two questions are always asked this night. This first being, *Why is this night so special?*"

Moshe answered. "Tonight this meal commemorates the Lord's deliverance from bondage through his deliverer Moses."

Eli continued. "The Lord Yeshua then expanded it to remember His sacrifice on the cross for our sins. He commanded that we do this in remembrance of Him until He returns."

Moshe now spoke. "Tonight, the Lord delivers us from the judgment he has sent over the world this night. He has passed over this house and all others that bear the sign of His sacrifice. For this we give thanks."

The host then began and led in the Passover meal. Throughout the meal Moshe gave instructions and illustrated the fulfillment of the meal in the coming of Yeshua the Messiah. The nearby audience sat and watched with undivided attention, amazed at the simplicity and beauty of the celebration.

Near the end of the meal Eli again spoke. "A second question is usually asked. Why is there an empty place at the table this night?"

Moshe answered. "It is for the prophet Elijah, whose coming is foretold before the coming of the Messiah."

Eli continued. "Tonight the chair is no longer empty. I come to you this night and proclaim that Yeshua, the Messiah is soon to return. Rejoice. Though days of difficulty are approaching, our Savior's coming and deliverance is near. Even so Lord, come quickly."

Those around the table answered in unison. "Amen."

They sang a song and finished the meal. It had lasted about an hour.

Those at the table got up and began walking among the people in the patio. The hosts asked about people's needs while Eli, Moshe, Brandon and Asher mingled.

Brandon and Moshe were having a conversation. Asher sat next to Brandon listening. Lanzig made his way in the shadows close enough to overhear.

Suddenly the calmness of the evening changed as the sound of screams rang out. They came from outside and around the house. At one point someone banged on the door. The host began walking toward the door but Eli signaled for him to not do so. A chill seemed to fill the air.

Hearing the scream, Brandon looked around the patio. He sensed a mixture of tension and personal guilt. It quieted him. A question stirred within. He turned to Moshe.

"Why am I here and not out there? What I mean is, how do you decide who gets rescued and who suffers?"

Moshe looked around. He understood the question. "First of all, I don't decide."

Brandon interrupted. "Listen, I get it. Since I've traveled with you guys I've seen it. There are some really bad guys out there. Evil is real, I get it. It's just…"

Lanzig's throat tightened as he listened.

Moshe looked away as if seeing something in the distance. "I remember how I used to evaluate my life. I thought of myself as a pretty good guy. I certainly didn't see myself as evil. But I also remember …" He began to choke up. "I remember on the Island when the Lord revealed to me the true nature of my heart. I saw it all, all the lies, all the dark nasty … the filthy deception."

Moshe had to stop to wipe his face. "But then I remember how He took it all away."

Moshe turned and looked directly at Brandon. "When you really look at it, it's not about us. It is never about our being worthy or unworthy. None of us are worthy of rescue. His rescue says everything about Him and His loving ability to save wretched men and women. He stoops down to give us life. He…"

Moshe had to catch his breath. He placed his hands over his chest. "I … I don't know why He never gave up on me. He should have. I was stubborn enough. But He didn't and I'm so glad … I'm so glad he didn't."

Moshe began to weep. He could say no more.

Brandon's eyes were equally tear filled. He looked away and softly whispered, "Yeah, I don't know either…"

Lanzig quickly looked away. He felt exposed. Even though no one looked at him, he sensed as if eyes were peering into his mind. He heard words screaming out. Descriptions that he would have once proudly admitted now shamed him. He saw faces of the dead he had once stood over in pride. He saw lives he had crushed, destroyed and triumphed over. The pride of his scheming and conquests had turned to degradation.

He wondered if anyone could detect his nervous twitching. He felt trapped. He considered running outside but a certain cunning cowardice kept him in place. He feared the unknown outside and wrestled under the weight of what pressed him from within. One word screamed in his mind, *Evil*. He was evil.

For all his prideful swagger, here he sat a cowardly evil man in the midst of truly kind, loving and real people. They were not afraid to admit their weakness. But Him?

A young girl got up and walked over to Eli, "May I sing a song I have written?"

Eli nodded.

She turned to those gathered. "With your permission I would like to share a song which has filled my heart tonight."

*I'm all alone. No one can see,*
*I'm by myself in misery.*
*I closed my heart, disguised the shame.*
*But eyes that move in darkened halls,*
*Now shines a light on hidden ways.*
*Help me believe that there's a way.*
*Beyond my sin to conquer shame.*
*Help me believe that there's a way.*

*My heart was dark. You brought the light.*
*My pain was deep. You healed the hurt.*
*Your love is real. You made me new.*
*I'm born again because of You.*

*Who could have known? I let no one see.*
*Who could believe it would happen to me.*
*I hide it well, deceived myself.*
*I played the part, conquered foes.*
*The promised prize I never found,*
*Only a shell of empty lies.*
*But then You came and helped me see.*
*You broke my heart and healed my soul.*

*My heart was dark. You brought the light.*
*My pain was deep. You healed the hurt.*
*Your love is real. You made me new.*
*I'm born again because of You.*
*I'm born again because of You.*

When she finished there were few dry eyes. As she returned to sit down people thanked her profusely. All around a shared grace bathed those who knew and understood the depth of the grace they had been given that night.

Lanzig's eyes looked into a place he had never ventured, his heart. For the first time he saw it in all of its darkness. The rest of the room disappeared as he remembered. He saw the death and destruction. The blood of so many seemed to surround him and scream out to him. He tasted the vile nausea that was his soul. He sensed the crushing weight of it and wondered if he could survive. It was like descending into a dark pit with no escape until … he felt a hand.

He looked up and wiped away tears. The young girl sat next to him.

Her voice poured out something he had never experienced, love. "Sir, are you okay?"

Immediately behind her he saw Moshe looking directly at him with the same look.

Lanzig struggled to form words. His voice broke with every attempt. Finally he managed a simple trembling phrase. "I'm an evil man. I have done terrible… terrible things."

Moshe breathed heavy as he answered. "I know."

"You know who I am?"

Moshe nodded as his eyes filled with tears.

"Is there a …" he fought to get the next words out. It took several times before he could finish. "Is there a … is there a way for me?"

"Yes." The words were more whisper than words.

He waited and then in hopeful pleading, "Really? Seriously?"

Moshe nodded. In that simple gesture a spark of hope leaped into Lanzig's heart. Somehow he knew what he must do.

He stood to his feet. "I ask your attention please."

Everyone turned to look at him.

"I am Hermann Lanzig. I'm an evil man. I am a liar, a thief, a deceiver, and a murderer. But I want to be a follower of this Yeshua, the Savior. I confess this to you all and I desire His forgiveness."

He fell to his knees and then face down to the ground. Suddenly the air filled with what could only be described as a Presence. Tiny flakes of light seemed to appear and float around the room. One of the tiny flakes gently fell on the fallen body of Lanzig.

Lanzig's weeping changed into the crying of a heart rejoicing beyond any other expression.

Moshe began to hum softly. The tuned filled the room and then he filled it with words.

*Mighty hand that rescues here*
*Safe from harm*
*And safe from fear.*
*We bear witness*
*To that hand*
*That rescues him*
*Who cried to You.*
*Make complete*
*With finished work,*
*In honor of Your name.*
*Heal the heart once broken*
*Whole within Your hand.*
*Heal the heart once broken*
*Whole within Your hand.*

In another place far away yet near, a tiny voice whispered, "Truly."

# Chapter 30

Eli and Moshe awoke before anyone else in the house. Despite pleas from the hosts, they insisted on sleeping by the door leading to the outside. It provided a kind of comfort as the screaming outside continued throughout the night.

A husband and his wife who had joined them in the park, more in panic than anything else, began asking questions.

"Can we leave now?" the husband asked Moshe.

"You need to stay inside until sundown. It will not be safe until then."

"But I looked out the window and up in the sky through the patio. It looks like it's moved on."

"The danger is not over yet. It's best if you do as we said."

He looked at his wife who seemed to be equally determined. "You can't make us stay."

Moshe lowered his eyes. "You're right. I cannot or will not make you remain in the house. But again, I would warn you against it."

Overhearing the conversation, others were puzzled why the couple would want to leave. The couple noticed the attention.

"Look." The man spoke loud enough for everyone to hear. "We're not part of your religious thing. We admit that all of this is strange and all but... but we have places to go. We got caught up in the mob thing yesterday. We appreciate the hospitality but we insist on leaving."

Moshe looked to Eli, who nodded. They both stepped away from the door.

As the couple walked toward the door Moshe asked, "Are you sure?"

The man smiled and nodded. "Thank you, but yes we're sure."

Moshe stepped back and let the man open the door for his wife. They both walked out.

The husband attempted to call the hotel and arrange a ride, but no one answered. He and his wife decided to walk to the hotel and enjoy the brisk April morning.

They noticed the lack of much activity on the streets that morning. They attributed it to the Passover holiday. When they reached the hotel the wife noticed a small boil on her husband's neck. It had begun for them.

That morning at the same hotel, Margit woke up alone in her room. She had marked her door as instructed. The night before, her husband Franz had refused to stay in for the night. Their earlier plans had included an evening celebration with others from the tour. Despite her refusal to go out, he scoffed at her fears and went out. She attributed his absence to an evening of drunkenness. He had done this several times on their trip.

Later that morning she heard pounding on the door. She looked through the peephole and gasped. She quickly opened the door. Franz staggered in. His arms and face were covered with boils.

## Rome

D'bar sat at his desk facing a wall of monitors. Assured that everyone had connected, he began.

"I want reports." His voice expressed his present misery. His arms and neck were covered in a cream.

When no one responded he screamed. "I said I want reports. I want to know what this is!"

Besnik spoke up. "Chancellor, preliminary reports indicate that a dust cloud carrying a pest ... or something is making its way around the globe. Satellite images show the cloud moving out from Jerusalem and spreading as it moves. It is traveling westward along latitudes 30 degrees north and south. Above and below that it turns eastward as well as north and south toward the poles."

Someone else spoke up. "This movement follows the dominant wind currents and the earth's rotation."

D'bar regained his composure. "What's the prediction on its spread?"

Besnik answered. "Observations indicate that the cloud is not dissipating. And given the speed of its movement it should completely cross the globe in twenty-four hours from its start."

D'bar looked at the sores on his arm. "Do we know the connection to these blasted boils?"

Someone spoke up. "Air samples are being studied and we should have an answer soon."

"How soon?" D'bar shouted in irritation.

"Not long sir."

He screamed. "I want answers and I want them immediately. If this pestilence is going to cover the globe I want something to say by the time it's hit everyone. I don't want delays and I don't want excuses. Is that understood?"

D'bar disconnected the feed. He clinched his teeth at the sheer agony. He had already discovered what happened if he touched or rubbed the boils. He took another pain pill.

✡  ✡  ✡

A week had passed. The sting of the plague had now covered the globe. No section of the earth remained unaffected. Even though warnings had gone out as the cloud spread, no precautions other than the ones issued by the *Two* successfully protected anyone. The pestilence affected everyone even if people shut themselves in, used gas masks, or filtration systems. The only ones unaffected by the plague were the ones who had obeyed the instructions given by the *Two*.

Asher had acquired a van for the group. They had grown by one member. The group left Jerusalem and like before remained out of the public eye. They had also admonished believers worldwide to avoid crowded areas. The absence of the plague's effects on them could put them in danger.

✡  ✡  ✡

D'bar called a meeting again. His personal misery and the scope of the plague irritated him to no end. He wanted answers.

He stood before the bank of monitors waiting for the connections to completely activate. If his personal pain was any indication of the severity of the situation, he knew he had a crisis that demanded action.

D'bar heard the signal indicating everyone's presence online.

"Alright, I want some answers. I don't care who starts, just do it."

Besnik began. "Well sir, we have isolated the cause." He paused as if expecting a comment.

D'bar shouted. "Don't stop. Go on!"

"Yes. Well, imbedded in the dust cloud were microscopic mites. They penetrate the skin and enter the lungs. They were small enough that any and all preventative measures proved insufficient." Besnik finished.

Someone else started before D'bar could react. "This species of mite had never appeared before. One theory is that it's a mutation."

D'bar rubbed his forehead struggling and waiting for the recent pain reliever to take affect. "What about the boils?"

Another member answered. "The mites carry an infective agent that attacks the body in a couple of unique ways."

"Really?" D'bar shouted.

"Yes sir." The speaker cleared his throat. "The infective agent, which is both viral and bacterial, attacks the nervous system. It most directly affects the pleasure centers in the brain. It is reported that whenever infected individuals attempt any sexual activity the pain increases even more. The infection also attacks the nerves of the body. The boils are a reaction as the body fights back the infection."

D'bar took a deep breath. "So what you're saying is that this infects the very parts of our body by which we experience pleasure?"

"Yes sir. That very much sums up the situation."

He shouted back. "No it does not sum up the situation. Do we have a cure in sight?"

Besnik nervously responded. "Well sir, our experts working toward that end say it would be pointless."

"*POINTLESS!* Did you just say pointless?" His rage was hardly contained.

"Let me explain sir. After examining the organism, our experts predict that since this is a mutation, the life cycle of the organism will end the problem on its own. They predict that this will pass in less than two months from when it started."

D'bar took a deep breath. He didn't want to lose control at this point. He waited as he thought.

"Ok. How sure are these so-called experts on their predictions about the infection going away on its own?"

"Almost completely certain. The infective agents have already begun to degrade and all models verify their conclusions."

"Ok." D'bar tapped on his desk. He smiled as an idea came to mind. "Here's what we're going to do. We will inform the world that a cure has been discovered. Tests are being run and will be ready for distribution at the time predicted. We'll say that the cure will be dispersed in the air overnight and no inoculations will be necessary."

The council members smiled and nodded at D'bar's plan.

D'bar continued. "Not only that, but we will distract them during the time that remains. We will declare that all forms of online entertainment will be free until the crisis is over. This will please advertisers and increase the population's connectivity."

The council members applauded at the plan.

D'bar rubbed his forehead again. He raised one hand toward the monitors. "Peace, Prosperity, and Order."

Each of the members repeated the mantra.

D'bar disconnected all of the connections except Besnik's.

D'bar looked up at the monitor. "I know we haven't mentioned it but I have a suspicion that these two Jewish prophets are behind all this. Have you made any progress finding them?"

They were spotted at the Knesset on the day the plague began. I sent another hit team to take care of them. They never reported back. Their remains were found and identified on top of the Supreme Court building. It seems they and their weapons were found fused together."

"What?"

"Some intense heat struck and killed them."

"Lightening or something like that?"

"Well… some kind of intense heat etched the building and perhaps struck them at the same time."

"Etched? Etched what?"

"A large cross was etched into the building."

"I'm sure that didn't please the Jewish government?"

"No sir, it did not. That's why they were immediately repairing it. It's also when my men were found."

D'bar puffed out his frustration. "Ok, what about Lanzig, anything on him?"

"No. We have no reported sightings. Knowing him, he's in disguise and won't be found unless he wants to be found."

"Well, stay at it. As for these two, we have to find a solution. My celebration is less than a year away and I don't want them spoiling it."

"Yes sir."

D'bar cut the connection. Besnik wondered why D'bar hadn't come down harder on him about the *Two* or Lanzig. He attributed it to the affects of the plague. He reached over and injected a narcotic to relieve his own personal misery.

✡ ✡ ✡

The group made their way out of Jerusalem. The *Two* remained out of public view while the plague continued. They spent this time among believers in Bethlehem and other villages southwest of Jerusalem. Due to the severity and spread of the plague, and its effect on people, the unaffected avoided daytime crowds. Across the globe people responded with violence. Many had taken advantage of the free entertainment venues provided as well as drug abuse to stem the pain and misery.

Reports from their sources around the world were the same. Very few had reacted to the plague by calling out to God for relief. It saddened Eli and Moshe that instead of turning to God, so many had either anesthetized themselves, or responded by cursing God.

Hermann used the time of isolation to pour himself into his new faith. He had an insatiable desire to learn everything he could. Moshe had no sooner given a reading assignment than he completed it and followed it with a stream of questions. He filled countless pages with notes and private observations. It amused everyone when they heard him shout or laugh to himself at some new discovery. Hermann's transformation and growth amazed all who witnessed it. The change surprised Hermann more than anyone.

Seven weeks passed. Just as predicted, the plague weakened and then played out. The boils faded but left scaring on anyone who had rubbed or scratched them. The persistent torture of the boils left few able to resist the temptation. Cosmetic remedies flooded the marketplace in an effort to cover up reminders of the plague. People drew some measure of personal comfort in the knowledge that practically everyone seemed to share the same problem.

The five of them sat on a patio on a hillside home not far from the village of Battir. A mild May evening breeze lifted a small cloud of dust as it raced through a valley below.

Brandon watched it and commented. "The ground is really dry. You would expect some greenery this time of year but…"

"Very dry, this is true sir," Asher finished. "It has not rained in so long. I think people have even forgotten what it looks like. Perhaps when it finally comes they will see it as God's tears."

Moshe and Eli traded glances.

After a few moments of quiet Eli spoke. "It's been seven weeks now. Tomorrow we go to Battir. Are you familiar with it Asher?"

"Somewhat sir. It is a Palestinian village on a hillside much like this place."

Hermann raised a hand. Moshe smiled. "You don't need permission to speak."

"Yes, of course. I'm sorry. Eli mentioned seven weeks. I remember from the time I followed you all around and made note of the pattern. After a plague there would be seven weeks of silence. Then came three weeks of your preaching. Then you would announce another plague. Is there some meaning behind this?"

Brandon reacted. "Wow, you really watched us closely?"

Hermann nodded almost embarrassed.

Asher chimed in, "Sir, what were your intentions in all of your snooping?"

The question caught Hermann by surprise. "I ah…" he choked up a bit. He paused while he swallowed back newfound emotion. He looked at the *Two*. "My intentions were two-fold. First I wanted to find out what was behind your abilities."

He paused again. He rubbed his face before continuing. "I ah... I was at the Dead Sea with Osgood. I almost followed him into ah ... if I had I would have died with him. What I saw there both frightened and drove me on."

He looked down to take a long breath. "I had also plotted your deaths. I worked for the enemy in trying to destroy you all. I'm ah..."

"We already knew." Moshe spoke.

"What?"

"We knew someone was out there following and watching us. And when you showed up we knew who you were and that you were the one."

"How?" He caught himself and chuckled. "That's a dumb question isn't it?"

Everyone laughed.

"Anyway, back to my original question. What is it with the pattern?"

Eli deferred to Moshe.

"All you have to do is look at creation to see that God is in the details. There is nothing random in anything He does. The very universe is a mathematical display of His genius. He is the one who set the pattern for us. The numbers seven and three represent completeness and perfection. So it shouldn't surprise anyone that God had chosen the pattern."

Hermann thought a moment. "So are there to be seven plagues?"

Eli nodded.

"And then what?"

Eli and Moshe traded looks with Brandon and Asher.

Hermann saw the looks. "What am I missing? What comes after the seventh plague?"

Moshe cleared his throat. "After that our mission is accomplished."

"And then what?"

Eli and Moshe looked back out toward the valley. Hermann's question hung in the air unanswered.

Finally Brandon took a deep breath. He looked at Hermann. "Then they die."

In the distance a jackal howled at the moonless night and a second one answered in the darkening night.

There were no more questions that night.

# Chapter 31

The plague of boils morphed much of human interaction to electronic relationships. People displeased with the physical scaring caused by the plague substituted doctored images of themselves. They began living alternate lives of fantasy and escape. Identities were hidden under the mirage of created lives substituted for the real. For so many it had become an addictive state of being. New categories of syndromes and disorders were created to label a variety of sell-inflicted neurosis. New international laws passed allowing individuals to redefine at will their self-defined identities. Many escaped the reality of the plague by entering into a love affair with themselves. The ever-expanding world-wide social media fed and nourished the erosion of human community. The electronic became the proxy for human.

As before, the *Two* renewed their proclamation. For the next three weeks they walked the streets and delivered the Word from the Lord in the towns of Battir, Even Sapir and Ora. But unlike previous times, they were mostly ignored. People paid little attention to them or their message. As they walked the streets, people seemed glued to their electronic devices. Individuals didn't talk with others standing right next to them. The occasional interaction only occurred when one person shared what they were looking at with the person next to them.

Whenever Eli would stop to shout out a proclamation, people put in earpieces for their devices. As the days passed, people were increasingly annoyed with any attempt to interrupt them.

✡  ✡  ✡

Besnik had not spoken to D'bar in over a week. He wanted to report some of the progress taking place in his region. It excited him to finally have something to report concerning the prophets and Lanzig. With all of the bad news around, it felt good to have something good to report. He placed the call.

D'bar answered abruptly. "Yacov, you better not be bothering me with any bad news."

"Quite the opposite sir. I have several good things to report. First off, progress on the Jewish Temple is moving along smoothly. In fact, we are ahead of schedule. We should meet your deadline without a problem."

"Very good. What else?"

"The two prophets have reappeared southwest of Jerusalem. We are making progress. With everyone enjoying personal social interaction, there has been little response at their recent appearances. I think the time has come to make a bold public move against them."

"Excellent."

"Oh, but sir it gets better. We have also picked up something more. Lanzig."

"What?'

"Photos indicate he is traveling with them."

"What do you mean? Is he shadowing them?"

"I don't think so. Everything indicates that he has joined them."

"What? Lanzig is with them? That doesn't make any sense."

"Sir, maybe he's actually joined them. Maybe he converted."

"That's hard to believe." D'bar recounted all he knew about Lanzig. "No, I can't accept that. I don't see how that's possible. He must be pretending in order to infiltrate their ranks. Yes, that's it. He's gone undercover. Very clever. I just wonder why he didn't tell us about it?"

"I don't know sir. The photos seem very convincing."

"Nonsense, Lanzig is extremely shrewd. Never underestimate his cunning. I watched how he took over Osgood's organization and eliminated all competitors. No, we simply have to find a way to contact him discreetly and discover his plan. He wants to hand these two charlatans over to me."

While D'bar went on, Besnik shook his head. He didn't believe D'bar's assessment. He couldn't explain it but he believed Lanzig to be a traitor. He'd make contact with him, hopefully with a bullet. He'd prove to D'bar that Lanzig had betrayed the cause. He'd show him what true cunning looked like.

D'bar's raised voice brought him back. "Yacov, did you hear me?"

"What was that sir?"

"I said to let me know when you make contact with him. Until then monitor them and keep me in the loop."

"Absolutely sir." After D'bar hung up he wondered how he could make it all work without it coming back on him. There had to be a way.

✿ ✿ ✿

Asher stood outside by the van. He knew they traveled to Jerusalem today.

Eli walked out of the house with the others right behind him.

"Asher, do you know Teddy Stadium?"

"Yes sir, I went there once to watch a match."

"That is our destination. There is an event there around noon. We should get there before then. The weather is warm. The sky is clear. We should find a good crowd for the Lord's proclamation."

Without another word everyone loaded up. Brandon sat in the front looking at a street map to help Asher. The *Two* sat in the middle row. Hermann mentioned that, as the newest group member, sitting in the back seemed fitting.  To see a humorous side of Hermann lightened the mood.

They pulled up to the stadium. Half the parking spaces were already taken. They parked and walked to the stadium entrance. They noticed everyone's preoccupation with their mobile devices.

No one even recognized the *Two* or the uncharacteristic way they dressed. Someone dressed like a Bedouin shepherd in a metropolitan area usually caught people's attention. But apparently not today. That would soon change.

Reaching the west entrance, the group stood in a small huddle and took a moment to pray together. When they finished, Brandon, Asher and Hermann stood aside. The *Two* turned to face those approaching.

Eli turned to Moshe and nodded. Moshe raised the Rod straight up and brought it down tapping the ground. The sound exploded from the ground like the sound of giant gong. The thunderous sound startled everyone in the lot and shook windows for some distance. No longer were people looking down. They had their attention.

Eli's forceful voice carried as if he was speaking with the aid of a sound system.

"For almost three years we have brought to you warnings from the Lord. The Lord has shut up the sky and you do not listen. Three times the Lord has judged your gods and yet you continue in your ways. Your bodies heal but your hearts are far away. You feel secure in worlds of your own making."

The people looked puzzled and almost bored. One shouted, "Shut up man. Leave us alone." Others nodded in agreement. One person took a photo to post.

"You desire to be alone?"

Several shouted, "Yes!"

"Then hear the Word of the Lord."

> Woe to those who add house to house *and* join field to field,
> until there is no more room, so that you have to live alone in
> the midst of the land! In my ears the LORD of hosts *has*
> *sworn,* "Surely, many houses shall become desolate, *Even* great
> and fine ones, without occupants." So the *common* man will be
> humbled and the man of *importance* abased. The eyes of the
> proud also will be abased. But the LORD of hosts will be
> exalted in judgment, and the holy God will show Himself
> holy in righteousness." **18**

Again Moshe raised the Rod and pointed it directly toward the
sky. A bolt of fire shot into the air and passed from sight.
Suddenly a loud rumbling roar echoed across the sky like distant
thunder.

People looked up as if watching a fireworks display. When
the roar echoed away they looked back down. The *Two* had
already walked some distance from where they stood. People
shrugged and went on their way.

It didn't take long. As people looked at the mobile phones
something had happened. Even though the phones worked, their
social applications didn't. People looked at each other and
noticed everyone had the same problem.

Someone spoke up. "Try restarting."

Anyone who tried found that the problem only got worse.
Various aspects of their devices began fouling up. The more
people attempted to fix the problem the more the cascading
failure increased.

Within an hour the majority of the worldwide web collapsed. The
interesting aspect of the network failure was in what remained intact.
Phone communications and banking seemed unaffected while all

other aspects of the web lay in disarray. The days that followed were ones of confusion and seclusion.

✡ ✡ ✡

"Alone? You are not alone." The deep dark voice echoed through the chamber lit by one single candle.

D'bar sat on the stone floor in the middle of the distinct shape of a pentagram drawn in old and long dried blood. In each of the five points of the star were four unlit candles and the singular glowing one in front of him. He had begun the private ceremony two hours earlier. Initiated by the ingestion of a potent and ancient elixir, D'bar chanted non-stop until the presence arrived as it always had. He smiled as he sensed the dark and alluring specter drawing him close. He fell face down and surrendered himself.

"Master, come to me. Reveal to me the ancient secrets of power. Infuse me and make me your instrument."

"You have done well. Soon I will not merely come to you. Do well and I shall dwell within you and you will know the true meaning of my power. Now hear and obey my words."

"Yes lord."

"There are two who stand in your way. They are thorns of pestilence. You must destroy them. Only then can I fulfill my destiny in you. They have power but it is nothing compared to what I possess which shall be yours. You must battle and defeat them."

"Yes Master."

"Now listen carefully and I will reveal to you about their ways and how you will defeat them."

Over the next hour the dark nefarious voice dictated instructions concerning four battles, which must come to pass before he could defeat his enemy. Suddenly the single candle went out.

Out of the darkness the voice spoke. "Do not fear the darkness. It is not your enemy. You will emerge out of the darkness victorious. I am with you until the end."

D'bar looked up and suddenly the other candles ignited and were consumed by immense red flames. Against the wall stood a giant silhouette with arms stretched out. Crimson light filled the room and danced up the walls.

"I am with you in the darkness." The voice shouted in what resembled the howling roar of a dragon.

The room fell into deep darkness. D'bar drank in the narcotic of the moment. His red eyes glowed like fired rubies. He lifted his outstretched fists and whispered, "Yes."

✡   ✡   ✡

"Whether we think about it or not, we want life to make sense. We either create a story for ourselves or we choose one that fits our inclinations. Rarely do we willingly agree to something that requires us to submit our wills." Moshe looked across the valley stretched out before them.

Hermann listened carefully before speaking. "So what did God have in mind with this last plague?"

"These plagues are judgments. Each of them are targeted to communicate to man's vain reliance on false gods. The True and Living God does not share His position with anyone or anything else."

Hermann scratched his chin. "Is God so insecure that He feels threatened?"

Moshe smiled at Hermann. "No, not at all. It's about truth. There is no one greater than Him. That's the truth of the matter. To say or accept anything other than that is false. He really is the greatest and supreme personality of the universe."

A light went off in his mind, Hermann smiled. "I get it. It's like the scripture I read. He is the first and last, the beginning and the end. He is the final reality. Everything else is built on Him. He is the Creator. Any other authority is a pretender."

"That's the message we are sent to deliver. It is the essence of the Story. He Is. Anything denying it shall be brought down and judged."

It seemed ludicrous that anyone would demand that the Chancellor convene the council. Such meetings came only by order of the Chancellor himself. Yet, D'bar sensed the panic among his leaders. At times, if he hadn't needed them for logistical purposes he would have eliminated them all. He knew they each saw themselves as powerful individuals. He knew better. They had no real idea of true power. He had to tolerate their fears and doubts. D'bar took it as part of the price for his position and ultimate purpose.

D'bar sat in the next room watching them squabble and debate their plans and solutions. He allowed them a few moments before he would show them how this and every crisis could be mastered.

He listened until he had had enough. He practically kicked the door open. The loud entrance had its intended result. They all found their seats. He waited for added affect.

"Gentlemen, what troubles you so?"

The Regional Czar from East Asia spoke up. "Your Honor, We are in a quandary over how to solve the collapse of the communication and connectivity of the world. Can you explain to us how this was allowed to happen?"

A hard and cynical smile crossed D'bar's face. Besnik knew the look well and braced himself.

D'bar took a deep breath. Again that smile. "Is it my understanding that you are making a demand?"

The Czar understood his error and regretted it. "My pardon sir, it was certainly not my intention. I spoke out of the anxiety of the moment. Again, I beg your pardon."

"Very well." D'bar cooled his demeanor. "We will use your momentary lapse as an example. You see gentlemen, there are some things you must understand. We are not here to stoop to the demands of the mob. We are here to control and manipulate them."

D'bar walked around the room. "You asked how this could happen? Things always happen. This world evolved out of chaos and things happen out of our control. The only valid question to ask is, *How can we use this to our advantage?*"

D'bar saw the puzzled looks. "Let me use the current situation to explain. It's all too obvious that people are feeling crippled at losing their connectivity. People desire explanations. I understand. I don't care, but I understand. We are looking into what happened, and if we discover someone is behind it, they will be punished publically and severely. But once things occur, you must find ways to use circumstances to further our goals. Is this clear to you?"

Eyes wandered in furtive glances. D'bar suddenly slammed his fist on the table. "I chose you to lead!" The primal rage in his eyes terrorized them into submission. D'bar turned to face the wall. He smiled. He loved the feeling.

He slowly walked back to his chair and sat. He glanced over some papers as if gathering his thoughts. In actuality, he knew exactly what to do. The plan had come to him earlier. As promised, it flowed to his mind clear and succinct.

"People are distressed so we shall aid them to our gain. They were addicted to electronics so we will make them dependent on us. We will anesthetize them and make them twice our slave. When things are restored, we will control their minds and bodies. You will all receive implementation prodigals before you leave."

D'bar rose as if leaving but stopped. He looked across the table. He waited until all eyes fixed on him.

His eyes hardened. "Don't you ever presume to question me again."

# Chapter 32

Strange time passes differently for individuals. For some it moves amazingly fast while for others it crawls painfully slow. Such was the case for the seven weeks of the current plague. Like sediments carried by the flowing waters and deposited according to weight, the gravity of time and events separated the hearts of men and women.

A giant sifting occurred and few recognized where it took them.

✡ ✡ ✡

Techno wizards across the globe worked feverishly to discover the reason and a cure for the informational shutdown. A multi-million dollar bounty prompted a flurry of privateers into the mix. After two weeks of meticulous scrutiny, the system failure remained a mystery.

One of the world's leading experts summed up his analysis; "I can find no reason in the system for the shutdown. It's as if someone flipped a giant switch and turned everything off. The problem remains in that we don't know where that switch is. In the state of people's present anger and frustration, I am thankful that the masses are locked out or they would have all of our collective heads."

Several days later that same expert suspiciously went missing. No private individual made any other such public pronouncements.

The Chancellor announced over televised media that the government would find a solution. In the meantime he recognized and sympathized with the strain brought on by the multiple crisis faced by the world. He proclaimed his multipronged relief plan.

Beginning immediately governmental mental healthcare facilities would provide life enhancement medications free of charge. This would continue until the current crisis came to an end.

Concerning the continued drought, the Chancellor noted that three months earlier his office had launched his worldwide water relief initiative. The relief would begin immediately. New deep well and desalination facilities had already begun delivery of the much-needed resource worldwide.

As D'bar looked directly into the camera, his well-rehearsed voice sounded caring and strong. "Together we will move past the obstacles before us. We will draw on the strength of our mutual courage and defeat any and all who seek to hold us back. We are stronger together. This is our resolve. Peace – Prosperity – and Order."

A field of flags bearing his symbol faded in while his face faded out. Grand and stirring music carried the force of his words as they were sung by what sounded like hundreds of voices. This scene then blended into a clear sky and the singular face of the Chancellor.

✡ ✡ ✡

"Oh my, he does seem impressed with himself." Asher seemed truly surprised.

Brandon chuckled at Asher's innocence at the Chancellor's use of the media.

Hermann scratched his chin. "He knows exactly what he is doing. Trust me. If there is one thing that defines the man, it is power."

"And it will be his undoing." Eli stood behind Hermann. They had all watched the Chancellor's speech. It was one of the rare occasions when the *Two* gave any attention to anything coming from the government.

Moshe shook his head. "Enough of that. Shut it off. We have tasks ahead of us."

Both Eli and Moshe moved to face the group.

Eli began. "Asher, tomorrow we begin our next three weeks. We will travel to Bayt Sahar."

Moshe then continued. "Brandon, over the next week we need to get word out to our brothers and sisters. Tell them that they must ready themselves. Each family is to gather containers for storing water. They need to store the amount of water required for their family for one day only. They may also store an additional amount to share. There is to be no hoarding in fear. The Lord will provide."

Hermann's face said what the others were thinking. Moshe saw the question on their faces.

"Brothers, people have become dependent on the empty promises of men and governments. They look to satisfy the desires of their bodies and have forgotten their souls. As the Lord declared, *Man shall not live by bread alone, but by every word that comes from God.* Danger is approaching. We anxiously await the Lord's return. Yet to the unbelieving, His return will bring inescapable judgment. This is part of our witness. We are called to warn them and declare the way of rescue."

Hermann's lips quivered as he listened. "I've never been a man of emotion. Calculated advances to further my own cause defined my whole life." He paused to catch his breath. "If God had not rescued me I would still be out there. I understand how they think. It's like being blind and not knowing it. How can we penetrate that wall?"

"We can't." Eli whispered loud enough to hear.

"Eli's right," Moshe added. "Only God can get through and reveal the way to men's hearts."

"Then why doesn't He?" Hermann eyes pleaded to know.

"Because He's a gentleman. He doesn't force His way upon us. He stands at the door knocking, sometimes pounding." Moshe remembered his own stubbornness. "I think we all remember our own journeys and resistance."

"Then we should pray." Asher's simple answer stopped them all.

"Thank you brother for reminding us where our true strength comes from." Eli was already moving to his knees.

They all knelt.

Silence dominated the next thirty minutes. One of them whispered a single word, "Jesus."

While nothing was visible, the presence saturated the room. One by one the men fell face down under the weight of unmistakable divine nearness. Within each heart the surrenders occurred. Each of them received insight as to what awaited them individually. And each of them yielded themselves to the unfolding Story.

After a time, one by one they got up and quietly exited the room. They each knew.

✡  ✡  ✡

Besnik decided not to send D'bar a message on the recent intelligence he had received. He wanted full credit for the action. The report revealed that the prophets had popped up south of Jerusalem. He smiled as he read how few were responding to their preaching. His media campaign against them had proven effective. The time to strike seemed perfect.

After all the previous failures he wanted to assure the success of his present plan. He decided he needed to carry out some personal surveillance.

✡  ✡  ✡

With all of his years of experience, Hermann understood surveillance. Whenever the group went out he couldn't help himself. He always evaluated the surroundings trying to spot it. After a lengthy conversation with Eli and Moshe, he decided to no longer remain incognito. Yet, he remained ever vigilant. His eyes inspected every person in whatever crowd gathered around them.

As the group made their way down a street of Bayt Sahur, Hermann spotted him. Hermann almost chuckled at Besnik's mediocre disguise. Through side-glances he saw Yacov focusing in on him.

When Eli stopped to talk to a small group, Hermann weaved his way around and stood directly behind Besnik.

In the soft and deep tone he had used in earlier days, Hermann whispered. "Yacov, how good to see you. Are you interested in what they have to proclaim?"

Besnik jerked his head back and looked into Hermann's grin. "You think that's funny don't you? I could ask you the same question, you know. It's no secret that you have been making company with this group. Have you become one of them?"

Hermann knew the day would come. He had never pictured it happening with his once vile adversary. Yet what he felt at the moment surprised him. The former feelings of disgust were replaced with pity. He saw his former self and wondered if Yacov could be reached.

Hermann answered directly. "Yes I have."

Besnik laughed. "You? Don't they know what sort of devil you are? Have you told them of all the blood on your hands?

Hermann lowered his head. He could not deny one accusation. The reality of God's grace hit him. "Yes, they know it all. And more importantly, God knows it all. And what's amazing is that He has forgiven me."

"Forgive you?" Besnik forgot himself and shouted. He looked around and lowered his voice. "There is no forgiveness for savages like us. The only way out for us is to eliminate all the accusers. Destroy the evidence and there is no crime." He laughed again.

"The One who judges cannot be destroyed. He is also the One

who has provided an answer to our guilt."

"Stop it!" Besnik pressed his glare at Hermann. "Don't hand me that religious baloney. You and your so-called prophets are temporary news. You cannot succeed. What you are selling, the people are not buying. What we offer is the security of the now. They will sell themselves into the bondage of our care."

"If you could only see."

"I said stop it! Don't you get it? You've chosen the losing side. The Chancellor is going to crush those two and anyone else that stands in his way. You know that you're a marked man don't you? I'll tell you what, leave this nonsense now and I'll make sure you don't suffer the same thing these saps have coming. Come on. You seriously don't think they can win?"

Hermann realized the futility. "Yacov, I want you to know that I will pray for you. It is you who has chosen poorly. You do not understand Who you are opposing. Even if you kill us all, you cannot win. The Lord is the Victor. He is returning and you don't want to be on the wrong side of that. I wish I could convince you. I wish."

"Get out of my face. I can't believe I once feared you. You're a shell of the man I once knew. You and your band of whatever will be easy enough to crush. And when it's all over, I'll see you in hell."

"I'm afraid not."

"Whatever!" Besnik turned and walked off.

✡ ✡ ✡

Their mood seemed subdued. The team had spent their last week in Bayt Jala with little response except passive hostility. Public opinion had definitely turned. The three weeks were over and they each knew what that meant.

"Where are we going today sirs?" Asher looked nervous.

"Are you familiar with a park southwest of the Old City called Gan HaPa'amon?"

"Yes sir, Mr. Eli sir."

"The government is dedicating a new water feature there today. We shall attend because the Lord has something to say." Eli breathed a long deep sigh. The last few days had wearied him greatly.

Since the park's new multiple water fountains would showcase newly sourced water under the Chancellor's program, Besnik would speak at the dedication. Dignitaries gathered all around the Regional Czar seeking his favor

When the group arrived at the park, they found a large crowd gathered around the podium. As he spoke, Besnik extolled the virtues of the Chancellor's concern for the plight of the world's people.

Suddenly Eli shouted out. "Why do you listen to the empty words of vain leaders?"

Faces and cameras turned. Gasps and jeers blended together. Every face communicated with nauseated scowls toward the unwanted guests. Four security persons drew their weapons with instant regret. The second they lifted them to aim, the weapons exploded in their hands.

Eli continued. "Listen while you have time. The days draw near when the Son of God shall come and all will see Him. Yet, you will not listen. You have turned your backs upon the True and Living God and His Savior Yeshua. You have put your trust in the empty promises of men. Do you think they can save you?"

Besnik shouted back. "Did you all see that? They attacked those who are here to protect us." He pointed his finger at Eli. "You come here spreading violence and we come to satisfy the thirst of the people. The world does not want you or your God. Look and see the water. We answer the needs of the people."

Eli looked up into the heaven. "O Lord God, show Yourself. Let men see and know the emptiness of their trust."

He then looked directly into the camera.

> "Be appalled, O heavens, at this, and shudder, be very
> desolate, declares the LORD. For My people have committed
> two evils: They have forsaken Me, the fountain of living

waters, to hewn for themselves cisterns, broken cisterns that can hold no water." [19]

Moshe stepped forward toward one of the newly constructed fountains. Eli cried out. "So that you may know that the Lord, He is God."

Moshe dipped the Rod into the fountain. Suddenly the waters of all the fountains in the park turned a dark red.

Several people screamed. One man walked over to inspect the water. He reached down and scooped up a handful. He put it to his nose and then gagged.

Someone asked aloud. "What is it?"

The man looked at his hand. "It smells like...blood."

People began running away. Besnik spotted Hermann slowly shaking his head as he turned to leave.

The fountains of that park were not the only ones affected. At the very instant that Moshe dipped the Rod, all of the Chancellor's new water sources were struck with the plague of blood. With most of the world's reservoirs nearly depleted by the continued drought, the new plague left no one untouched.

The coming days would challenge the world's civility and display the believer's generosity. The stories of both could fill volumes. Only the records of heaven would record the full extent of greed and the grace of the days to follow.

# Chapter 33

**D**esperation and anger were the prevailing moods across the world. The government scrambled to cope with the water situation. At first, filtration efforts provided rationed amounts to the populace. Over the weeks the supply slowly increased with minimal relief.

The Chancellor launched a vicious propaganda campaign against the *Two*. He openly accused them of terrorist attacks in both the water contamination and the Internet collapse. The relentless hostile disinformation created a toxic atmosphere across the globe.

As for believers, the Lord provided as promised. The emptied water containers miraculously re-filled overnight. And as directed by the Lord, they shared their supply in grace. For even through the flood of hatred spewed out by the government, the Spirit of the Lord moved among the desperate. The eyes of many were opened to the true thirst in their souls. Both the Light and the darkness were having their days among the hearts of mankind.

"In my previous life … it sounds funny to say it that way. Anyway, previously I concentrated on gathering information. I was a man of action. It's so different to be dedicating so much time to learning. In many ways I feel like a kid. And that's saying a lot for a man of my age."

Moshe chuckled as he listened to Hermann. "I think we all know the feeling. Except for Eli, none of our group were raised in the faith. Let me ask you, what about all of this has surprised you the most?"

Hermann scratched his chin. "The change. By that, I mean the change within. It came so suddenly and thoroughly. There's no way I could do this on my own. It's like starting over."

Brandon now laughed. "Yeah, it's pretty wild isn't it?"

Asher chimed in. "Yes indeed sirs. I am but an ordinary man. I have no great education and yet great and marvelous ideas come to my mind as I read God's Word."

"It's like someone told me. It makes you smarter than you are." Moshe added.

Hermann suddenly seemed pensive. He attempted to say something but stopped as he collected his emotions. Everyone saw and waited. "I was cruel man. I never cared about what I did to others and how it hurt and destroyed them." He had to stop to catch himself.

The silence filled with their own memories. He continued. "I care now. I know myself well enough to know that this is not from within me. God has placed it within me. It shocks and amazes me. I want others to know this. Isn't that something? I care."

Eli finally spoke. "Yes, God is pretty amazing. What's equally amazing is the stubbornness of people's hearts. Each of us is thankful that God penetrated our hearts. But so many are hard set in their course. Their will is so heavily invested that they will not turn away. Even while seeing clearly the hand of God, they will follow it to their own destruction."

Moshe reached over and picked up the Bible he always carried.

The binding and pages were well worn. It had belonged to his wife. "Mary often wrote quotes from things she had read or heard. This one sort of hits at what Eli said. It's from a man named G.K. Chesterton."

"For Carthage fell because she was faithful to her own philosophy and had followed out to its logical conclusion her own vision of the universe. Moloch had eaten his children."[20]

"Then she wrote this on her own. *Their gods ate them.*"

Hermann's hands were shaking. "They almost ate me."

✡  ✡  ✡

With so many people breathing down his neck, including the Chancellor, Besnik had neglected much attention to Lanzig or the *Two*. He wondered how long before the Chancellor called again. At least now he had some news of progress. He didn't have to wait long.

Besnik took a deep breath as he saw the light blinking.

"Good morning sir. How are you today?"

"Cut the smoke, Yacov. Things are going better but your area is still the sore thumb in the world. Report."

"Yes sir. As you said, things are getting better. The water contamination has subsided and should be cleared up completely within a day or two. As you know the banking remained unaffected during the recent breakdown. My experts tell me people will have access to the whole social media realm in the same time frame. You should be able to announce your success in bringing these problems to an end."

"Yacov, I know all of this. I want to know about the two renegades you have in Israel. I've labeled them terrorists. Why haven't you apprehended or destroyed them yet?"

"Well sir, their ability to..."

"Enough with the excuses!" D'bar's shouts were loud enough that anyone in the room could have heard it. "It's November and my Jerusalem event is in February. You are running out of time. Do I make myself clear?"

Besnik's throat tightened. He felt his heart racing. "Yes sir."

"Use whatever force is necessary. Destroy them and the world will congratulate us. Get it done." D'bar hung up.

"Whatever force is necessary, that's what he said." Besnik whispered to himself. "Maybe it's time for open action by the military." He made the call.

✡   ✡   ✡

The seven weeks had ended and Hermann knew what came next. He also knew other things. He went to Eli.

"I've found out that the Regional Czar Yacov Besnik has activated the military to deal with us. Do you think it's wise to go out?"

Eli put his hand on Hermann's shoulder. "God's promise is certain. They cannot harm us until our work is completed. They are the ones in danger. Strengthen your faith. You and Brandon will need it after our departure."

Hermann understood but it made him nervous to think about it. He had never shied away from a challenge but this was different and he knew it. He prayed he would be ready.

"Please let Asher know we are leaving for Bethlehem in an hour."

Word reached Besnik about the group's presence in Bethlehem. He had them followed. After his last encounter, he had decided to move with force against the group. He assembled a specialized death squad for a late night assignment.

He had instructed the squad leader to report to him personally the next morning. He felt relieved to hear that the squad leader had arrived.

The man's expression did not look promising as he entered Besnik's office that morning. The man did not speak immediately after sitting down.

"Well?" Besnik asked.

"We were unable to complete our mission."

"Why not? Are your men dead? What happened?"

"Two of my men followed the group to their evening destination. We set up a perimeter to assure that no one left. The house remained under constant surveillance. By midnight all the occupants were asleep. We planned our raid for two-thirty in the morning. Everything seemed perfect to carry out the mission. We had even silenced any dogs in the area to eliminate any detection." The man stopped to take a breath.

"We approached the house from four different positions. About eighteen meters from the house we encountered their security detail."

"Wait, what? What security detail? You never said anything about a security detail."

"They weren't there before. As I said before, we kept the house under constant surveillance. But suddenly they were there all around us. There were well over a hundred of them."

"What kind of security team were they?"

"Yeah, well that's the other thing. They were not only overwhelming in number and surrounding us, they were huge. On average every one of them were at least eight feet tall. We were commanded to surrender our arms and leave. The situation left us with no other choice."

"Wait a minute, this doesn't make any sense. Where did these men come from? Why didn't you spot them earlier? And why did you surrender without a fight?"

"I don't have an answer for the first question. It's like they came out of nowhere. As for the second question…" He paused to consider his words. "My men are hardened professionals. But the enemy we encountered were…they were frightening. Every one of my men had the same reaction. They dropped their weapons in terror and ran."

Besnik didn't know what to think. The look in the man's eyes said it all. The confident killer had been replaced with a broken and confused man. With hard eyes and a wave of his hand Besnik wanted the man out of his presence. The squad leader sheepishly departed.

Besnik's only consolation came from the fact that he had not informed the Chancellor of his plan. He pressed his fingers hard across his forehead. The more he thought about it the more he seethed. He shook his fists into the air and whispered through gritted teeth, "Why is this so hard?"

✡  ✡  ✡

For two weeks the group walked the streets of Bethlehem. Eli practically pleaded in his warnings to the people. They received little response. After every message Eli would look over to Moshe with tears across his face and shrug his shoulders. Both of them sensed it. A foreboding reality was closing in around the world and so many didn't even realize it.

✡  ✡  ✡

Besnik reviewed construction reports on the Jewish Temple and his phone rang. He had expected the call, surprised that it hadn't come earlier.

"Yes, your Excellency, and how are you today?"

"Yacov you know why I'm calling?"

"I just finished reviewing the construction details on the Jerusalem monument. Everything is on schedule for your visit."

"Really? Everything? Do you think I do not have eyes and ears in your region? Those two renegade loud mouths are still running around loose. You do know that they aren't the only ones stirring up their propaganda. We've identified over one hundred and forty thousand similar advocates. But your two are at the center of it all. Their continued presence fuels the others. And how is that possible when the rest of the world's networks are down?"

"We've not been able to identify how they are communicating. Phone communications are closely monitored. As for the social networks…"

"Yes I know." D'bar interrupted him. "They'll be up in the next day or two. I'm making a worldwide speech to celebrate it. I don't want those two ruining it. Get them under control or you will force me to come down and take care of it myself. Trust me when I say, you don't want that. It's the end of November and I am coming in February. You are running out of time."

The line went dead. Besnik mulled over the Chancellor's words. The more he thought the more he understood his predicament. He realized that the time for subtlety had ended. The time for overwhelming brute force had come. He merely had to decide when and where.

✡ ✡ ✡

The last day in Bethlehem had come. The next day they would move on to Ramat Rachel a kibbutz community south of Jerusalem. Hermann seemed anxious and waited for Eli with Asher by the vehicle. Moshe and Brandon were finishing their farewells to their hosts.

When Eli walked out, Hermann went right to him. "Can we talk?" Eli nodded.

"I received word from a contact in Bethlehem."

Eli chuckled. "Hermann you do surprise me. Even now you have contacts. Nevertheless, what troubles you?"

"There's something going on in Bethlehem. They are evacuating the same area where we are going. It's like someone knows our plans."

Eli put his arms around his shoulder. "More likely they have watched us and seen our pattern. It wouldn't be that difficult."

Hermann shook his head. "But don't you see? They are evacuating because they are planning an attack and don't want collateral injuries."

Eli looked directly at Hermann. "It means they are getting desperate. But they will not succeed. Don't fear, the Lord is watching over us. Now, let's go."

Besnik did have something planned. He had planted an assault team, of over two hundred heavily armed men in the evacuated homes. A weaponized drone flew overhead. Even if property or some of the team were lost in the assault, this mission would not fail.

As they drove to their destination, Asher noticed things that piqued his curiosity. He wanted to point them out, but Eli had instructed him about not getting diverted.

Besnik positioned his command station two kilometers away. He watched everything through the camera mounted on the drone. It pleased him that everything was going according to plan. He looked over to the team commander. "Have them move in as soon as they park their car. I want this done quickly." The commander nodded.

Asher pulled over to park the vehicle. "Sirs, the area looks deserted. Where is everyone?"

Eli looked at Moshe and nodded. "Hermann, Brandon, Asher, you three stay in the vehicle."

Eli and Moshe exited and walked a few feet to the rear of the vehicle. Eli looked up and spotted the drone. He pointed directly at it and shouted. "Do you suppose that the Lord does not know and see? It is you who sees and does not comprehend."

At that moment Moshe spotted armed men running towards them one hundred meters away. He bowed his head and whispered a short prayer.

The men began to lower their weapons to fire.

Moshe took the Rod and swept it at arms length in a circle.

Besnik moved closer to the screen and watched in shock. He couldn't believe his eyes. As the man whirled around his long stick, fire seemed to be flying out of his mouth.

"Widen the view!" Besnik shouted.

The fire attacked all of the assault team. Even if they ran around corners the fire chased them. The fire not only attacked them, it completely engulfed and consumed them. Panning the entire area Besnik spotted no survivors.

Besnik stood back from the monitor. His mind boiled. He turned to the commander. "Does the missile have a camera on it?"

"Yes sir."

"Good I want to see it up close. Fire the missile."

"But sir, it is a very powerful weapon. We agreed only to use it as a last resort."

Besnik stood face to face with the man. "Commander, I gave you an order. I will accept full responsibility. Now, fire the missile!"

The commander nodded to the technician. The technician acknowledged. "The weapon is launched."

Besnik moved in close to watch.

Moshe heard the sound and looked up. He nodded. He took the Rod and pointed it at the incoming missile.

Besnik backed away from the monitor. The technician checked his instruments.

"Commander, we have a problem."

"What is it?"

"The weapon is malfunctioning."

"What is it?"

"We've lost telemetry control and it has armed itself."

"How is that possible?"

"I don't know sir. I'm running diagnostics right now."

"What is the weapon's course?"

The technician checked the computer readings.

"It's locked on us, sir!"

Besnik watched the screen in shock. He knew.

"It will strike in a few sec…"

Moshe and Eli watched the smoke rise in the distance and sighed deeply.

# Chapter 34

**D**'bar read the report on Besnik. He growled out his anger. "Idiot."

He thought for a moment and then knew his next step. It would take a day or two, but he had no choice. He sent out the notice.

✡ ✡ ✡

As they made their way through the streets of Ramat Rachel, the curious came out. Rumors of the events in Bethlehem had spread. The news reported the incident as a training exercise accident. As instructed, they highlighted the fact of no civilian casualties.

Unofficial narratives leaked out portraying an all-together different narrative. The two who now walked their streets played a central part in those stories. The small crowds came out to listen in both fear and inquisitiveness. In caution they listened from a distance.

Concurrently, the government made an announcement that the social media network had re-launched. That news alone reduced the crowds even more. People found themselves once again glued to their devices. By the end of the week the group walked the streets with almost no one coming out. Yet, Eli faithfully and loudly made his proclamations as they walked.

That night, the group gathered for prayer after the evening meal. Brandon felt compelled to say something.

"With the reaction you have received lately, how do you guys stay motivated?"

Both Asher's and Hermann's facial expressions communicated equal curiosity.

Eli and Moshe traded looks. Eli answered. "This does not surprise us. We were told to expect this reaction. In fact, after tomorrow we expect to see a greater hostility. You should as well."

Hermann rubbed his chin. "I began to ask why but then I caught myself. I remember my own blindness. Pity's not the right word. It makes me sad for them. They are helpless and hopeless at the same time."

Moshe nodded. "Let's hope some see before it's too late."

✡  ✡  ✡

Unlike other times, as the council members entered the room, D'bar sat in his seat. Seeing him, they rushed to take their seats. When the final member took his seat, they glanced at each other waiting. D'bar busied himself with papers and never looked up.

Finally he placed his hands over the stack of papers. Without looking up, "Thank you all for coming on such short notice. I'm sure you all know of the loss of our associate, the Middle-Eastern Regional Transition Czar, Yacov Besnik. Despite what you may have heard in the media, Yacov died out of his own negligence. He acted foolishly and paid the price."

D'bar looked up to scan the members. "Nonetheless, it is a strategic loss. That region is a hot bed of trouble that feeds resistance elsewhere. So for the time being, I will take charge of the region until I can find an adequate replacement."

One of the members raised his hand. "Yes, speak up."

"Your Excellency, earlier Besnik had sent out an invitation to an event in Jerusalem in February. Can you tell us about that?"

"Yes, of course. As you all know, as part of the regional peace agreement, the Jews have rebuilt their holy shrine in Jerusalem. They have begun using it but the upcoming event is the formal dedication. I have decided to make a change on my Monument of Unity, which I spoke of earlier. It is finished, but not in place. As part of the security for my appearance I will close the Temple grounds for several days preceding my arrival. It is then that I will have the monument placed inside the Temple itself. What better way to make the point that the ways of the past are over."

"But Excellency, won't that cause intense reaction?"

Fire filled his eyes. "Let anyone try. I will make sure my presence is felt in overwhelming fashion. We must demonstrate to the world that resistance to the new reality is futile."

D'bar smiled in self-satisfaction. "Perhaps Besnik's departure is providential. This region and the world will come to see the full force of my power. After all, what I bring is Peace, Prosperity and Order."

D'bar looked across the table. "Is that not right gentlemen?"

Like so many parrots they echoed the chant. "Peace, Prosperity, and Order."

"I'm so glad I can count on your undying support. Read the instructions I have provided for each of you. Good day." D'bar got up and walked out, leaving a room of nervous leaders.

✿  ✿  ✿

The group waited by the vehicle. They wondered about the day's destination and what would follow.

Eli and Moshe walked straight to the vehicle and got in. The others looked at each other and followed suit.

Eli immediately asked. "Asher, do you know where the Israeli Broadcasting Corporation is located?"

"I think it's up in the northwest part of the city. They recently moved into a newer location. I'll find it."

While Asher checked a map, Brandon couldn't hold his curiosity. "Why are we going there?"

Moshe answered. "As you all noticed, people stopped coming out. They are now all reattached to their mobile medias. We have a message to deliver and we are going to utilize the means available to us."

Hermann smiled. "Earlier when I watched you, I always knew you were savvy. But now I admire it even more."

They all laughed.

When they arrived, Eli and Moshe stood right across the street from the front door. Eli immediately began. His voice thundered loudly.

Someone on a second story happened to look out. "Hey guys, come look at this. Isn't that the two guys who have been causing so much trouble?"

A few people joined him at the window. "Yeah, that's them. Maybe we ought to go check it out."

An executive noticed the group standing by the window. He walked over to see. He watched for a moment before turning to one of his associates. "Sam, get a camera crew. We're going down and doing some filming."

"But isn't there a restriction of covering these two?" The young man wanted coverage for his own career.

"Well, I'd rather get forgiveness than seek permission. Anyway, I heard that when these guys pop up they put on a show. I don't want to miss it. So, let's get with it."

Within minutes a crew stood across from the *Two*, filming. Hermann had to laugh when he saw them come out. The media were notorious at manipulating events. Now Eli and Moshe were playing it against them. He loved it. Some of the crew even used their private mobile devices to capture the moment.

Eli looked directly at the camera crew. "You purveyors of information pretend to declare reality. Yet, the world has abandoned reality and escaped into a world that robs them of the truth. For truth can be both liberating and harsh. But if mankind will turn to the ultimate reality, they can be set free. If they do not, the truth accuses them."

Eli looked over to Moshe briefly before continuing. "Hear and comprehend the words of the Lord."

> "For God will bring every act to judgment, everything which is hidden, whether it is good or evil. Behold, the LORD'S hand is not so short that it cannot save; nor is His ear so dull that it cannot hear. But your iniquities have made a separation between you and your God, and your sins have hidden *His* face from you so that He does not hear." [22]
>
> Seek the LORD, all you humble of the earth who have carried out His ordinances; seek righteousness, seek humility. Perhaps you will be hidden in the day of the LORD'S anger." [23]

Moshe lifted the Rod and pointed it directly at the man filming with his mobile phone. The man suddenly felt the device heat up in his hand and he dropped it. Moshe and Eli then lowered their heads, turned and walked away.

The executive present frowned. "What was that all about?"

The man picked up his phone and checked it for damage. With shock in his voice, "What?"

Someone saw the look on his face. "What is it?"

"Nothing.'" The man quickly placed his hand over the screen. He looked around to see if anyone had viewed what appeared on his phone.

A young woman looked at her phone and screamed. "No!"

Someone else checked their phone and shouted. "What in the world?"

As the group drove away from the area, Brandon had to ask. "What happened back there?"

Moshe answered. "Mankind has surrendered themselves to the Babylon of social media and the cyber-world. They go there seeking to find meaning. They have literally laid out their whole lives in that existence. Today the Lord has exposed them to the truth. He has chosen to humble them so that some may repent and come to Him before it is too late. Soon there will be no escape from the judgment of the truth."

Hermann didn't understand. "Okay, but what happened exactly?"

"For those of us who know the Lord, He has separated us from the judgment of our sins. They are forgiven. They are gone. But today, the Lord has opened the floodgates. All the individual information people have on their devices and in the cyber-world is pouring out in the open. What was hidden is hidden no more."

Brandon and Hermann's eyes widened. Brandon whispered, "Who can stand under the weight of such revelation?"

"Only those covered by the redeeming payment of God in Christ that takes away our sins."

Everyone remained silent for the rest of the drive out of Jerusalem.

✡ ✡ ✡

The shock waves moved quickly around the world. Increased cases of suicide and violence spread and increased. Anger, retribution, revenge, despair, and isolation, these and many more reactions came as a result of the unveiling of people's lives worldwide. Within two days the web networks again shut down, but the damage had been done. Countless lives had been turned upside down or laid to ruin. Several local governments toppled by both the revelations or through reactionary violence.

After a week of staggering informational bombshells, D'bar formed a response. He appeared in a supposed spontaneous Q & A interview. In truth, D'bar completely controlled the appearance.

"Chancellor, I want to thank you for agreeing to come on live and respond to the latest crisis facing the world." The attractive female interviewer's face expressed deep concern.

"Molly, I welcome the opportunity. First of all, let me say that we in the government are both grieved and appalled. We are grieved at the senseless exploitation of privacy that has occurred. While some crimes have come out, for the most part, we have witnessed the violation of sacred and intimate information." The female nodded with a look of empathy.

"Secondly, I am appalled at this heartless act of terrorism. These monsters attacked us at the most vulnerable point of our souls. What gives them the right to rape our private lives for their own enjoyment."

The interviewer lowered her head. When she looked back up, she was wiping away tears. "Chancellor, I know you speak for all of us. Everyone I know has felt the sense of being violating. Do we have any idea who is behind this horrible act of terrorism?"

"The investigation is continuing. And while the method is still unclear, we have evidence pointing to some persons of interest."

The woman nodded. "Yes, in fact we have some footage provided that shows the first reported instance of the attack. Let's look at it."

The video clearly displayed the *Two* standing in the street. Moshe stood pointing the Rod and then the reporter shouting as he looked at his mobile phone.

"And you are certain that this is the first incident?"

"Oh yes. The electronic signature is very clear. The attack started here and exponentially spread across the globe."

"And what measures are being taken?"

"Now that the networks are shut down. We are destroying the contaminated data and will reboot through backups as soon as possible. Security reinforcements are under construction with a view to privacy. We are also seeking to apprehend the terrorists and identify their cells worldwide. They cannot hide from us."

The woman smiled at the last response. "Chancellor it certainly makes us feel safe knowing that you and others are working to solve and rectify this situation."

"Molly, we are doing our best. Our main goal is to save our planet from the assault on our well-being. I know you heard it before, but we really mean it. Peace, Prosperity, and Order."

She nodded and repeated it. "Yes indeed, Peace, Prosperity, and Order. Thank you sir."

The cameras went off. D'bar smiled. "Molly, that was excellent work. You convinced me and the whole world as well."

Almost giggling, "Excellency, thank you so much for the privilege. And truly, thank you for watching out for us."

D'bar smiled as he walked off the stage. He loved how easily people were manipulated. His plan was succeeding. In the next few weeks he would have complete control. Now to put his final solution into play.

# Chapter 35

In the remaining weeks in the judgment of humiliation, the *Two* and the group remained completely out of the public eye. The government launched an intensive search for them. The group accepted the hospitality and refuge among the faithful. Eli made it clear that they were not in danger but nonetheless they exercised caution on behalf of those who sheltered them.

Knowing that their time was short, Eli and Moshe used this time to intensify Hermann's and Brandon's training. The *Two* understood what leadership role both men would play in the future. They each paired off in the training, Eli with Brandon and Moshe with Hermann. In those weeks, the bond between the men knitted like fired metal. After a few weeks you would have thought they had known each other for a lifetime.

✡   ✡   ✡

In a partnership of mutual benefit, D'bar had groomed and promoted a religious confederate. The enticement of power never ceased to impress D'bar in its ability to compromise the mighty.

D'bar had chosen this unlikely ally for a specific purpose. D'bar's plan needed something more from the populace. He needed their adulation. He chose a religious leader as the best advocate to promote such devotion. Culture had already abandoned the other gods. They loved to worship celebrity. D'bar would now offer himself.

He smiled as he thought how easily he manipulated people. They truly were like sheep.

✡ ✡ ✡

Eli and Brandon sat on a back porch. Brandon could sense a difference in Eli's mood. "Brother, what is it? You seem extra burdened today."

Eli smiled. "You've gotten to know me pretty well haven't you? We need to begin some preparations for what comes next. Tomorrow the government will announce the re-establishment of the network. The people don't realize that they have only tightened the grip they have on their lives."

Brandon nodded in agreement. "So what does that mean for us?"

"I want you to begin instructing the faithful. In three weeks the next and last judgment is coming. They need to prepare. They will have neither power nor light for seven days. Whether it's fuel or batteries, they need to secure enough to last for one day only. Beyond that, the Lord will supply. This event will affect the entire world."

Brandon thought for a second. "No power I can understand. But what do you mean, no light?"

Eli only smiled.

Brandon nodded. "I get it. Don't spoil the surprise?"

"One more thing. I know that you have secured your communications and you need to maintain that. But I want you to find a way to leak something out. At mid-day on the last day, we will be on the Mount of Olives."

Brandon squinted his face. "But won't that invite a confrontation?"

"Yes, most likely. The Lord wants us to make the message very clear. His judgment is coming and there will be no excuses."

Brandon felt his heart beating quickly. He nodded as he listened to the sobering words.

✡  ✡  ✡

A security chief knocked on D'bar's door. "Enter."

As the man sheepishly entered, D'bar's face displayed his irritation. "Don't simply stand there, what is it?"

"Your Excellency, we have intercepted a coded message from the network of the insurgents." The man waited for a response.

D'bar puffed out his disgust. "Well, are you going to tell me or must I interrogate you for the answer?"

"No of course not." His hands shook as he lifted the memo to read it. "Leaving out all of the religious messaging it seems that the two leaders are planning an appearance."

He confirmed the information before handing it to the Chancellor. "The time is on the memo and the place is the Mount of Olives east of the old city."

D'bar looked at the memo. "Those fools, they have created a trap for themselves. I want that area secured from all directions. I want overwhelming force with no means of escape, is that understood?"

"Absolutely your Excellency. I will have plans drawn up immediately for your review. As the Americans once said, shock and awe."

D'bar smiled. "Make sure that's exactly what happens. The dedication is coming and I want these trouble makers out of the way."

The chief felt at ease. He smiled. "Yes sir. All of the religious authorities have been informed of the enhanced security preparations. We will have adequate time to set up the monument and secure the area for the dedication."

"Excellent. Make sure those two rascals are eliminated and you will reap a great reward."

"I will do it."

D'bar nodded and waved the man to leave. Once he had exited the room, D'bar closed his eyes and breathed slowly as he chanted dark phrases. The lights in the room flickered before dimming to near darkness. The air became cold and damp. D'bar continued his chanting.

As if coming from out of the floor, a dark voice whispered. "You are."

D'bar responded. "I am."

He repeated it over and over until the words slowly appeared on the walls as if etched by clawed fingers. A dark shadow began to emerge up from the ground. It floated along the wall and began to circle D'bar as he continued to chant the words.

The form grew and swirled around D'bar in a whistling dark mass. The speed intensified until it knocked D'bar face down on the ground. The mass then rose and fell upon him.

D'bar screamed as if crushed by an immense weight. He remained on his face for several minutes. When he finally arose he stood straight up with his eyes closed. He inhaled as if he were taking in the entire air of the room. When he finally opened his eyes in the darkened room they glowed like burning coals. D'bar twisted his neck muscles feeling the power that now penetrated every cell in his body.

He took another deep breath before slowly speaking the words once again. A dark voice spoke the blasphemy. "I AM."

✡   ✡   ✡

The crisp morning air gave no hint to the coming events. Brandon and Hermann spent the early morning in prayer. They both knew of an impending judgment but little else. It made for a somber morning. When Eli and Moshe emerged from their time together they greeted the group with quiet smiles.

Eli cleared his throat, "Well gentlemen, let us go do the Lord's bidding."

Asher had chosen the route. The group loaded up and headed out."

✡ ✡ ✡

D'bar had decided to monitor the assault from an office north of the old walled city. He sat and reviewed the plan. The security chief stood nearby awaiting D'bar's assessment.

"The plan looks very good."

"Thank you, your Excellency. A heavily armed contingent of five hundred men has every entrance and egress covered. They will be out of sight until the targets enter the zone. They will then move in and await the go order."

D'bar smiled. "Excellent. I have a camera drone that will capture the whole thing. We will delay broadcasting it until we have edited it to our liking. This is going to be beautiful. When this is done, no one will question my power and authority."

D'bar looked at his watch. "If they are on schedule this should start up in the next hour. This is going to be spectacular." His grin hid none of his evil intent.

✡ ✡ ✡

Leaving Abu Dis, Asher drove north before heading west toward the mount. He looked into the rearview mirror. "Sirs, where exactly on the mount do you wish to go?"

Eli answered while looking out the window. "Do you know where the Tomb of the Prophets is?"

"Oh, yes sir. I have been there many times."

"That is our destination."

Moshe saw the questions on Brandon and Hermann's faces. "It is the reported tomb of the prophets Haggai, Zechariah, and Malachi."

296

"Very good, sir. You could be a guide yourself."

"Not hardly, Asher. Eli told me all about it." The small humor helped ease the moment.

Nearing the Chapel of the Ascension, Asher felt his nerves tingling. "Sirs, you do realize that there are very limited ways in and out? This is a very popular place and the traffic is absent. It almost seems like a trap."

"That is their plan my friend. Do not be troubled. They are the ones who should run away in fear." Looking up he spotted the drone. "But they will not."

"Asher, find yourself a spot to park. We will walk down to the tomb. As you said, there's no one out so there are plenty of spaces." Eli seemed calm but saddened.

Brandon had to ask. "Brother Eli, you look so troubled. What is it? It's not yet time is it?"

Eli looked at Brandon. His half smile tempered by his sadness. He glanced over to Moshe as his eyes moistened. "So many people are going to die today. I wish there was some other way, that's all."

Moshe's eyes held back their own tears. He simply nodded his agreement.

✡   ✡   ✡

"Excellency, they have passed all the check points. The units are on the move awaiting your orders."

Looking at the video feed D'bar grinned. "They have come to a stop. What is that location?"

"It is the Tomb of the Prophets, sir."

"Those fools have cut themselves off. Look at them. They're walking down to the place. We'll have them completely surrounded. Move everyone in and ready. Let them start their little show and then we'll slaughter them."

"Yes sir."

Asher remained with the vehicle. Reaching the tomb, the four stood outside, circled and prayed. After the prayer, Brandon and Hermann walked away but stood nearby. Eli and Moshe turned and faced the city.

Moshe heard the drone. "They are watching."

Eli nodded. "They shall see and hear."

Eli took a deep breath. "O Jerusalem. The prophets come to you and proclaim the word of the Lord and yet you do not listen. You forge alliance with the Lie and thus share its pain."

He looked directly at the drone hovering high, between them and the city. His voice rang out as if amplified and shot out toward the city.

> "Enter the rock and hide in the dust from the terror of the LORD and from the splendor of His majesty. The proud look of man will be abased and the loftiness of man will be humbled, and the LORD alone will be exalted in that day. The pride of man will be humbled and the loftiness of men will be abased; and the LORD alone will be exalted in that day," [24]

✡ ✡ ✡

D'bar heard every word. His face distorted in rage. "Now!"

The chief passed the order. From every direction hundreds of men poured out from their positions.

Eli saw them and sighed. Moshe lifted the Rod above his head and stretched it out. He then spun around in a circle. A wave of fire flew out toward the attackers. Before they could lift their weapons, in mere seconds the flames covered and consumed them in place.

D'bar fell back into his chair. Everyone in the control room watched in stunned silence.

✡ ✡ ✡

Eli again looked up toward the drone. "The Lord is the Light of the world. Yet, you have chosen to walk in darkness. For seven days in darkness you shall remain. This is the declaration of the Lord."

Moshe took the Rod in both hands. He raised it high and then brought in down in a thud.

Immediately, everything went dark. In that instant across the world, all electricity ceased to work. Simultaneously, as if a veil had fallen over the sky, the sun was blotted out. Even the stars could not penetrate the blackened sky across the earth.

Eli and Moshe looked toward the city. Small pockets of candle lit windows began to appear.

They turned toward Brandon and Hermann who stood dazed in the dark with their mouths open. Moshe raised the Rod and it became a torch. They used it to find their way back up to the road. Asher waited faithfully. He had locked himself in when the troops ran past him down the hill.

They all got in the vehicle and drove out of the city. Cars headlights lit the road. People stood outside their houses staring up at the shroud of darkness that had replaced the mid-day sky.

✡   ✡   ✡

D'bar screamed. "Get the lights back on!" Not wanting to trip in the darkness, he remained seated.

"There's no power sir. I have a crew looking into it, but they are first trying to locate some flashlights." Someone responded.

It took a moment before someone remembered that the control room had windows. "Why is it so dark?"

The chief answered. "Because we lost power you idiot."

"But sir, it's mid-day and there's no light coming in through the windows."

Several people made their way to the windows. The sky was coal black. Only scattered tiny flickers of light peppered the landscape.

In the room a woman voiced what everyone thought. "What in God's name is happening?"

D'bar sat in his chair seething. If anyone had approached him, they would have seen the hate pouring out of his glowing red eyes.

Across the city and circling the globe, a mixture of screams and soft wailing rose to meet the black air. The last of the judgments from the *Two* had arrived.

# Chapter 36

For seven days the darkness prevailed. No light from the sun, moon, or stars penetrated the black veil encompassing the earth. The worldwide electrical grids also suffered complete failure. Scientists could not adequately describe or explain the phenomena. Hypothesis ranged from space debris to rapid shifts in the earth's magnetic fields. No theories provided a coherent solution. In reality, the event unnerved the experts. This event produced the emotions associated with encountering the unknown.

Reactions among the populace varied. Some exploited the event and exercised wanton violence and lawlessness. Riots exploded worldwide. Every major city fell victim to the chaos. The darkness provided the perfect cover for the rampage of evil across the globe. For many cities, the fires of destruction provided the only illumination in the stygian night.

Many experienced raw fear. Rumors of the end of the world, invasions from space, or other explanations spread like a virus in the hearts of many. The lack of authoritative communication only added to the horrid blackness. Accounts of phantom visitations fueled the terror of the unbroken night. An apocalyptic panic drove many into paralysis. Mass cases of suicide pacts grew as the days passed.

Contrasted to the prevailing milieu, the flickering presence of hope pierced the darkness. Prepared from beforehand, pockets of the faithful shared their light. Songs of peace and praise could be heard penetrating the black nights. In the darkest of nights, souls were encountering a light so vivid and strong it could be compared to the blind receiving sight. Wails of fear were transformed into tearful joy. The story of the light conquered the night and souls were set free.

✡ ✡ ✡

"The battle is coming." Eli's voice almost trembled as he uttered the words.

The days of darkness allowed them to slip out of the city. Moved by the Spirit of the Lord, they traveled southeast of Jerusalem away from the turmoil. Six days of darkness passed. One day remained. The four of them crouched by a fire.

Brandon and Hermann nervously sat silent. They understood the current situation. The reality of it bore down on them like an impended verdict. Every sense of adequacy melted away and left them withered by what lay ahead.

Eli and Moshe also felt the inner trembling. The certainty of coming events pressed hard on their hearts. They both experienced the preference of unexpected death over having read for themselves their fate. Unspoken questions ricocheted in their minds. *"Would it hurt?" "Will I bear it well?" "Would it last long?"* They sensed their resolve eroding. They both felt as if they would collapse any minute in emotional exhaustion.

And so they each sat silent staring into the flickering campfire.

A snickering dark presence sat nearby. Kept at bay by two tall guardians, all he could do was sneer and mock. He felt self-satisfied that his enemy felt shaken. His lust for blood desired satisfaction. His cruel laughter dripped with vile hatred that had no limit.

Suddenly the two guardians straightened themselves before falling to their knees. The dark one turned to look. In holy terror he made a screeching retreat.

Soft footsteps barely disturbed the dry ground. Tender hands touched the shoulders of the two guardians inviting them to rise. "Keep watch."

"Yes Lord."

Moshe saw Him first. He gasped before falling to his face. Eli quickly joined his friend on the ground. Brandon and Hermann looked in shock. Their whole bodies trembled not knowing how to react. Quickly they joined the *Two* on the ground.

"Arise, faithful servants of the Most High." His voice familiar yet so new, lifted their hearts and faces from the ground. Each whispered, "Lord."

"The day of testing is coming for you all. I come so that you may know. You are not alone."

They all bowed their heads, feeling their inadequacy.

The Lord smiled, knowing their hearts. He walked over to Brandon and Hermann. He put His hands on their shoulders before touching their chins to lift their faces.

"My two jewels of grace."

Hearing the words, both men's eyes filled with tears. The power and truth of the words showered their souls in light.

"You are My workmanship. Do not fear for the days ahead. They will be filled with times of trouble, but I am with you. I will guide you and give you strength. And you in turn will lead many and provide them with courage until I return. Help one another and do not fear. Look to the heavens and await My return. My strength will be perfected in your weakness and My light will trace your every step. Do not fear."

The Lord stepped between them. He pressed their heads together in a circle. Softly He whispered a gentle prayer. Their souls lifted beyond anything imaginable as they heard their own name from the lips of their Savior.

When He had finished, He looked at them. "I love you both. You shall see Me when I return."

He smiled as He patted them on the shoulders. "Now I must speak to My *Two* messengers. Peace to you both."

Without further instruction, Brandon and Hermann turned and walked away arm in arm.

The *Two* looked at the Lord. Understanding His eyes, they ran to the Him and He embraced them. After a brief moment, the *Two* stood facing the Lord.

The Lord placed His arms on their shoulders. "I understand the anguish you are sensing. It is never easy to face your own death."

They felt embarrassed that He compared their situation to His. Without looking up Eli whispered. "Oh Master, our position is nothing in relation to Your..."

The Lord stopped Him. "But the agony of soul is real, is it not?" They both nodded.

"I am so proud of both of you. You have carried out your missions faithfully. Do not allow the enemy to steal the moment. When the time comes, I will be there with you. Have no doubt in that matter. You have each other and the Spirit. No one can harm you until you have completed My task."

He saw the relief on their faces and smiled. "Trust Me. Your questions are resolved in that trust. Now, I have some instructions. In three days you will go to the Temple and make your final proclamation. All truth must be accomplished. Do not allow fear to touch your hearts. You will bear witness once more and the whole world will see. The battle comes, the victory is Mine and you will see it. Soon your hearts will taste the glory of your rewards."

Even in the dim light His eyes glowed in indescribable brilliance. "I am so proud of you both, My Two Olive Branches."

He vanished.

They could hardly feel the ground beneath their feet. They fell to their knees in quiet worship.

✡ ✡ ✡

Emergency generators maintained minimal operations for the Chancellor and his team. Communication from his office worldwide remained equally minimal.

During the previous days, D'bar had plotted his response for the moment when light and power were restored. Even in the interim, propaganda leaked out forming the framework for D'bar's plan. It had taken several days, but he now had a means of communicating with the council members. The meeting would soon begin.

D'bar sat before the monitor waiting for the meeting. The flashing light indicated everyone was online.

He took a deep breath and looked directly into the camera.

"Gentleman, we find ourselves in an unprecedented situation. I know that the world and our plan seem to be unraveling. Let me assure you nothing could be further from the truth. The situation has provided us the perfect opportunity to take full control."

He recognized the look. "I understand your doubts. But you need to know that all of this is about to change."

"How?" someone said.

"I am about to destroy the perpetrators of all of this chaos. I have shaped public opinion to make sure that the blame for our misery is clearly connected to them. And then I will destroy them."

Someone asked. "How will you do that when previous attempts have failed?"

D'bar closed his eyes for a moment. He breathed slowly, concentrating on the voice within. He looked back into the camera. The tone of his voice darkened.

"First you will learn and then the world will learn. My power is not to be questioned."

He again closed his eyes. Suddenly each of the council members felt it. Their throats tightened. They each gasped for a breath. They struggled in vain to inhale.

His voice echoed as if through a deep tunnel. "My power has no limits. Do not ever question it. Prepare yourselves to hail my victory and my power. You owe your very breath to me."

He slapped the table in front of him. The fear in their eyes said it all. One by one they all whispered two words, "Yes, Master."

"Excellent. You will receive detailed instructions. The minute the light returns, initiate the campaign. Never doubt me. Peace, Prosperity, and Order." He ended the meeting.

D'bar stared at the blank screen. He stretched out his arms and embraced the darkened air.

Slowly he began chanting ancient and dark words. He swayed as he repeated the arcane ritual. The longer he did it, the darker and colder the room grew. After a time two glowing phosphorous eyes appeared in the corner.

A hissing voice spoke. "Bow before your master."

D'bar fell face down to the ground.

"Many have aspired for it, but the power I give you has never belonged to any man. You are my vessel. Together we shall conquer the enemy and subdue the world."

The phantom moved toward D'bar, its hideous shape only detectable by the glowing edges of its form. It hovered over D'bar like a grotesque mass of pitch-black evil. The simple proximity to D'bar made him shake uncontrollably. When the mass collapsed upon him he convulsed for several minutes.

Finally he lay still. D'bar opened his eyes and scanned the room. He touched his arms and face as if the sensation was new.

Suddenly he grinned. He stretched his arms up into the air. With a wicked shout he uttered only one word. "Yes!"

# Chapter 37

When it happened, the experts chose silence over empty or embarrassing explanations. To the very second, seven days from the moment the world went dark, the heavens opened up. The sun appeared, the moon, and the stars were visible. Reactions ranged from shock, fear and excitement. The world also regained full power and media connections. Worldwide celebrations broke out as the news spread across the globe.

The media played up the return and regaining of order. Stories and news commentaries portrayed D'bar as central to ending the nightmare. They promoted the narrative revealing D'bar's part and his further plans for worldwide security. Strategic placement pointed to his dedication in a week of the Jewish Temple and his message of unity and peace.

On the second day, the next step of the Chancellor's plan began. A barrage of reports launched a searing campaign with one goal in mind. Story after story insinuated the *Two* as the culprits behind the recent worldwide events. They and all who followed after them were painted as terrorists involved in crimes against humanity. Leaks reported the possibility of trials before the world court.

By the third day worldwide protests erupted demanding that the *Two* be brought to justice. The world had moved from celebrations to seemingly spontaneous pogroms against anyone suspected as associated with the *Two*.

As D'bar watched it all unfold, he couldn't help but smile. The instructions he had received had worked perfectly. The world hated the *Two*. The campaign would force them to come out of hiding. And as promised, when they did he would crush them.

✡   ✡   ✡

The group had spent the three days in fasting and prayer. They were aware of the current climate. None of it surprised them. It all made sense to them. Each of them had their own inner battles concerning what lay ahead.

On the last night they gathered around a table. They shared a simple meal in silence. Afterwards, Eli led them in celebrating communion. The humble beauty of the time lifted their hearts in hope. The sublime worship completed, they sat silent for a moment.

Ever so quietly Moshe began to hum a slow melodic tune. He then added the words he remembered so well.

> *Protect the time*
> *I walk in darkness*
> *Provide a light*
> *To guide my way.*
> *And if by chance*
> *The darkness find me,*
> *Provide the light*
> *To lead me home.*
> *Lead me home.*
> *Lead me home.*
> *Give me light*
> *To lead me home.*

*And in my heart*
*I hear You calling*
*To take the hand*
*That guides my way.*
*In every breath*
*I trust the promise*
*The one*
*That takes me safe to You.*
*Lead me home.*
*Lead me home.*
*Give me light*
*To lead me home.*

At the conclusion they were all looking up at the ceiling. It seemed to them that they could almost hear distant voices echoing the tune. They each took a deep breath, got up and went to bed with unexplainable peace.

✡ ✡ ✡

Security forces all across the city were on high alert. Word had gone out to inform the Chancellor if the *Two* were spotted. A "no action" order had been issued. Only by command of the Chancellor would any steps to approach or apprehend the suspects be taken. Anyone disobeying the order would face immediate execution.

✡ ✡ ✡

As Asher drove toward Jerusalem from the east, he awaited final instructions from Eli. Everyone noticed the increased security forces at almost every intersection.

Hermann noticed Asher's apprehension. "Don't worry Asher. If I know D'bar, none of these forces will apprehend us. He has something spectacular in mind."

Eli nodded. "Asher bring us into the city along the southeast section of the Old City. I want you to drop us off on the Ruta Haofel just past Zachariah's Tomb. You know where I mean?"

"Oh yes sir. I know it well."

"Good." Eli looked to Brandon. "Only Moshe and I will be getting out. I want you and Hermann to begin alerting the faithful to prepare to leave the city. You know what's coming."

Eli's took a deep swallow. "You're too important at this point. Come back in three days. We'll look for you."

They each shared uncomfortable smiles.

✡  ✡  ✡

"Headquarters, this is station 27. The suspects have been spotted. They are heading into the city from the east. They seemed to be heading towards the Old City. I have assigned a tail on their vehicle."

D'bar responded quickly. "Excellent. Have them light it up with a laser marker. Our drones should pick it up."

✡  ✡  ✡

Passing Absolom's Pillars and approaching Zachariah's Tomb, Asher slowed down. He turned on the caution lights as he pulled over.

No one in the vehicle knew what to say. Finally Hermann spoke. "Dear Brothers, thank you so much for helping me find a way home." He broke.

Brandon struggled to speak. "I too am thankful to God for your guidance. We pray for you. Pray for us." He too broke.

Eli and Moshe each took a deep breath. In unison they spoke. "We will see you in three days."

The *Two* got out of the vehicle. Moshe tapped the roof as a signal to move on. Asher drove off.

✡  ✡  ✡

"Sir, drone six has them. They have exited a vehicle and are walking toward the new Temple area."

D'bar slapped his hands together. He shouted. "Ready my vehicle. Alert all security forces in the area to converge on the

310

Temple area. I should arrive in ten minutes. Wait until I get there."

The orders went out.

✡   ✡   ✡

Eli heard and then spotted the drone. He simply nodded. He and Moshe approached the Temple's outer court. They spotted security forces. The soldiers identified them immediately. As they walked, soldiers gave way to their approach.

When they reached the courtyard, the *Two* looked around before kneeling to pray.

Waiting for the Chancellor's arrival, the soldiers noticed how the sky began to darken. It had been so long since any of them had seen storm clouds. A few speculated the meaning of it all.

✡   ✡   ✡

The sound of screeching tires alerted everyone of the Chancellor's arrival. Over two hundred soldiers now encircled the *Two* who had remained in prayer.

Hearing the fanfare and shouts, the *Two* rose to their feet. Their movement startled many among the security forces. The recent encounter of similar security forces was no secret to them. Many of them were in no hurry to battle powers they did not understand.

As the Chancellor approached, Eli pointed directly at him. "Cursed one, son of the devil, now you come. Like your father, you are a liar and deceiver."

Several closest to D'bar raised their weapons. The Chancellor directed them to lower them. He wickedly grinned.

Eli continued. "Who can deliver you from the judgment to come? No one. For it is declared and it will come to pass."

He then swept his gaze to all of those around them. "Hear and bear witness. The Lie and its Liar has deceived you all. Repent while you can. Soon all the world will see and know. The Lord, He is God. This is our witness. The Lord Himself will vindicate our words."

D'bar's eyes boiled with rage. He listened and waited for the voice within.

Moshe raised the Rod. Thunder rolled loud across the city. Soldiers backed away in fear.

Moshe's hands shook ever so slightly as he slowly lowered the Rod and softly laid it on the ground.

The voice exploded within D'bar's brain. "NOW!"

Startled, he shouted it himself. "NOW!"

Soldiers hesitated.

D'bar raised his hands into the air. Thunder again roared. He pointed toward the *Two*. Lightening crashed down next to the *Two*.

D'bar shouted in a voice that echoed in a volume exceeding expectation. "Kill Them! Kill them NOW!"

The *Two* stood with hands by their sides.

The soldiers suddenly seemed emboldened. Immediately a hail of bullets rained toward the *Two*.

Like straight line rain the bullets poured into the bodies of the *Two*. The force and volume of the barrage held them in the air, not allowing the bodies to fall.

After a minute deluge of gunfire stopped. Almost in slow motion, the bodies of the *Two* crumbled to the ground. The result seemed obvious.

The soldiers looked at each other almost surprised to be alive themselves.

Unexpectedly, someone spotted movement. Eli opened his eyes toward the sky. Through dried lips he whispered his last words. "Let it rain."

Instantly the skies opened up. Rain came down in a torrent.

Soldiers who had heard Eli looked at each other.

D'bar noticed the looks. He shouted. "The curse is lifted. The enemies are dead. We are free! Celebrate the day."

He repeated his shouts until all around him joined in. Soon the crowd of soldiers danced and shouted the words over and over.

The hovering drones had captured the whole event. Editing out the unwanted footage, the celebration chant soon crossed the globe. Rain had begun to fall all over the world.

Footage of people celebrating in the rain and chanting D'bar's words filled the lips of people everywhere. The narrative of the event portrayed D'bar as the one who had brought the *Two* to justice. News stories fawned over his accomplishments and his leadership. The Chancellor had declared that the bodies of the *Two* were to remain unburied in plain view as a reminder of their crimes against humanity.

The Chancellor declared a worldwide holiday. He called it "World Freedom Day." He invited people to share their hopes for the future and to give gifts to one another.

His leadership seemed unquestioned. In either awe or fear, the view in the world seemed unanimous. There was no one like him.

As D'bar watched the news reports he soaked in the adoration. He sat back and closed his eyes. The voice within whispered the delicious chant and he repeated it. "Who is like me? Who can make war against me?"

After repeating it several times, he broke out in a wicked laugh that echoed within the dark room. He barely noticed the snickering dark voice whispering the words to his puppet.

# Chapter 38

The revelry continued unabated day and night across the globe. Fueled by unending propaganda directing the emotions of the populace, a festival of triumph and vengeance prevailed over the hearts of mankind. To insure its success, D'bar had prearranged massive celebratory events everywhere. The nights were filled with all manner of debauchery and drunkenness.

✿   ✿   ✿

Back in Jerusalem the bodies of the *Two* remained where they had fallen. Cameras provided continuous broadcast of the so-called *"Judgment of the Seditious."* Accompanying stories provided footage of the events and catastrophes attributed to them.

D'bar's initial intention included only a twenty-four hour display of their bodies. A failed attempt to remove the bodies changed that plan.

On the first evening one of the security detail was ordered to seize the fallen Rod lying beside the body of Moshe. The second he touched it, the man collapsed and his body immediately burst into flames. Footage of the incident never came out. No one again attempted to get near the bodies.

To prevent any information of the incident leaking out, D'bar had the security detail eliminated. The bodies would remain in the open as decaying reminders. They were left as food for the birds. Yet no birds would even come close. They circled but never descended.

Unseen by anyone, two ominous guardians stood watch over the bodies. Their assigned duty prohibited any disturbance of the bodies. They had personal interest in the ones they protected.

✡ ✡ ✡

The Chancellor's inability to possess the Rod frustrated him endlessly. He remembered Eli's words and the rumors. He could not allow any interference with the upcoming dedication ceremony. He increased security. Film producers created alternate footage for broadcast. The bodies had to be gone before the dedication.

✡ ✡ ✡

The revelry and celebrations provided the needed cover for Brandon and Hermann to re-enter Jerusalem. They knew of the government's desire to apprehend them. Yet, they were equally determined to get back into the city before the third day. They arrived and found refuge within the Old City where the intricate web of streets shielded them from detection.

✡ ✡ ✡

D'bar had yet to assign anyone as RTC to replace Yacov. A young Jordanian had come into prominence. Bashir Weisel had the unique quality of sharing heritage from Jewish and Jordanian parents. He applied himself aggressively to promoting D'bar's plans. The Chancellor had assigned him to handle the security of the dedication. Bashir sat in D'bar's office.

"Young man, I am impressed with your diligence. I have received good reports about your dedication to our program."

"Peace, Prosperity, and Order your Excellency. It is the only way in these troubled times."

"Yes." D'bar stared at the young man trying to detect any duplicity, yet all he saw was another sycophant ready to do his bidding.

"The dedication is in four days and there is an unresolved issue."

"You are speaking of the corpses of the terrorists?"

"Exactly. I would prefer to let them rot in the sun, but I need them removed. They are an affront to the world and to the upcoming dedication."

"Excellency, you need not concern yourself. The bodies will be gone. I will see to it myself."

D'bar cleverly smiled. "Make that happen, Bashir. I see great things in your future."

"It is my honor sir." Bashir raised his right arm. "Peace, Prosperity, and Order."

D'bar bowed his head ever so slightly and returned the salute. He thought to himself. *"This is too easy."*

✡   ✡   ✡

In three days the world had exhausted itself in revelry. The *Two* were dead, the drought had ended and weather patterns worldwide were returning to normal.

As the sun reached mid-day, Bashir watched the bodies from the control center. His plans for disposal of the carcasses were in place. It puzzled him that no birds had attempted to feed on the bodies. Nevertheless, a local mortuary would cremate them by days end.

Bashir knew of the resurrection rumors. He had resources in place to thwart any attempt at a body snatch and claimed resurrection. He would apprehend and expose any such charade. No false resurrections would occur on his watch.

By afternoon, Bashir knew that no attempts to whisk away the bodies were coming. He made his way to the area of the carcasses.

✡ ✡ ✡

Hermann surveyed the so-called concealed security. They had convinced a nearby vender to hire him and Brandon for the day. This put them less than thirty meters from where the *Two* lay. Hermann took one of the guards a complimentary afternoon snack. The guard looked around before accepting it. Walking away Hermann could see the *Two* on the dry bloodstained ground.

✡ ✡ ✡

Seeing the afternoon sun sitting low on the horizon, Bashir grunted. "So much for their fake miracle."

The two guardians spotted Bashir leaving the vehicle and approaching. They glanced at each other.

Bashir walked over to a guard filming the scene to provide some instruction.

"Start with a wide angle and then focus on me. I want this whole thing recorded."

Bashir sneered. "We will make it clear to the world what awaits all who challenge the new reality."

He looked toward the bodies. A rage suddenly coursed through him like wildfire. The inflamed surge of emotions pushed him toward the bodies.

He began to scream. "I will show the whole world. You are dead and dead you will remain."

Marching toward the bodies, he pulled out his pistol. He knew what he wanted to do. A wicked grin crossed his face. He pictured himself putting multiple shots through their heads. It would provide the finishing touch before the bodies were incinerated.

As Bashir moved closer, one of the guardians started to raise his hand. His companion stopped his friend. He signaled for him to wait.

Hermann watched Bashir approaching the bodies. He saw the pistol. He saw the fire in the man's eyes.

A cloud moved over the softened amber light of dusk.

Bashir's march slowed when the ground softly trembled. He regrouped and moved on.

He reached the bodies. He snarled as he cocked the pistol. He looked at the camera and shouted.

"Let everyone see and know what happens to the enemies of our leader and his kingdom."

With all of the guards watching Bashir, Hermann and Brandon moved inside the security zone.

Bashi grinned, relishing the moment. He took aim and emptied the weapon into the heads of the corpses. When he finished he shouted out, "Ha!"

Suddenly the ground shook. Bashir stepped back to regain his balance.

Instantly a bright light crashed down from above and filled the area. Bashir stepped back even further.

He fell completely back when all at once both of the towering guardians were visible. They stood over eight feet tall like ivory towers of power. Bashir trembled in the presence of these enormous warriors.

The two guardians chanced a look at Bashir with a mixture of warning and pity. They quickly shifted their attention toward the *Two*.

An extraordinary breeze glided across the area. It carried the fragrance of newly budded roses.

Brandon and Hermann felt the breeze. They saw the guardians and recognized the fragrance. They immediately locked their gaze on the *Two*.

Bashir's ashen face darted back and forth trying to plan an escape. Movement caught his eye.

Moshe stirred first, quickly followed by Eli. Both men's arms moved to lift and turn themselves over. Each man took in a deep breath before looking around. They rose to their feet. Moshe picked up the Rod.

Bashir began shaking uncontrollably.

The ground again rumbled.

Around the perimeter the guards screamed and dropped their weapons. They too could see the giants standing behind the once dead men. Most of them scattered in panic.

Brandon and Hermann fell to their knees, lifting up praise to God.

Then it came. A voice exploded like the sound of monstrous thunder.

"Come up here."

The ground lifted and fell.

Bashir began to scream as the *Two* commenced to lift off from the ground.

The light around them intensified as the two guardians accompanied them into the clouds.

Brandon and Hermann fell face down. A voice whispered to them. "I am coming soon, prepare and persevere."

For reasons he could not explain, Bashir ventured a glance up into the light surrounding the *Two*. His screams exploded as a sudden flash of the light struck him. He collapsed to the ground.

The rumbling intensified. A remaining guard looked to the east. The earth rolled like an incoming wave. He pointed at it before running away in terror.

Hermann looked up, knowing what to do. He got up and ran toward Bashir. When he reached him, he found the man weeping, trembling and mumbling incoherent sounds. He called Brandon to come help. They each grabbed an arm and lifted him up. Seeing the approaching catastrophe, they ran away practically dragging Bashir.

When the full strength of the quake hit the city, it thundered like a fleet of roaring trucks. The ground growled as it rose and fell in cascades of destruction. Buildings and walls around the city collapsed in dust and death.

Within his command post, D'bar had watched the whole thing. Everyone in the room sat stunned and silent as the events unfolded on the monitors.

D'bar seethed. With every passing second his anger intensified.

Voices whispered as the ferocity of D'bar's rage deepened.

When he spotted Hermann on the screen, he screamed. "Noooooo!"

The quake struck. The lights went out.

✡   ✡   ✡

The light enveloped the *Two* like a cool cushion of peace. Only as they passed through the clouds did they notice the accompanying guardians.

Moshe reached out his hand. "Keeper."

Eli did likewise. "Shamer."

"Our little brothers," they responded.

It wasn't so much that the surrounding light diminished but rather that a greater light overwhelmed it. The *Two* sensed their movement yet didn't feel air striking their bodies.

They also knew when they had arrived. A cloud surrounded them. No, not actually a cloud, instead it was the presence of the glory, best described as light and substance. Moshe remembered it. Shekinah.

In front of them, like a picture coming into focus, they saw a vast crowd stretched out as far as they could see. Some were walking toward them.

As they drew nearer, they saw them clearly.

Eli cried out. "Momma, Dad!" He broke out in a run toward them. Reaching them, the three embraced.

Moshe trembled. There stood Mary and his Mom. On Mary's shoulder jumping up and down, Snoop. He leaped off and ran toward Moshe. Reaching him he leaped up into the air.

Moshe caught Snoop as he scurried over his shoulder.

He squealed out. "Oh Oliver…oh I mean Moshe."

Moshe's smile widened. "No Snoop, please call me Oliver."

"Yes, very well. Oh, Oliver, I have so many stories to tell. I have met your Mary and your mother. Oh, the wonders we have shared. Is not the Maker's joy amazing?"

"Yes Snoop, it truly is."

Mary reached Moshe. She stopped and looked at him a moment.

Moshe trembled at the sight of her. "Oh Mary, my dear sweet Mary, you were so right and more so."

Her eyes glistened in love for the man, her husband, and her brother. They embraced. She whispered softly to him. "My Ollie, my dear Ollie, how the Lord has completed His work in you."

After some moments, Oliver opened his eyes and looked over Mary's shoulder. His lips whispered, "Mom."

Her tender smile said it all.

He released Mary and stood before his Mom. She took his hand. "My dear son, to see with my eyes what the Lord whispered to my heart is beyond words. The Story is written in you and the many you have touched."

They embraced. She whispered words to her son once held back, but now set free.

After a time, Eli and his parents joined Oliver and his group. Then came the procession. They had waited for the right time. Animals from the Island, large and small came forward and issued their manifold greetings and introductions.

Who could say how long this went on? Time seemed to not exist. But after a time, the multitude spanning the horizon shouted, "Greetings in the Name of the Maker and His victory."

Then the very air trembled. Like a sea of parting waters they all began to fall down in a wave. The air filled with a roaring shout. "Hail to the Lamb."

Light became a shadow before Him as He walked among the multitude. Repeated shouts echoed, "Hail to the Lamb!"

When He reached the *Two*, everyone all around lay prostrate on the ground.

"Arise Servants of the Most High. Arise all."

He looked at the *Two*, "Well done, good and faithful servants. Enter into the joy of My victory."

Turning to the multitude, "Rejoice in the celebration of Joy and reunion. Sing the new song, for the Victory of the Lamb comes."

Roaring shouts echoed over the multitudes. "Glory to the Lord Most High. Rejoice in His celebration."

For what seemed like years wrapped up in moments, the celebration continued. Stories and songs bounced from person to person, group to group. With each telling came cheers and worship.

After time undefined, the moment arrived. A thunderous sound of a trumpet exploded in the air. All eyes turned.

A voice rang out. "Prepare, for the Victory of the Lamb has come."

Across the horizons, the redeemed and the host of heaven all clothed in white prepared themselves. As the departure climaxed toward a final moment, shouts of praise and excitement filled the air.

Again, a trumpet sound introduced a declaration. "Victory to the Lamb, let all the earth rejoice."

Antiphonal voices shouted, "Victory to the Lamb, for the fear of His glory comes."

Again a response poured out, "Victory to the Lamb, let the heavens declare the Story."

Multiple times the multitudes shouted, "Victory to the Lamb!"

✡ ✡ ✡

In a large cave, created by the great Jerusalem quake, clusters of the saints gathered. Suffering from hunger and loss they held close to each other. The years had been filled with both adventure and pain. The relentless attack against them had been vicious and wicked. Yet, in spite of their shared persecution and heartache, the communion of love and joy wrapped them in peace and comfort unknown to others.

Time to time, soft weeping would inaugurate whispered prayers. Though the toll was great, the ointment of grace penetrated their hearts and provided sufficient strength.

Whispered songs became a congregation of the praise of light in the darkness.

In a small crevasse near the entrance sat a small group of men.

Bandages covered the right arm of Asher, who nevertheless smiled in effervescent joy.

Young Bashir squinted, trying to read one of the few remaining copies of the Scriptures they possessed.

Brandon and Hermann sat next to each other. They both scanned the ones gathered.

Brandon smiled. His left leg was wrapped in a bloodied bandage. A stray bullet from a recent chase had found its mark.

Hermann had his left arm in a sling. The mob of that same chase had broken the arm with a large rock thrown at them.

The two looked at each other and chuckled. Hermann had to comment. "Look at us."

Brandon responded. "Yeah, who would have ever imagined it? Here we are, a rag tag group of misfits and yet the things we have seen."

"I know. I can hardly remember my life before. It seems like another life. Wait, it was."

They all laughed as they considered their own stories that had brought them there.

Hermann looked out from the cave. "It shouldn't be long." He sighed. "It shouldn't be long at all."

✡ ✡ ✡

In his headquarters, D'bar was overseeing the military campaign. Screaming out orders, his desperation lay just below the surface in the stampede of events crowding in on his empire. His best-laid plans

had collapsed in a torrent of catastrophes. He dared not admit his
fears, but they were there. He trusted no one and hated anyone who
dared question his power. But only his arrogance powered him. He
realized that even the previous power he had sensed, mocked him.

All of this together inflamed his vile heart of evil against everyone
around him.

One of his newest assistants came into the room with his head
bowed low.

Seeing the defeat in the man's face infuriated D'bar all the more.

"What?" he screamed.

"Excellency, we have been unable to locate Lanzig and his
associates."

"But you had them. Worthless. All of you are worthless. One
simple thing and you can't accomplish it."

His rage finally exploded. "No, no, no!" He reached for his pistol
and shot the man.

The ground trembled.

✿　✿　✿

Those huddled in the cave felt the ground move. It did not
frighten them. Their hearts quickened as they sensed something. The
cave didn't seem as dark as before. Someone whispered, "He's
come."

✿　✿　✿

In D'bar's headquarters, those watching quickly backed off from
the monitors. Someone shouted, "What's wrong with the sky?"

The thick walls of the bunker could not hold it back. The room
exploded with light.

D'bar screamed, "Noooooo!"

✿　✿　✿

Some to terror, some to praise, every story is engulfed into one
Story.

Light.

In the end, everyone will know and understand The Story.

# QUOTATIONS NOTED

1. Isaiah 29:15
2. Isaiah 43:10-13
3. Isaiah 45:5,6
4. Isaiah 51:12
5. Isaiah 66:18,19
6. Isaiah 64:1,2
7. Isaiah 42:8,9
8. Isaiah 45:22,23
9. Isaiah 47:10-15
10. Isaiah 55:1,2
11. Isaiah 10:3
12. Isaiah 33:1,2
13. Isaiah 43:10-12
14. James 5:1-3
15. 1 John 2:15-17
16. 2 Peter 2:5-7, 9,10
17. Isaiah 26:19-21
18. Isaiah 5:8,9; 15,16
19. Jeremiah 2:12-13
20. G.K. Chesterton, *The Everlasting Man*, (Wilder Publications, 2008), Kindle Edition, Location 2226.
21. Ecclesiastes 12:14
22. Isaiah 59:1-2
23. Zephaniah 2:3
24. Isaiah 2:10,11, 17

## ABOUT THE AUTHOR

E C Lartigue is currently the Missional Pastor at a church in the
Tulsa, Oklahoma area. His senior Pastor describes him as "a pastor
with a poet's heart and a storytellers mind." His work has taken him
to countries across the globe on mission with God. His experience
has taught him that "story" translates across cultures and generations.
And the greatest "Story" of all is the Gospel. Communicating that
"Story" is his passion.

His prayer is that the reader will enjoy the adventure of story,
especially the one God desires to write in their lives. For only God
writes great non-fiction.